About the Author

JO GALLON is an experienced journalist and editor wh r the years has covered topics ranging from crime trials and global warming to terrorism, the Middle East, European and US politics. He has written for *Reuters*, *The Economist*, *The Times*, *The Telegraph* and *Newsweek*. He now divides his time between freelance journalism, preparing lobby reports for the indi ry and (more recently) writing *The Prophecy*, his debut novel.

THE PROPHECY

JOHN KILGALLON

First published in Great Britain as a paperback original in 2010 by
Allison & Busby Limited
13 Charlotte Mews
London W1T 4EJ
www.allisonandbusby.com

Copyright © 2010 by JOHN KILGALLON

The moral right of the author has been asserted.

A CIP catalogue record for this book is available from
the British Library.

10 9 8 7 6 5 4 3 2 1

13-ISBN 978-0-7490-0799-7

Typeset in 11/15.5 pt Sabon by
Allison & Busby Ltd.

The paper used for this Allison & Busby publication
has been produced from trees that have been legally sourced
from well managed and credibly certified forests.

Printed and bound in the UK by
CPI Bookmarque, Croydon, CR0 4TD

*For Sean, Marilyn, all my family
and friends close at heart, and to the memory of
my mother and father. They would all, I'm sure,
raise a glass and smile at new life being
put to an old name.*

CHAPTER ONE

ONEIDA, NEW YORK STATE. NOVEMBER, 2007.

Sam Tynnan had no idea how close to death he was; after all, he was used to writing those scenarios for his characters, not himself. But he was tense, breath held, for an entirely different reason at that moment; everything around him seeming suddenly suspended. The faint rustle of tree tops in the breeze on the forest edge a hundred yards back from the house, a dog barking somewhere in the distance, the muted strains of Paco de Lucia's 'Concierto de Aranjuez' from the next room.

Suspended, expectant – the clawing hope and ambitions of the past eighteen months now honed down to just a few moments – as Sam Tynnan mentally grasped for the perfect paragraph on which to finish the book that might earn him a million.

Sam knew more than most what a lottery it was. Writing full-time now for nine years, he knew that a manuscript could garner you anything from a 20 cent rejection slip, through advances that wouldn't feed a secretary for a month, to low- and high-five figures, low and high-six, to the pinnacle, seven-figure advances.

His agent, Elliot 'Elli' Roschler, had read Sam's initial outlines and had seemed really excited, 'Looks like this could be the big one.' But that term in itself had changed meaning in the past few years. Since the publication of Adam Dayne's *Magdalen Code*, the market had been turned on its head. Suddenly religious and mythology thrillers were flavour of the month and foreseeable future. Dayne himself had earned over forty million dollars from the book, but there'd been a score of sky-high advances and royalties riding in its wake.

Sam looked at the words on his computer screen with due reverence. No more worries about mortgage and credit card payments, no more concerns about holidays and the money and time lost taking them, no more asking Kate if she could hold on for the maintenance payment until his next advance came in.

It felt so close now, so tangible and real. He could imagine Elli's exuberance as it came through and he read it. Then days later the calls would start: the first bid, another one or two topping, then the juggling and Elli playing one publisher against the other to stoke the fire for the final auction.

But despite the heady figures Elli had projected seeming unreal – especially after such a long dry spell – a part of Sam felt as if they were not only real, as if already half in the bank, but also fully deserved.

Because this particular book had been a battle. A harder battle than any book he'd written so far.

And his at-home office was strewn with the remnants of that battle: chapters and segments written and re-written, deconstructed and reconstructed, spider-scrawl writing in the margins and often continuing on the back of pages; countless filled notepads, which had accompanied him even on shopping trips and dinner dates and were by his bedside every night, in case a chain of thought hit him that he feared he might not get back in quite the same way again.

Then there was the mountain of books and papers: fourteen volumes on Nostradamus alone, the *Bible* and *Koran*, Steinsaltz's *Talmud*, Bukhari's *Hadiths*, Tahawi's *Aqeedatut*, *The Clementine Vulgate*, and countless reports, commentaries and quotes from the Internet.

But the other reason Sam felt he deserved this now was because, after all these years of writing, he knew that ideas as good as this rarely came along. In fact, often they didn't come along at all. If he hadn't by chance stumbled across a Nostradamus passage while researching something else, then linked that to a chain of current events, he might never have hit on the idea. Coming just four months after his mother's death, it was as if she was reaching a hand down from heaven. '*Here*. Here's the jigsaw piece in your life that has so far been missing.'

So tangible, so real now. *So close.* Sam reached out one hand and touched the screen, as if that physical contact might help the last words flow. Just a few more lines now and he was finally there.

'What's the hold-up?'

'Don't know.' The computer operator, mid-twenties, looked up only briefly from his screen. He shrugged and smiled lamely. 'Takes time to finish a book, I guess.'

'You guess, huh, Cali?' There were twelve years between them, but most importantly three levels of rank. The younger man's smile faded as his section commander leant over the desk. 'Why don't you do me and everyone else here a favour and remind us what the last communication said?'

There were another six men in the room – a dingy, bare-walled warehouse unit with a desk, computer, three chairs and two benches its only furniture. No one said anything, but there were a few faint smiles.

They'd been with Washington a little longer; long enough to know better. Or perhaps because they were the front end of any ops. One slip from favour and Washington could make sure that you were first through any door, the first to face a bullet.

And now also because they were playing out the final scene of an op; long months of planning boiled down into a few hours, then those final frantic minutes when one foot wrong or a split-second mis-timing invariably spelt death. No second chances.

Washington, Cali, Ohio, Illy, Montana, Utah, Nevada, Texas... When their section had first been put together fifteen months back, they'd each been offered a choice of state name to mask identities. 'So choose any you like – but *not* the state you live in. And *not* Washington – that's already taken. That's me.' Clear reminder of rank positioning at the outset. And three- and four-syllable States could be shortened to easy nicknames, but *not* Washington.

Cali held one finger by his screen. 'Says here in his last email... "Up to page 434, just a page or so to go now. Hope to finish later this afternoon and get the whole thing through to you before you head off."'

'And what time was that?'

'Two-eighteen.'

Washington checked his watch. 'Three and a half hours just to write a page or so?'

'Endings could be like beginnings, I suppose – the hardest part. Got to make sure everything's wrapped up neatly – no loose ends. Then there's final polishing and—' Cali broke off as he caught Washington's withering look. He nodded. 'But, *yeah*, it's a long time.'

There was still nothing from the six apart from a faint shuffle, a creak from one of the bench seats. Weight being shifted, unease settling deeper. They'd already been waiting over three hours on a knife-edge, and now might face another hour or so.

Stocky and broad-shouldered, their Kevlar vests made them look larger still. The only light in the room was from a desk lamp by the computer, and with their black combat fatigues they made ominous shadows.

'Any indication of whether Roschler has left his office yet?' Washington asked.

'Not really. All his link says is that he's online, but may be away from his computer. Which could mean anything: simply doing something else at his desk, he's somewhere else in his office, or in fact he *has* left, but kept his computer on overnight to link to from a home computer.'

Nevada, the strike team leader and second in command to Washington, spoke for the first time.

'If he *is* linking from a home computer, that'll mean a last-minute shift Wyo's gonna be none too happy with.'

'Yeah, I know.' Washington grimaced.

Wyo, head of the second team, was waiting with similar white-knuckle anticipation four hundred miles away. And while they'd covered that eventuality and a score of others, it was a gentle reminder that *still* something could go wrong.

But from his years of running ops like this, Washington knew the weight behind that comment. Consoling themselves in these final tense moments that someone, somewhere, was in more danger and with more at stake if it all went wrong.

Washington knew that on this particular op, more than any other, that was far from the truth.

'Where are you now?'

'Just crossing thirty-eighth.' Glancing through his taxi window, Elli Roschler picked up on Sam's intimation. 'But if I head back now to pick it up, I'll be late for this early dinner meet.' Elli checked his watch. 'Already looks like I might be a few minutes over. I'll grab it straight after – should be no more than a couple of hours. You say just three minutes ago you sent it?'

'Yeah. I tried your office line first to see if it came through OK.'

'Just missed me. And Maggie left ten minutes before me tonight.' Elli eased out a slow, satisfied sigh. 'My, my, Sam. Finished...*finished*! You must be on cloud nine.' Elli chuckled. 'That is, when you've pinched and shaken yourself out of that haze of unreality that you *have* actually finished.'

'A couple of Carlos Terceros should do that for me.'

'I'll raise a glass to that too over dinner.'

'Anything exciting?'

'Nah, not really. Warts and all bio. Fallen soap star. Mother beat and abused her, drugs and drink later which she blames on that. AA and rehab, gets married then discovers she's a lesbian, more drugs and rehab. Oh, and her dog, from the trauma of all this, is now in therapy too. You know, the standard American success story.'

They both laughed. In the past nine years of their association, they'd become more than just agent and client, they'd become close friends. Elli and Mike Kiernan – a fellow writer of Sam's and Oneida, NY State resident – had been the first to offer their condolences and shoulders to cry on when three years back Kate had left him and headed for the West Coast with their son, Ashley, then only six, to pursue her career. After a decent period of mourning for the relationship, Sam's friends had done their utmost to play matchmaker for him. But invariably the set-ups had left Sam feeling all the more lonely and out of sorts, thinking of how both Elli's and Mike's marriages had stood the test of time, their homes full of the photo evidence: anniversaries, family holidays, Christmas and birthday snaps with their sons and daughters. But Sam knew that they meant well. Good friends. And thankfully all of that had stopped when Lorrena had walked into his life a year ago.

'And I daresay you'll be raising a champagne glass or two with Lorrena tonight?' Elli commented.

'Yeah, sure will.' Sam glanced at his watch. It was still an hour or so before she was in. She'd recently started taking Italian language evening classes; a sudden desire to learn her parents' native language.

'I'll pick it up on my way back from dinner and start reading straight away tonight. So looks like a midnight-oiler.' Elli chuckled, then became more serious. 'And Sam?'

'Yeah?'

'Well done. Because I know at times this one hasn't been easy for you.'

'Thanks.' Sam sighed, as if finally shedding the last of that burden. 'Let's just hope you're still saying "well done" when you've read it.'

'I'm sure I will...I'm sure I will.'

After they'd said their goodbyes, the house felt even stiller, more silent. There was nobody else to talk to until Lorrena came in, and no manuscript to dive into any more. He'd *finished*! He felt suddenly at a loose end, slightly empty, as if someone close who he'd spoken to every day had just walked out; pretty much how he'd felt when Kate had left with Ashley, in fact.

The TV was on a news channel on mute – Sam often did that to relieve the solitude; it made him feel plugged into and part of the world outside, but without the disturbance. The classical CD he'd been listening to had finished.

He went into the lounge to slot in another. He wanted something with energy now to kick him out of his mood, start celebrating that he'd actually, finally finished. Fifth down in the CD rack he found *The Police – Greatest Hits*. Perfect. Took him back to his teens. He selected track four, 'Message in a Bottle', and he swayed to it on his way through to the kitchen, joining in on the chorus as he grabbed a Bud from the fridge. He took a swig as he part-danced his way back to the lounge.

With the song's heavy bass and percussion, at first the sound of glass smashing didn't fully register; and when it did, Sam's head swivelled sharply back to the kitchen – perhaps the fridge door had swung open and one of the other bottles had fallen? But a stark beam flickering haphazardly through his lounge disorientated him, and he'd only just started to react to the silhouette lunging towards him, when an arm was clamped around his neck, yanking him back again.

The grip was strong, rigid. Sam's legs felt suddenly like molten jelly, ready to give way, but the arm held him firm as he was dragged back, shuffling frantically to keep up, to his office.

'*Khoob, computeresh hanooz mutassil ast. Mohkam giriftee-esh?*'

'*Baley, man daaramesh!*'

Sam could now see another two men: one taking a seat at his computer, another at the end of the lounge by the front door, no doubt in case he decided that escaping that way was an option. Sam didn't know what they were saying, but he'd heard enough from his research over the past eighteen months to recognise the language: Arabic or Farsi. But the man by his computer now addressed him in English.

'The book you've just finished. Who have you sent it to so far?'

'I...I don't know,' Sam stumbled. 'Can't remember now.'

He was in shock but there was also another sharply rising panic: if they took his copies of *The Prophecy* from the computer *and* got hold of Elli's copy – that was it. No more copies out there.

'Let's try that again, shall we?'

Heavily accented, but still American English – as if they were Arab immigrants from New York or Buffalo who'd arrived in the USA five to ten years back. Not the clear but lilting cadences of the Saudi and Egyptian nationals he'd spoken to while researching.

Sam felt the air shunt out of him as his back hit the floor and of the men straddled him, pinning him down. A hand was clamped tight to his throat and a gun thrust into his face, its barrel inches from his nose.

'Where, mister? *Where?*' the man straddling him

shouted, speaking for the first time. Computer-man was suddenly busy, eyes fixed to the screen as he sifted through Sam's files. The gun was cocked.

Last copy then gone! And he couldn't send a mob like this Elli's way. What if they went to his house while Miriam and the kids were there and...?

Sam's breath came out with a shuddering gasp as the trigger struck home with only a click. Computer-man's chuckle rode its hollow echo.

'Where did you buy that gun, Hadi? A Gaza marketplace?'

'Never given trouble before.'

The gun was prodded closer, the man's leer fading as his eyes took on a fresh, pinprick intensity.

'For the *last* time, where...*where*?'

Computer-man already had his email file history up, and Sam realised the futility of holding back; they'd find it any second in any case.

'Elliot Roschler – my agent. I sent him a copy a short while ago.'

A couple of key taps, then a slow sigh from computer-man. 'OK, got it here. Elli Roschler. Sent nine minutes ago.' A gentle nod to the man towards the front door out of Sam's vision, then he half-turned to Sam again. 'Anyone else?'

Sam thought for a moment. 'No...no. That's it.'

'And no other copies sent to Roschler before?'

'Ah, wait – yes.' Sam suddenly remembered. 'An

outline and the first three chapters when I started – then this, just a few minutes ago.'

The hand gripped tighter around his throat, as if punishing him for the momentary forgetfulness, gunman's teasing leer rising again as the cold of the gun barrel was traced below his left eye. Sam shuddered, his body's trembling tipping into overload.

'And nobody else?'

'No – he was the *only* one. Nobody else.'

'And apart from the hard copy we see here,' computer-man gestured towards the papers strewn across his desk and a side cabinet, 'any other disk or CD copies?'

'No, no...that's it.' Sam swallowed hard, feeling his Adam's apple pulse against the hand on his throat. 'It's all here.'

'Sounds like a story to me,' gunman said. 'No other copies sent out in all that time. And *no* disk copies.'

Computer-man raised a quizzical eyebrow, and after a second gave a gentle, submissive nod as he turned back to the screen.

'Where else, fuckhead? *Where else?*' gunman screamed, and Sam felt some of his spittle land on his face. 'There *have* to be other copies somewhere.'

'No, there's no more – I *swear!*'

At the far end of the room, the third man was talking in Farsi to someone on his cellphone. Sting was singing about sending an SOS to the world, but nobody was listening.

The trigger was pulled. Another empty click.

Sam swallowed back sour bile.

Computer-man sniggered. 'That really is one whore of a gun, Hadi.'

'Or maybe I just didn't put in enough bullets.' Sly, concessionary smile from gunman.

'Ah, the old Russian roulette routine. Never fails.'

'Except I can't remember how many bullets I put in – two or three.' The smile widened, but his eyes stayed fixed coldly on Sam.

'Bound to hit one soon, I suppose.'

'Yeah.'

The third man, finishing his call, came over with a paper shredder, plugged it in, and started feeding in the loose manuscript pages from Sam's desk and side cabinet.

The trigger was cocked again.

'For the last time – *who else*?' Gunman glared malevolently, all trace of humour, teasing or otherwise, suddenly gone. 'And think *very* carefully before you answer this time.'

'I swear – nobody else. Nobody!' Sam glanced pleadingly towards computer-man, sensing that he held the main sway. 'We had to keep everything tight on this one – as you can imagine.'

Computer-man's eyes searched his long and hard.

Then, after a frozen moment that felt like a lifetime, again that gentle nod.

'Yes, I *can* imagine, Mr Tynnan.' He blinked heavily and sighed. 'I think he's telling the truth, Hadi. So just finish it.' He turned back to the computer, as if Sam was no longer of any relevance, and slotted in a re-start disk to wipe it clean.

Sam's heart sank. He should have guessed that they'd kill him anyway once they had what they wanted. A moment ago he was desperately clinging to eighteen months' work, now life itself was slipping from reach. Tears welled in his eyes, the gun and the man beyond suddenly blurred through them.

'*Please!*' he pleaded, but his voice sounded distant, disembodied.

'That is, if there's a bullet up next,' gunman said, ignoring him.

'Oh, Hadi, you've no heart – enough torture for the evening.'

21

CHAPTER TWO

LONDON, ENGLAND.

'There's been another increase in activity, Adel.'

'How much?'

'Fourteen per cent since yesterday.'

Adel nodded thoughtfully. 'How about the other TAME sections?'

'Section one is just waking up. But for TAMEs three through seven, much the same. Some even higher.'

Adel cast a brief eye around the room: seventy-nine other computers, each with their own operators, with most of the on-screen text in Arabic, Farsi or Urdu.

Pre-9/11, there'd been less than forty Arab translation operatives between the USA and Britain.

Echelon could sift through millions of phone and email messages worldwide and pass that on to the NSA and GCHQ and, in turn, CIA and MI5; but when Arabic, Farsi and Urdu keywords were added to the pot, that extra flood of messages had to be read and analysed. And that had been half the problem. Swamped by the sudden deluge in Arab-language 'activity' in the run-up to 9/11, those operatives had been unable to sift through and find those few vital messages – at least in time.

They weren't making that mistake again.

Adel Al-Shaffir, born in Dumyat, Egypt, but for the last twenty years, ever since his LSE days, considering himself very much a Londoner, headed TAME2. His counterpart, Jalil El-Abinah, New Jersey-born to Lebanese parents, headed TAME1 in New York. TAME3 was Paris, 4 Berlin, 5 Madrid, 6 Rome, and the other twelve TAMEs – Terrorist Activity Monitoring and Evaluation centres – were spread between Tel Aviv and Jakarta.

Recruitment had been key. Arab nations such as Egypt, Jordan and Saudi Arabia had keen self-interest in combating terrorism. But then Arafat had been half-Egyptian, Al-Zaqawi Jordanian, and Bin Laden Saudi. What if you got a rogue operator, one who made sure those vital messages were overlooked? So, apart from a strict vetting process, areas of responsibility were changed regularly so that it would be practically impossible for a terrorist cell to ensure their particular messages hit a 'sympathetic' computer.

Few felt the pressure of that more than Adel Al-Shaffir, responsible for this room full of mostly Muslim men balancing dual moral ethics: on one hand that they were tracking the bad guys, yet on the other were betraying their own.

So Adel had to act not just as their boss, but as an adviser, friend and confidant, so that he was close enough to gauge if that latter moral ethic became too much for them. Correspondingly, secrecy was more vital in their department than any other: they could never talk outside about what they did. Because while they might have come to terms with that latter ethic, others might take a different view – so such talk could be their death sentence.

At times for Adel the pressure of it – balancing not only his own shadow life and ethics, but that of all his men – was too much, would bring a tremble to his hands, wake him in the dead of night in a cold sweat. *Was there something he'd missed?*

Adel considered the stats. *Fourteen per cent?* On its own, it wasn't too much to worry about. But there'd been ten or eleven per cent increases now every day for a week, with five and six per cent increments for a few days leading up to that. A good hundred and twenty per cent increase overall. Something was happening out there.

* * *

Sam heard the shot this time, felt the sticky warmth of his own blood on his face and neck. But the pain seemed to be in his chest rather than his head, and the man pinning him down was slumped against him.

And through a blurred, watery haze – some of the blood had run into his eyes – he became aware of other gunshots and frantic activity: a flurry of footsteps and sharp, urgent voices, computer-man raising his gun just before two shots ripped into his chest and threw him back a yard, three more shots from deeper in the room out of sight – one of them thudding into the body against him as Sam felt it move a fraction; perhaps a last death spasm rather than him trying to raise up again.

And then a figure in dark combat fatigues was leaning over him. 'Are you OK?' One hand grabbed the shoulder of the body slumped on him and hefted it brusquely aside.

'Yes, I...I think so. For...for a minute I thought...' He swallowed back the sour tang where some blood had trickled into his mouth. Sam tried to quickly, desperately adjust to what had happened, while his still-racing heart drum-tattooed it home: *still alive, still alive...alive!* 'That...th—'

The man gripped Sam's shoulder, pressing reassuringly. 'Don't worry, you're OK! Rest easy.' He gave a quick scan of Sam's body to make sure he hadn't missed anything on his first assessment. 'We got here just in time.'

'Certainly does look that way, Mr Tynnan,' another voice added.

The man who'd spoken was in his mid-forties, thickset with a touch of grey at the sideburns and a healthy tan, as if he topped it up with regular trips to Florida or the sunroom at his local health club. He wore the same combat fatigues as the others, but without the automatic rifle or helmet, and his jacket was loose at the top to show a crisp white shirt and tie beneath. As if this was just a tiresome distraction from his office duties.

Nevada moved aside and started directing his men on clean-up as Washington crouched down, taking his place.

'We'd in fact hoped to get here sooner.' Washington's easy smile pulled into a tight grimace. 'We've been on to them for a while now, but they still caught us on the hop. Our plan was to cut them off while they were at your back door – not already through it with a gun at your head.'

Sam sat up, wiping the blood from his eyes. Washington proffered a hankie, which with a nod of thanks Sam used to wipe away the rest.

'*They?*' Sam glanced towards the nearby bodies, one of them being zipped into a plastic body bag.

'Extreme jihad cell. Like I say, we've been tracking

them for a while.' Washington sighed softly. 'And they've been tracking *you* for a while, too. Checking your emails back and forth, *anything* regarding *The Prophecy* they could pick up on. That's why they came in now – you sending the final copy to Roschler.'

Sam shook his head as he struggled to make sense of it all. An extreme jihad cell? And now an anti-terrorist squad? It was all too much. 'But if they knew already who I'd sent to – why all their questions?'

Washington contemplated Sam soberly. 'Oh, they *knew* all right. They just wanted to see if you'd tell them the truth. Also to find out about any loose disk or hard copies they might not know about. If you lied about the electronic copies they knew about, then there was a good chance you'd lie about the rest.'

Sam closed his eyes as a shudder ran through him. All that would have meant was more toying with him, more Russian roulette and empty chamber clicks before he finally snapped.

'*Elli!*' Sam's eyes flicked open again, Washington's mention of Roschler sparking the thought. 'They've probably sent people there too. You've got to get to him!'

Washington held out a calming hand. 'Don't worry. Already taken care of. Another of my teams should be there soon.' Washington patted the cellphone in his breast pocket. 'They'll call me the minute they have news.'

Washington asked if Roschler might still be in

his office, and Sam related their conversation of ten moments ago.

Washington grimaced. 'One consolation, at least. His not being there when they visited. *If* they have.'

Sam nodded numbly. Except that if they *had* visited, that would be the last copy of *The Prophecy* gone. Eighteen months of work down the drain. Though right now, Sam reminded himself, he was lucky to be alive; adjusting to losing *The Prophecy* and all the possible knock-on wreckage from that was stage two. One step at a time.

'Are there any other copies of *The Prophecy* out there, My Tynnan?' Washington asked, bringing a furrow to Sam's brow: *replay of the earlier nightmare questioning?* Washington held a hand out. 'I need to know, Mr Tynnan. Truly I do. Because if there *are* copies out there, these people will find out and come for you again. And next time, we might not get here in time.'

Sam looked at Washington levelly. He wished there were more copies out there, but having a gun in your face, and now panicking that the last copy might have already been lost, somehow focused the mind. With a tired sigh, Sam repeated what he'd said at gunpoint: no spare disks, the only electronic copies were with him and Elli Roschler, and no full paper copies, just odd pages and part chapters. 'What little they might have not shredded.' From the look of it, he'd be lucky if there were thirty intact pages left.

Washington joined Sam briefly in scanning the desk and side cabinet. 'And nothing else anywhere?'

Again that uneasy déjà vu as Washington's eyes searched his. Sam started to shake his head, then suddenly remembered those first three chapters sent to Roschler. '...Almost a year ago now, and the same way: email file attachment. But apart from that, nothing else. That's it!' Sam sighed, the stark reality settling: if they got that last complete copy now from Elli's computer, he was sunk. Even if Elli had kept those three chapters separate somewhere – he'd still be missing a giant four-hundred-page hole in the manuscript. He'd *never* be able to rewrite and knit it all back together.

Washington fired a quick look round the room, part of it taking in the activity of his men, then, bracing his hands with an audible slap on his thighs, stood up. 'Right. We've got to get you out of here.'

The last of the three body bags was being carried out, and Sam joined Washington briefly in looking at them, as if they might hold the answer to why they had to leave. Then he remembered Lorrena. 'My... my girlfriend's due back here soon.' Sam checked his watch. 'About forty minutes.'

'Don't worry. When she arrives, my people will still be here cleaning up. They'll bring her to the hotel where I'll take you now.' Again that sobering stare as Sam grasped for any semblance of the reality that had been brusquely yanked away from him only moments

29

ago. 'You *can't* stay here, Mr Tynnan. It's not safe. A back-up man, or even a whole team, could come back to check what happened to their friends – and we can't take that risk with you. *Or* your girlfriend.'

'OK. *OK*.' But still Sam looked around numbly, as if unsure what to do.

Washington snapped him out of it by telling him he'd need to grab a few things for overnight, and minutes later they were heading quickly up Sam's driveway. It was mid-November, but already the night air was brisk as Sam followed Washington and another of his team towards a grey Chevy Tahoe. A long black SWAT truck sat behind it. Sam could see a driver at the wheel of the Tahoe, but the windows on the truck were too heavily tinted for him to see inside.

The other man sat in the front by the driver with Sam and Washington in the back. They turned at the end of his road heading away from Oneida towards Syracuse, and neither of them spoke for the first few minutes of the drive.

The lights each side thinned as Oneida's residential outskirts gave way to farm fields, Sam's mind and the pit of his gut as dark and empty as the night landscape rolling by. Whether from the motion of the car or the butterfly nerves still raging in his stomach, Sam started to feel queasy. He bit at his lip, swallowing it back as he looked at Washington.

'Who are they? You said that you've been tracking

them for a while. Do you know exactly what within *The Prophecy* might have made them target me?'

Washington applied thought for a second, a faint smile touching his lips. 'We thought you might be better able to answer that, Mr Tynnan. After all, *you* wrote it.' He met Sam's eyes steadily, but his smile carried no trace of tease; simply softening a home truth. He was about to add something more when his cellphone rang. He checked the display before answering and exhaled heavily. 'It's my Roschler team.'

Sam looked at Washington expectantly as he started speaking. He'd just escaped with his life; now he'd know just how much of it was left worth living for.

CHAPTER THREE

FIVE MONTHS LATER.

'Are you OK?'

'Yeah, I'm fine...*fine*.' Sam held Mike Kiernan's searching gaze for a few seconds to lend assurance.

In the first couple of months after that day, that question had hardly ever been asked, because it was patently clear then that he was far from OK. Night after night he'd drink himself into a stupor to try and forget that he'd lost *The Prophecy*; half his days were spent sleeping it off and hiding away from the world so that he didn't have to face just what he was going to do next.

'Come on, Sam, don't let what happened crush

you,' Lorrena would cajole. 'You're stronger than that. *I* need you, and if you haven't realised so does young Ashley. You've only spoken to him twice on the phone since this happened.' Before, he'd speak to his son every weekend.

And he'd get emails from Elli, unconsciously adding weight to Lorrena's pep attempts, or perhaps they *had* spoken together: 'Work and focus on a new project could be just the thing to lift you out of this slump.' The final clincher had come from Mike: 'If you don't snap out of it soon, Sam, I swear you're gonna lose yet another good thing in your life you won't easily replace: Lorrena.'

Crowd roar and applause distracted Sam for a moment. That night's Patriots game was on a large-screen TV at the far end of the bar. A group at the pool table also looked up briefly at the on-screen action.

'We'll be there next week,' Mike commented.

'Yeah, looking forward to it.' Sam forced a smile, trying to show enthusiasm for the upcoming get-together with Mike's old Boston pals at the Gillette stadium.

They were at Vaccarelli's, their favourite local watering hole for the past few years, a roadhouse bar just outside of Canastota on the 365 to Syracuse. Where Sam and Mike sat it was all Tiffany lamps, oak panelling and secluded booths: the saloon end for more private, sedate conversation.

Mike dragged his attention from the screen and looked back at Sam. 'Anything more from your saviour SWAT man?'

'Nah, nothing much. Only spoken to him a couple of times since he sent my computer and those last pages back.' Washington had taken both away to check and sent them back ten days later. Nothing traceable had been left on his computer, everything already wiped clean, as Sam had feared.

Sam struggled to keep the worry from showing on his face. 'I think, like everyone else, he's mainly been checking that I was OK. Once he felt settled that I wasn't going to do anything rash and jump off a tall building, the calls stopped.'

Most of the early calls had in fact come from Sam. A secure-line number Washington had left him. 'You won't be able to speak to me directly on it, but leave a message and I'll always get back to you within forty-eight hours.' And, true to his word, Washington always had, and he'd become Sam rather than Mr Tynnan after a couple of calls. But Sam couldn't help thinking about what happened in the interim, imagining a team of CIA spooks running his voice through all sorts of stress analysis programmes, with Washington probing before he phoned back: 'What sort of state is he in? How best should I handle it?'

Mike nodded thoughtfully as he topped up their beers from the pitcher.

'Possibly best if he doesn't call any more. One sign at least that it's all finally over.'

'Yeah, suppose so,' Sam agreed as he sipped at his beer. He'd shared his dilemma with Mike Kiernan probably more than anyone else; partly because, as a fellow writer, Mike might relate stronger to losing a manuscript that had consumed his life for eighteen months. Not that they were anything like in the same league when it came to their careers. Mike Kiernan's crime thrillers were regularly in the *NYT* top ten, whereas Sam was just a contender.

Mike had also built up a reputation as one of America's 'earthier' crime writers; one who actually knew first hand the mean streets of South Boston and the characters he was writing about.

They'd first met twelve years ago at a Bouchercon writer's convention in Monterey. At the time Sam had still been living in his native UK, but when five years later Kate's acting career took off, with a Broadway break that precipitated their move from London, Mike had been the main reason they'd settled in Oneida: they'd have a friend there. Mike had enthused about the area's plus points: good schools, great community spirit, and, most importantly, one of America's lowest crime rates. Mike himself had moved there three years before from his native Boston when a friend's teenage son had been shot in a mugging gone wrong. 'I made the move primarily thinking of my kids. And I daresay you might feel the same about Ashley.'

They'd become good friends over the years, closer still by default of the split with Kate – and more drinking and drowning-sorrows time together – and they shared the same sly, caustic sense of humour, '*Once I got you to shake off that shy, British reserve,*' Mike had jibed.

'*Oh, fuck off.*'

'*See. It's gone already.*'

Mike took a longer slug of his beer, sighing faintly as he set the glass back down. 'So how's it going with the new book? More into the rhythm yet?'

'Yeah.' Sam shrugged. 'You know what beginnings are like, always the worst part, and this one's doubly difficult because—' Sam broke off. He always found himself tiptoeing around the minefield of what had happened. 'Well, while it might not have the same short-term gain as *The Prophecy*, the long-term prospects could be great. *If* I hit the formula right.'

Mike nodded with an understanding smile. 'I think Elli's given good advice.' Sam had gone into more detail the last time they'd met about his plans to revive a popular main character, Toby Wesley, from a past book to develop a series. 'It's the right move.'

'Let's hope so.'

Mike glanced absently towards the on-screen game before returning to Sam.

'And no thoughts about *The Prophecy* any more?

Trying to piece it all back together again?'

Sam snorted lightly. 'Seems that's the main thing everyone's interested in these days.' Washington had asked him the same on their last couple of conversations.

'Yeah, but this is *me*, Sam.' Mike held Sam's gaze. They'd picked and probed at the subject before, but never whether that door was firmly, once and for all closed: it was too painful. 'I more than anyone else understand what it's been like for you losing that manuscript. Especially having seen what you put into it.'

Sam nodded numbly, recalling Mike's words at the outset: 'Must be like losing your left leg, your best friend, and having your soul ripped out and nailed to the fridge door – *all* at the same time!' Mike had mentioned reading about H.G. Wells losing a manuscript on a train, and couldn't imagine how he'd ever come to terms with that.

Sam eased out a slow breath. 'At first I just didn't know if or how I'd be able to make it out of that grey tunnel. All those days drinking, hiding away from the world, trying to blot out what happened and feeling sorry for myself. But I was only thinking about what I lost, not what I *almost* lost. And when I finally focused on that, how close to death I'd come – never being able to see Ashley – *nothing* is worth that.' Sam took a hasty slug of beer, feeling his eyes moisten with the memory. 'And once the inclination had gone, the rest was easy. Because even if I *had* wanted to, it was always going to be a hell of a mountain climb – maybe an impossible one – to piece back together and write *The Prophecy* again.'

Mike nodded slowly. 'In a strange sweet-and-sour way, that's good to hear.' Mike lightly gripped Sam's forearm across the table, and Sam swore he could see a faint glistening in Mike's eyes too; or maybe it was just the soft, rose-tinted lighting of the saloon section. 'Because it's good to have you *fully* back, my friend.'

They left the bar almost an hour later, their banter freer – perhaps because they'd put to bed the last of Sam's ghosts hanging between them these past months. And because for the first time Sam had fully opened up on how he felt about losing *The Prophecy*, he felt freer too within himself, as if a weight had been lifted. He found himself humming along to the radio on the two-mile drive back home, and was still faintly humming as he shut his car door and heard the jangling of the house phone.

He ran the last short stretch: key in the front door, then five manic, stretched paces to grab the receiver. Lorrena was no doubt already in bed. He was breathless as he picked up, heart pounding from the rush. Then his heartbeat raised another notch as he heard the voice at the other end: *Washington!*

'We've been able to pick up something that we

couldn't get from your computer – because, as you know, that had been wiped clean. It took a while for your service provider to get back to us with a list, but on that – sent just ten minutes after you emailed Roschler – there was one last email, with attachment, sent to an IPA in Bahrain. So there's still a copy of *The Prophecy* out there somewhere, Sam – *if* we're able to trace it.'

ANTALYA, TURKEY.

The Ashna Mosque in Antalya, Turkey, was not regarded as one of Islam's most beautiful and coveted mosques. And what beauty it did possess was not easily admired because the city had encroached so closely around it, leaving only narrow cypress tree-lined paths each side separating it from the surrounding three-storey grey stone buildings.

But it was nevertheless one of Islam's earliest-built mosques, built in the reign of Sultan Keykubat in the thirteenth century, preceding Istanbul's Blue Mosque by three hundred years, and its fluted minaret spearing high above Antalya's rooftops – considered its most impressive feature – was first to catch the dawn sun as it broke the horizon.

That caught-breath moment between night and dawn. The four men observing the mosque from across the road, tucked in the recessed shadows of an alleyway, also held their breath in that instant, timing.

There was only one guard for the whole building and only two weak spotlights on each flank, but it was the brighter, two thousand watt security lights which presented the main problem. Motion activated, they'd switch on like stage spotlights heralding the main act as he paced the mosque's perimeter. Three minutes in front, then a steady pacing around the building – the back took thirty-six to thirty-eight seconds, they'd timed it – before he reappeared the other side.

They needed to move in and set the explosives as he approached the back – otherwise he'd see them moving away as he reappeared the other side. The problem was that the brighter security lights flicking on behind him might make his head turn; unless, that is, their brightness was dissipated and merged with the rising sun.

Their leader held one hand up expectantly as he measured that rising light: the guard was just coming to the end of his three minutes in front; would they have to wait until his next circuit, or could they move in now?

He watched the guard start pacing, fourteen measured strides before he turned and started down the flank of the building – but still the man stayed his hand, uncertain, the light was still too weak.

He lifted his eyes to the sky and saw the first

orange dapples tingeing some cloud wisps – the guard was already halfway down the side, he'd have to decide quickly. But then a second later the sun touched the minaret, spilling golden light down the mosque front. He waited a moment more, counting the guard's paces, then gave the signal.

Two of his men ran across, half-crouching, low and silent.

Meanwhile the third man had his rifle trained on the guard's back, watching through his telescopic sights for his head turning, picking up any movement behind him. If the guard did, then he'd switch on the red tracer and a split-second later three 9mm bullets would follow that path. But he hoped not to have to; that would partly defeat their aim.

The front security lights flicked on. His finger tensed on the trigger, watching for even a millimetre of movement or reaction – but the guard kept pacing steadily, only four paces to go now down the side.

The two men were already by the main columns either side of the mosque entrance, starting to attach the C4.

Then they were gone again from rifleman's side vision as he focused back through his sights. Tense, heart-pounding seconds as the guard turned – rifleman fearing that he might catch the brighter light in his side vision – before he was finally gone from view. With a faint sigh, rifleman's trigger finger relaxed.

The group's leader and rifleman watched intently as the two men set the C4 and connected its detonators, anxious that they'd finish and get clear before the guard emerged from the other side. The leader checked his watch as they finally scampered away: thirty-two seconds since the guard had gone from view.

The four ran at full pelt along the alley towards their car parked in the first cross street, and hardly had the last car door slammed when the explosion boomed from a block away, causing a flurry of birds to alight from the surrounding rooftops. Their car's revving lost in the reverberations of the explosion, they drove off.

Sam watched the rising dawn light play on Lorrena's back.

Her braided dark-chestnut hair coiling halfway down, the soft down of wheat-gold hair in a neat line from the nape of her neck to the small of her back – contrasting against her rich olive skin – a few faint freckles across her shoulders, the gentle fall of her breathing through half-pouted lips as she slept.

He'd noticed these features before, but never in quite the same detail as now in these frozen dawn moments. Perhaps because there'd been some snow overnight and the reflected light was brighter than normal. Or perhaps because now, recalling Mike's warning about how he'd have lost her if he hadn't shaken himself out of his slump, he was appreciating how much she meant to him; how he wouldn't have been able to cope without her – with or without dramas over Kate and Ashley or *The Prophecy*; how good she was for him; how much he truly, desperately loved her.

They'd first met on one of his regular visits to Albany Library. He was looking through books on Egypt and Syria, and she was right next to him, two books already tucked under one arm and a take-out coffee in that hand, the other reaching at full stretch to the top shelf. And as the book she'd been teasing out slipped from her grasp, she jerked to catch it, spilling half her coffee over Sam.

Red-faced, she'd apologised and insisted on buying him a coffee. 'I've got to get another one for myself in any case.' He'd declined, but when he looked at her fully for the first time and saw how beautiful she was, he'd found himself nodding, 'OK.'

One coffee became two, and over an hour spun by in which time they'd swapped stories and half their lives. She was a receptionist at a medical centre in Utica, and she was enlivened to hear that he was a writer, yet without either the open-mouthed gawping or the trite put-downs – 'Can you actually make money at that?' – which he sometimes got. She got the balance right and seemed genuinely interested in the process.

Lorrena was at Albany Library to get some books on southern Italy because in a few days she was flying off to see her father there for two weeks. Both her parents were originally from Taranto, settling first in Brooklyn when they emigrated, then later Syracuse, where she was born. But when her mother died her father had gone back to Taranto, where he still had some family. Sam said that he came to Albany Library practically every other week. 'Research. Except for the occasional book I can't get there and I have to go to Boston or New York.'

As they were sipping the last of their coffees, he was still getting up the courage to ask to see her again when she did it for him. 'We must do this again. It's been fun.' She clasped his hand gently across the table; a touch that promised much more, sent a tingle through him. He said he'd like that, and she scribbled down her number on a paper napkin. 'I'll be back from Italy early next month. Give me a call then.'

She was tanned and smiling when she returned and looked even more beautiful. They saw each other three times that first week back and halfway through the second week became lovers. Things moved quickly after that and less than a month later she was moving in with him to live.

That was how it had begun.

And practically every day since, he'd feared losing her. Perhaps because of her beauty, perhaps because, at twenty-six, she was eleven years younger than him, or maybe a combination of these things and his still-lingering feeling of inadequacy since Kate had left him;

the sense that he just wasn't good enough.

But what had made their relationship grow so strongly in the fifteen months since that day at the library, had been her tender insight and understanding, as if they'd known each other years.

She'd been the most remarkable emotional bolster to lift him out of his pit of gloom after losing *The Prophecy*, had rocked and soothed and comforted him more times than he dared count – until that day when Mike had warned that he risked losing her if he didn't snap out of it. 'You've already plumbed her emotional well, tapped her dry. Nobody can keep doing that day in, day out. You're lucky to have her, Sam – but you're pushing that luck right now.'

And then that fear was back squarely in his lap: the sense that she was too good for him – too young, too beautiful, too caring and understanding – or that he simply wasn't good enough for her.

Almost lost her.

Sam felt himself gently trembling with that realisation as he reached out and touched her, tracing one finger lazily down her spine. He kissed her gently in the small of her back and she stirred.

Perching on one elbow, she blinked slowly a couple of times as she focused on him.

'You OK?'

'Yeah, fine. Woke up early, so I thought I'd just admire the view.'

She smiled lazily. 'You were restless last night too.'

'I know.'

She reached out and gently clasped his hand. 'Don't worry. I'm sure he'll call soon. It probably takes time to track down something like that, and it's only been a couple of days.'

He closed his eyes for a second and slowly nodded. *So caring, understanding.* Only two days, but it had felt like a lifetime. Just when he'd finally managed to push it all away and get his life back on track, it was back to haunt him again. He wished now that Washington hadn't phoned. Raised his hopes again, only to leave him hanging. And as much as Lorrena was there, as before, reaching out a hand in solace, he was aware that he was starting to burden her again.

'Suppose you're right. I shouldn't worry so, torture myself.' He shrugged. 'Already done that once, got the T-shirt.'

She squeezed his hand once more in reassurance, but he could tell that she wasn't convinced.

That was the other thing she was good at: telling whether or not he was lying.

'Seven-two-four.'

'Cairo?'

'Eight-six-one.'

'Jeddah?'

'Five-four-eight.'

Adel tapped the data into his computer as his team called out the past four days' 'message activity' for each of their assigned areas.

The news of the Ashna Mosque bombing three hours beforehand had whipped Adel's office into a frenzy: phone lines burning to Turkey and the Middle East, frantic keyboard tapping as his team sifted through using the keywords Ashna or Antalya. Every message, seemingly innocent or otherwise, was under the microscope; because certainly whoever was behind it wouldn't use overt words like 'bomb'. Even phrases such as 'plans for' would be too obvious. Usually it was hidden in innocuous, casual conversation: 'Does your father still go to the Antalya Mosque? I hear the best sermons are by Imam Sadettin.' Look up the date for Sadettin's sermons, and the last one would coincide with the bombing.

With a last flurry of key taps, Adel looked at the results, then hooked his jacket from his chair and dialled out on his cellphone as he announced to the flurry of activity in his wake, 'I'll be gone an hour or so.'

To the voice answering as he stepped into the lift, Adel said simply, 'Place four.'

'What, *now*?'

'Yes. I'm heading there as I speak.'

'OK.' Resigned exhalation. 'I'll see you there.'

Adel closed his eyes and tried to relax as his taxi

sped through the London streets, the frantic key-tapping of the operations room still playing in his head.

Their arranged meeting place was a riverside pub in Southwark, The Anchor. It was one of six pre-designated rendezvous – in this case a rambling tourist pub – away from London's main Arab stomping grounds of Queensway, West Kensington or Knightsbridge. They could lose themselves amongst the tourist throng and hopefully not be noticed; at least, not by anyone who'd attach any significance. It wasn't so much of an issue for Adel, but his contact, Fahim Omari, was well known in London's Arab community.

Adel ordered a Perrier for himself and a Campari and soda for Omari and took a terrace table with a view over the river and St Paul's. He had only taken the first couple of sips of his Perrier when Omari appeared.

At six-two, Adel stood a full head above Omari as they embraced.

'The rush, I am presuming, is because of the news from Antalya?' Omari asked, once they had sat down.

Adel nodded with a tight-lipped grimace. 'Any noises which might have reached you?'

'No. Nothing that might tie into that, at least.' Omari took a sip of his drink. 'Target like that, might just be Kurdish separatists.'

'Certainly one of the stronger options. But I also wanted to check sources – in case it might be something more ominous.'

'If there's another in the coming weeks or months, also in Turkey – then you'll know pretty much for sure.' Omari shrugged. 'That is, if there *is* another one.'

Adel looked out at the view. A weak sun had broken from behind cloud cover, reflecting off the river and the dome of St Paul's beyond. But both he and Omari were aware of the flip side: if there was another mosque bombing and it wasn't in Turkey, or indeed Iraq – where it could also be put down to internal sectarianism – then they were looking at something entirely different and more worrying.

Omari took a fresh breath. 'Any claims of responsibility yet?'

'No. You know how it works. They go for the publicity jugular first – put it out on the Internet or through Al Jazeera. We're usually the last to know.'

Omari nodded thoughtfully.

The two of them went back a while – in fact, to twelve years before Adel's birth. Omari and his father had been old clients of Adel's father, a marble and stone merchant from Dumyat, Egypt. In 1958, at the age of nineteen when his father died, Omari took over his father's burgeoning Cairo construction company, which included a sizeable land portfolio. Omari's father had survived the 1952 land reform, but the 1961 act was another matter, and worse still there were accusations that his father had circumvented the 1952 reforms through fraud and bribery; Omari was quietly informed that if the case went against him, which looked likely it would, his company assets and land would be confiscated. 'Quietly', because those telling him also conveniently had a few contacts, lawyers and ministers allied to Nasser's regime, who would be willing to buy everything from him before that calamity occurred. At half price. Half was better than nothing; Omari took his half-wealth and, with a chain of properties between Lancaster Gate and Queensway which had rocketed in value since he'd bought them in the Sixties, had many times over made up for what he lost in Egypt.

Omari was one of the most stylish men Adel knew, even though much of it was from a bygone age: the Mahawat he now slid out of an elongated silver cigarette case was straight out of *Casablanca*; his subtle-toned grey or beige-check sports jackets contrasted against navy or maroon polo necks, as if he'd lifted Steve McQueen's wardrobe from *The Thomas Crown Affair* and hadn't bothered to update it since. No need: on Omari it worked. Now in his late sixties, Omari still cut a dashing figure at London's clubs and casinos.

Westernised on the outside – but by reputation hard-core Islam on the inside – Omari had been a good friend of Arafat's, regularly courted the more outspoken imams, and was a heavy patron of two of Palestine's more suspect 'charities'. Adel had seen Omari's name appear more than a few times in MI5 files as a terrorist-financing suspect. But there was a good reason, one known to only a handful, why Adel knew he could stake all on Omari being a reliable source of information.

Adel focused back on an earlier comment. 'You said "nothing that might tie into *that*". Why, was there something else?'

Omari lit the Mahawat, blew out the first plume of smoke. As always, outwardly assured and in control. But Adel caught a flicker of unease in Omari's eyes.

'I didn't want to say anything – not until I was sure.' Omari stroked his chin. 'Because while it looks unlikely Abu Khalish was involved in the Turkey bombing, I've heard that he might be planning another "spectacular". This time in northern Italy.'

'Which town?'

'That's the problem. I haven't been able to pin it down beyond that – it could be Turin, Milan, Genoa... Bologna. Indeed, I don't know for sure if it *will* go ahead.' Omari shrugged. 'Which is why I hadn't yet said anything – until I knew.'

Abu Khalish. With little heard from Bin Laden for five years, Khalish had over the past four years firmly taken over the 'terrorist king' mantle. The first 'spectacular' had been three trains bombed in Amsterdam: eighty-one killed; then two trams in central Vienna: thirty-eight killed, including bystanders and passing shoppers; a similar attack in Copenhagen: Danish Intelligence, PET, had intervened at the eleventh hour, six dead. And the last attack, three metro trains in Paris, had also been partly thwarted by French Intelligence and GIGN. One bomber was shot dead as he tried to set off his device, another escaped and was never found. Then it had all thankfully gone quiet for eight months. But Adel should have known Khalish would try again, especially after having been thwarted in Paris.

'Through his normal cells in Italy?' Adel queried.

Omari nodded, and took a sharp draw of his Mahawat.

'When?'

'Again, not yet pinned down enough to be certain. Could be only days or a week from now, could be as much as a month. But not longer than that.'

Adel closed his eyes as he slowly exhaled, as if the weight of the information had pushed the air from him. When they'd first rendezvoused at this pub, Omari, who considered himself something of a history buff, commented that there used to be a plague pit behind the pub, and it was also where Samuel Pepys made the first recorded entry of viewing the Fire of London. *Plague and fire.* Almost four hundred years ago, but with the likes of Bin Laden and Abu Khalish bent on destruction, it hardly seemed as if anything had changed since that age.

They exchanged pleasantries about their respective friends and family while they finished their drinks, then embraced again as they parted.

CHAPTER FOUR

ALBANY, NY STATE.

Decatur Island, Lopez Island, then Shaw and San Juan, finally Orcas, sailing anticlockwise, east-west.

Sam knew the sequence pretty much off by heart from his previous book, but it was the position of the outlying islands like Sucia and Patos he wanted to get clear.

Rights of Passage, published five years ago, had been Sam's most successful book to date. Toby Wesley, a quarter-Japanese – the rest Anglo-Irish – detective covering the Pacific Northwest San Juan Islands. There were scores of New York, Boston, Philly, Miami and San Francisco detective novels, but the

San Juans were rarely done. Possibly because there wasn't much serious crime there. But when there was, the impact was immense. A murder didn't just hit the immediate family, it became a seismic community event – whereas in a big city it was often little more than another stat and a few column inches. Sam had played those small community shock waves like a Stradivarius, pumped them for every ounce of pathos and handkerchief wringing, and now the game plan was more of the same again, to build on that success in a series.

Sam could see the good sense in Elli's advice, and now – treading some of that same ground with those old characters, researching the San Juans again at the library – Sam also felt a part of himself shift to five years ago; as if the gap in between had been hardly any time. Or, better still, hadn't happened at all.

Washington had finally phoned again the night before.

'It all hit a dead-end I'm afraid, Sam. Whoever picked it up paid cash at an Internet café in Bahrain and used a false name to set up a hotmail account. They'd put it on disk and disappeared within minutes. Our chances of tracking down where that copy has gone now are slim to none. So sorry, Sam. How are you coping?'

It was the first time Washington had asked it, and Sam had to think for a second.

'Getting into a new book now. Probably the best thing to push it all away, put it behind me.' He didn't mention that he'd barely written two sentences in the five days since Washington's first call about the Bahrain IPA. Five more days of his life trashed.

'I understand. Well, if there's anything you need from me, Sam, don't hesitate. You know where to reach me.'

But his words had one of those reverse-play goodbye rings to it: *don't call me again unless it's really important.*

Sam closed his eyes for a second as he sipped at his coffee. *Routine.* Yeah, that was the best way to forget it all: the library at Albany and picking up books on the San Juan Islands, going back to a theme from five years ago that would hopefully fade out events in between – and maybe subconsciously that had been a side tactic of Elli's, Sam thought ruefully. A leisurely walk through Albany's Washington or Lincoln Park, sometimes stopping to rest for a bit, then finally coffee or lunch at Ramona's, where he'd make notes from what he'd picked up at the library.

But the problem was that part of it hopscotched. Five years ago, Kate and Ashley had still been with him; and sitting in Lincoln Park half an hour back, he'd suddenly had a flashback to playing there with Ashley as a toddler, his high-pitched giggling as he chased a ball piercing Sam's heart, so clear again now in his head that it felt like yesterday. And apart from the last couple of visits to Albany Library, every time he'd been there over the past eighteen months he'd been researching *The Prophecy*.

Oh, God. Was this what it was like when your mind finally snapped? Sam steadied his grip on his cup as he sipped, but kept his eyes open now, didn't trust what images might assault him; just hoped the brightness of the day beyond the café window and the people milling on Lark Street would—

Sam jerked, some of his coffee spilling as a face suddenly leapt out from amongst the street scene of passers-by. He focused more intently.

The man across the far side of the road turned away, offering only a part profile as he talked with another man while walking along. It was harder to tell for sure from that angle.

For only a couple of seconds, as the man had glanced at something across the road a few yards to Sam's left, his face had almost matched the image indelibly etched on Sam's brain: that warped leer beyond the gun barrel as the trigger struck empty chambers! *Almost*. Still Sam wasn't sure, and as he realised in panic that they were moving out of view, he hastily slapped a few coins on the table and signalled to the waitress. He hustled out and started following.

They were forty yards ahead on the opposite side.

The second man was shorter and fatter with a heavy paunch, also Arabic or Mediterranean-looking, and had short, dark, curly hair and a cheroot moustache. He seemed to be doing most of the talking, with the occasional effusive arm movement.

Sam prayed that his sidekick, *gunman*, would turn again, so that he could know for sure – but not too much. Despite the distance and other people on the pavement and the passing traffic, Sam was aware that if gunman fixed on him directly, he'd probably recognise him. The game would be up.

They stopped at that point, the arm movements becoming more elaborate. A half turn from gunman as he contemplated what was being said – but still not enough! And suddenly the madness of it all hit Sam. *He'd seen the man shot, his corpse zipped into a body bag.* It couldn't possibly be him, it was simply someone who looked like him. Was this the final stage of your mind crumbling: projecting your assailant's face on everyone who looked even remotely like him?

But as the two men started moving again, Sam, almost mechanically, continued to follow them. Just a chance that it might be him. He'd felt almost certain with that first front-on glance his way. One more look like that and he'd know.

Gunman half turned again, talking now. Then – the movement so quick and fleeting, Sam had trouble taking stock – he swivelled his head Sam's way and past him, taking in the oncoming traffic as the two men stepped into the road.

For a second Sam's heart leapt. Had gunman picked him up in his side vision and was heading across to confront him? But then he saw the door release lights flashing on a dark blue Toyota Highlander just ahead of them.

They got in, gunman in the driver's seat, looking round at the traffic as he edged out.

Sam turned as well, looking in the same direction; the Highlander's glass was faintly tinted, he couldn't pick out much. He desperately needed a cab otherwise he'd lose them. But there were none in sight.

The Highlander waited for two cars to pass, then pulled out.

Still no cabs. Sam became frantic. He was losing them!

But when the Highlander was sixty yards away, a cab finally turned from the next side street.

Sam waved it down and leapt in. 'Follow that car! The dark-blue Toyota SUV four cars ahead.'

The driver grinned over his shoulder as he started moving.

'You're kidding, right? This ain't New York, this is upstate.'

'Deadly serious. And not too close – I don't want them to know they're being followed.'

'OK. But they start doing any crazy speedin', I ain't keeping up.'

They didn't speed. They kept at a steady thirty to forty miles per hour practically all the way out of town, until they reached a sedate residential area – trimmed lawns, cherry trees and maples, though most of the houses were modest, forty-year-old, aluminium-sided A-frames.

Sam asked the cab driver to ease back. With less traffic, they'd be more conspicuous. But at one point, Sam feared they'd lost them: turning into a street eighty yards behind the Highlander, he could no longer see it ahead. They coasted along. It wasn't visible looking up the first side street, either – but halfway towards the next turn-off, Sam spotted the car in a driveway. Gunman had his key in the front door of the house and his friend was behind him with a briefcase. They paid the cab little attention – stocky-cheroot giving them only a passing glance as the door opened – but still Sam signalled the cabby on a full hundred yards before asking him to stop.

Sam felt suddenly open, vulnerable as the cab left. There were no other people or passing traffic to distract from or partly shield him. Stark reminder that if it *was* gunman and he spotted Sam, the gun chamber this time would no doubt be full.

But having come this far, he couldn't just leave without knowing for sure; just one front-on glance from gunman through a window should do it. He'd just have to make doubly sure to keep concealed, out of sight, as he played spy.

Sam closed his eyes for a second to steel himself, then started back towards the house.

CHAPTER FIVE

MILAN, ITALY.

Only twenty-one, dressed to the nines in a crisp cream linen suit and clutching a brand-new leather attaché case, he looked like he was heading for his first day at work.

Except that he knew it would be his last day on earth.

He merged easily with Milan's morning rush hour as he headed along Via Manzoni. Not too fast, not too slow. But with purpose. As if he was heading somewhere important. A new job interview, or maybe his first day at work.

That's what his handler, Youssef, had advised when

he'd asked what to do if he felt nervous, concerned that people might pick up on his agitation.

'You won't be the only anxious person heading to work. You could have a difficult boss, a tough negotiation to handle, or some work you're late handing in. Or maybe you're heading to a job interview or it's your first day at work. Yes, your first day at work. Just think of that if you start to feel anxious.'

Certainly, he should blend in otherwise. His skin wasn't too dark; his mother was originally Palestinian, but she'd been married to a Jordanian and had herself taken that nationality so many years ago now. Nobody would find that link, at least not easily. And he'd been brought to Italy when he was only seven. So now he was more Italian than Arab in language, dress and mannerisms, his skin colour no different to most Italians born south of Rome. And there were a lot of those in Milan. Perhaps if people knew his name was Ahmed rather than Antonio, they might revise that opinion.

His shirt was chocolate brown, contrasting against his suit *and* his skin – making it look lighter still – and his tie a light-tan natural leather. His black hair was gelled tightly back and his tie matched his tan Gucci slip-ons. No socks. He could easily pass for a new recruit at any of Milan's fashion houses, magazines or advertising agencies.

Yes, he thought, bringing the first tremor of a smile

to his lips: first day at work, and dressed to kill.

And the consolation that he was not alone; at that moment two others just like him were in Milan's city centre for their first day at work.

Sam wasn't able to broach the subject with Mike until after the first quarter.

It was Mike Kiernan's regular get-together – whenever there was a big Patriots game he'd invite his old South Boston 'crowd' to watch the game from his executive suite at the Gillette stadium.

Many of Kiernan's old 'crowd' were straight out of a rogues' gallery: Lyle Cullen, a twenty-year veteran Boston safe-cracker; Craig Macfarlane, who'd run a sizeable tri-state auto-chop operation. And Barry Chilton, right-hand man to Vince Corcoran, Boston's leading mobster. And to add to the eclectic mix was Robby Maschek, a retired police officer, now a South Boston gumshoe.

Kiernan had met them for past research and they'd stayed friends – if indeed Kiernan needed an excuse – because he found them 'characters'. It was the sort of gathering that might raise a policeman's eyebrow, except that half of the guys were 'officially' retired.

'Two legs, Jackson! *Two* legs!' Barry Chilton screamed. 'Use 'em!'

'Maybe his third's gettin' in the way,' someone joshed.

'Yeah, well.' Chilton grinned. 'He's gotta learn to keep that for the bimbos and supermodels – *not* to fuck his game.'

A few chuckles descended quickly into a collective groan and an 'Oh *Jeez*!' from the crowd as they watched Willie Andrews get creamed and flattened by two heavy Titans linebackers.

Lyle Cullen was slightly built and a few inches shorter than Macfarlane and Maschek at six foot. But all three were dwarfed by Barry Chilton.

As the Titans pushed back through three successful downs, the room became more subdued. The Titans onslaught was finally stopped ten yards short of the end zone to a few gasps of relief – then the whistle blew to end the first quarter.

Mike smiled at a quip from Macfarlane and turned his attention again to Sam. He put a hand lightly on his friend's shoulder as they pulled away to the side of the room.

'OK, Sam...what's happening? Some guy in Albany?'

Sam had started to explain before the game started, but then Lyle Cullen had come over. But what few words he'd got out had obviously piqued Mike's interest, and there'd been a couple of tight, apologetic smiles across the room, as if to say, 'Sorry, buddy, I'll get to you as soon as I can.'

And so Sam, not wishing to dampen Mike's evening, and eager to finish before the game started again, blurted out in a rush the saga of possibly seeing the Arab gunman in Albany and following him to a nearby house. 'I hung around for almost two hours outside for a better look before finally giving up the ghost.'

Mike was sceptical. 'Are you sure it was him?'

'That's the trouble. Not a hundred per cent. Eighty, ninety per cent even, when he hit a certain angle. But not the full monty. That's why I followed him – to try and nail it for sure.' Concealed by either the neighbour's hedgerow or parked cars across the road, Sam had caught a couple of glimpses through a front window – he assumed the lounge or dining room – but neither had been full-on-front-facial enough for him to be certain.

Mike still wasn't convinced but Sam could see he was trying to be supportive.

'And you can't even phone your friendly SWAT man. Because if it is your Arab trigger-man, that means SWAT-man is in on it too.'

'I know.' Sam nodded dolefully with a tight smile. 'That was the *first* thing I thought of.'

They were silent for a moment.

'And are you sure you're not just seeing things? Because of the shock of that day – seeing that face where maybe you shouldn't?'

'And that was the *second* thing I thought of.' Sam smiled crookedly. 'Or, actually, the first. But thanks for the reminder that I might be going mad.'

'That's OK. Anytime.' Then more seriously, on the back of a sigh, '*Sorry*. So what's the plan now?'

'Another visit to the house. Another stake-out to see if I can get a better look this time and know for sure.' Sam shrugged. 'All I can think of.'

Mike grimaced tightly. 'Are you sure that's wise, Sam? Let's say it *was* him. You were probably pushing your luck as it was on the first stake-out – but *another*?'

'I know.' Sam lifted a helpless palm. 'And that was the *third* thing I thought of. But I don't know what other options there are.'

They fell silent again, Mike shaking his head, and then the rising roar of the stadium crashed in.

'The girls have stopped shaking their booties!' Chilton called out.

'Yeah, they're lining out again,' Maschek confirmed.

Mike held a hand out towards them. 'OK, *OK*,' he said, probably sharper than he intended. He looked back at Sam. 'Shame there aren't any pics of this guy. Then you could use the likes of Robby.' Mike hooked a thumb sideways. 'Someone who, if eyeballed by this guy, wouldn't cause a problem. SWAT-man would certainly have some photos of the guy, if like he says he's been tracking this group for a while. But obviously difficult to contact him without making him suspicious.'

'Yeah.' Sam nodded numbly. He couldn't think of an excuse to ask for a photo that might wash with Washington. 'Probably not the wisest move.'

'Christ-on-a-Harley!' Macfarlane exclaimed, gesturing with his Coors can. 'How could you miss that pass? Get some sunglasses and become a jazz musician, willya!'

'Apparently Elton John's got a walk-in wardrobe just for his sunglasses,' Cullen commented. Since quitting safe-cracking, he'd become a master of trivia.

Mike tempered a brief smile towards his friends as he turned back to Sam. 'I can see you're set on it. And you're not going to rest easy until you *do* know for sure.' He braced a hand on Sam's shoulder. 'Just be careful, Sam, that's all. You've only just found your way out of hell. Don't head back there.'

SALON, PROVENCE.

He sat at the back of a Routiers café in Salon's Place Crousillat. Pale and gaunt, ponytailed, early thirties, with an elaborately embroidered tunic top – the café owner and its regulars knew him as Jean-Pierre Bourdin, one of the town's more eccentric Nostradamus experts.

Four years ago he'd been a leading technical engineer at Aerospatiale in Toulon, where he'd joined straight after leaving Montpellier University. Then one day he'd fallen from an airframe platform. A bolt had worked loose on the airframe scaffolding, causing the platform to tip with his weight.

He'd suffered heavy spine and some lighter head injuries and for two months doctors feared he might not walk again; but, in the end, he was 'lucky' – if that was the appropriate term. The only remnants of that fateful day now were a heavy limp, occasional mind-numbing headaches, and half the €1.2 million payout from Aerospatiale's insurance company.

He decided not to stay at Aerospatiale – not least because he couldn't face getting up on an airframe platform again and had developed a fear of heights in general. Instead he'd used a chunk of his insurance payout to buy an old manor house in Salon-de-Provence, the town that Michel de Nostradamus had called 'home' for much of his life.

Jean-Pierre had first developed an interest in Nostradamus at Montpellier University, when he'd discovered that the astrologer and prophet had been their most renowned past student.

Having read his way through Nostradamus's early Almanacs and all later seven volumes of his *Centuries*, he put together a thesis in his last year at Montpellier.

Then, having read everything he could that interpreted Nostradamus's work, he went back through the seven hundred quatrains of the *Centuries* for deeper or alternate interpretations which hadn't previously been extrapolated.

Three years into his work at Aerospatiale, he had his own Nostradamus website and regular blog pages, and had written two books on the subject which were published by a minor Paris press.

Then came the fall from the airframe platform. After the long hospitalisation and a spell of feeling sorry for himself, he started to see it as an opportunity. *Divine intervention!* He could use the insurance money to pursue his main interest – though some would term it 'obsession' – which had increasingly made his work at Aerospatiale play a poor second.

He bought an old manor house only eighty metres from Nostradamus's old house. Built in 1783, it was the closest old residence he could find to match the ambience from that era. He converted the downstairs into a mini Nostradamus museum and bookstore, lined the walls with aged texts and manuscript pages, and headhunted an equally aged woman from a local charity shop to tend it.

But it was upstairs where Jean-Pierre's main work took place: tilting and aligning astrolabes, quadrants and armillary spheres to the planets and stars – exactly as Nostradamus would have done in the 1500s. He lived Nostradamus's life as closely as it would have been then; and, in doing so, more importantly took his predictions to the next level: renewing, embellishing and updating those prophecies in the light of what had come to pass in the interceding four and a half centuries.

Jean-Pierre nodded as the waiter took away his finished roast brie on salad starter and put down his venison *pot au feu* main course. Henri, the café owner behind the bar, held up a half bottle of house red by way of asking if he wanted a refill. Jean-Pierre shook his head. '*Non, merci.*' Canal Plus lunchtime news was on the TV at the end of the bar, but Jean-Pierre paid it little attention as he ate.

The final icing on the cake of Jean-Pierre's 'new life' had been inspired by a programme about a medieval family living for a year in a seventeenth-century Loire Valley chateau, very much as they would have done in the time of Louis XIV. Similarly, Jean-Pierre reasoned that if he dressed as Nostradamus had then and observed many of his daily rituals and habits, perhaps he'd be able to get even closer to the spirit of his prophecies and their interpretations.

He'd found some garments at a medieval-costume shop and had the rest custom made. His garb raised a few eyebrows in town and from Henri's regulars, but after a short while bleary eyes settled back on domino games and *le Figaro*. '*Mad Jean-Pierre again, take no notice.*'

He had kept up the full costume for almost two years, but had now settled for just a symbol of that era with period tunic tops – no different to what you might find in many hippy flea markets – over jeans or trousers.

Jean-Pierre paused mid-mouthful as an item on the TV news drew his attention: a mosque bombing in Antalya, Turkey.

He remembered getting a call, almost a year ago now, from an English writer with an 'in progress' novel centred around Nostradamus, part of which had involved some mosque bombings.

Jean-Pierre had given advice on what he felt were the most pertinent quatrains to that chain of events – but hadn't that first proposed mosque bombing been in Turkey?

The bombing was probably just coincidence, nothing to worry about, but Jean-Pierre found himself wolfing down the rest of his meal, eager to get back and check his notes.

Two possible targets at the same time.

The thought preoccupied Adel increasingly after meeting Omari. In particular how it might have affected their 'activity' figures, possibly given them false readings.

Certainly it might help explain why a sharper spike in activity in Turkey or the Middle East hadn't immediately leapt out at them. An intended European target would have levelled out that playing field; the sharp rise in activity of the past two weeks would have been spread more evenly.

As he'd walked back into the room, Karam, whose main responsibility was for east of the Bosphorous and Middle East, thrust the latest printout into Adel's hand.

'Fifty-six per cent increase in Antalya activity over the past week.' Karam paused for emphasis letting the information sink in. 'But we've got a forty-eight per cent rise for Istanbul too – though that could have been a linked operations base. The rest of Turkey was lower.'

Adel ran one finger rapidly down the stats printout. '*OK*. Twenty-nine per cent. So, nineteen per cent above the average for Istanbul, but almost double that for Antalya?'

Karam shrugged. 'The *average*. But places like Izmir and Amasya at the other end of the scale showed only twelve and nine per cent rises respectively.'

Adel grimaced. He knew what Karam was saying. They should have picked up on it earlier. But it was always easier to find the signs retrospectively, when you knew what you were looking for. Until then, the information would have been graded by overall region, then country, then the major cities. A city like Antalya simply wouldn't have figured, because it wasn't the first place you'd expect a terrorist attack. It would have got lost in the averaging of general country data.

Yet this time, Adel reminded himself, they might well know what they were looking for in advance.

'Thanks.' Adel went over to Malik, responsible for European operations. 'Something possibly bubbling in northern Italy. Milan, Turin, Genoa or Bologna. See if anything stands out – using Rome, Venice and Naples as your baselines.'

'OK, boss. Right on it.'

'Oh, and get input too from T6 in Rome. See what extra shades Rani can put to the base stats.'

'Yes, boss.'

At first, Adel had thought the term had been out of respect, until he realised that Malik called everyone 'boss'. A five-stone-overweight Lebanese Druze, Malik invariably wore bright shirts with contrasting braces – today it was yellow braces with blue stars over a crimson shirt – and in that same spirit had the habit of shouting stats and information across the room, as if he was in a busy Wall Street trading room.

It was Malik's language ability more than his unbridled enthusiasm that had assured his rapid rise up the ranks. Aside from his north London kebab-shop English, he was also fluent in Arabic, Farsi, Hebrew and French.

Malik put the stats in Adel's hand eighteen minutes later.

As Adel read them, he felt a tightening at the back

of his neck, rising swiftly so that his whole head felt suddenly hot and pressured.

Malik leant over, pointing. 'Notice the thirty-nine per cent rise just in the last two days in Milan.'

Adel nodded numbly. His eyes were fixed on little else. 'Looks like it could be the one.'

'Fourteen of that has been monitored by T6 in just the past five hours. Even without that, it's still a good eighteen points above the next highest, Rome, and twenty-six above Turin – with the rest lower still. So whatever's happening there – it looks like it could be sooner rather than later.'

Adel nodded again. This was the cutting edge of their expertise, what it all finally boiled down to: calling an alert at the right time. Too early, and after a few days the security services became listless – all the edge and focus lost. After a few false alerts, it swilled away even faster. But make that call even a minute too late, and the price was simply too high to pay. Adel laid the stats on his desk and looked up at Malik pensively, as if still unsure he was making the right decision.

'Get back to Rani and advise him to go straight to critical, code red, with all GIS and *carabinieri* in Milan – with particular focus on transport networks.'

Ahmed could still hear the sirens of the *carabinieri* echoing in his head as he headed along the tiled underground passages at Duomo Station.

He wouldn't have worried so, except as he'd made his way down the last of the subway steps, he'd heard sirens coming from the other direction too, and more still in the distance. It sounded as if half the city was suddenly alive with *carabinieri* sirens.

Just after he'd gone through the ticket barriers and was approaching the escalators, he'd seen a group of three *carabinieri* appear at the bottom of the steps he'd descended only a minute before. Razor-keen and alert, earpieces in and MP-5 semi-automatics part raised, their eyes darted rapidly around the milling crowds, as if they were looking for somebody specific.

Ahmed's heart leapt in his throat. But their eyes drifted past him, one of them finally settling on a twenty-something with a mini Afro and a rucksack approaching the ticket barrier. He signalled his colleagues to follow his lead, and then they were gone from view as the escalator carried Ahmed down.

Ahmed breathed a sigh of relief. Youssef had been right about their dress choice. But still those sirens echoed in his head as he paced the tiled tunnels. Every other sound also seemed somehow amplified: the echo of the milling crowds bouncing off the tiled walls; the rumble of the train as it finally arrived, sounding like deafening thunder accompanied by a hurricane wind rush; the hiss of the doors as they closed behind him; the strained electric whine as the train started again, its clatter and rumble bouncing back at him off the tunnel walls as it gained speed.

A trickle of sweat made its way down his forehead. He wiped at it with his free hand, aware of a couple of people looking at him. He closed his eyes, letting the gentle rocking of the train soothe him.

First day at work, first day at work. People were simply looking because he was dressed smartly, not because they'd noticed the panic written across his face, the sweat on his brow, the nerves dancing wildly in his stomach.

Oh merciful Allah. *Allah.*

Halfway after the first station stop, Youssef had instructed.

It seemed no time that the train was slowing again – his few moments to himself abruptly cut short as the brighter station lights struck his eyelids like a strobe. He opened them again.

Doors hissing open, more people getting on.

A fat man in a brown suit pushed back against him with the surge. Beyond him, two middle-aged women, one draped in cheap costume jewellery, were chattering loudly.

Her gold cross on a chain amongst the pearls and bright beads caught Ahmed's eye. It flashed and glinted at him with the reflected station lights, as if teasing, taunting, as the train pulled out. He was no longer upset or offended by them. He knew that for many people they were just casual fashion accessories; those carrying them as symbols of what they held most dear, most sacred, were less and less each year. Unlike his own religion; and certainly not enough to die for.

Most dear, most sacred. His mother had worn the key round her neck for the first four years in Italy. Until two years after his father died, and nine months after she'd met her new husband.

'*We shouldn't wear our past, our shame, around our necks for all to see*,' he'd said.

From that day on, she'd kept the key in her jewellery box.

His stepfather, like his mother, was originally Palestinian – except he was from the West Bank and so had the option of being Jordanian, which he'd taken in 1974. Whereas she was from Beersheba, so her only route out of the refugee camps had been to marry a Jordanian, her first husband. Ahmed's father.

His new father saw himself as a 'progressive' Palestinian. He had turned his back on his country's problems, considered this his sacrifice in order to forge ahead in the Western world. '*However painful, we must forget all that – otherwise it just drags us down. We just become slaves to a cause that has no place in our new lives here, in Italy.*'

But that wasn't what the imam at the mosque said, or his handler, Youssef. They said that we must *never* forget. Otherwise that history and birthright would be lost too.

Ahmed had been careful, secretive with his mosque visits. He didn't want his father to discover that he might not be a 'progressive' Palestinian. As careful as his mother was not to take the key out of her jewellery box while he was around.

But when she thought nobody was looking, Ahmed had seen her take the key out and finger it reverently, slow tears running down her cheeks as she recalled their lost home.

The same tears she would no doubt shed when she heard the news about her son.

Except she'd *know* why he'd done it. She'd understand.

Because while her new husband might have day by day crushed that spirit and will to remember out of her – so that now she was afraid to even mention anything about her past life in Palestine in front of him – she'd know that her son hadn't forgotten.

He'd kept that spirit alive for *both* of them.

CHAPTER SIX

Sam paused mid-sip of his second coffee of the morning as he heard the repetitive starter motor whining from the driveway.

He shook his head. Third time this month it had happened. Probably the cold mornings.

Churn...whine, whine, whine...clunk. Churn... whine, whine, whine...clunk.

He'd better get out there before she burnt it out. He took one more quick gulp of coffee, and headed outside to help Lorrena.

'When are you going to finally call it a day on this—'

She held one hand out in a stop motion through the car window. 'Don't say it! We agreed, remember?' She smiled wryly.

The pig. The heap. The junk pile. He'd run the gamut of name-calling on Lorrena's car, but it didn't matter. Lorrena's mother had bought her the baby-blue Volkswagen Jetta second hand as her first car seven years ago. Then four years later she and her father were burying her mother. Angina-linked heart failure. So now the car had sentimental value; it was an inarguable case.

Sam hardly bothered any more and just mumbled, 'I know, it's *your* heap – and you love it.' He placed his hands on the hood, shoulders bracing as she took the handbrake off, ready for the push out the driveway.

At least they both knew the routine by now. A sharp twist of the wheel to swing out into the road as they gained momentum at the end of the driveway. Then he'd get behind and push and after thirty yards she'd slip into gear and *the pig, the heap* would finally splutter to life.

Except that today it didn't start on the first try, and it took another twenty-yard run before it finally did, by which time Sam was out of breath.

'Thanks, sucker!' Lorrena shouted through the open window, giving a quick wave. 'Just think, if you had a car like this, you could get me to do the same for you!'

And with a couple more splutters and a backfire which left a plume of black smoke in her baby-blue wake, she was gone.

Sam grimaced. *She was impossible.* But it was probably part of the attraction. He headed back to the house, smile fading as his thoughts turned back to their earlier conversation.

'I'm going out after work with Ruby and Lisa. Girls night out. So I might be late.'

'I'll probably meet up with Mike for a quick drink.'

'Vaccarelli's?'

'Yeah.'

'No danger of us bumping into each other then. We'll be heading for a place with loud music and young studs gyrating in satin posing pouches.'

He smiled weakly, the best he could muster considering that he had no intention of seeing Mike that night.

He hadn't told Lorrena about possibly seeing *gunman*. After months of her soothing his brow over the nightmare and the burden it had put on her – and their relationship – he didn't want to worry her that the nightmare might be back again. Not yet. Not until he was sure.

And maybe not even then. *'You've already plumbed her emotional well, tapped her dry. Nobody can keep doing that day in, day out. You're lucky to have her,*

Sam – but you're pushing that luck right now.' He'd cross that bridge if and when it came to it.

Having given up on talking Sam out of going back to the house again, Mike advised him to at least try and observe more at night. 'Lights on in the windows will give you a better chance of picking him out – plus you're more obscured.'

It had been awkward observing in daylight. He'd found a position half obscured by a hedgerow and not too visible to other neighbours thanks to a parked van. But when late afternoon the van moved, he'd felt more exposed, and didn't stay longer than another half-hour.

Sam had visited twice since, picking up a rental car at Little Falls on the way – different models, both with tinted windows – and had sat outside for almost four hours each time, an hour of which was after sundown. No show for his Arab friends either time. He hadn't wanted to stay beyond that, otherwise he'd be late getting back to Oneida and Lorrena might start asking questions.

But tonight she'd be expecting him late, so he'd be able to hold his vigil longer.

Sam didn't want to head off until midday, but it was hard to get into writing with the planned trip filling his thoughts. He found himself staring blankly at the computer screen for long spells, in the middle of which Elli Roschler phoned.

'How's it going?'

'Fine. *Fine*,' he lied. He'd been staring at the same paragraph for the past half-hour, having changed the last sentence already four times. And that had been the pattern since Washington's call of two weeks ago, which he hadn't told Elli about; nor did he intend now to tell Elli about this new panic with *gunman*. Worrying Elli that the nightmare might be back and his focus was once again shot to hell.

'Still on for delivering the first hundred pages the middle of next month?'

'Pretty much. Well, maybe closer to the end of the month.' A bit of time-buying. He doubted he'd even make that the way things were going. 'You know what beginnings are like. Always a bit slower.'

'Yeah. I know.' But there was something else Sam sensed in Elli's tone; as if he had some underlying concerns, but didn't want to say anything. Or there was something else he wanted to say, but decided it could wait. 'Let me know when you're there with the hundred, Sam. We should lunch.'

'Yeah, great. Look forward to it.'

And then it was just him and that same on-screen sentence again. Sam gave it two more tweaks before deciding he was finally happy with it. But as his thoughts shifted to the next sentence, he found himself equally stuck with that; and after ten minutes staring at the screen with no fresh inspiration, he'd had enough.

He grabbed his car keys and headed to Albany, his fingers tapping anxiously on the steering wheel only minutes into the drive. *Lying to Lorrena, lying to Elli.* The only person he'd confided in was Mike. And what if *gunman* didn't appear this time either? How many more no-shows before he finally gave up?

He changed to a dark maroon Chevrolet rental car at Little Falls, a light rain beginning to fall as he approached Amsterdam.

It was 3.46 p.m. as he pulled into the street. He parked on the opposite side twenty yards back from the house; angle-on, but still with a clear view. There were no cars in the driveway and no sign of life in the house. And that remained the case for the next hour. And the next. Sam had turned on the radio after half an hour, but still the minutes dragged. He started to stifle off yawns.

The light faded early with the cloudy skies, the rain steadier, heavier, as it hit dusk. There had been an increase in car activity in the road not long after Sam first arrived – the school run – and now there was another: people returning home from work. Sam found himself tensing with each fresh set of lights – but they'd either stop short to turn into driveways or drive past.

After an hour and a half of the same, Sam's nerves were worn. His sleep had been fitful since his first sighting of gunman and he could feel himself drifting off.

He snapped to attention as another car passed. The song had changed on the radio so he knew he'd fallen asleep. Suddenly, he sat bolt upright. The dark blue Toyota Highlander – the same car as last time – was parked in the driveway.

How long had he been asleep? He checked his watch. Eight or nine minutes at most. Still, if they'd been suspicious of his car, they might well have approached close enough for gunman to have recognised him through the tinted glass. Swift bullet to the head and he could have been dumped at the nearest patch of wasteland.

Sam shuddered. There were two lights on in the house: the dining room where the curtains were drawn, and the kitchen with only thin laces each side. Sam had a seventy per cent clear view of the kitchen, but there was nobody in it right now.

He waited. Ten minutes. Twenty. As he stifled another yawn, he switched from the easy-listening channel. He didn't want to risk drifting off again. Finally, there was some activity visible through the kitchen window.

Gunman's fat-gutted friend, waving one hand as he spoke. Gunman was a yard or so behind, but not close enough – and not looking Sam's way directly – so he still couldn't be sure.

A slight head tilt as gunman started speaking, but

still not enough. Just a bit more, Sam willed him on. Move closer to the window. *Closer*.

Sam peered hard through the rain streaming down his windshield. While it helped further obscure himself inside the car, it also masked a clear view of his target.

With a dismissive wave towards his friend, gunman turned away and Sam eased out his held breath.

He could hear another car approaching. Sam expected to see it stop short or drive on, but it slowed down just thirty yards ahead as it came alongside gunman's house. And as Sam picked out its shape and colour beyond the headlamps, along with its unmistakeable engine rattle, his heart froze.

His mouth and throat were suddenly dry, unable to swallow, his temples taut with his pounding pulse, as he watched Lorrena's car, *the pig*, *the heap*, turn into gunman's driveway.

In case there was possibly another car just like that, Sam desperately checked the registration. Then he felt the lead weight in his chest, trapping his breath, fall rapidly through his stomach.

As Lorrena killed her engine and headlamps, gunman finally moved closer to the window to look out, and Sam was sure.

At the very moment that he was unsure about everything else in his life.

* * *

The woman reminded him of his mother.

Ahmed didn't notice her until she lifted the young boy, no more than four or five, into her arms as if to protect him from the surge of commuters pressing in harder and closer around them.

Not as his mother was now, but how Ahmed remembered her when she was younger and he was a child: jet black, slightly wavy hair a foot past her shoulders, large brown eyes with a tinge of sadness that would quickly lift whenever she saw him – the same look the woman now gave to the child in her arms as she kissed him on the forehead, smiled and hugged him close.

And Ahmed wondered whether that's why he hadn't noticed her until she lifted up her son. In that moment the boy symbolised how he and his mother had been then; a sudden, poignant recall of happier days.

A hot day on the edge of Adh Dhahiriya, his mother holding him on her shoulder as she pointed into the distance.

'You see there, that village in the distance. That's where your mother's home used to be.'

He hadn't seen, at least not clearly. They were on a small ridge which afforded a view into the distance, but the bus ride from East Jerusalem, where her brother now lived, had taken over two hours, the heat rising steadily all the way. Now, a heavy heat haze hung over Beersheba, half obscuring it.

Though sensing the excitement and enthusiasm in his mother's voice, and not wishing to dampen it, he'd answered with equal eagerness, 'Yes, *yes*. I see it.'

She'd kissed and hugged him tight then. But what had stuck in his mind most about that day was a light and spirit in her eyes that he'd never seen before.

'We'll return one day. You'll see. *You'll see.*'

A light and spirit that had year by year been dulled, until now that dream of returning was distant, out of reach. Relegated to a chain around her neck for thirty years, and now a jewellery box that she dared not even open while anyone was looking.

But with a tight cramp to his chest, something else suddenly hit Ahmed: the mother and son were only four paces away. *They'd be caught in the blast!* In that moment, they represented to him a second chance at life and spirit and happiness that for his mother and himself had long gone; and by killing them, he'd be killing that also.

He started moving away from them, pushing his way through the tightly packed throng. And this time, people did openly stare at him: at the heavier sweat beads on his forehead, at the obvious panic in his eyes, as if he'd just seen a ghost.

Set the device off midway between Cordusio and Cairoli Station, Youssef had instructed; but they must already be past that point now. Ahmed looked back: seven or eight paces away, the blast would still catch them. The end of the carriage was only four paces away. If he could just make it to there, they might stand a chance.

The train rocked and swayed as he pushed through – a middle-aged businessman cursing under his breath as Ahmed caught his ankle.

The train slowed, some brighter flashes coming from the side. Ahmed turned to them like a startled animal caught in headlamps, fearing that he'd mis-timed and they were already pulling into Cairoli Station. But it was only electrical flashes.

He pushed on through the tightly packed crowd – only two paces from the end now – when suddenly there was a harder, sharper braking. Ahmed lurched forward as the train came to an abrupt halt.

He could hear his own breathing falling steadily in the lull, and another fear suddenly gripped him: one of the other bombs had already gone off, and they had shut down the network! The train would wait here idling for the *carabinieri* to come along the tracks, open the doors and arrest him. He'd face years ahead in an Italian jail – or perhaps he'd be sent to Guantanamo Bay.

What should he do? Set the device off now – half the operation completed better than none? Or wait until the *carabinieri* came along – hope that he could set it off before they tasered or shot him. Grab some extra glory by at least taking some of them with him.

He closed his eyes, muttering a silent prayer to Allah for guidance and to his mother for forgiveness.

But picturing her as she would be later when she heard the news about him, he couldn't tell whether that light and spirit was back in her eyes beyond the tears.

A sudden jolt broke him out of it. He opened his eyes. The train was starting to move again.

CHAPTER SEVEN

Mike was the only one he told. Mike was the only one he *could* tell.

Sam related the woeful chain of events as calmly and factually as he could, watching Mike's wide-eyed and open-mouthed reaction.

Mike asked a few questions to get everything clear in his mind, and as he repeated '*Are you sure?*' one time too many, as if Sam's state of mind was again in question, Sam finally lost it, his voice rising.

'You think I haven't asked myself that a thousand times over the last twenty-four hours? That I'm wrong about the man? That it might have been someone else's car, not Lorrena's? Or that I'd read the number plate wrong? Or she'd lent her car to someone else? Anything...*anything* not to have to accept what I saw!'

Mike looked around anxiously. They'd gone to a nondescript diner on Highway 90 near Whitesboro, somewhere where nobody would know them. It was close to midnight, so there were only a few other people in the diner – as before, engrossed in their own food or conversations. Bright fluorescent lighting seemed to suck the life out of the room and the people in it. It looked like it would take more than a few sharp, raised words to grab their attention.

Mike volleyed a few more questions to get everything clear in his mind. 'OK, *OK*. Let's accept that it was her, *and* him. Let's see where else that leads us.'

Sam nodded and Mike's first comment was that they were obviously somehow working together. 'And if gunman is suddenly alive and that attack was staged – that means SWAT-man and his team are all in on it too. Full circle. They've all been working together from the start.'

'Yeah.' Another nod from Sam. Hopefully soon Mike would get to something he *hadn't* already worked out.

'So the thing now is to trace back and work out how and why they first latched on to you. When did you first meet Lorrena?'

'Uh, just over a year ago now.'

'And how long had you been working on *The Prophecy* then?'

Sam thought for a second. 'Two, maybe three months.' Sam saw a shadow of consternation cross Mike's face, and added, 'But I'd been working on research for four to five months before that.'

The shadow lifted after a second. 'OK, right. That's the lead-in time. Now to who. Contact a lot of people over that time for research?'

Sam shrugged. 'Thirty-five, forty, I suppose. Maybe more.'

'Many American based?'

'No more than eight or ten. And slightly more than that across Europe: England, France, Germany...one guy in Holland. But over forty per cent were Middle East-based Islamic scholars. The best sources were in Egypt and Saudi, but I also found a few good sources in Syria and Oman. And one even at Haifa University.'

Mike nodded slowly, thoughtfully. 'And that's the *people* lead-in. One of those contacts got concerned about something you were writing in *The Prophecy*. They made a phone call, concern turned to alarm, and Lorrena was sent in. Where did you say you first met her again?'

'Albany Library.'

'Figures.' Another nod. 'Somewhere they know you visit regularly.' He was on a roll now, piecing it all together. 'And her background? I know she's second-generation Italian, and I remember you telling me about her mom dying a few years back. But what about her father and the rest of the family?'

'Her dad moved back to Taranto a year after her mum died. And she's got one older sister been living in San Diego the past eight years.'

'So nobody you can check out locally, huh?' Mike raised a sharp eyebrow.

Sam blinked slowly in submission. Stripped bare like that, it seemed so obvious. He looked up after a second; one factor didn't sit right.

'But if it was her job to monitor what I was up to with *The Prophecy* – why didn't she just take the manuscript herself and wipe it from my computer?'

'Two reasons.' Mike held the fingers up. 'First, she couldn't be sure that you hadn't made a copy disk while she was out and stashed it somewhere she didn't know about. That needed some hard questioning to flush out. Second, if she'd taken it, she'd have had to disappear at the same time. Yet she had to hang around to make sure you weren't inclined to try and write the whole thing again – *and* to make sure you were telling the truth about any spare disk copies. That you wouldn't suddenly twirl one out of a bottom drawer. "Hey, look what I got! I managed to dupe those stupid Arab gunmen, *and* Washington!"'

A faint shudder ran through Sam. Revulsion as the

strata levels of deception and the fact that he'd been sleeping with the enemy the past year struck home.

'So, you're saying that once she's a hundred per cent sure I'm not going to try and rewrite *The Prophecy* – which must be close to a given by now – she'll be gone.'

'Yep. She'll tell you that her father's ill in Taranto, or make some other excuse – and you won't see her again.'

Sam cast a sideways glance at the lifeless diner and the equally lifeless people, but nobody could have felt emptier than himself at that moment. 'Can't wait,' he said with an edge to his voice, bitter at being duped for so long.

Mike smiled warily. 'That's the thing, Sam. You don't want her to leave – not right now. Because she holds the key to everything you want to know: the people she's working for, why you were targeted and, most importantly, just where a copy of *The Prophecy* might be right now.' Mike paused, watching the uneasy realisation settle with Sam. 'The clues to that are all there somewhere – she must have notes, names and contact numbers, perhaps in her diary or laptop?'

Sam met Mike's gaze levelly. Everything he said made sense, in fact was what he'd hoped for from Mike, that ability to rapidly strip bare and get to the core of a problem or plot. But acting on it would be another matter.

He shook his head. 'I don't think I could do it. Besides, I thought you said it was dangerous?'

Mike shrugged. 'Well, if you're happy to let slip what might be your last chance to trace *The Prophecy* – *fine*.' He leant forward. 'But you're in danger either way, Sam. If Lorrena thought for one second you might be onto her, she'd hightail it anyway and call SWAT-man before she'd even reached the end of your road. And this time there'd be no empty chambers.'

Sam closed his eyes as the shudder ran deeper this time. He'd wanted the advice, but wished now that Mike had spared bludgeoning him with its harsher edges.

'I don't know,' he said as he opened them again. He shook his head. 'I just don't know.'

But Sam *did* know.

The night before he'd drifted from bar to bar to kill the time, so that he could be sure Lorrena would already be home and in bed by the time he returned. Not only so that he wouldn't have to face any questions or conversation, but also her touch. He found himself trembling at even the thought of that, wasn't sure how he'd respond; whether he'd just freeze rigid or push her away – and she'd know immediately something was wrong. Or perhaps he'd just lay there gently trembling under her touch, and she'd still know.

He'd had a couple of stiff whiskies at the first bars,

then had switched to soft drinks. If he was out of his head when he got back, he wouldn't know how to react. He'd need his senses about him.

It was 12.34 a.m. by the time he put his key in the door. Lorrena's Jetta was in the driveway, but there were no lights on in the lounge or kitchen. It looked like she was already in bed.

Still he moved quietly, stealthily up the stairs, and used the second bathroom rather than the en suite so that he didn't disturb her.

Slipping beneath the sheets alongside her, she murmured gently and turned over, and Sam feared for a minute that she'd fully rouse and reach across to him.

But she didn't fully waken, and after a moment he eased a silent sigh of relief.

Though tonight as he headed away from the diner and it struck him that he faced the same again, his foot eased on the gas pedal, once again delaying, hoping she'd already be in bed by the time he got there.

Key in the door. 12.46, twelve minutes later than last night. Footsteps light on the stairs, though somehow his legs felt even more leaden tonight, as if he was taking the last steps towards his execution.

Breath held as he finally eased into bed. A muted groan from Lorrena, then silence, and he thought for a moment he was home free. But then the groan returned more fully, throatily, and she rolled towards him, draping one arm across his stomach.

'Uuuhmm – late again tonight.'

'Yeah, met up with Mike. Problems with a couple of scenes I wanted to run by him.'

'And was he much help?'

'Well…we got most of it sorted.'

Silence, only the steady fall of her breathing, and Sam wondered what she was thinking. Had the story washed, or was she suspicious?

Then: 'You're trembling.'

He swallowed silently, imperceptibly. 'It…it's cold outside, and I ended up talking with Mike in the car park longer than I realised.'

'Vaccarelli's?'

'Yeah.'

He bit his lip as soon as he said it: one lie she could easily uncover.

'I'll warm you up,' she said, and he felt her reach down to him. Limp, lifeless.

'And I…I had a couple more beers with Mike than I should.'

Uneasy silence again. Had she bought the story? Or was she already laying plans to leave at first light and phone for a SWAT team?

'Try not to drink so much with Mike next time,' she said, as, with a teasing pat to his groin, she rolled away. 'And come to bed a bit earlier tomorrow night, big boy.'

'OK.' He turned to his side after a second, but the tightness didn't fully ease from his chest for another eight or nine minutes, when he could tell from the fall of her breathing that she'd fallen asleep again.

OK. Looked like he'd managed to ride out tonight with a story. But what about tomorrow night and all the ones after? And if he was having trouble just getting into bed with her each night, how on earth was he going to summon up the courage to start playing spy games with her?

Sam stared into the darkness for almost two hours thinking about that, the only accompaniment the steady fall of her breathing, before he finally fell asleep.

CHAPTER EIGHT

MILAN, ITALY.

The black Lancia Thesis carrying the head of Milan's GIS, Colonel Giuseppe Muzzio, cut through the bedlam of Milan's early morning traffic.

Hectic at the best of times, the shutting down of the city's train and subway network had thrown twice the number of cars onto the roads.

A GIS *maresciallo,* warrant officer, drove and the Lancia's siren wailed incessantly, but often it got lost amongst the frenetic beep-beep arguing of the traffic, so headlamps were constantly flashed as well.

It took thirty-eight minutes to arrive at Cairoli Station when normally it would take half that time.

More bedlam. Police cars. SUD vans. Fire engines, ambulances and medics. And beyond a taped-off, police-guarded cordon, press cameras clicked and microphones jostled with two mobile broadcast units which had already arrived. A pressing mass of people watched the station entrance expectantly, some openly crying and wailing.

Muzzio had already ascertained that a Captain Bruno Castaldi of the *polizia di stato* headed the operation. His *maresciallo* quickly sought out Castaldi from the throng.

Muzzio nodded back towards the fire trucks as he headed down the station steps alongside Castaldi.

'Has there been a fire?'

'No. They've been solely for the cutting equipment.'

Castaldi brought him up to date as they walked through the main ticket concourse and started down the escalator. Eight dead, including one of Muzzio's men. But a dozen or more critically injured, 'Any of which could add to the fatality list over the next forty-eight hours. Including, I'm afraid, possibly another of your men.'

Muzzio nodded sombrely. The explosion near Rovereto Station had been more serious: the train had been travelling faster and had resulted in twenty or more fatalities. But this incident had directly involved some of his men. So he'd come here instead and directed his second in command, Captain Endrizzi, to Rovereto.

'Why did the train start up again once the network had been shut down?'

Castaldi shrugged, grimacing tightly, as if to say the decision wasn't his or he'd have called it differently. 'The train driver worked out that he was only three hundred metres from Cairoli Station. He asked his network operator for permission to continue that short distance so that he could offload the passengers. The operator said yes, as long as he kept his speed low. He did, edging along at no more than 20 kilometres an hour.'

They both knew the rest: four of Muzzio's men had already cleared everyone from the station platform and were awaiting earpiece instructions as to what to do next when the train coasted slowly into view. As the third carriage, the one carrying the bomber, came alongside them, he'd set off his device.

Muzzio stifled a cough as acrid fumes and dust hit the back of his throat. And it seemed to be getting denser as the escalator took them further down.

'I thought you said there was no fire.'

'No, no fire. Just dust.' Castaldi waved one hand theatrically. 'Amazing how much of it there is. Forty years of dust accumulated from when the station was first built. One explosion, *puff*, and it all suddenly becomes airborne.'

Muzzio stifled another cough. Dust motes hung thick in the air, dimming the overhead fluorescent lighting.

Then two-thirds down, the lighting ended abruptly, the only illumination from lamps strung on cables along the walls and the flickering of torches from people below. The hum of a generator became evident as they neared the bottom, visibility now down to no more than a few metres. The explosion had obviously taken out all the electrics from here onwards.

A fireman stepped through the gloom, shining his torch on them.

'You'll need these to advance any further.' He held out two respirator masks.

Muzzio put on the mask and followed Castaldi and the fireman deeper into hell.

Rani Hemakah of Rome's T6 tracking unit got the call from Milan at 11.14 a.m., almost two and a half hours after the bombings, then phoned Adel in London.

Adel cradled his head in his hands as he heard the news: twenty-three dead at one location, eight at another, and that toll could easily rise by ten or twenty per cent over the next few days. 'There are a lot of critically injured,' Rani commented.

'OK. Thanks, Rani.' He sighed tiredly. 'We both did our best. We got the information to you as soon as we knew, and you acted on it as quickly and as best you could. Nothing more we can do.'

'Yes, I suppose so.' Rani sounded equally defeated.

Nothing more we can do. But as Adel hung up, he

felt those words hang heavy in his chest. What if he'd got the information from Omari earlier? Rani might then have had time to set off suspect-raid alerts to disrupt their plans at the eleventh hour. And with too many pre-empt raids, what was the risk? A hundred of his Muslim brothers saw high-powered lawyers, screaming about their civil rights being abused. Against the lives of those thirty-one? No contest, even if it might save just *one* of those lives.

There was a lull in the operations room over the following hours. To be expected. There weren't any fresh activity spikes, nor any anticipated – major bombing incidents rarely occurred close to each other – and apart from casualty and mortality updates, nothing more was expected now until forensics had identified the two bombers, then hopefully pieced together the CCTV footage of them getting on the trains.

But the lull was also a winding-down, a coming to terms with what had happened: *we tracked an activity spike, but still didn't manage to stop it happening*. Or, as Adel found himself now doing, clinging to small mercies: *at least that second train was stopped and then only moved slowly. If not, three times that number might have been killed on that train.*

Just after lunch, Adel's wife, Tahiya, phoned.

'You haven't forgotten?'

'No, no. Baklawar, karabeej and tahini humos. I'll pick them up on my way home.'

'Oh, and some of their halva. The one with pistachios.'

Adel scribbled a quick note. 'Don't worry, I'll get them. I won't forget.'

'Because I know so often you have a lot on your mind.'

Adel closed his eyes for a second, said nothing. *You have no idea.*

'I'd get them locally, if I could,' she continued.

Mawlid an-Nabi. Mohammed's birthday. They were no longer strictly devout themselves, but indulged these festivals mainly for the children's sake. In the same way that many lapsed Christians still observed Christmas or had hot cross buns at Easter.

'Don't worry. I've made a big note to myself. I'll see you later.'

Adel grabbed a water from the cooler, then went back into the Italian activity stats to see if he could glean anything new. Twenty or thirty minutes later – he'd lost track – Malik was by his shoulder.

'You'll want to see this.'

The sound reached him as the TV was turned up. He stood and moved closer to the large plasma screen, most of the room already swivelled from their computers towards it: Abu Khalish was on Al Jazeera TV.

They'd shown the same photo now for the past five years, as if he was a war zone correspondent; no video. All that changed each time were the words, though the substance was the same: Khalish's high-pitched, slightly cracked voice in rapid Arabic claiming responsibility for – though most would say gloating over – the latest atrocity.

In the photo he had a heavy beard and moustache, and a mocking smile; some time had been spent choosing the right photo to mirror his messages. His dark eyes seemed to stare right through you, until you noticed that his left eye was focused slightly off centre and its iris had a faint yellow tinge – an injury dating back to Shatila, word had it.

But halfway through Khalish's speech, Adel also started to smile. Abu Khalish had just made a mistake in his prepared speech. A serious mistake.

And Khalish rarely, if ever, made those.

The September 1982 raid on Shatila refugee camp by Lebanese militia was the first main defining event in Abu Khalish's life. Only fourteen at the time, he was partly blinded by his injury; a bullet had glanced off his left cheekbone, but the impact rocketed a splinter of bone through his retina. Though he was by far the most fortunate: his father and elder brother were both killed in the raid.

The second defining event was the November 2001 attack by coalition forces on Mazari Sharif, Afghanistan, in which he lost his younger brother. Abu's Palestinian father and Egyptian mother had raised three sons and two daughters, but within a year of 9/11, Abu was the only son remaining.

The shaping of Abu Khalish's life had its roots even further back, in the days of Black September when in 1971 the PLO *fedayeen* had their final showdown with King Hussein's Jordanian army before being exiled to refugee camps in the Lebanon.

Both Abu's father, Fayez, and his uncle, Majed, were high-ranking commanders in Arafat's newly formed Palestine Liberation Organisation (PLO). Fayez was mainly involved with on-the-ground operations – strikes across the border against Israeli *kibbutzim* and Lebanese right-wingers during the civil war – while Majed handled 'external planning': ensuring funding and arms ran smoothly to support those operations.

Years later Majed Khalish was attributed as the main person responsible for Arafat's extreme wealth at the time of his death, with multimillions stashed in Swiss bank accounts. And as the PLO's most effective funds and arms raiser over the years, Majed Khalish had himself sorted away a sizeable stash.

When Abu's father and elder brother were killed at Shatila, Majed decided that the refugee camps were no longer the place to raise a family, and used his money to move them to Paris. It was not uncommon within Islam to help a brother's family who'd lost their breadwinner; Majed's wealth ensured it was done in a style that was not so common.

Abu proved a good student, so funds were provided for him to go to the Sorbonne, where he studied economics and politics. Abu's Uncle Majed became not just a replacement father, but his mentor; and, in turn, it quickly became apparent that Majed was coaching Abu to follow in his footsteps.

Upon leaving the Sorbonne, Abu started work with one of his uncle's main trading companies, specialising in fine, rare Arab art. Extensive travel was involved, meeting with wealthy buyers, but it was little secret that it was a thinly disguised cover for PLO fund-raising.

And eight years later when his uncle died, Abu, along with his uncle's eldest son, took over the running of Majed Khalish's sprawling trading network.

Urbane and charming, he far preferred his playboy lifestyle over getting married. And with his beard and moustache always neatly trimmed, he was far removed from radical Islamists like Mullah Omar or Bin Laden.

Though that all changed with the death of his youngest brother, Raji, in Afghanistan. Raji *had* become radical, joining an extremist religious school in Oman before heading to a Taliban training camp seven months before the coalition war started.

When Abu learnt how his brother had died, trapped

in a school building and gunned down like a dog along with five hundred others, it broke his heart.

Abu stayed in Afghanistan for four months after the funeral, shared tea and prayers with Raji's fellow Taliban fighters and commanders, and rumour had it offered them considerable finance and arms support.

And shortly after he left, his beard and moustache now long and unruly, that infamous photo was taken and Abu Khalish's war against the West was set in stone.

Secretive to the last, it was never revealed whether Abu, born and raised Sunni Muslim, had himself adopted the more radical Wahhabi code, or whether it was purely revenge for his brother's death – or, thinking more strategically, to take Bin Laden's campaign to the next level.

That was a singular war against America stemming from, as Bin Laden saw it, their unholy, *infidel* presence on sacred Saudi soil. So Abu Khalish's battle cry became for the removal of *all* foreign troops from Islamic soil. '...*For while they remain there, they represent not only an insult to Allah, but to the sanctity of Islam itself.*'

The smart money had it that unlike Bin Laden, he wouldn't be holed up in a cave in southern Afghanistan or across the border in Pakistan. He'd probably be clean-shaven, hair gelled back, and with his fluent Spanish as well as French was now a José or Eduardo buried in the depths of Bolivia or Ecuador.

Sharp-witted, smooth, chameleon-like, the smart money also had it that Abu Khalish would never be found.

Because Abu Khalish never made mistakes.

Except now, Adel thought, his smile rising as he listened to Khalish's Al Jazeera speech.

'...and so we pray, *inshallah*, that the actions of our three brave *shahids* today will bring our endeavour of reclaiming the sanctity of Islam a step closer. May Allah's blessing be on their souls, and on yours.'

Three brave martyrs.

Khalish had obviously sent his tape to Al Jazeera a few hours ago. Yet with the bedlam, the traffic, and the fact that initially other bombings were suspected – for the first few hours news reports had simply stated, '*A number of bombings reported on Milan's metro network.*' Adel wasn't sure if even now they'd modified those reports to just *two* bombings. He turned to Malik.

'Relay this clip to Rani if he hasn't already seen it. Looks as if one lamb has slipped from the fold, and Khalish himself has been kind enough to let us know about him. Let's see what messages might be out there as he tries to find his way back home.'

Sam leant his head out of the kitchen. The TV was on mute, Lorrena still at her laptop.

'Looks like we've run out of both herb seasoning

and tomato puree.' He smiled wanly. 'I should have checked before I started cooking.'

Lorrena looked up from tapping the keys. 'Oh, right. You want me to get them?'

He shrugged. 'If you don't mind. Unless you take over tending the pot for me, and I go?'

'No, no. It's OK.'

A last flurry of key taps and Lorrena got up, reaching for her keys on the end of his desk. The ploy had worked. But had she merely finished up some notes or logged out and off? Sam couldn't tell: her screen was angled away from him.

Lorrena grabbed her jacket. 'I won't be long.'

'Thanks.' Sam retreated back into the kitchen.

A second later he turned off the extractor fan and paused in his pot stirring so that he could hear the front door slamming, her car starting up and heading out the driveway.

He went to the front lounge window; her car lights were approaching the end of the road, indicator flashing for the turn.

He went over to her laptop. She'd switched it off. More support for her having something to hide, worried about leaving it accessible for any time.

He switched it on, glancing at his watch as he grabbed the lap-link cables from a desk drawer and linked his computer to hers. Eight to nine minutes to the nearest 7-Eleven – Sam had timed it earlier.

Two minutes to shop and pay.

Three minutes to get the software rolling, then the estimate to find a password match was six to eight minutes. Another minute to close down and disconnect – so only eight to ten minutes to hunt through and hopefully find something.

But there'd been little other option. Lorrena took her laptop with her everywhere, and as far as Sam knew it held all her files and notes. He'd rifled through bedroom drawers the day before in search of other notes and papers, or a diary, but found nothing.

Even that had taken him two days to work up the courage to do. In the end his curiosity, his desperate need to know, won out. Plus the fact that he felt he was living on a knife-edge every day, every hour, in any case.

The password finder software screen came up. Sam clicked START and watched as hundreds, then thousands, of possible options scrolled rapidly down his screen.

The night before had been the first time they'd made love since he'd seen her car in gunman's driveway. But despite his best efforts to push all the wrong thoughts and images from his mind – fill it solely with her breathless, naked beauty below him – it had ended disastrously, a flop, halfway through.

He'd rolled off with a defeated sigh. 'I suppose one thing they don't tell you about losing eighteen months work is that it can affect your libido. Or maybe it's because I'm having problems with some scenes in this Toby Wesley book now. Fear of writer's block, and suddenly you get blocked in every other way.'

She'd reached across and gently stroked his cheek. 'It's OK. It'll get better. It takes time.'

Except that he knew it would never get better, no matter how much time. *How many more lame excuses before she caught on?*

Or perhaps she already knew, was just saying the right things to keep him sweet: *I know you've been going through my drawers. Things aren't how I left them. It's part of my training to pick up on even the smallest detail or thing out of place. You won't see me again after I head off tomorrow morning. You're Washington and gunman's responsibility again now.*

For the third night in a row he found himself gently trembling alongside her, taking hours to finally fall asleep.

And the next day after she left for work, he found himself jumping at every small sound from outside: people passing, their neighbour closing his car door. When late morning a FedEx messenger rang the doorbell, he'd hidden away in the kitchen out of sight until he was gone. He'd left a card through the door: CALL OUR DEPOT TO PICK UP YOUR PARCEL. *Your bomb?*

Oh God. He couldn't live like this day after day. He *had* to know, if nothing else for it all to come to an end.

Sam sat up as his computer pinged. A password match had been found: LOR18614NA6.

First three letters of her Christian name and her birthdate run backwards, but Sam had no idea what NA6 stood for.

He tapped it into her computer and started browsing through files: first her emails, then main document folders.

Nothing with Washington or any Arab names that he could see. He tapped *Washington* into a filename search, then just *Wash*: nothing. Then he tried *Washington* with random word search: two documents came up, but the references were in its city context. Nothing suspicious.

Sam noticed a lot of files with initials followed by four or five digits. He clicked on a few starting with W. Nothing alluding to Washington or anything suspect, even in shortened or code form, in those either.

The egg-timer delays with each search and file opening seemed endless. He checked his watch. Almost half his search time gone already. Only five to six minutes left.

He started opening random files with other initials: notes or letters to work colleagues, particularly her closest friend, Ruby; one to her father; one a list of

Utica Medical Center patients organised by zip codes. Again, nothing.

He clutched at his hair, becoming frantic. Think, *think*!

Maybe files with his name in it. Her reporting to her paymasters what *Sam* was up to.

He keyed *Sam* into word search. The delay was longer this time. Finally: eleven documents. He started clicking through them: a couple of casual notes to friends at work...*hope to twist Sam's arm to come to the Christmas office party*. One to her father: *Sam's a lovely guy, but no, no plans for marriage just yet*. For a plant, she'd certainly built up her history well. Then finally some personal diary notes to herself: *This weekend Ashley is visiting for the first time since I've been in the house, so Sam's anxious and on edge. Understandable, I suppose – concerned whether Ashley will like me or not*.

Sam's nerves bristled at the sound of a car engine. He looked round sharply, but it was only a passing car.

He brought his attention back to the screen, starting to open the rest of the *Sam* files: more casual, day to day, personal diary entries, or quick lines to friends, then on one diary entry a reference to *The Prophecy*: *Sam's become far more intense as he nears finishing* The Prophecy. *We've hardly been out the last couple of months and he's testy and on edge much of the time, more difficult to talk to. Anyway, it'll soon be over and hopefully back to normal!*

The Prophecy! His progress on *The Prophecy* would be what Washington et al were most interested in. Four more *Sam* files to check, but he decided to jump ship. He typed *The Prophecy* into keyword search: five documents.

Sam started clicking through them as if his index finger was on fire. First, another personal diary note: *Although Sam spends more time at his computer and less time with me as he gets deeper into* The Prophecy, *it's nice to see him so enthusiastic, so alive! And at least I haven't lost him to another woman!!* Second, a note to workmate, Ruby: *Don't know if we'll be able to make it to your barbecue this weekend. Sam's set a crushing work schedule to finish* The Prophecy *and get it to his agent; seems to work through most weekends now too.* Third, the previous *Sam* diary entry he'd already viewed. Fourth...

Sam jolted as the engine rattle reached him just as the fourth document was opening. He hastily clicked CLOSE. Egg-timer again.

Car door closing, footsteps approaching.

He clicked TURN OFF COMPUTER. More egg-timer. Finally: WINDOWS IS LOGGING OFF...

Key in the door, turning.

Even if it fully shut down before Lorrena walked in, he still had to detach the lap-link cables.

He wasn't going to make it in time.

CHAPTER NINE

KENSINGTON, LONDON.

Olives, humos, karabeej, dates – stuffed with almonds, dusted in cinnamon or finely ground nuts – it was the smells that Adel remembered most as he browsed.

It reminded him of the local store in Dumyat where his father used to take him as a child: the smell of sweetmeats, syrup-soaked baklawar, dates, nuts and candied fruit so heady at times that he'd feel dizzy with it, and his mouth would be watering even before his father had slipped two baklawar and four candied almonds into his palm as treats for helping him with the shopping.

'You OK there, Mister Adel?' the store owner, Sahir, prompted. 'You need some help?'

'No, no. It's OK. Just making sure I get the right baklawar for Tahiya.'

Sahir leant over, pointing. 'I think you'll find it's one of those two.'

Sahir probably knew his wife's tastes better than he. His shop, Sehwanar, had become one of his and Tahiya's favourites when, as a young couple, they lived only three blocks away in a West Kensington flat. Not least because in Sahir his wife had found a fellow Syrian. They'd talk, swap stories and reminisce and she'd laugh at his often ribald quips. If Sahir had been twenty years younger and as many kilos lighter, Adel would have sworn he and his wife were having an affair.

Adel selected a dozen of both, just in case; and, along with the humos and karabeej, put them on the counter. His phone started vibrating in his pocket, but the main call he was expecting he couldn't take now. 'Oh, and some of your halva.'

The halva was in a round slab a foot high, encrusted with pistachio nuts, on a silver tray at the end of the counter.

'This much?' Sahir poised his wedge knife.

Adel widened two fingers a fraction. 'A bit more.'

As he added up on the till, Sahir asked, 'Good day at work?'

Adel made a face. 'A bit hectic.' As much as he dared ever share of his shadow life.

'Letting in too many bloody foreigners,' Sahir quipped as he put it all in a bag and took Adel's money.

It was a private joke of theirs from years back when Adel had told Sahir he worked at the Foreign Office – his standard cover story now, but indeed where he *had* worked then. Sahir had asked whether Adel might be able to help with a young Syrian cousin of his trying to gain immigration, and Adel had clarified that that was the Home Office.

'I left them to it. Had to leave early today to get all this back for the family for *Mawlid*.'

Sahir gave a small, solemn bow. 'And Allah help anyone who doesn't return home on time with their baklawars on such an occasion. Give my regards to your beautiful wife.'

'I will.' Adel smiled and lifted one palm in parting from the doorway. He checked his cellphone as soon as he was out: *Malik*. But Adel didn't make the return call until he was at least a dozen paces clear and nobody else was in passing earshot. *Shadow life*. 'Tell me?'

'Thirty-two suspect messages for the Milan area. Nearly all of them ambiguous – *I couldn't make the appointment this morning. Can you give me a new time?* Also: *The location you gave me, I couldn't find. Can you give me new directions?* But then we expect that.'

'What's the linguistic breakdown?'

'Forty-seven per cent in Arabic, eighteen per cent Farsi. The rest were in Italian, but the IPAs or phone networks trace back to Arab names.'

Adel sighed. 'I don't know how Rani feels about it – but that's a long list to call raids on. I'd say try and pare it down a bit, but in the end it's his call. Let me know what he decides.'

'Sure. Oh, and there's also been another activity spike in the Middle East. Cairo, Alexandria and Gaza. Fourteen, seventeen and eight per cent respectively.'

Adel pondered the information. Another bombing planned hot on the heels of Milan seemed unlikely. 'Could well be a winding-down of network sources for the Milan operation – so might be something worth looking at there. Or perhaps just organisation of an arms shipment into Gaza.' A regular occurrence left for Israeli intelligence to deal with. 'But let me know if it develops any more.'

Adel hailed a cab as he hung up and stared blankly through its side window at the passing shops. A half-mile stretch of mostly Lebanese-, Jordanian-, Syrian- and Iranian-owned shops and cafés, some patrons sitting outside to have coffee, smoke *shisha* and read *Al-Hayat* – and the only place Adel would ever visit in that stretch was Sehwanar.

Always too afraid that as he left a café, someone might pick him out and ask, who is that? '*That's Adel, works at the Foreign Office. Also, like us, originally from Egypt.' 'That's strange. My cousin works at the Foreign Office and he thought he was the only Egyptian working there.'* The cancer strands that might lead to his exposure would be seeded.

So he'd arrive like a thief at Sehwanar, grab what he wanted, and leave as quickly again in another cab. And similarly he'd pass the *shisha* cafés and Arab delicatessens of the Edgware Road and Queensway without stopping, glancing with a stab of nostalgia at this Arab-London life he and Tahiya had kept at arm's length these past years – ever since he'd moved from the Foreign Office to MI5. *Shadow life.*

When he'd made that transfer, the only way they felt they could successfully cut themselves off from their past Arab-London life was to move away from West Kensington – though partly that had also been due to the birth of their second born, Farah, and the need for more space.

They'd moved to an upmarket Surrey suburb – because posh also meant *private* – with stockbroker neighbours who minded their own business. You could smile and wave to them in passing for years without them ever really knowing who you were or what you did; or *ever* asking. And the schools for Jibril and Farah were good.

Nineteen minutes into his train journey home, Malik called again.

'You do the talking,' Adel said as he answered. Clear indication that with commuters sitting close by he couldn't say much his end.

'Rani's got the list down to fourteen.'

'Sounds more workable to me. But as I said before, this is his call – so what does *he* think?'

'Rani thinks the same, it's more workable, and is ready to give the green light to the GIS on all fourteen addresses.'

'Then I would go along with that.'

Adel closed his eyes for a moment after he'd ended the call, resting his head against the side glass as he thought about those people in Milan on commuter trains ten hours earlier. And the one person now loose in that city who could provide the key to that and a possible trail back to Abu Khalish.

That one person was Irfan Shohani. He was twenty-two and a regular at the same mosque as the other two train bombers, Ahmed and Katib, which was where their handler, Youssef, had first recruited them.

While GIS teams, each five-strong, were shining spotlights on front doors or ramming them open across the city, including Shohani's, in the Via Padova area – he was over a mile south meeting up with Youssef.

He'd left a discreet email message for Youssef mid-morning, but the reply came to his mobile phone – equally discreet – and not until late afternoon. Youssef suggested that they meet up near Linate Airport at 6.00 p.m.

He'd suggested a section where the A51 Highway was raised on stanchions, with an industrial estate one side and the taxiways of the airport the other; the area underneath was shadowy and private.

After their greetings, *Salaam*, Youssef left a moment's appropriate pause, glancing absently at a 737 landing at the airport before asking, 'So, what happened this morning?'

'The train stopped. It was stationary for almost half an hour, then we were led out by firemen with torches and had to walk over half a kilometre to get out at Moscova Station.' Irfan shrugged. 'There was no opportunity then.'

Youssef mirrored the shrug. 'So with the train stationary, it hardly seemed worth setting off your device?'

Youssef's tone had a lift to it, as if he was in agreement, but still Irfan was cautious; he continued with the rest of his pre-arranged story.

'No. Not just that. Many people had got off at the last station. There were only seven people left in my carriage. And one of those was a woman in full jilbab and hijab, another a child. When the train stopped for so long, I saw that as a sign that I wasn't meant to set it off.' Irfan clasped his hands below his chin and glanced heavenward. 'That I was meant to serve in other ways. And that is what I am here now to pledge myself to, *inshallah*. Another assignment or duty, whatever you might divine as Allah's wish for me.'

Youssef looked down thoughtfully for a moment. Finally, 'You did the right thing, my friend. Setting it off with such small numbers, and with one victim an *Abid* female. The press would have had a field day. But it might be a while before another spectacular is planned, and for that you might have to travel. Or with the ingenuity you have shown, it could be you will be asked to help in other ways.'

'I understand.' Irfan nodded, closing his eyes briefly in humble acceptance. 'In whatever way I might be able to serve.' He felt the weight lift from his chest that Youssef had accepted his account so graciously. In truth, there had been more than a dozen people in the carriage and the woman in the jilbab had been in the next carriage, which he'd purposely avoided when he got on. The spirit of what they were doing had seemed so strong when the four of them had all been together, planning. But when he found himself walking alone through the city with the bomb in his briefcase, his resolve seemed to swill away like a receding tide. His mother hadn't helped. He'd told her he was dressed smartly because he had a job interview, and she'd hugged him and wished him well. So he was already looking for an excuse not to go ahead before the train stopped.

'No worries, my friend. You did the right thing.' Youssef smiled comfortingly, patting Irfan's shoulder. But then he grew concerned again. 'And after the train stopped and you were led out, the *carabinieri* didn't stop you and ask questions? Or search you?'

Irfan shook his head. 'No, no. Of course not. I still have the device, don't I?' He lifted the briefcase. Youssef had instructed him to bring it so that he could dispose of it; nothing possibly incriminating, not to mention dangerous, should be left with Irfan.

'Yes, you do. You do.' He gripped Irfan's shoulder reassuringly as he said it, but it was mainly to hold the young man steady as he rammed home the ice pick.

It slid cleanly between Irfan's ribs and pierced his heart. Youssef could tell from Irfan's eyes that he'd died on his feet, but still he twisted the ice pick around to make sure. The puncture wound was small and clean, so no blood had spilt on Youssef's clothes.

He took the briefcase and twenty minutes later was eating *kibbeh* and *fattoush* at his favourite café on Via Oropa, washed down with a glass of grape juice.

When he walked back into his third-floor apartment two blocks from the café, eighty-two minutes had passed since he'd left it.

The first thing he noticed was that his computer had gone. His eyes shifted to a side cabinet: his spare cellphone and charger as well. A jacket he'd left hanging on the wardrobe doorknob was also no longer there. He went across and opened the wardrobe: empty.

What he didn't notice as he crossed the room was the motion sensor on the ceiling, or that it had started flashing red. It was set on a three-second timer.

As he reached for the adjacent chest of drawers, everything was whited out, the explosion ripping apart every fibre in the room and carrying it to the extremities of that blast before turning in on itself, the maelstrom of debris sucked back with equal force into the vacuum created.

Then, apart from some loose cement dust and plaster still trickling from the floor above, silence.

Because of his height, Adel Al-Shaffir carried a slight stoop from constantly leaning over to greet or listen to people.

So he was already halfway there when he walked through his front door and leant down to pick up his five-year-old daughter, Farah, and hug and kiss her on both cheeks.

Jibril, three years older, already saw himself as too grown-up and macho for kisses and hugs, so all he got was an affectionate hair ruffle.

Tahiya was in the kitchen and Adel went through to give her the same both-cheeks kiss.

'You didn't forget?' she asked as he pulled away.

'No.' He held up the bag, 'All right here.' He

put an arm around her. 'Smells good.'

'Lamb *shakreeyeh*. Ready in about forty minutes.'

He smiled teasingly. 'I meant *you*.'

She reached for a tea towel to flick at him, but he escaped and went to change.

She was almost a foot smaller than him with the warmest, softest, most alive eyes Adel had ever seen. Or maybe it was just when they rested on him their dark intensity lifted. That same look across an LSE classroom fourteen years ago when they'd first met, and still now Adel found himself melting.

She lit candles for dinner and they seemed to make her eyes even softer and dance all the more as she looked across at him.

He said that he had to take one call later that was important, just one; and after a pause she nodded in acceptance, 'OK,' then held one finger gently to her lips. He wasn't sure whether the gesture meant 'No need to say any more' or 'When you take that call, make sure it's not in front of the children'.

They'd made a pact that he shouldn't bring his work home with him. Work-related calls should be rare or hopefully never. And when they couldn't be avoided, they shouldn't be in front of the children.

It was a trade-off of sorts for his work having already separated them from much of their past lives, exiling Tahiya to suburbia; she didn't want it to *completely* control their lives. Nor have their children subject to the backdrop of the latest terrorist bombing or atrocity.

The children couldn't seem to wait for the humos and lamb courses to be out the way so that they could get to the baklawar and halva, and it was good to see them so enlivened, so happy. Not long ago Adel's elder brother in Egypt – still close to their family home of years and running their father's old business – asked whether Adel had stayed devout, hoping London life hadn't led him astray so that his faith took second place. In response Adel had recited the prayer regimes, mosque visits and Islamic festivals they still adhered to, including *Mawlid*, Mohammed's birthday. His brother, Namir, was the last person he'd want to tell that they did it all now purely for the children's sake – but Namir quickly rejoined that to certain sectors of Islam celebrating Mohammed's birthday was seen as far from devout. Indeed, for a Wahhabi Muslim, as with all forms of music and dancing, it was banned. His brother had studied for three years to become an imam before taking over their father's business, so knew about such things.

The call from Malik, informing him that the fourteen Milan addresses had been raided but nothing suspect had been found, came halfway through the main course. He held one hand up in apology as he left the table to take the call, and Tahiya nodded her understanding – but the mood when he returned, perhaps because Tahiya could tell that he was still preoccupied with the news he'd received, had changed. The magic of the evening had been broken.

So when only twenty-five minutes later the second call came to tell him that Irfan Shohani, resident at one of those fourteen addresses raided, had been found dead, and there'd also been a nearby apartment bombing, Tahiya's look of concern changed to an impatient frown.

With the third call, Adel knew what was coming with Tahiya and so got there first. 'Look, Malik, I'm having dinner at home with my family. That's why I said anything else should wait until morning.'

'I know, boss – but I thought you'd want to know about this. They're running it on Al Jazeera every half-hour.'

Adel got up from the table and walked into the hallway. '*What?* Another announcement from Khalish?'

'No. There's been another mosque bombing. This time in Egypt. And it doesn't look like Khalish is behind this one.'

As Malik told him and fleshed out some of the details, Adel felt his blood run cold. At least with Abu Khalish they knew what they were dealing with. With this, they were in totally uncharted waters.

Tahiya fired him a stony stare as she hustled the

children past him. 'I thought we had an agreement, Adel. I don't want to spend any more of my evenings like this. I'm putting the children to bed.'

And then he was left alone. Truly alone.

BAHÌA DE SALINAS, COSTA RICA.

It was early afternoon and approaching siesta time when the man received the call in Costa Rica, a remote stretch of coastline close to the border with Nicaragua.

'*Dígame.*'

'That second trading option has now also been closed. There are no others for now. I'll let you know if and when other options arise.'

'Thank you for calling. *Hasta la próxima.*'

A nondescript call totally in Spanish between two supposedly South American businessmen, Abu Khalish knew that even *Echelon*, the USA's all-encompassing network-spy computer, would be hard-pushed to pick up anything from that.

To locals he was known by another name, a Mexican businessman. He was three stone heavier than his last photo as Khalish; clean-shaven, his hair dyed light brown, and his eyes were now a limpid green. He bore little resemblance to Khalish and his papers would pass the most scrupulous examination, though the only person he'd had to show them to so far had been the local estate agent when he'd rented the property.

Still, it might be time soon to move on; shame, he thought, taking in the sweeping bay view and the palm jungle beyond. He was just starting to settle in, feel at home. But then for him a sense of complacency quickly instilled the opposite reaction: unease. Guilt perhaps at having such feelings when he thought about his two brothers and the momentous, chess-game war he was waging as a result. A sense that he had no *right* to have such feelings. But his instincts hadn't served him wrong so far.

CHAPTER TEN

'Not far now.' Mike Kiernan looked across as he drove.

'OK,' Sam acknowledged. Then added with a faint sigh, 'Let's hope we're doing the right thing.'

Mike had noticed Sam's hand clasping repeatedly at his own thigh on the drive. Maybe nerves because of who they were heading to meet, but Mike had picked up on Sam's increasing agitation the past week. His friend was falling apart, cell by nerve cell before him, only he didn't have the heart to tell him.

'You need help, Sam – have done for a while, but perhaps don't want to admit it. And this kind of help is a lot better than the kind you'll need if you *don't* do something.' There, he'd said as much as he dared.

'But still, *Vince Corcoran*. I still can't help feeling it's like using a sledgehammer to crack a nut.'

'In case you haven't noticed, Sam, you're up against some pretty big guns. CIA spooks and SWAT teams, with a few jihad madmen thrown in for good measure. I'd have thought that might call for some big guns in return, don't you?' Sam nodded, but Mike noticed his fists were still clenched.

Mike let the Plymouth County farm fields roll by without speaking for a moment. Vince Corcoran's turf might be South Boston, but for the past ten years he'd lived forty miles away among the golf courses and riding stables of Lakeville.

'Robby Maschek could pass it to any number of minor hoods he's known over the years, but he's got a gumshoe's licence to protect, and he can't be sure they'd bury the traces. With Corcoran, he *can*. Corcoran simply passes it down the rungs as he thinks fit, and that action in itself cuts all links to Robby.'

As Lorrena had walked back in from the 7-Eleven, Sam still had the lap-link cables in his hand; though thankfully he'd detached them from her computer and it had shut down. '*Mike's got some new software he thought I might find useful. Just checking I've still got the link cables here in the drawer.*'

She'd just nodded and handed him the shopping

bag with the herbs and puree. No indication whether or not she'd suspected anything. But again Sam had faced another anxious day wondering whether she'd phone for a SWAT team and not return.

Two hours after she'd left, he couldn't stand it any more and headed to Syracuse, killing time between shops and cafés before going to Mike's for the last few hours. Her Jetta was in the driveway when he'd returned and he'd breathed a sigh of relief. All he had to face now was the bedroom vigil if she reached for him again that night. *More 'writer's block impotence' excuses; but for how much longer would that story wash?*

Mike had made the call to Robby Maschek while he was there. '*You've done what you can, and it doesn't look like you're gonna easily get another peek at her laptop.*' Maschek had kept tabs on Lorrena for four days, but she hadn't gone anywhere suspect in that time, not even gunman's house again. And gunman's blue Highlander registration he'd also drawn a blank on. '*Good news is that it traces back to a rental company. Bad news: it wasn't listed as rented out that day. My bet is that they made a duplicate plate on another Highlander.*' So now it was time to involve Corcoran as well.

'The nickname Corky?' Sam asked. 'Short for Corcoran?'

'That's one theory. The other is because most of

his enemies end up bobbing in Boston harbour.' Mike risked a smile, and despite his uneasy mood Sam managed to join him.

Corcoran's house, set eighty yards back from the road behind high video-entry gates, was a smaller version of Hugh Hefner's Chicago mansion; though not by much. Mike prided himself on his car, a two-year-old Jaguar XK, but he was seriously upstaged as he pulled into Corcoran's driveway: Bentley Azure, Porsche Cayman, vintage Hispano-Suiza J-12 and a Hummer H3.

Mike paused halfway in opening his car door. 'Oh, inside you'll notice all the curtains are drawn and there are no lights on. But don't worry, you'll be able to find your way through. Vince is just a little different, even for a mobster.'

They got out and entered Vincent Corcoran's world.

Adel couldn't help admiring the ingenuity: whoever was behind the two mosque bombings had planned the Turkey and Egypt attacks either side of Milan so that the Middle East stats merged with the European stats; helped mask it.

Or perhaps it was Khalish playing masquerade: he'd got wind of the planned mosque bombings through his network, so planned his Milan spectacular at the same time to hopefully shield the activity spikes.

Guesswork. And unless or until there was a 'responsibility claim' announcement, the answers could remain elusive.

Adel brought his attention back to the photos Karam was going through with him: computer JPEGs fresh from TAME in Cairo of the El-Qelef Mosque in Alexandria.

'That one's taken just six minutes before the fake imams come by. One guard in front, the other patrolling down one side. Notice the floodlights are all on and the two CCTV cameras are operative – and remain so throughout. Timing for each photo is in the corner.' Karam pointed with his pencil. 'Now on the next one we see the two imams come into view – by which time both guards are in front.'

Adel nodded pensively. 'With the assailants so clearly visible, we see the reason for the disguises.'

Karam grimaced. 'Posing as imams provides good cover: heavy beards and moustaches, long black robes. But I daresay beneath all that spirit gum and fake hair, there are some prosthetics too for good measure. The CCTV shots are fairly distant – even with image enhancement, I doubt we'll pick up much.'

Adel frowned and turned to the next photo.

'Here we see imam-one asking the first guard for some directions. Then, as he lowers his rifle to point, imam-one grips the rifle and touch-tasers the guard. As the second guard starts to raise his rifle' – Karam paused for Adel to flip over – 'imam-two takes a deft step back, grabs the rifle to ensure it stays low, and swings round to taser the guard's neck.' Karam sighed tiredly, but his worn smile carried a hint of admiration. 'All over in seconds.'

Adel flipped through the rest in pace with Karam filling in the details: the guards' prone bodies dragged to one side, the C4 set, the final explosion. The mosque's entry portico was completely destroyed and half of its dome, but only the top third of one of its two minarets had fallen.

'Seems at least they're caring in that respect,' Adel commented. 'Wanted to make sure the two guards weren't caught in the blast.'

Karam nodded. 'Yeah, that at least.'

Adel groaned inwardly at the intimation. All the other factors – well organised, professional, and not even a sniff of who they were or their allegiances – were going to make them tough nuts to crack.

Again Adel was struck with just how much they were groping in the dark without any responsibility claim. Without that, they had nothing to link to, no idea of their affiliations or aims.

He didn't have to wait long.

And when that announcement came on Al Jazeera four hours later, he was reminded of that old adage: be careful what you pray for, because God, *Allah*, may well grant your wish.

There was no personal photo or identity, just a taped voice in Arabic with scrolling text and an English translation beneath a photo of the El-Qelef Mosque.

Everyone in the operations room was transfixed by the large screen, as they had been for Khalish's announcement the day before claiming responsibility for the Milan bombings. Except Khalish clearly wasn't behind this action; quite the opposite. So just who was this newcomer daring to take on Khalish?

And as that clear, strident Arab voice got to the main body of his prepared speech and the aims and demands of his group became clear, Adel closed his eyes for a moment, cradling his forehead in one hand. One thing was certain: the war on terror would never be the same again.

Sam saw the news clip on one of the last TV screens on their way out of Vince Corcoran's house.

Corcoran's eyes were light-sensitive, so he permanently wore dark glasses – not just to appear 'cool', as was often touted – and kept the curtains drawn and the lights off. The only light as you walked through the corridors and rooms of his mansion were from TV screens – hundreds of them from different ages, practically a TV museum. Most were showing old Cagney, Bogart and Edward G movies – Corcoran was an ardent film buff – but every sixth or seventh screen would be tuned to a TV news channel or daytime soap.

There was no sound on any of them, just that eerie light playing a silver-screen and TV history of the past seventy years to guide you through.

As he and Mike were leaving – with Barry Chilton, Corcoran's right-hand man, leading the way – Sam saw the El-Qelef news item on a screen tuned to CNN.

Driving away, Mike noticed that his friend was quiet, the colour drained from his face. 'Well, don't say I didn't warn you that Vince was *different*,' Mike shrugged. 'But at least we got what we wanted.'

'No, it's not that. It's something I saw on one of those screens. Possibly linked to *The Prophecy* – but I can't be sure until I've seen the full news item.' Sam stared blankly ahead as if shell-shocked, still trying to assimilate and make sense of what he'd seen. Maybe Mike was right; he *was* going mad, starting to see imaginary things: *gunman* across the road, Lorrena's car in his driveway, now another mosque from his manuscript on CNN. He sighed. 'Can we maybe find a bar nearby with a TV tuned to a news channel?'

'Sure, *sure*.' Despite the tremulous, hesitant timbre, Mike could tell it was no lightweight request. 'In fact, I can go one better than that.'

Minutes later they were sat in a lay-by, the occasional passing truck buffeting the car as Sam viewed Mike's cellphone screen, waiting for that news item to come up again on CNN.

'*Rival terrorist group lays down the gauntlet to Abu Khalish...*'

If Mike ever wondered what mind and body reserves his friend had left after the bit-by-bit falling apart of this past week, he saw those last vestiges crumble away now as Sam's hand fought to hold the screen steady. The breath shuddered out of him as the news item came to an end, but it was a full ten seconds before he pulled himself back to the world around, and with a still-trembling hand, gently closed the cellphone and passed it back to Mike.

Sam was silent for a few moments as they drove on. Then he started to explain.

'As you know, *The Prophecy* centred around Nostradamus prophecies, but at its core was also a chain of mosque bombings. The sharp-end "physical" representation of those prophecies, if you will.'

Mike just nodded, said nothing. Sam had shared with him solely the bare bones of the plot, not its intricate detail. The only thing he'd given advice on had been structure with individual scenes.

'When I saw the news five days ago about the first mosque bombing in Antalya, Turkey, I didn't attach too much significance. I thought: it's just a coincidence, there have been a number of mosque bombings in Turkey before, and usually they end up put down to Kurdish separatists.' Sam closed his eyes for a second, shook his head. 'And with what I had on my plate with gunman and Lorrena, I didn't really have time to give it more thought.'

'So that first mosque bombing in *The Prophecy* was in the same place: Antalya, Turkey?'

'Yeah.' Sam shrugged after a second. 'OK, I changed the names of all the mosques in the book so as not to offend anyone's religious sensibilities, and there's a number of small mosques in Antalya. But it's pretty evident in *The Prophecy* that I based it on its largest mosque, El Ashna – which was where the bombing took place five days ago.'

They were silent for a moment, only the thrum of the wheels on the road.

Sam took a fresh breath. 'Now with this second bombing in Alexandria, it's just too much of a coincidence. *Two* bombings exactly as in *The Prophecy* – place *and* sequence.'

Mike was still searching for an alternative explanation. 'But Alexandria is a much larger city, with more large mosques. Surely the coincidence factor might come into play even more?'

Sam shook his head. 'No, don't think so. Equal-sized minarets either side of a central dome – it's pretty clear that I based that second bombing on the El-Qelef Mosque.' Sam sighed. 'Besides, I thought *I* was the one meant to be in denial.'

'Never let it be said that I'm not right there for you,

batting on the same side.' Mike was keen to lighten the mood, if nothing else to diffuse the tension.

'Even if there was the possibility of putting that down to chance, there's no escaping the announcement that's now come with it and the demand made. Almost exactly as in *The Prophecy*.'

'*Almost?*'

'A few words changed here and there, but the substance is the same: the demand for Abu Khalish to give himself up, and in return the bombings will stop.' Mike cocked an eyebrow as he glanced across, and Sam filled in the details. '...All of it as if a supreme test of the "sanctity of Islam" proclamation which launched Khalish's own bombing campaign. Full circle, hoisted by his own petard.'

'As with all good thrillers.' Mike grimaced. 'And how, may I ask, did it all end up? In *The Prophecy* who is the mastermind behind it all?' As Sam told him, Mike stared blankly ahead for a moment without speaking; suddenly he had a better understanding of his friend's panic. '*Jeez.* And you wonder why you were targeted?'

'Yeah, now you mention it.' Sam's tone was suddenly firmer, more sure of his ground. 'Because that was the one thing I was careful about – *not* offending Islam. In fact, one of my protagonists – the main man responsible for tracking the bombers – was a very sympathetic Muslim character.'

'Maybe. But it certainly looks like you've upset *somebody*.' Mike looked at Sam aslant. 'And now it seems there are only two possibilities: you've either hit on the most incredible piece of future-telling ever known in fiction, or whoever has your manuscript is using it as a blueprint for Armageddon.'

CHAPTER ELEVEN

'You will have witnessed with your own eyes the contrast between our own actions and those of Abu Khalish in Milan. Our circle of brothers embraces both Sunnis and Shiites, but we are united in our love of Islam and so have ensured that no lives have been lost through our actions, and will continue to do so. For it is written in the Koran that life is sacred, the creation of Allah, and so only Allah may decide when it should end – not the likes of Abu Khalish.

'So it follows, as naturally and inarguably as does a river unto the sea, that in displaying such contempt for human life in his war, Abu Khalish is defaming the good *name and spirit of Islam. A religion of understanding and compassion, yet he is connecting it in the minds of many with something which it is not: with evil, with destruction.*

'*Yet we hear Abu Khalish proclaim that he is a true defender of Islam, that he is fighting to protect its sanctity. So let us now see if this is the truth or just empty words. For if Abu Khalish truly believed in the sanctity of Islam, then in penance for that aforesaid defamation he would cease his war and surrender himself in order to stop any more of its sacred monuments being harmed. That would be the action of a true shahid, my friends – one who sacrificed themselves to protect Islam.*'

Adel rubbed the bridge of his nose as he looked up. He'd read the brief transcript several times earlier before going back over individual sentences for deeper subtleties or messages. Now, he gave it one last skim through as his section leaders grouped in front of him.

'OK. With Abu Khalish, we know exactly what we're dealing with – his full history. But here, we're fighting in the dark. So while we now finally have a mission statement, there's still no real background or texture. And no photo, only a voice. So that's going to be the first thing: honing in on every cadence and inflection of that voice to find out where it might come from, or indeed have *been* through the years. So that'll mean running it through every voice and linguistic program between here, GCHQ and the NSA.' Adel surveyed the group of eight. 'But any initial thoughts?'

Isam, responsible for Africa, half-held up his hand. 'My guess would be Yemen or possibly Oman from the dialect, although there's something else there – as if he's spent time in Morocco or Tunisia. There's a faint French inflection on some words.'

'I don't know about the Yemeni part,' Malik offered, 'but I picked up on the French lilt too. Although you get that also in the Lebanon or indeed Syria – so he could equally have spent time there.'

'OK.' Adel nodded. 'Yemen or Oman, with possibly some later Moroccan, Tunisian, Lebanese or Syrian influence. Or perhaps the other way round: he originated in one of those last four, then spent some time in the Yemen or Oman?'

'Yes, possibly,' Malik said.

Isam gave a concessionary shrug.

'But not France itself, French Canada, or any other Western influence?' Adel pressed. As Isam and Malik applied thought, Adel's eyes shifted fleetingly around the group.

Finally from Malik: 'If it was a brief influence. The inflection is very slight. Or, if he did spend any time in France or French-speaking territory, he was buried deep in an Arab community where that remained his main language and he spoke French rarely.'

Isam agreed, and Adel scanned the rest of the group. No other input.

'Well, we'll soon know. And hopefully improve on that and with any luck narrow it down to within a couple of blocks of where he used to live. Or, better still, *now* lives.' Adel gave each instructions on their areas of pursuit, then turned back to his computer.

Western influence? This possibility concerned Adel.

It was an audacious, fantastic coup: stealing Abu Khalish's thunder over Milan and laying the gauntlet at his feet in the same motion. Putting a spotlight and pressure on Abu Khalish that half the world's intelligence networks and billions spent hadn't so far achieved. But that was half the problem: it was almost *too* good a coup, and it didn't take much to work out that the main beneficiaries were the West rather than Islam.

So Adel wondered just how long it would be before someone in the Pan-Arab world claimed a possible Western influence, whether it had substance or not. *And what if something his team uncovered then lent that substance?*

Adel rolled that scenario forward in his mind and didn't like what he saw. For the first time he was as concerned by what his team might uncover, as by what they might not.

* * *

Strange. Sam had just arrived home to find Lorrena's Jetta in the driveway, but the house was in darkness. He got no answer when he walked indoors and called her name, and started to feel uneasy. *Maybe she was doing some of her own snooping, or had some other surprise waiting for him in the shadows.*

The phone rang, making him jump.

He picked up after the first ring. It was Kate.

'Hi, Sam. I was trying to get hold of you. I'm coming to New York.'

'When?'

'Tomorrow, with Ashley.'

The kitchen light flicked on and Lorrena emerged from the shadows, half-lit in the glow. She pointed and mouthed, '*She called earlier.*'

'Oh, right,' Sam said into the phone. He thought he knew what was coming.

'I've got this really important meeting with the new Broadway producers of *Nevada Angel* – you know, that play I did when we first came over. Well, they're adapting it for film.' She paused for a response, then rolled on halfway through Sam's mumbled congratulations. 'It's been in the pipeline for a while now so I already knew about it, *and* I've already got approval from the Hollywood end – but apparently the Broadway producers also have a say. And so I wondered, while I was there, whether you might want to see Ashley? Have him stay with you?'

Sure enough. But he could have done without the preamble before she got to the key question. Kate's usual breathless my-rising-career-before-all-else monologue – London, Broadway, finally Hollywood – and somewhere en route he'd lost his son. For her first two films she'd commuted from Oneida, catching a flight back every weekend, because Ashley was already settled in a good school. Then suddenly it became every other week, then every month.

He'd blamed all that time apart on their failing relationship, though the final straw had been her starting a relationship with someone else, a scriptwriter. Forever fated to fall for writers.

'I don't know,' he said. 'How long are you over for?'

'Just a couple of days.'

Sam would have loved to see his son; he grabbed every possible opportunity. But now wasn't the ideal time with these new dramas with Lorrena, Vince Corcoran and the mosque bombers' announcement.

'You know normally I'd love to have Ashley stay, but it's a really bad time right now what with—' Sam broke off as he noticed Lorrena's quizzical expression. She knew little of the real story – aware only that he had some writer's block problem with his new book, part of which was spilling over into the bedroom. Passing up the opportunity to see his son would hint at something more serious than that, could make her suspicious. Sam lifted his tone. 'But, *hey*, I hardly get to see him as it is – so I can certainly shift the rest of my life around to accommodate.'

Kate gave him the time of their flight arrival and Sam arranged to meet them at the airport.

Lorrena was smiling as he looked across. The Sam she knew and loved was back. She went back into the kitchen and Sam shook off a faint shudder as he hung up.

Yeah, *fine*, he hoped he'd played the subterfuge well. But now involving his son like a pawn in his game was something else entirely. A sign that things had gone too far.

SALON, PROVENCE.

Jean-Pierre worked best at night.

The bookshop below had long closed and Madame Pelletret left for the day on increasingly unsteady legs.

Finally, he now had the solitude. And the darkness.

He lit twelve candles – four groups of three to represent the zodiac and the seasons – spread out the charts and set the angle of the armillary sphere. To the right of his desk a shutter was left open so that he could see part of the town beyond his study window: Salon as it verged into farm fields beyond.

There was little electric light visible there, the

few new buildings obscured by the darkness, so it was easier to imagine that part of town as it would have been in the 1500s. When Michel de Nostredame would have looked from his candlelit study at a similar view.

Pinned to Jean-Pierre's study walls were several key Nostradamus quatrains – copies from the original manuscripts in quill on vellum – but holding pride of place above his desk was arguably his most notable quatrain, from which all else had stemmed:

The younger lion will overcome the older
In single combat in the field of war
His eyes will be pierced in a cage of gold
Two breaks made one. He then dies a cruel death.

Nostradamus had accurately predicted, by four years, French King Henry II's death in 1559 during a jousting tournament, in which a broken lance pierced his gold helmet and went through one eye, causing a brain haemorrhage which led to his death ten days later.

From that moment on, Nostradamus's notoriety as an accurate soothsayer spread. And none helped that process more than Catherine de Medici, Henry II's widow. Having witnessed first hand his accurate prediction of her husband's death, she sought his counsel on predictions for their children; and by natural extension, he became sought by her wider court and French aristocracy at large.

But in doing so, Catherine de Medici became more than just a main benefactor; she became his protector as well. For this was the age of the Inquisition, when fortune-telling was seen as akin to sorcery and punishable by death. Yet while the French royals held Nostradamus in such esteem, *inquisitors* would be loath to move against him.

Nevertheless, with his published work – not just private whispers in palace chambers and attendance rooms – Nostradamus was more cautious. Aware that overt, controversial prophecies might alarm the Church, encourage them to wrest control over that royal favour, he peppered his quatrains with allegory and Latin and Greek phrases to mask specifics. That way, if he was ever confronted over a controversial prediction, he could claim an alternate meaning.

For over four hundred years since, countless scholars and academics had deliberated over those predictions to try and define their 'true' meaning.

So, keenly aware that he was just one more in a long succession of Nostradamus 'experts', Jean-Pierre set his cap on being different, setting himself apart. The core of that was partly reliving Nostradamus's life so as to hopefully add new light and interpretations; but he quickly discovered that this meant becoming more involved with prophecies of current and near-future events. After all, there was little point in updating or reinterpreting the past.

Which was no doubt why, from among the countless other Nostradamus experts, that English writer last year had put him high on his contact list. Of particular interest had been Jean-Pierre's research into Mabus, the Islamic instigator of the Third World War, and how that might tie into current-day events.

So when he'd seen the news about that first mosque bombing, and it matched his scribbled notes after their conversation – Turkey, but no mention of a specific city, had also been the location for that first fictional bombing – he'd immediately felt alarmed.

He was about to phone and check whether that planned bombing sequence might have since changed, or what city in Turkey had finally been decided upon, when news came of the second mosque bombing: Alexandria, Egypt. He'd checked his notes again and breathed a heavy sigh of relief: Islamabad, Pakistan, had been the planned second bombing.

The third news item with the mosque bombers' demands which might make him revise that opinion, he hadn't yet seen. There was only one room in the house with a TV, and as soon as Madame Pelletret left at 4.30 p.m., he stoically avoided it, pulled himself away from all modern distractions. He felt the decades, then centuries, fall away increasingly as night fell – until finally he was back in the 1500s.

Feeling as Michel de Nostredame felt then, seeing as he saw.

So while, as every night, Jean-Pierre delved into the darkness of the past for the clues to the future, the real future went on outside his window without him knowing.

CHAPTER TWELVE

Sam was waiting by arrivals at JFK airport when he got Lorrena's call. On the board, Kate and Ashley's flight from LA had shifted from 'landed' to 'at the gate' twelve minutes ago.

'I'm going to get my nails done after work tonight – so I'll be late home. Seven-thirty or eight.'

'OK.' Nails being done, Italian language classes. Sam wondered now just how much of that was real. Something else for Robby Maschek to check out. She usually went to the same place.

'You already at the airport?' she asked.

Obviously she could hear the background

announcements and crowd echo. 'Got here fifteen minutes ago. Just waiting for them to get their baggage.' He sighed. 'It'll probably be late too by the time we get back, and after the drive I reckon I'll be too tired to cook – so I'll just grab takeaway. Pizza or Chinese never fails with nine-year-olds.'

'You're finally learning, Sam. Lesson one of being a good dad: make sure never to cook, just grab takeaways.' She chuckled. 'See you later.'

The noise and bustle pressed back in as he hung up, but her chuckle stayed with him for a moment. It made him think of happier times and he started to have second thoughts about what he'd set in motion.

He quickly shook it off as he saw Ashley and Kate emerge amongst the throng of fresh arrivals. He smiled, waving to get their attention.

Adel spread the photos out in the 'long table' room. Originally designated as a boardroom, it only got used for meetings which couldn't be covered by quick desk huddles or calling instructions across the main operations room – which was rarely. So its main use now was for meeting visiting MI5, MI6 or foreign agency brass, or as a lunch canteen.

Now, mid-afternoon, with lunch finished over an hour ago, Adel had the space to himself, so he could spread out the photos.

There were over twenty from the two stations

bombed, then four different angles of Irfan Shohani's straggled body and half a dozen of Youssef Rehlik's bombed apartment.

Following the photos through in sequence put life, or in this case *death*, to the trail of destruction Abu Khalish had left in Milan. The whole thing had been ordered from a distance, and now not a single part of that trail could lead back to Khalish. Just how he liked it.

But the photos, beyond the cold statistics of the numbers killed, also told a deeper story: the keen twenty-two-year-old footballer – not much older than the bombers – who'd lost his legs, the fourteen-year-old girl who'd been blinded, the mother who in protecting her young son from the blast they feared had crushed and smothered him; but then discovered, miraculously, he was still alive, had suffered only a couple of broken ribs. '*Then came the hard part*,' Rani had related when he sent through the photos. '*Telling that little boy that his mother had died in saving him.*'

And Adel wished he could have taken those bombers by the hand and led them through that carnage, let them hear those heartbreaking stories first hand. 'See, *see* what you've done. And you think for *this*, you're going to heaven?'

Yet Adel also partly saw them as victims. For their actions had little to do with being *shahid*s in the name of Islam, they had more to do with leaving no possible traces that could lead back to their terrorist paymasters. Nobody left alive who could possibly talk about arrangements and money and explosives trails. When they died, the operation and all links died with them.

And when the operations went wrong and someone was left alive – as in the case of Irfan Shohani – they were quickly dealt with. No traces left.

Murder and suicide, as with other religions, were decried in the Koran. Trying to excuse them within the context of jihad as some sort of holy war was also a much-stretched interpretation, and so usually pushed only by extreme fringes for their own purposes. When his brother had been studying to be an imam, Adel had many conversations with Namir about the true nature of jihad. And so he understood all too well that rather than a fight of a physical, violent nature in the name of Islam, it was more one of inner conflict; that same, age-old moral battle to always strive to do the right thing – often against impossible odds and temptations – that most people endured at some stage, whether religious or not.

Adel looked up from the photos as the door opened. Karam.

'GCHQ on line four. They've got that voice analysis on the mosque bomber.'

Adel had been waiting for the call from the

Government Central Communications Office. 'Thanks.' He pressed a button on the speakerphone to one side. Hopefully better news.

It had started to rain when Lorrena got to the nail salon.

By the time she left an hour and twenty minutes later, it was heavy enough for her to turn up her coat collar and keep her head down as she attempted a quick sprint to her car fifty yards away.

Fishing for her keys in the last few hustling steps, she swung her car door open and slid in swiftly so that she didn't get drenched.

She didn't see the two figures emerge from the shadows until it was too late.

One opened her passenger door a split-second after she got in, the other slid into her back seat. She felt the press of a gun barrel against the nape of her neck as the man behind spoke.

'Just do as we say and you won't get hurt. Now start up and drive – we'll tell you where to go.' The gun barrel was eased off an inch.

The man in the front passenger seat with his gun trained on her said nothing. He was wearing a dark-grey ski mask with just eye slits. Risking a glance in the mirror as she started up and edged out, she saw the man behind wore the same. He directed her to take a couple of turns after a moment, then sat back as they came onto one of the main roads out of Utica.

The rain was heavy, so she put the wipers on rapid. They kept a metronome beat with her pounding heart.

'What do you want?' she felt brave enough to ask after a while.

But that silence simply lengthened as she drove. No answer.

Finally, when they'd gone almost three miles and the thinning street lights of Utica had completely faded: 'Turn here. *Here!*'

The turning had loomed up swiftly, and she had to squint through the rain to see it clearly. She braked and made the turn.

'OK...' he prompted after a moment. 'Pull in here.'

She'd driven barely two hundred yards into the road, but already it felt completely isolated. Pitch-dark, no street lamps. Woodland one side, farm fields the other, the last homes on the edge of Utica over a mile away. Nobody was likely to stumble upon them.

The man in the front seat started rifling through her handbag, but then she watched him do a strange thing: having checked what was there, he took out only her cellphone – left her credit cards and money – then simply clasped it shut again and kept it in his grip.

And it struck her in that moment: this wasn't

just a couple of young punks mugging for their next quick fix. The whole thing seemed too planned, organised; and while she couldn't be sure with the ski masks, her kidnappers seemed older. The man in the front seat was maybe late twenties, but the other was in his thirties, possibly forties. A carjacking she'd immediately discarded: no way for an old Jetta. And as she arrived at the next obvious conclusion, her heart sank: this was a hit! It might be made to look like a robbery gone wrong, but she wasn't going to get out of this alive.

In her mirror she saw the man behind take her laptop from its case, which seemed to attract more interest.

'This yours?' Obviously. She didn't nod or answer. 'Looks a nice one.'

Still trying to sell the robbery. But who had sent them? *Washington?* No. He still needed her to keep tabs on Sam for a while. But maybe some other department had sidelined him and decided to cut the operation early. Bury all traces at the same time.

'Look, you don't have to do this,' she said, exhaling to ease the tension coiled in her chest.

'Do *what*, lady? I told you straight – you play ball, we ain't gonna harm you.'

There was a heavy pause, and Lorrena tried to pick up any slant or tease in the voice. Or whether their faces were creasing into smiles beneath the ski masks:

playing her for a mug. From just eye slits, she couldn't tell much: their eyes were flat, expressionless.

'Now out of the car.'

She got out. The heavy rain was strangely welcoming, cool against her skin, easing the band of heat suddenly clamping her skull.

'Move forward away from the car.' She went seven or eight paces before the voice came again. 'OK, fine.'

She looked back at the ghostly silhouettes in the beam of her car lights, both guns pointing at her. She knew this was her last chance.

'There are things Sam has told me that I haven't passed on yet,' she said. 'Things that are vital for you to know.'

Again a long pause, only the sound of the rain pattering around them.

'That'd be wonderful, except – who the hell is *Sam*?'

And this time she was sure there were smiles beneath the ski masks. They weren't buying it. She'd played her last card and failed.

'Now turn away from us.'

But as she looked back at them with one last silent plea in her eyes, she saw a set of car lights behind them turn into the road. The car moved steadily their way, and the two men turned too as its lights hit them.

It slowed and finally stopped forty yards away.

Obviously wondering what on earth was going on ahead. And Lorrena thought: *thank God*. Her prayers had been answered. They weren't going to do anything now with someone watching.

The headlamps were on full-beam. She couldn't make out any shapes inside the car, had no idea of who or how many.

But then she watched its headlamps flash twice and when one of her assailants acknowledged it with a wave, her heart sank back again. They were all together! They'd followed them from town or arranged to meet here to pick them up from their hit.

'As I said, turn away and don't look back.'

And so, all hope gone, she did as she was told, feeling the last raindrops on her lips as she waited for the bullets.

In London, Adel's team were still frantically trying to pinpoint the accent of the man who'd claimed responsibility for mosque bombs.

'Inflection and accent point to Yemen, with Oman not even coming into the picture,' voice analyst Paul Cunningham said. 'And lean towards Lebanese or Syrian influence rather than Moroccan or Tunisian.'

'Any favour between Lebanon or Syria?' Adel asked.

'Lebanon slightly ahead. But it's a minute difference – only four per cent in it.'

Adel stroked his forehead. Yemen citizens who'd also resided in either the Lebanon or Syria. Might be a hundred thousand or more.

'And was Yemen the first influence, or could that have been later?'

Cunningham was circumspect. 'That's where it becomes interesting, dear fellow. The main reason we're so sure the Yemeni residence was previous rather than latter: Mehri influence on some words.'

'*Mehri?*' Adel quizzed.

'A fast-dying south-semitic language, more akin to those of Eritrea or Somalia; it's unlikely anyone would pick it up or be influenced by it in later life. It's only present in the inflection on a few words, but our bet is that our man was born into a Mehri-speaking family and spoke it as a child; then later, as he learnt Arabic, lost most of it.'

'And Mehri is native to Yemen?'

'Yes, but only in a few small regions, and spoken by no more than seventy thousand people. Even taking the clock back twenty or thirty years, that number wouldn't exceed ninety thousand.'

Adel sat up. Now they were cooking. Seventy or ninety thousand cross-referenced against more recent Syrian or Lebanese residents might give them a figure in the low thousands. Adel passed on his thinking, and three hours later Cunningham phoned back with the results: 1,462 names.

'Official censuses of Mehri speakers were a bit patchy twenty or thirty years ago,' Cunningham observed, 'so fingers crossed our man is in there somewhere.'

'Yes, fingers crossed.' But just that morning they'd been fishing in a sea of millions, now they were down to a list of under fifteen hundred.

'Hooong Kong-style noodle, chicken saaatay...'

Sam smiled encouragingly at his son as he struggled through the takeout menu. Whatever Ashley lacked in pronunciation, he made up for with confidence and overstatement. Obviously he'd inherited his mother's acting skills. The Chinaman behind the counter was striving to be cordially patient but Sam could see it starting to wane. '*Why you think we give you numbers?*'

'Prawn Shanghaaiii...Chicken Kuuung Pooo.'

'That last one's a little hot,' the man pointed out.

Ashley looked back at the menu, lost in thought again.

'That's OK,' Sam said. 'Whatever he can't eat, we'll have.'

'I'll be all right,' Ashley said defensively. 'I think I've had that before.'

Sam shrugged. Big boy now. He'd be ready for Szechwan soon.

Deliberation completed, Ashley picked out a mixed chow mein and some prawn balls. Sam added a plain and fried rice to round off the order, and paid.

They were silent for a moment as they sat and waited. It had been a long drive, and Sam had already been updated on most of the news. Kate's boyfriend, *the prick*, had moved to a seafront house in Capistrano Beach, so now Kate saw him just at weekends. Sam wasn't sure if that was a sign of things cooling between them – last thing he'd heard they were meant to be moving in together – or just the distance factor. He wasn't sure either why he was interested, or if he even still cared, but now enough time had lapsed since those juicy snippets to get away with asking it casually.

'Things OK between them?'

'Suppose so.' Ashley looked towards the counter and the kitchen beyond, the rapid clatter of wok frying suddenly more interesting than talk about his mother's relationships.

Ever the diplomat. But it couldn't be easy being nine in the middle of see-saw relationships, Sam thought. He wouldn't press any more.

As long as Tom wasn't an ogre or mistreating Ashley, that was all he should be concerned about. Ashley had conceded that Tom was 'OK' – or maybe he was just playing the diplomat again – and his house was 'cool'. It sounded little more than a shack, but seafront shacks in Capistrano Beach probably didn't come cheap, and to a nine-year-old *anything* on a beach was 'cool'.

Ashley had already talked about his school and new friends, so Sam went back to that safer ground, asking who were his best friends and any girlfriends yet? Ashley singled out two 'for sure' best friends and one 'maybe', and had just started on the more difficult part, *girlfriends* – when Sam's cellphone rang.

Sam stood up and took a couple of steps away as he heard who it was: Lieutenant Millen, Utica PD.

'Is that Mr Tynnan? Mr Samuel Tynnan?'

'Yes, it is. Speaking.'

'And is a Miss Lorrena Presutti known to you?'

'Yes. Yes, she is. What's this all about?' Though, with a rising lump to his throat, Sam feared he already half knew.

'I'm afraid there's been an incident, sir.'

CHAPTER THIRTEEN

QUEENSWAY, LONDON.

Fahim Omari had his opponent on the run.

Three of his pieces were now trapped on the middle bar, the first for now the last eight moves. Omari stroked his chin thoughtfully as he made his next move; he'd soon have to move his own markers trapping them in order to help propel his own advance. Otherwise they themselves, as back runners, could get picked off and trapped.

Mahbusa – literally translated *imprisoned*, referring to that entrapment of an opponent's markers on the central bar – was Omari's favourite game. Around them at the café in Queensway's Whiteley's Centre came the sound of chequer slapping and dice rolling from other games: *infranjiah*, similar to backgammon, and *Gul bara*. Exclamations of joy or disillusion at key moves, as with arm movements, were effusive, some hands grasping skyward in entreaty at how *Allah* could possibly allow such a thing. Coffee was strong, black and often sweet, and the newspapers being read were *Al-Hayat*, *Al-Arabi* and *Asharq Alawsat*.

It was a café scene more befitting Cairo, Beirut or Tehran. If someone opened up a *Daily Mail* or *The Times*, a few eyebrows might arch: '*I think you want the Starbucks around the corner, my friend.*'

The café visits had become a regular Tuesday and Friday morning ritual for Omari. A game of *mahbusa* or *infranjiah* along with three or four black coffees and a slice of *basboussa,* a semolina syrup cake with almond topping. And as an added advantage, if the weather was fine, as it had been this morning, he could walk the half mile from his home in Lancaster Gate.

His opponent, an Iranian who'd left within days of the Shah being deposed and was now a carpet and ceiling fan importer, tapped one finger against his grey moustache as he saw the game slipping away from him.

Towards the end of the game, Omari was distracted by a figure entering the café past his opponent's shoulder: Wajd Masahran. As he caught Omari's eye, Masahran touched a finger to his forehead, then pointed to one of the back tables.

Omari left a discreet gap at the end of the game for small talk and to finish his coffee, then patted his playing partner on one shoulder in parting and went to join Masahran.

Masahran was a recruitment consultant specialising in oil-rig workers, constantly on flights between London and Bahrain. But he was also a collector for three Palestinian charities, two of which had been investigated for arms-linked funding.

'Of course, the main problem we have right now,' Masahran explained, waving one hand above his coffee, 'is a shortage of funds after the long embargo on Hamas.'

Omari nodded. The history he knew well, and he waited patiently through Masahran's preamble of woe to get to the meat of his pitch: a Nablus school which had all its computers taken and one wing bulldozed by the Israeli army because of suspected terrorist links.

Masahran shrugged. 'Because of those suspected links, our usual funding routes have been blocked.'

'What's your target sum to put things right there?'

Another shrug, as if to make light of the figure. 'A hundred thousand pounds.'

Omari made the decision quickly. 'OK. Put me down for thirty thousand of that.' He knew that within days, Masahran would have raised the rest. 'Transfer details as before?'

'Yes.' Masahran smiled and clasped Omari's forearm across the table. 'And thank you for the help, my friend. Those who can still be counted upon are less and less these days.'

'No. My pleasure.' Omari nodded graciously. 'And the school terrorist link was unfounded?'

Omari had said it as if an afterthought, but Masahran knew it was no light issue. The parameters of Omari's donations had been made clear at the outset: while he wished to help the Palestinian people, he drew the line at funding arms or terrorism. His aid was therefore restricted solely to orphanages, schools and some community build projects.

Masahran appeared mildly offended at the suggestion. 'Of course, my friend. Yet another wild claim – no substance at all. If I suspected any such link, I would *never* have mentioned the project to you.' Masahran gave a smile of reassurance and then lowered his voice. 'Though there is something on that front which I need to pass on to you. Something important.'

To any onlookers, if the import of those final words wasn't apparent from the way Masahran leant across the table to utter them, it certainly was from the shadow still lingering on Omari's face after they embraced and parted.

Omari meandered through the mall shops for ten minutes to give Masahran time to get clear, then on his way home stopped at a phone booth on the Bayswater Road to make the call.

'We need to meet,' he said as he heard Adel's voice. 'Urgently.'

'OK. I need a couple of hours to finish something here. Place three any good for you?'

'Yes, fine. Place three. Two hours.'

Lorrena was still shaking as they got into bed that night.

'It was terrible, Sam...*terrifying*. I was sure they were going to kill me.'

Lorrena hadn't wanted to go into any detail in front of Ashley, so now was the first time he was hearing the full account: how the two men had come out of nowhere as she left the nail salon and forced her at gunpoint to drive out to a remote spot; how she'd closed her eyes at the last second in anticipation of the gunshots, but instead heard a strange tinkling fifteen yards ahead, then the sound of their footsteps rapidly receding.

'I didn't work out what that tinkling was until they got into the car behind and headed off: they'd thrown my car keys over my head.'

As he listened, Sam found himself trembling too – the first time he and Lorrena had been in tune this past week.

He bit his lip. It was the worst possible timing with Ashley staying. He should *never* have agreed to it; should have known that once he did, he'd have little control over how it happened, let alone when.

The sole aim had been to get hold of Lorrena's laptop and cellphone. And since she always had those with her, Robby Maschek didn't see any way round that apart from a staged robbery, which was why he'd recommended Corcoran. Too risky, too *illegal* for Maschek's blood.

When he'd been sitting in Corcoran's drawing room in the ghostly glow of forty or so TV screens, Corcoran must have sensed his unease, because he'd leant forward and lowered his sunglasses for a second, as if sight of his eyes might lend assurance.

'Don't worry, my men are professional.' He'd smiled wryly. 'She'll be shaken, but not stirred.' Half-Irish from his father, half-Sicilian from his mother, Corcoran, according to Mike, saw himself as some sort of matinee idol; albeit he was now in his late fifties.

Amongst the proliferation of Cagney, Edward G and Bogart movies playing, Sam also noticed some

175

more recent classics: *Goldfinger*, *Silence of the Lambs*, *Goodfellas*, *The Shining*, *Reservoir Dogs*.

'If you can get past the eccentrics and the corny movie quotes, Vince is actually a great guy,' Mike had voiced after the meeting; then, with a shrug and dry smile, 'his psychopathic tendency to kill anyone who crosses him aside.'

Over the next couple of days, as Robby Maschek went through Lorrena's laptop files and cellphone records, they'd know if it had all been worthwhile.

But the evening with his son had been ruined. They'd spent half of it waiting at a police station for Lorrena to finish her statement and the boy had also been caught up in the whole drama as an ashen-faced, tearful Lorrena emerged. 'Oh God, Sam...it was a *nightmare.*' Now, with her still trembling alongside him, his strongest emotion was guilt. *What the hell was he thinking of going down this route with Maschek and Corcoran?*

Then he reminded himself of gunman firing empty chambers an inch from his face, which Lorrena had obviously been party to. And, as with every other night this week, suddenly he couldn't bare her touch. It made his skin crawl.

Though at least, with the recall, it made it easier for him to also slip into an act. He hugged and gently rocked her.

'It's OK...it's *OK*. It's all over. You're safe now.' And he kept hugging her until finally the gentle quaking of her body subsided and she fell asleep.

They were *both* playing roles now, Sam reflected; and with part of his manuscript being played out in real life, it looked like someone else had the script.

CHAPTER FOURTEEN

Place three was an Irish pub eighty yards from Leicester Square.

There were a few Arab-owned cafés and shops in the area, but none of the owners would be found here; and the trade of the area was seventy per cent tourists and out-of-towners.

Omari was eight minutes late. He made his apologies as he sat down.

'Had to go through a shopping list for Akram. He said the best fish would go if I left it too late.' He smiled indulgently. 'Always so particular.'

'How is he these days?' Adel had never met Omari's

long-standing servant, only seen photos of him from Omari's MI5 file. But the poignancy of how that association had been forged, dating back to Omari's days in Egypt, had stuck in Adel's mind, and Omari often mentioned Akram when they met.

'Apart from being more picky, fussy and particular than a score of mothers-in-law,' Omari waved one hand theatrically, 'fine.'

Adel grinned. 'You wouldn't have it any other way.'

'You know me too well.' Omari gave a concessionary shrug. 'Unfortunately.'

Despite the servant-master relationship, the two men were similar in age, so Adel often pictured an ageing Lemmon-Matthau 'odd-couple' relationship. It seemed that most of their arguments took place over the cooking, with constant debates over where to get the freshest ingredients and how best to cook them, right down to best tobacco flavours for the *shisha* and even likely suitors. '...*When I might be lucky enough to have a lady friend visit the house.*' But beneath the casual shrugs, easy smiles and entertaining stories, Adel knew the scars that lay there: Omari had lost his only son, just nineteen at the time, from a drugs overdose; then six years later his brother's son, Layth, who'd stayed with Omari for years in London and become like a second son, died in a tragic accident. And Omari's strongest solace and emotional bolster through those periods had been Akram: ever-faithful, ever-constant Akram. One of the *only* constants left in Omari's life, Adel considered. Omari had saved Akram from a fire when he had been a young beggar on the streets of Cairo and Akram had strengthened that bond by seeing Omari through his emotional turmoil.

Raucous laughter from a group of three at the bar distracted Omari for a second. The place was busy and boisterous, the music loud. They were sitting in a far corner, only visible if you made your way two-thirds through the bar crowd.

Pleasantries exchanged, Omari's expression now became graver. Despite the music drowning out their voices within two feet of their table, he leant forward.

'I've received information about another possible incident.'

'Where?'

Omari leant even closer as he passed on the details, in much the same way that Masahran had earlier.

As the implications sank home, Adel took a swig of his drink to quell a sudden dryness in his throat. 'And you think it can be trusted?'

'It's the same contact who passed on information about three of Khalish's past operations, including the last one in northern Italy.' Omari held out one palm. 'But hopefully with a specific location *and* time frame this time – we'll have more luck than with Milan.'

Adel nodded slowly, mechanically; still caught up with his own thoughts. 'The tenth or eleventh of this month, you say?'

'Yes. He was very specific about that.'

Five or six days time. *London*. With those specifics, yes, they should have more luck than with Milan. But that, and the fact that it was home soil, also brought added pressure. No possible excuses if it went wrong. *We didn't have enough information...it wasn't on my patch, so I didn't have control over security manpower deployment.* This time Adel held all the cards.

'There was something about a couple of mosque bombings on the news the other day. Did you see it?'

'Yes, I did,' Sam said. Lorrena had mentioned it casually, as if it was of little import. He'd wondered, *dreaded*, over the last couple of days whether that question might come up. And, despite having run through a few ready answers in his mind, he still found his nerves bristling. Perhaps because he still hadn't fully decided which of those answers was best. He turned as Ashley shuffled in carrying his suitcase, glad of the distraction. 'You got everything in there? No socks or an iPod left under the bed? You know what your mum's like – she'd make me fly all the way to California with it if you have.' Sam grinned, just in case Ashley missed the sarcasm.

'Yeah, I got everything.' Ashley rolled his eyes:

spare the dramatics or humour; or perhaps: iPods are sooooo last year.

It was the tail end of breakfast and they were all getting ready to leave: Lorrena to work, and Sam soon after to drive Ashley to JFK. Possibly why she'd chosen now to broach the subject: casual, in passing, and he might be too distracted with the rush to think through a good answer.

Lorrena took a sip of coffee before picking up the thread again. 'Because I remember you mentioning you had some mosque bombings in *The Prophecy*.'

Sam sighed. 'Yes, there were. *The Prophecy*'s first bombing was in Turkey too, coincidentally, but I can't even recall the sequence after that. All I remember is that Turkey was the first and Medina the last – everything in between is a blur.' He tried to smile convincingly. 'I finally took Elli's advice to put *The Prophecy* behind me so I can focus on this new Toby Wesley book. And it *has* been six months now.'

Her eyes stayed on him for a second as she swallowed her last gulp of coffee.

'Oh, I'd better move.' She grabbed keys, bag, coat, and halfway through her whirlwind exit bent down to hug Ashley. 'Don't forget, if your dad starts to bore you silly with his talk on the way to New York – you tell him!' She smiled and Ashley beamed back. 'And next time you're here, I'll make sure to keep clear of police precincts.'

She pecked Sam on the cheek as she left. 'Bye.'

Ten minutes later as he headed off to New York with Ashley, Sam was still raking over the ashes of their conversation and wondering about that last-second lingering look.

Had she accepted his answer? Maybe it had been one final test: *ask him about the mosque bombings on the news. If he answers in any of the following ways, then get out of there and call in the SWAT and clean-up team.*

After all, that had been a crucial reason she was still around: to see how he reacted as events unfolded. But it was a delicate chess game. One part of that, the bombers' challenge to Abu Khalish, she couldn't get away with mentioning. He couldn't remember going into that much detail about *The Prophecy* with her. So as Lorrena, his girlfriend, she wouldn't know that, but as Washington's spook she'd know every last detail; she couldn't cross that divide without giving herself away. But had that been part of the test? She'd expected *him* to mention it as a natural follow-on to the mosque bombings? Or could it have washed that if he'd forgotten the finer details, he'd have lost that too? Or simply that he hadn't seen that news item yet?

'You OK, Dad?'

'Yes, fine. *Fine.*' He tried to relax. This business with Lorrena, Washington, the mosque bombings and Abu Khalish. It had swamped all else, and stifled these precious hours he had alone with his son. *Pathetic*. He sighed. 'Lorrena's mugging has still got me rattled. *Sorry.*'

No doubt Kate would call as soon as Ashley was back in California. *What's all this about Lorrena getting mugged? I thought where you lived was meant to be safe, Sam? Sounds to me like it's fast becoming like downtown Detroit.*

He made one last effort to push it out of his mind and get back to what he should be doing with these precious hours – talking with his son.

They chatted about a skateboard park Ashley had found near home and a ju-jitsu class he'd enrolled in – Sam raised an eyebrow, at least Kate had stopped *totally* wrapping him in cotton wool – then about two of Ashley's favourite teachers, one of whom sounded wildly eccentric. '...Half the class call him Kurt Cobain's madder brother.'

'Makes him different, bit of a *character*, I suppose.'

'Yeah, I guess,' Ashley conceded.

The conversation had finally started to flow more easily until he got a call from Lorrena.

'With the rush this morning, I forgot to mention that I've got another Italian language class tonight. I'll be late back.'

'Oh, right.' He felt his heart sink; but at least he had the answer to his question. Having mulled over his answer, she'd obviously decided that he hadn't passed the test; or perhaps she'd conferred with Washington and *he'd* reached that conclusion. With Ashley gone, he'd be on his own: what better time to call in the SWAT team than that night? His throat tightened. 'OK, see you later.'

From then on the conversation with Ashley was once again strained – short answers, half-sentences, long silences; he found it impossible to detach his thoughts from the SWAT team awaiting his return home.

And as they hit the outskirts of New York, Ashley asked again, 'Are you sure you're OK, Dad?'

'Yeah, sure. I'm OK. Just that call from Lorrena reminded me what she went through the other night. She didn't sound good.'

But as they met up with Kate at the airport and he said his goodbyes, Sam found himself hugging his son tighter and for longer than usual. And once he'd waved Ashley through checkout, his eyes lingered on the spot he'd been standing in, as if it might be the last time he'd see him.

Because he knew then that it probably was.

CHAPTER FIFTEEN

'...Which then strikes off another two hundred and forty-eight.'

'So what's the total down to now?' Adel asked.

Key-tapping at Cunningham's end. 'We're down to eight hundred and thirty-four possibles.'

Adel rubbed his forehead. In three passes – too young, too old, or according to records not left either the Lebanon or Syria for the past ten years – Cunningham had taken almost six hundred names off their mosque bomber voice-trace list.

'Leave the last batch in there,' Adel said as he was struck with the thought. 'There's a good chance he'd be using assumed names for this – if in fact he even travelled to the operation areas – so that's not going to show under his real name.'

'True.' Cunningham took a fresh breath. 'All we can hope for is that something else now leaps out to throw a spotlight on his name from that list.'

'Yes, let's hope. Let me know if you think of anything else to pare it down.'

But Adel knew that their main hope was through matching travel records from mosque-attack cities to names from that list; yet with aliases probably used, no such match would be possible.

And as Adel knew all too well, a miss was as good as a million miles: they had Abu Khalish's name *and* what he looked like – but in four years were *still* no closer to finding him.

And if Omari's information was correct, Khalish had certainly given his answer to the mosque bombers: *Not only am I not going to give myself up, but I'm planning another bombing.*

Adel couldn't think of any other reason but sheer defiance for Khalish planning another bombing so soon after the last. The closest previous gap between bombings had been nine weeks, the longest eight months. This planned London attack was only twelve to thirteen days after Milan.

Adel checked his computer. There was still no activity spike for London. Probably too early; but that would no doubt come over the next forty-eight hours.

* * *

Robby Maschek got to the house just before dusk and had been outside now for over two hours. He'd made the call to Sam Tynnan mid-afternoon to bring him up to date.

'I didn't have much luck with her laptop, I'm afraid. All just day-to-day stuff, it looked like everything juicy had been put on a couple of online file links – *both* heavily encrypted. But I did finally manage to break the codes on one and get through.'

'Oh, right.' Sam's tone lifted.

'They'd already wiped everything. Almost as if they knew someone might come looking, or at least weren't taking the risk. I could keep trying to break the other, but I reckon it'll be the same.'

'Did you find her diary on there?'

'Yeah, but again didn't see anything untoward. Lot of blank spaces – so maybe that's when she was doing something she shouldn't. We're just left to guess.'

'And her Italian language classes?'

'Thought about that. If I contact them, there's a good chance they'll tell her, and then she'd be on to us. And even if we find she only had one class a week, yet she told you *two* – we already know she was other places now and then. Because you saw her with Arab gunman.'

'What about her cellphone records?'

Hearing the faint desperation in Sam's voice, Maschek trod softer, left a lifeline. 'Well, maybe if you go through those numbers with me, we might find something.'

They arranged a time for Sam to go to Maschek's office the next day, but then Sam was back on the line again just ten minutes later.

'I forgot to mention: talking about Italian language classes, I got a call earlier from Lorrena saying that she's got one tonight. And the last time she said she'd be late was when she visited the gunman's house in Albany. Might be worth following up.'

Maschek sighed heavily. 'Look, Sam, I'm as disappointed as you at not being able to find anything so far. But I don't see what—' He stopped himself; suddenly he *did* see a point in going there. Even if she didn't show, with a long lens he might get a good shot of gunman to run through police photo files. He'd already run one of Lorrena through: nothing. And if nobody was around, there was something else he might be tempted to try. He sighed again. 'OK, it might give us something useful. Especially if gunman turns up in a different car, or a new face shows up. Where will you be later if there's anything worth reporting?'

'Not home, that's for sure. But wherever I am, you'll be able to get me on my cellphone.'

Maschek picked up on the intimation. 'Why not home in particular?'

Sam explained that that might be the other reason

Lorrena had made the excuse about her Italian language class. 'They might have decided it's time to shut down the operation and for her to bail out. In which case I could well find a SWAT team on my doorstep.'

'Oh, *Jeez*. Not good.' Maschek was reminded that for himself it was just another case, but for Sam Tynnan his life was on a knife-edge. 'You want me to phone Vince to get some muscle down there?'

'No, it's OK. It'd be midnight before they could get there from Boston. I'm just going to nip in for a few minutes to grab some things, then head over to Mike's for the night.' He'd phoned Mike an hour ago to explain.

It was still a three-hour run to Albany, and Maschek said that he'd better get weaving. 'I'll phone you later with any news.'

Maschek looked back at the house: *still* no signs of life. He checked his watch: 8.46 p.m. It was starting to look like nobody would show.

The street was quiet, most people had already returned home and settled down for the night. He waited another twenty minutes – still no arrivals – then approached the house. There had been nothing on her laptop, but maybe there'd be something in the house itself. Papers, notes, *anything*. If he had to cross the line by breaking in a window or door, nobody was going to know.

He went round the side of the house. The back door felt like it was double-bolted when he tried the handle, but then he noticed a top window an inch open.

He opened it wider, took the slip wire from his pocket and fed it through. He looped it onto the larger window handle below, and pulled. It gave. They hadn't locked it.

He didn't hear the rustle until it was upon him – his heart suddenly in his throat. But it was only a grey cat come to sniff around for food. Slowly, Maschek exhaled.

He closed his eyes for a second to compose himself, then climbed in through the window.

He found himself in a small bedroom. One bed, side table and a wardrobe. He checked the side table drawer: empty. The wardrobe the same, no clothes.

The bedroom door opened onto a bare, empty corridor: no furniture or a single mirror or painting. Three doors led off it.

The first was another bedroom; again, nothing in the drawers or wardrobes. The second was the lounge: no TV or stereo, and nothing on two side cabinets. He opened the drawers of the cabinets: all empty. He went through to the kitchen to make sure: fridge empty, every cupboard bare. He bet too that they'd cleaned and sanitised every surface for prints.

Sam was right. Looked like they were closing

down the operation, bailing out. Which meant he was probably right too about a SWAT team waiting for him. He took out his cellphone and dialled Sam's number.

Adel checked his computer straight after lunch. Still no London activity spikes. He went back over the hour-by-hour fluctuations for the day: up four per cent by late morning, but had now slipped back two points. Nothing to speak of.

The core of that 'activity' and 'chatter' list had originally been no more than fourteen thousand names worldwide. Known terrorists, their contacts and affiliates, arms suppliers, activists and radicals. Every phone or Internet line connected with them was monitored. And each year that list had expanded: extreme imams, those photographed among their regular congregations, more photos and names still from 'death to the West' street demos, radical-Islamic Internet sites and virulent anti-West bloggers and message board posters.

Yet by far the biggest expansion had been the various contacts of those core names; two or three calls to the same person who was not a relative, and their names would be added to the list. Sometimes, in turn, their contacts too. Now that list was over a hundred thousand strong. In addition, random keywords would raise a flag amongst billions of conversations monitored by *Echelon*, whether part of that list or not. But to a large extent, they worked on the basis that most conversations would be coded and disguised as innocent.

If there was 'chatter' in one or more locations, a need for those names to talk to each other more than usual, then invariably it meant something was happening out there.

Adel's line buzzed, and he noticed a colleague waving from across the room, phone in hand. He picked up.

'Ghali of TAME Cairo on the line. Another call in on the Alexandria bombing.'

'OK. Thanks.'

Adel made notes as Ghali passed on the details. He'd heard from a professor at Cairo University, Amir Muhaimin, who'd been contacted last year by an English writer, Sam Tynnan. Research for a novel.

'...Muhaimin apparently didn't think anything of it until the Alexandria bombing the other day. You see, amongst a series of mosque bombings in this English writer's planned book, he remembers that one of those was in Egypt.'

'Alexandria?'

'I'm afraid he doesn't have exact recall, what with it being a year ago. But he did still have this writer's contact details – if you thought it worth pursuing.'

'OK.' Adel made a note of them. 'Thanks, Ghali. We'll follow it up.'

Adel tapped a finger thoughtfully on his notepad after he hung up. There'd been fourteen calls already about the mosque bombings. Half of them had headed nowhere, the other half so loony tunes that they were hardly worth checking out. This one would probably be no different.

Sam had to pull over to the side of the road halfway through the call from London. He stayed there for several minutes afterwards, trying vainly to bring his life back into focus. The call continued to prey on his mind on the rest of his drive back to Oneida.

What was this then? A follow-up to Lorrena's questioning that morning: get someone loosely based on a character in *The Prophecy* to come at him from a different angle, see if he said something different?

Professor Muhaimin? Sam remembered him, *vaguely*. Mike's theory was that Washington's team had initially latched on to *The Prophecy* through one of his early research contacts. Could Muhaimin fit that bill? Probably not. They wouldn't have used the name of their contact, they'd have stuck someone else in the frame.

But how would they know who else he'd contacted for research? There'd been a fair few referrals, he reminded himself. And he'd also dropped a name or two along the way. '*Your counterpart at Sultan Qaboos University, Professor Asimah, holds a slightly variant view to that...*' Or the simplest explanation of all: Lorrena had gone through his computer notes or the Arab assault team had copied them at the same time as wiping *The Prophecy* off his computer.

Perhaps choosing someone akin to a character from *The Prophecy* was simply to throw him off kilter? Blur that line between fiction and reality all the more. Real mosque bombings mirroring those in his manuscript, now the characters too?

In the end he'd played safe and followed much the same line as with Lorrena.

'In your book, where was your mosque bombing in Egypt?'

'I don't remember now. I had Cairo, Qena and Alexandria in my notes – I don't recall which I finally used.'

'And where in your sequence was the Egypt mosque bombing?'

'Again, I can't be sure – but I think third, fourth or fifth.' If this was a real enquiry fed through Professor Muhaimin, then in his original notes Alexandria had been the third bombing and Islamabad the second; he'd only switched them round later.

'You keep saying "can't recall or be sure" or "in your notes". Aren't you able to simply check your manuscript?'

'I'm afraid in the end the project was scrapped.' That was one thing he was sure he wasn't meant to share: Washington had said at the outset not to confide in anyone that he'd been raided and the manuscript taken. *It would open up too many other awkward questions.* 'It *is* over a year ago, and I'm working on another project now.'

'And in this now "scrapped" project, if you don't mind me asking – what was the purpose of these mosque bombings?'

The key question. But was he meant to tell the truth or fumble it? Washington had also said he should be careful who he shared his core plot line with. *'That's no doubt what got you targeted in the first place.'* Was that what this was all about? To see whether he was toeing the line or not.

Option two: 'Simply an escalation of Sunni-Shiite conflict which the West hoped to be able to play to advantage. But that never really got to the stage of being clearly defined. Partly why the project was finally scrapped.'

He was asked to then fill in some details, including his recall of any other mosque bombings in his sequence, and then the questions stopped. 'Thank you for your help.'

But Sam was rattled after the brief exchange. Had he handled it right, or had he just put the last signature to his death warrant?

His hands gripped tighter on the steering wheel as he hit the outskirts of Oneida, his eyes darting to his rear-view mirror. Was it too risky now to venture back home to pick up some things before heading to Mike's? No, he was sure he still had time. Four blocks from home, he slowed, checking every side street he passed for parked vans. By a block away he was at a crawl, then eighty yards from his door he pulled in and stopped.

No vans in sight, his driveway empty, three parked cars in the road, the closest four houses away. He spent a moment mentally attaching those to neighbours or their visitors, then drove on. Slowly. He did a close-up sweep of the nearest car to his house, a silver Pontiac Grand Prix, as he rolled past – it was empty.

He paused for a second as he pulled into his drive, scanning eighty yards past: two more cars, but they also looked empty.

And from there it was a frantic rush. Key in the door, four strides and he was at the top of the stairs. He grabbed his washbag, some underwear and clothes and threw them all in a sports bag.

Halfway through his stumbling run down the stairs, his cellphone rang. He checked the display: Robby Maschek.

'Where are you now, Sam?'

'Home, why?'

'Because I was about to say – *don't* go there.' Maschek was slightly out of breath, as if he was walking rapidly. He rattled on without pause. 'I got to the house in Albany, and it's been stripped bare. No TV, clothes, food. *Nothing*. So I think you're right. They're shutting down the operation, bailing out.'

Sam's stomach sank. 'Don't worry. I'm only here for two minutes to grab a few things – then I'm out of here.' He went over and grabbed his address and notebook from his desk.

'Wise thinking.'

'Yeah. Speak to you again later once I'm at Mike's.'

But three strides from his desk, halfway back towards the front door, he saw them: a shadow of movement through the front window – black fatigues, black helmets – but enough.

Despite his precautions, they'd seen him arrive and moved in. It was too late.

CHAPTER SIXTEEN

Lorrena took the call just before lunch at the medical centre.

'Mr Willerby speaking. I've got an appointment with Dr Savanson at three-thirty.'

'I'm sorry, but we don't have a Dr Savanson here.'

'Ah. I see now from my appointment card that it says High Cedars Medical Centre. Sorry about that.'

'That's OK. No problem.'

Similar message each time, and *always* just before lunch.

When Lorrena went out for lunch ten minutes later, she called Washington back.

'What news?' She suspected it was about her laptop links. Twenty minutes before Sam arrived at the police precinct, she'd made an excuse that she needed a cigarette – she didn't smoke – then called Washington from a nearby payphone to warn him her laptop had been stolen.

'We wiped everything on both links straight away – but somebody got through on one early this morning. Nothing yet on the other.'

'Incidental, or do you think someone's been purposely snooping?'

'Hard to say. Could be innocent. But it does mean we might have to put some extra precautions in place. We should meet.'

Lorrena picked up the hint that Washington didn't want to go into any detail on an open line. They arranged to meet at a diner four miles out of Rochester. Washington didn't want to risk anywhere nearby where they might be seen together by someone she knew.

Lorrena phoned Sam straight after to tell him that she had an Italian language class that night and left for Rochester when work finished.

She glanced over at Washington getting their coffees at the counter. She'd asked for a double-shot latte. A two-hour drive on top of a busy day at work, she could do with the extra hit.

She looked around – it was starting to get busy

with an early dinner crowd. Washington was wearing a brown windbreaker over a grey jumper. Casual, colourless, blended in – nobody in the diner would remember him, which was the way he liked it.

Even she, as part of his team, knew little about him. All she knew was that he was a veteran of the first Gulf War, then spent two years in Homeland Security before setting up this unit. But that left several shadowy years in between in which it was rumoured Washington ran various, mostly overseas, black-ops for the military and CIA. But that's all they were: rumours. Nobody knew for sure; again, the way Washington liked it.

They'd taken a table at the far end with empty tables each side: nobody within close earshot. But then a group of three came in and took the table behind them.

Lorrena noticed Washington glance round at them, then lean over and say something to the girl preparing their coffees. She put them in polystyrene cups and Washington paid.

'Not that private any more,' Washington explained as he brought them over. He nodded towards the front window. 'You got your car outside? Maybe we'd be better sitting there.'

It was cold outside and Lorrena's windscreen had misted up. She started the engine and put the heater on, sipping at her coffee for instant warmth.

'The first thing to work out,' Washington said with a slow exhale, 'is whether he's on to you or not. Certainly that mugging doesn't quite sit right.'

'I know.' Lorrena shrugged. 'Maybe they just didn't feel right doing it there – so close to the nail parlour and the other shops. But are you thinking that way also because of that link being accessed?'

'No.' Washington shook his head. 'That could have been innocent. They were set up to look innocuous, like online banking accounts or similar. A thief could easily have thought funds were there to access and grab. He sees one's *not* that and has been closed down in any case – he doesn't bother with the other.' Washington took a swig of coffee, raised a brow. 'What about how he seems with you day to day? Any telltale signs to point to him being on to you?'

'No, none. Unless he's a very good actor.' Lorrena held out one palm. 'Besides, why now? If he was going to get suspicious and think I might be involved, surely that would have come in the first month or two after the raid? *Not* six months later.'

'Anything you can think of that might have brought about a change?'

'No, nothing.'

They were both silent for a moment. Taking stock, drinking their coffees, warming hands on their cups.

Lorrena's windscreen had mostly cleared. At the side of the diner car park, she could see Washington's

Chevy Tahoe. Ohio was sitting behind the wheel, nobody else in the car.

Washington always preferred one-to-one meetings, nobody listening in. *Cuts the chances of information being passed on*, was his theory.

'Did you test him out over the mosque bombings?' Washington asked.

'Yeah, *eventually*. Had to leave a day or so's grace after the mugging. He might have thought it odd I had the presence of mind to ask about that straight after.'

'How did he react?'

'He said the bombing in Turkey was probably just a coincidence, and in any case he couldn't recall the sequence any more – says he pushed it out of his mind to get on with his new book. Can only remember the site of the first mosque bombing and the last in Medina. The rest's a blur.'

Washington cocked an eyebrow. 'And you believe him?'

Lorrena thought about it, then nodded. 'Yes, I do as it happens. As I say, it's been six months. And *everyone*, me included, has been pushing him to forget about it.'

Washington held her gaze for a moment before staring ahead again, letting out a slow plume of air. *Acceptance?*

In truth she wasn't sure, either way. *Had Sam truly moved on or did he think it was more than just coincidence?* She wanted to hang on to know. More critically, once Washington had sufficient doubt he'd cut the operation. And when he did, he'd also send in a team to take out Sam Tynnan. Close the final chapter.

The one thing she could never admit to was developing feelings for Sam Tynnan, *strong* feelings. So she wanted to delay the inevitable for as long as possible, desperately hoping that once the whole operation wound down, that action would no longer be necessary.

It's the first thing they warn you about: *never* fall in love with the mark. But they also don't tell you just how to avoid that. Nothing in the manuals about that one. And if she'd admitted that back when she first became sure, eight or nine months ago, Washington would have probably cut the operation then.

'And the bomber's demand that Abu Khalish give himself up?' Washington asked.

'He never mentioned it. And, of course, I couldn't ask.' Lorrena shrugged, and for a second everything seemed to blur. She blinked to bring Washington back into focus. 'To be fair, his son from California arrived around then, and he's been spending every hour since with him. So I don't even know if he's seen that news item yet.'

Washington nodded slowly, pursing his lips as he looked back at her. 'I think you're right. I don't think there's anything to worry about.'

Again his image blurred and Lorrena felt almost seasick as she watched him nod. Now his hand was reaching towards her, gripping her shoulder – yet she couldn't feel his touch!

'You're right...you're right,' he said. 'Everything's OK.'

A soothing mantra. Washington looking at her intently, trying to gauge when she might be fully under.

A dull, treacly warmth seemed to spread through her muscles and joints, making every limb feel numb, leaden.

And then it hit her: Washington switching to takeout coffees and suggesting they sit outside. He'd slipped something in on the way, had already made his decision before they talked.

She instructed her arm to reach for the door handle, but it refused to move, felt like a ton weight.

And as that numb weight reached her eyelids, so that even they were impossible to keep open, the last thing she saw was Ohio getting out of Washington's car and walking towards them.

She had only a couple more lucid moments.

At one point she recalled awaking to see Washington driving her car. She was in the front passenger seat.

The next waking moment she was back in the driver's seat and Ohio was wedged in awkwardly alongside her in the same seat; and she had trouble for a moment explaining that in her mind.

Then she noticed the barrier a hundred yards ahead and the black expanse of water beyond, and caught the strong alcohol whiff from her clothes – brandy or grappa – and realised what they intended to do with her.

And she thought: if they're doing this now, they'll be sending a team to Sam at the same time. She closed her eyes as a slow tear trickled out. 'I'm sorry, Sam,' she murmured, lost amongst the revs of her engine. '*So sorry.*'

The revving wavered higher and higher on each peak, and finally Ohio eased back the clutch, and the car lurched forward.

Ohio had only one hand on the wheel, the other gripped to the door frame, holding it an inch ajar through the open side window.

The wind-rush through the open window made her feel the acceleration all the more, an icy blast which brought a tingle to her cheeks. A tingling too now at the back of her neck with the rapid motion, a reminder that her senses were returning; though she wasn't sure if she wanted them back at this moment. Warm, welcome darkness would have been preferable.

She noticed she was able to move her arm again, but shifting her body was impossible with Ohio wedged in on top of her.

Four yards from the barrier, Ohio executed his stunt move perfectly, swinging the door wide and rolling out.

As the car hit the barrier, Lorrena felt her seatbelt cut into her and something ram against her left calf. A suspended moment as the black lake filled her windscreen before smashing through it – snowdrop glass fragments striking her face on a frothing burst of water. Then darkness.

Washington and Ohio stood by the lakeside for a few moments, surveying its inky blackness under a weak half-moon for any signs of movement. *Nothing*. They turned and walked away.

CHAPTER SEVENTEEN

A faint mist rose off the water.

Though Fahim Omari couldn't see the pool area from where he sat in his small steam room; copious billows of hot steam obscured everything beyond a few feet.

When the heat got too much he moved to the pool, closing his eyes as he sank fully into the water. It felt cool in contrast, even though it was constantly kept between 80° and 82°F.

Modelled on a Cairo *hammam* he used to go to with his father, this was Omari's favourite room in the house. Three archways ran the twenty-foot length of the pool, the pillars and walls brightly mosaicked for two feet above the waterline and then continuing on through the pool.

The only thing lacking from the original was light and aspect due to it being in a basement. So when Omari had heard about an Andalusian artist who did the most wonderful lifelike murals, he paid for him to fly over and paint one of the walls: a courtyard of the Alhambra Palace with the Sierra Nevada as backdrop. Brightly lit, the mural radiated sunlight and had 3-D layering, the pool area appearing to verge into the courtyard and its vista beyond.

Omari opened his eyes as he heard movement.

'I've brought your towels and robe,' Akram said, placing the towels at the poolside and his robe on a gold hook on one of the pillars. 'Tea will be ready in twenty minutes.'

Omari nodded and smiled. If Akram didn't time the tea, he knew he'd stay in there half the day. 'And what flavour for the *shisha* today?'

'Plum and cinnamon.' It was one of Omari's favourites.

Omari nodded again as Akram made his way out. They knew each other so well, like a foot and an old shoe.

Omari felt that life was made up of key transitional events – events after which things were never quite the same – and one of those first had been with Akram.

Akram had been a twelve-year-old Cairo street beggar when he first met the Omari family. He used to collect the old cardboard from their sites to sell on, then after a while they let him take the wood pallets as well.

On January and February nights, the temperature often dropped sharply, so they would let Akram sleep overnight in the warehouse which adjoined their Cairo house. They told him if he slept close to the cement bags he would benefit from their radiated heat.

After a while Omari suggested to his father that they let Akram sleep in the house instead, that it wasn't safe leaving him in the warehouse yard. But all he got from his father was a lecture about maintaining respective levels. *'He's a street beggar, Fahim. Who knows what he would steal from the house if we let him inside?'*

Then one night thieves broke into the warehouse. The screams were the first thing to awake Omari and, as he looked out at the yard, he saw the flames and Akram's prone figure on the ground, his *thobe* still burning. Omari moved faster than he ever had in his life, running down to the yard and smothering the flames with some nearby empty cement sacks. It turned out the thieves had lit a small oil lamp to see inside the dark warehouse; then, when Akram had woken up, startling them, had thrown it at him.

Only sixteen at the time, Omari spent the following weeks and months changing Akram's bandages and tending his burns, and the keystone of their long friendship was cemented.

When Akram recovered he stayed in the house and became his father's servant; then three years later when Omari's father died – the second key transitional event in Omari's life – he'd travelled with him to London.

The other key events were the birth of Omari's son, Nasib, his death nineteen years later from a drugs overdose, and the death of Omari's nephew Layth.

Omari had promised his brother on his deathbed that he would take care of the boy, yet within a decade of his promise Layth too was dead.

Strange, he'd shed more tears over Layth's death than he had over his own son. Possibly because of that promise; possibly because he'd seen Nasib's steady demise with drugs and so saw that final overdose as sadly inevitable, like a slow train wreck. Whereas with Layth, he'd been there one day, happy, vital, full of spirit – the *only* light left in his life after Nasib – then the next he'd been taken in a tragic accident.

He never knew that a man could cry so much; and Akram had cried too as he'd offered solace and comfort. Akram had become close to Layth as well from the years he'd spent in their London house.

Omari's divorce from his wife, Jannah, twelve years ago, hadn't been a transitional event; simply another slow, inevitable train wreck, and so almost a welcome release when the decree absolute came through. Akram said that he too was glad to see the back of her; though, ever the diplomat or perhaps afraid Omari still had feelings for her, it took him four years to get round to admitting it.

But Omari sensed that something was troubling Akram of late. He knew Akram didn't approve of one of his recent lady friends; maybe that was it? Or perhaps Akram had found a lady friend of his own – it would certainly be about time. In which case he wouldn't want to talk about it, so hardly worth prying.

Omari swam to the side and got out, started to towel down. No, just let things be, he concluded, and no doubt the old reliable, easy-smiling Akram would return. It was just a matter of time.

'I think you *should* make the call. If nothing else, to put your mind at ease.'

Jean-Pierre nodded thoughtfully at the attractive brunette sitting across the table from him. He'd first noticed Corinne at the back of the room on one of his Nostradamus lecture nights. Afterwards she'd approached him with some questions.

They'd kept in regular contact since and shared notes about that shared interest: Nostradamus. And at some stage Corinne became enough of a regular contact and friend that Jean-Pierre felt he could confide in her. It was then that it struck him that might be because he had nobody else to confide in, how lonely he was. Then came the thought that she too might be lonely, that she kept seeing him not just for that shared interest, but because she might be seeking something beyond just friendship.

But he'd never been bold enough to put that to the test, desperately afraid that if he read it wrong it might be the end of their friendship and then he'd be back to having nobody to share his private thoughts with, confide in.

'One mosque the same out of two, could easily be just a coincidence.' Corinne shrugged. 'You could of course wait for the third bombing – *if* there is a third. But if it's troubling you in the meantime, probably best to make the call.'

'Yes, I suppose you're right.' As ever, that invaluable voice of balance, reason, that so often eluded him. Left to himself, problems would rotate in his mind endlessly – never able to make that final bold step one way or the other. Pretty much what his relationship with Corinne had boiled down to, in fact. 'But my concern was also because of this mention now of Abu Khalish.'

'What did this writer tell you about that?'

'That's the trouble – not much. Just that the mosque bombings ended up linked to Khalish, but he didn't share any details as to how.'

213

'A noted terrorist featuring in a book about terrorism; not that unusual.' Corinne shrugged. 'But you're never going to know for sure unless you ask, are you?'

'Yes, I suppose. But what if it's all an elaborate hoax, and by getting involved I tarnish my name?'

'What – like the 9/11 quatrains?'

'Exactly.' Within days of 9/11, false quatrains attributed to Michel de Nostredame had appeared on the web and millions had been suckered in by them.

Corinne was distracted for a second as their starters were put before them, then brought her focus back. 'You knew immediately those quatrains were false and in fact were one of the first to go public with saying so, debunking them.'

'I know. But to this day millions *still* believe that they're real – so in the end how effective was that?'

Corinne waved a hand dismissively. 'Some people will believe what they want to, Jean-Pierre, no matter what. But you did your bit – distanced yourself from it. And I'm sure if this starts looking suspicious, you'll be able to do the same. Or, as you say, it might all just be a coincidence.' She reached across the table and lightly touched his arm. 'But I can see meanwhile that it's going to nag at you – so make the call.'

'I…I will.' But all he could think about right then was that touch on his arm and what it might mean, his mind suddenly numb to all else.

And it was still on his mind as he returned to the office and Madame Pelletret said she had three phone messages for him.

Two were calls he was expecting, nothing of import, but the third, from a Claude Vrellait, a *maître de livres anciens* in Montpellier, intrigued him. He didn't know the man.

'Did he leave a message or a number?' Jean-Pierre asked.

'Neither I'm afraid. He simply enquired what time you'd likely be back and said that he'd call later.' Madame Pelletret passed across the other two messages.

Jean-Pierre took a second to detach his thoughts from Corinne and that touch. 'I see...thanks.'

Make the call.

But as he reached the top of the stairs he heard the phone ring, then seconds later Madame Pelletret was buzzing his office line. 'It's Monsieur Vrellait again.'

Jean-Pierre picked up and Vrellait said that he was passed his name by a colleague, Bernard Lafin, 'In regard to possible verification of Nostradamus scripts.'

'Yes, I recall speaking with Monsieur Lafin.' But Jean-Pierre had to think for a second; it must be almost two years.

'In particular any side notes to his quatrains

which might turn up in the marketplace?'

'Well, yes. Any fresh documents which might surface are of course of keen interest to specialists such as myself.'

As Vrellait went on to explain what he believed he had in hand and what he required, Jean-Pierre fell silent. Vrellait finished, 'If this isn't quite your thing, I'd perfectly understand.' He paused. 'I can go to one of the other names on my list.'

'No, no. I *am* interested. Very much so. I was just caught by surprise, that's all.' *Surprise* was an understatement; if Vrellait's documents were authentic, it would be a discovery of unrivalled importance. But he didn't want to build up hopes too quickly, for Vrellait or himself.

Vrellait filled in the details and they finalised arrangements. He'd go to Vrellait's shop in Montpellier the following afternoon.

'No doubt you can appreciate my caution about letting the scripts out of my hands,' Vrellait commented. 'Even copies.'

'Certainly, I understand. I look forward to seeing them.'

After putting down the phone, Jean-Pierre wasn't sure whether to continue to sit there in stunned silence or jump up and down with excitement, the call and its import almost surreal. He couldn't fully focus on other work and didn't remember to call Sam Tynnan until forty minutes later; there was no answer.

He tapped one finger pensively on his desk as he hung up. He wasn't that bothered about the mosques any more anyway. Suddenly he had bigger fish to fry.

CHAPTER EIGHTEEN

'Where did they say her car went over?' Mike asked.

'Lake Ontario. Eight miles north-east of Rochester.'

'But no body found?'

'No, not yet. She's gone, Mike...*gone*! I went over this a dozen times with the police earlier. Her car door apparently burst open on impact and the currents are strong there. They might find her body ten or twenty miles downstream in a couple of days, they might not.'

Mike nodded slowly. 'And you say they're sure that she – or someone else – was in the car when it went off the edge?'

'Yeah. Hundred per cent. They found blood on some of the windscreen fragments and hair caught in a seatbelt rivet.'

Earlier, as the two figures had approached the house, Sam had pulled back deeper into the lounge; but he had the feeling that they'd already seen him through the front window. Then they did a strange thing: they rang the bell. A SWAT team wouldn't do that, Sam considered. They'd just burst through the front and back at the same time, as before. It was then that he went to the front window, looked out and saw the squad car. State troopers. He opened the door.

Forty minutes and two coffees later, he had the full account.

He was numbed rather than distraught or tearful; maybe that would come later. But he couldn't exactly say to them: *'She was a spook and planted here, that's why I don't know what to feel yet.'*

An accident was their main theory, suicide a slimmer possibility.

'Did Miss Presutti leave a note or anything?'

'No. No, she didn't.' Slimmer still as he watched their reactions.

'And we notice from records that she was the victim of a mugging just days ago. You think there might have been some connection there – she was upset about that?'

'Sure, she was rattled by that,' Sam conceded. 'But not enough to take her own life.'

Their questions wound down and they left soon after.

But now, convinced that Washington was involved, Sam was thinking again about that mugging connection.

'If we hadn't pulled that stunt with taking her laptop and cellphone, this would never have happened!' Sam swirled his Scotch, staring absently into the glass. 'Washington feared she'd been compromised – so she had to be taken out. We might as well have sent him her signed death warrant.'

'Don't beat yourself up so, Sam – you don't know that for sure.'

Sam looked at Mike levelly. 'Can you think of any other likely explanation, given the timing?'

Mike closed his eyes for a second in resignation. 'OK. That may well be the most likely explanation. But what's the point in driving yourself mad when you don't know for sure? Besides, what was the alternative? Just sit around while Lorrena kept tabs on you? Waiting for the moment when she decided that Washington should take *you* out? It was a dog-eat-dog situation, Sam, and you know it. Still is.' Mike put his Scotch glass to one side. 'Which is why we're here now rather than at your house.'

Sam looked at the room: a couple of prize stuffed

salmons, a steelhead trout, crossed fishing rods and nets, then beyond the log cabin window a small veranda overlooking the lake where they'd been caught. It wasn't safe to stay at his own house, and it was past midnight by the time he arrived at Mike's, his wife and kids already in bed. Mike had sensed it was going to be a long one, so he'd grabbed a bottle of Scotch from the cabinet on the way out. *'You'll need somewhere to stay for a while – so now's as good a time as any.'*

They'd gone to Mike's 'writing retreat' – a lakeside cabin twelve miles north. Few people knew about it and this time of year – a month shy of the summer season – it was quiet.

'You're right,' Sam said with a deflated sigh. 'It's just everything seemed to be closing in on me at the same time.' He told Mike about the earlier calls from Salon and London. 'The first one from France, I recognised the number so didn't answer. But the other I've never heard from – so I fluffed it, fed him a few lines.'

'Let me get this straight. The French guy is a real past research contact. But the London guy is simply someone who appears to be *based* on a character in *The Prophecy*?'

'Yeah, that's right.' Then, realising that sounded flippant: 'It's almost as if they already knew Lorrena wouldn't be around any more to keep tabs on me – so they've thrown in someone else to ask me questions.'

Mike shrugged. 'Again, Sam, you don't know that

for sure. And if this guy *is* real – then by feeding him a line, you've just done the opposite of what you should.'

'Yeah.' Sam smiled wanly. 'We're finally getting to the nub of it: Arab hit team not what they seem, then my girlfriend. Then real events mirroring those in my manuscript – now a character too. And I don't know the dividing line between fiction and reality any more. So when someone *does* turn up – no surprise I don't know what to say to them; whether to tell them the truth or simply spiel them more fiction.'

Mike wasn't sure if the Scotch had been such a good idea – when at this moment more than any other they needed clarity. But in a strange way, with the heat of the day's events and their equally heated words – perhaps partly fuelled by the Scotch – they were finally making some headway.

Mike leant forward. 'But don't you see, Sam – that's the thing. There are two sides to this coin. And, sure, if this character's just another plant, then you've done the right thing feeding him a line. But if he *is* real and you give him the right information, you've got a shot at guiding and influencing some crucial events in real life. Something us writers rarely get the chance of doing.' Mike read Sam's questioning look, as if to say '*I thought I was the one meant to be going mad*', and realised he'd run ahead of himself. He held up one hand. 'But to do that successfully, you're gonna have to play a pretty cute shadow game yourself. And if I'm going to help you with that, I'll need to know more. A lot more.'

'There were eight mosque bombings in total in *The Prophecy*, each mosque of increasing significance within Islam, with the final two in Damascus and Medina, two of the most important mosques in the Islamic world.' Sam paused as Mike started making notes on a pad. 'The bombings also tied in with some ancient Islamic texts, but most notably Nostradamus prophecies, or quatrains as they're known. Over nine hundred in total, dealing with everything from the French Revolution through to Hitler, Hiroshima and the collapse of the Berlin Wall. And there's a good deal of controversy over interpretations of Nostradamus's quatrains – not made easier by the fact that he included allegory as well as Greek and Latin phrases. One camp says that it was simply the style at the time, the other says that he purposely masked interpretations to protect himself from claims of sorcery and heresy; that, in effect, those parts were written in code.'

Sam took a fresh breath. 'But the most vital Nostradamus predictions in relation to current history – and those at the centrepiece of *The Prophecy* – are about 'Mabus' and an impending World War Three. In those predictions, Mabus is depicted as a child born out of the Arabian peninsula or Iran, who later unites the Islamic world in a war against Europe and the West. In the book, there's speculation that the first bombings are Shiite instigated, because the mosques targeted belong to their Sunni rivals. Then comes an announcement from the terrorists that although they're Islamic, they have no specific Sunni or Shiite alliance. "Our allegiance is only to Allah himself, and to countering the defaming of Allah by deeds and actions in his and Islam's name by Abu Khalish." They release a tape to Al Jazeera and *Al Hayat* calling for Abu Khalish to give himself up in order to stop the bombings.'

'So far, so good,' Mike said. 'Or *so bad*, depending on your viewpoint. Everything's pretty much following your manuscript.' A couple of Mike's past books had involved heavy interplay with the Feds, so perhaps Sam thought that would put him one step ahead with this sort of spy game.

'Then the third mosque bombed is Shiite,' Sam continued, 'which pushes aside any thoughts of Shiite allegiance and also backs up the bombers' claims. But at that point Iran's leading cleric, Bahsem-Yahl, the book's chief villain, comes to the fore. He's the hard-line successor to Khomeini and long regarded as the main power behind the throne of all Iranian leaders since. Bahsem-Yahl announces that he doesn't believe the bombers' claim. He states that no true son of Islam would ever desecrate a mosque, and it's his firm belief that the bombers are actually agents of the West. He starts to gain wide support for this in the Arab world – in the same way that many crackpots believe that 9/11 was an "inside" government conspiracy. But with far more weight to his claim: billions have so far been spent on wars in Afghanistan and Iraq, and all you do is create your own little terrorist group and Abu Khalish comes out with his hands up. And if you also set up that group with, on the face of it, only Islamic links – hopefully there's no backlash to the West.'

Sam took a swill of Scotch. 'Though as a result, in the Islamic world, they increasingly believe Bahsem-Yahl's claim that the terrorists are "Western agents", and as he becomes more vocal that support grows.' Sam exhaled tiredly. 'So the race is on to track down the bombers and hopefully prove that they *are* Muslim – with no Western links – before they can get to those final two all-important mosques.'

Mike cradled his forehead as he took it all in, the nightmare scope of his friend's dilemma weighing heavy on him. 'And in *The Prophecy* the main guy tracking these bombers is this Muslim agent who happens to be a dead ringer for the guy who just phoned you?'

'Yeah. Like I said, the only difference is that my man hailed from Fairfax, Virginia, this guy's from London.'

Mike pursed his lips. 'One pointer in favour of him being real, I suppose. If Washington wanted to faze you he'd have put forward someone from exactly the same place. And Fairfax, and the accent, would have also been easier for Washington to arrange.'

'I suppose.'

But Sam didn't sound convinced, and Mike realised his friend was still shell-shocked, unable to grasp the finer points of what was happening to him. 'So, *The Prophecy* concludes with the mosque bombers being Islamic with *no* Western ties. And this is a good thing?'

Sam nodded eagerly. Firm ground again – the fiction of his book. It was the reality of what was happening in life itself that was proving tough to grasp. 'Yeah. Because that then disproved the claims about Western involvement, stopped that dangerously rising fervour within Islam before it reached the brink.'

'And in the book your Muslim agent and his team managed to stop the bombers before they got to those two last crucial mosques?'

'Yes, they did.' Sam smiled thinly, shrugged. 'Got to have a good ending.'

Mike nodded thoughtfully as the final pieces slotted into place. But then he was struck with something he'd said earlier: *two* sides of that same coin. And as he considered that scenario, he felt a cold tingle run up his spine. He just hoped he was wrong.

'And pray tell me,' Mike said slowly. 'What if they

didn't manage to save those last two mosques, and the bombers *had* ended up having ties to the West?'

Sam closed his eyes for a second and nodded solemnly. 'Then that would have been the last straw to break Islam's back: the West being involved in bombing its most prominent mosques. Bahsem-Yahl would have been proven right and would gain even more support in uniting Islam against the West, and all of Nostradamus's predictions about Mabus would have come to pass. It would be World War Three.'

Silence. Stone silence. A single light glinted from across the lake from another cabin. Aside from that it was ink-black outside.

Mike took a moment to collect his thoughts. '*OK, OK.* We've covered your London man, but what about this French research contact? Why did you avoid him?'

'Partly, it goes back to what you said: that someone I'd contacted for research was probably the first information feed to Washington. So when one of those contacts phoned, I thought: *Could it be them?*' Sam shrugged. 'Even if their contact's innocent – how am I to respond if they say, "*Hey, I notice some of those mosque bombings you mentioned are taking place in real life?*" I can't exactly tell them the truth, tell them my manuscript's been taken and I've found myself in the middle of some weird spy game. So best in the end to just avoid it – not have to say *anything*.'

Mike nodded in understanding. 'And what part did this French contact play in it all?'

'Jean-Pierre is one of two main Nostradamus experts I contacted. I asked them both the same question: out of five possibles I'd nominated, who did they think was the most likely fit for Mabus? They both picked different names, and I went in the end with Jean-Pierre's choice: Bahsem-Yahl.'

'OK. We can probably test to see if his contact's kosher. Let me think on that. But for now let's get back to your main London man. What line did you feed him about the next mosque bombings?'

'I said I wasn't sure – couldn't even recall whether the Egypt bombing *was* Alexandria or where it fell in the sequence. But I thought Bizerte, Tunisia and Sharjah, UAE were in there somewhere.'

'And the real locations for the next two?'

'Islamabad and Muscat, Oman.'

Mike noted them on his pad. He looked up pensively. 'That's the other problem, apart from any possible connections to Washington. Because if you pass these on, and this guy *is* real and the mosque bombings end up where you say – he might well think you're in collusion with the bombers.' Mike grimaced tightly. 'After all, what other rational explanation is there? If you tell him you've written a novel that's being used as a blueprint for these bombings, he's unlikely to believe you. That's why I said before you might have to play

228

some cute shadow games of your own.'

Sam nodded numbly. Yet another thing he hadn't thought of. But the mention of *shadow games* made him anxious: he'd just played one of those with Lorrena, and look how that had ended.

Mike tapped his pen on his pad. 'Just because your Muslim friend ends up saving the world in your book, doesn't mean he'll be able to in real life. You might have to give him a helping hand.' Mike smiled crookedly. 'But that's one advantage you have in all this, Sam. In fact, your *only* advantage. You *know* what's going to happen next – *if* you can work out just who to trust with that information.' Mike knocked back the last of his Scotch and leant forward. 'OK, here's the plan.'

CHAPTER NINETEEN

Adel felt the hours and minutes ticking like a metronome in his skull.

Three days until the London bombing and still no sign of an activity spike.

The only thing Adel didn't need to note to remind himself. On other issues he was juggling, he'd made brief self-questioning notes.

Mosque bombers' spokesman. Ways of further narrowing the list? Cunningham's team had chopped another hundred and forty-two names through work records: government agency, civil service and hospital records of those present on the days in question.

Western influence? So far only one extreme Arab newspaper, *Al-Watan*, and a minor correspondent in one of the pan-Arabs, *Asharq-Alawsat*, had suggested they might '*have a hand*' behind the mosque bombings. Little to worry about. The bulk of the Arab press, along with the Western press, so far accepted the mosque bombers' claims at face value.

Could Middle East activity spikes be linked to the planned London bombing? A rise in some cities had been noted late the day before, most notably Bahrain, Islamabad and Kandahar. But they'd made that mistake before with Milan. And if it might be another mosque bombing, which of those three cities might be the target area and which were merely operation centres? And which mosque? Each city would have at least a dozen prominent mosques and another thirty or more also-rans.

They needed something else to guide their hand but all the calls so far had ended up being wild goose chases. So when a lead came in late afternoon, Adel didn't pay it much attention, assuming it was probably like the other eighteen '*I think so-and-so mosque might be next*' calls so far received. But Malik, who'd taken the call from MI5 central routing, pressed him to take a closer look.

'The call was made from a phone booth on Charing Cross Road, so we've got a CCTV visual as well as voice.'

Adel looked at the freeze-frame CCTV shot on Malik's screen. The sunlight reflections from the booth glass partly obscured the person inside.

Adel nodded. 'OK. Let's see what we've got.'

Malik hit visual play, then the voice recording.

'*I've got some information about the next mosque bombing.*'

'*Who may I say is calling, and where are you calling from?*'

'*That's not important. Just pass on the message that I believe the next bomb will be the Kalatahn Mosque in Islamabad.*'

'*One minute, sir – let me put you through to someone else.*'

'*No. I'm not hanging on the line. Simply pass on that message – Kalatahn Mosque in Islamabad.*'

The same MI5 operator stayed on the line. There was a brief silence, then: '*And what makes you believe that, sir? Where did you get that information, if I might ask?*'

'*I'm sorry. That's all you're getting. Just make sure to act on it. Goodbye.*'

Dialling tone, but the door to the booth had already opened; the visual and voice were out of sync. Adel got a clear look at the caller for the first time: mid-thirties, wavy blond hair, serge green jacket, maroon scarf. A second later he was out of shot.

'*And...*' Malik clicked on his bottom bar and

brought up another CCTV image box. 'We've got him again here.'

It was a cam-view from further down Charing Cross Road – with the distinctive jacket and scarf, he was easy to pick out amongst the milling crowd.

'Just here he turns off,' Malik said. 'Litchfield Street by the looks of it.' Malik waited for the figure to move out of view, then clicked again on his bottom bar. 'Then we pick him up again here – halfway along Monmouth Street.'

A sharper angle, Adel noted, and a briefer view: ten strides and he was out of shot again.

Malik sat back with a faint sigh. 'Then we lost him.'

'How long ago were those CCTV shots?' Adel asked.

Malik checked back. 'Eleven minutes ago when he phoned; seven minutes for the last on Monmouth Street.'

Adel stroked his forehead. If it hadn't been for the Islamabad activity spike, it probably wouldn't have been worth paying much attention to. But the caller was also different from the others: half of those claimed to have got the information in a dream or a 'vision', and also didn't mind passing on their name and details; their fifteen minutes of fame if they were right. This new caller had also avoided staying on the line too long, sidestepping their normal holding tactics. Many a time when they played that right, they'd get a police car to pull up by the phone booth while the caller was still on the line.

Adel took a fresh breath. 'Get a live link to every CCTV within a five-hundred-yard radius, and also check back on their last ten minutes of footage. Let me know if he shows up on any of them.'

Malik arched an eyebrow; it was a twelve-man operation at least. But Adel was already heading across the room towards Tariq – responsible for India, Pakistan and Afghanistan – to get him to alert the security services in Islamabad.

ISLAMABAD, PAKISTAN.

For the three guards in front of the Kalatahn Mosque, it had been a quiet night so far.

And when at nearly 1 a.m., a rusty, dirt-encrusted open truck – its number plate illegible from mud splatters – dropped something as it rattled past, it was a source of amusement rather than alarm.

It was an old Bedford, and looked like it had kept going with second-hand parts and rubber bands for the past thirty years. One of the guards shouted after it, but it was already sixty yards past, and his voice was lost amongst its heavy engine throb and a belching plume of black diesel smoke.

Another guard approached the object and kicked

it tentatively with the tip of his boot: it was a rusty exhaust muffler. He looked round, as if deciding where to throw it, but when he crouched down to pick it up his colleagues realised there was a problem.

The guard's legs buckled at the knees and his rifle clattered to the ground as he held out one hand to break his fall.

Colourless and odourless, the methylfentanyl gas inside the muffler had started dispersing the instant it had left the truck. The furthest guard, seeing its effect on the other two, was the only one who stood a chance of getting clear.

He made it four full strides before his legs turned to jelly, and thankfully his whole body was numb by the time the pavement swung up and hit him in the face.

But he was far enough from the capsule to be the only one of the three to remain conscious; and so he looked on, eyes blinking slowly, as the two gas-masked figures ran in. All he could do was stare, mouth half-open like a landed fish.

Setting the C4 took only two minutes, shifting the three guards clear of the explosion another forty seconds. Everything was going well, according to plan.

That is until a jeep, armed by four officers from the nearby Kohsar police station, approached. They'd received the alert only minutes ago, so were ill-prepared – but they had the element of surprise on their side.

The mosque bombers' leader, Faraj, considered that if they'd arrived only minutes earlier, he'd have been able to adjust his plans; now, all he could do was make split-second decisions as the drama played out. His sniper, Dhakir, crouched a foot away awaiting his signal, had a clearer view through his rifle sights.

They were both concealed forty foot back in a narrow, unlit alleyway opposite the mosque and its wide, brightly lit boulevard, and so were shrouded in darkness.

They both watched as one of the policemen, caught on the edge of the gas's spread, faltered in his run and fell to his knees. The other three kept up pace in pursuit of their two gas-masked colleagues racing back towards the alleyway.

A van and a car flashed by between them on the main boulevard; then as the view cleared again one policeman started firing his handgun while another fell to one knee and aimed his rifle.

Dhakir took out the rifleman's right shoulder with a single shot, then swung across to the other policeman. But as he squeezed the trigger, one of those pistol shots felled his furthest colleague six yards short of the alley. His friend fell with a leg wound as the policeman's shoulder jerked back, gun thrown from his grasp.

His other team colleague ran breathlessly into the

alley, ripping off his gas mask after only a few yards.

Then the explosion came, spewing out a plume of rubble and dust.

The last uninjured policeman looked round at it, then at the alley, uncertain what to do. His gun was drawn, but only half-raised.

A warning shot from Dhakir whistling two inches past his head cemented his decision: they couldn't do more until they had back-up.

Faraj and Dhakir could hear sirens approaching. It sounded like they were only a couple of minutes away. As Dhakir watched two of the policemen pick up his injured colleague and start scurrying back with him across the boulevard, he looked expectantly at Faraj.

Faraj closed his eyes for a second before nodding. 'OK. Make the change.'

Dhakir slotted the fresh bullet into his rifle and beaded his red sight dot on one of the policemen. Then he shifted eighteen inches sideways to the back of his friend's head and squeezed off the shot.

'We've picked up Blondie again, boss!' Malik called out to Adel, beckoning with one arm. Malik had assigned a team of fourteen – eight tracking live feeds, six going back over the last ten minutes' footage. Halfway through, someone had referred to their cam-view suspect as 'Blondie' and the nickname had stuck.

One of the live-feed team, Bahir, was first to pick up their subject, forty-eight minutes after the last sighting on Monmouth Street.

Adel joined Malik, watching over Bahir's shoulder as on-screen Blondie crossed a broad pedestrian area, café tables in the top corner of the frame.

'North side of Covent Garden, coming off of James Street,' Bahir said, pointing. 'He's headed either towards the Opera House or the South Plaza.'

A dozen more paces and he'd stepped out of view.

'...And then we pick him up again on one of these.' Bahir moved his mouse and brought up two more screen frames.

There was a tense, expectant wait before they finally saw Blondie appear in the right-hand frame.

'OK,' Bahir said, leaning forward and tracing one finger on screen to work out Blondie's direction. 'Looks like he's headed towards Tavistock Court.'

Bahir clicked off his left-hand box and brought up a Tavistock Court feed in its place.

Adel asked, 'What roads follow on from Tavistock Court?'

Bahir enlarged a map from the top corner. 'Tavistock Street and Burleigh Street.'

Adel turned to Malik. 'Let's see if we can get him picked up. Nearest local squad car will do. Give them his description and direction headed, then feed them the best close-up CCTV shot.'

Malik nodded and went over to his desk to make the call.

Bahir commented, 'I've only got the feed heading west on Tavistock Street towards Southampton Street.' He looked round, calling out, 'Who's got the feed for Tavistock Street East and Wellington Street?'

Five desks away, Siraj, hair cut in descending layers like Javan rice plateaus, nodded. 'That'd be me.'

'OK, Blondie...' Bahir poised a finger in the air as he waited to see which way he headed. East. He brought the finger down towards Siraj. '...coming to a screen near you.'

'Got him!' Siraj said at length.

But again there'd been a taut sixteen-second wait while they worried that he hadn't gone the direction anticipated, or had ducked into a shop or restaurant with another side or back entrance, and they'd lost him.

Adel went over to Siraj's screen. Twenty yards along, Blondie stopped by a restaurant window – perusing its menu or looking for someone? – before continuing.

'End of Tavistock Street,' Adel called out to update Malik, phone in hand with the police on the other end. 'Approaching Wellington Street.'

'Aaah, that's where we might have a problem,' Siraj said. 'We've only got feeds at each end of Wellington Street. Nothing in the middle and nothing on Exeter Street.'

'What are the options?' Adel pressed.

Siraj tapped a few keys. 'If he heads north, we'll pick him up on Russell Street. South, we'll pick him up at the end of Wellington Street or when he hits the Strand.'

They both watched as Blondie stepped out of the screen frame, and Adel started a count in his head: thirty seconds, fifty, one minute.

'How long before he should appear again?' Adel asked.

'Russell Street, he should be there by now. The other end and the Strand, thirty seconds more. But if he's gone into Exeter Street – another minute or so before he shows at either end.'

...*Ninety seconds, two minutes. Three.* Still nothing.

The operations room was expectant, hanging on a knife's edge. Malik had his phone in hand with the police waiting on the latest position.

Four minutes. Adel made his decision.

'OK. Two options: he's either grabbed a cab in that block or he's still there somewhere. Let's go for option two for now before starting to worry about the first.' He looked towards Malik. 'But it's going to need more than just a local squad car. We'll need at least four armed SO19s for each possible exit, and double that plainclothes to go door to door.'

* * *

It had started to drizzle as the squad descended on Covent Garden.

Five SO19 officers in a black Met van and ten plainclothes Counter Terrorist Command, SO15, in three squad cars.

The squad cars swung broadside at the ends of the cross-shaped block they had to search, the Met van blocked the last exit. Four SO19 men – black nylon fatigues over Kevlar, black PASGT helmets, Heckler and Koch rifles – stood by the vehicles, the fifth at the central cross street.

They'd sealed the roads because the last thing they wanted was Blondie grabbing a cab out of the area under their noses while they searched.

The SO15 team, headed by Bob Losey – a twelve-year Special Branch veteran before he took the sideways step – were all in casual plainclothes: jeans, chinos, windbreakers, crombies, leather jackets. Whatever would conceal their shoulder-strapped Glock 9mms.

Losey hated this type of operation. Most vehicles emptied from the street within minutes and the armed guards at the street ends cut ghostly figures in the dusk light. People had started to group behind them, thinking it was a bomb scare.

And at this time of night the bars and restaurants of the area were heaving. Split into teams of two, they found themselves pushing past heavy crowds through practically every doorway.

It was always easier for those inside to eyeball them first, Losey thought; after all, they'd just swung through the door, bold as brass.

Losey felt his nerves tighten with each doorway entered. His eyes darted frantically, trying to take in a hundred or more people in four or five seconds. The jostling motions, bursts of laughter, sudden arm movements, banging of beer mugs on bar tops; each brought a nerve-jump.

Losey's eyes rested on a blond thirty-something man a moment too long, wondering if it could be their mark. The man, sitting with two other rugby-shirted beer-mates, stood up with a threatening, '*Yeah, want something?*'.

Losey eased his jacket aside to show his gun and badge. 'Take it easy,' he mouthed above the bar noise, and the man, red-faced, sat back down. Lucky his partner Micky didn't eyeball him first, Losey thought; he'd have fired the second the arm lifted.

As they were about to push open the next door along he heard a shout on his earpiece: '*I think we've got him!*' Ken, team three.

'Where?'

'PJ's.' Heavy sigh. 'The only problem is, he's with a girl.'

'She's not part of our remit. Just leave her there.'

There was a commotion then as a door swung open forty yards along. Losey ran towards it.

'That's not the problem. She's—'

'Don't worry, I'm there,' Losey cut in. He could hear the problem from where he was. The woman, a brunette in her late twenties, was still shouting about police brutality and how her barrister 'Daddy' was going to 'sue their bums off', as he approached.

Losey held a hand towards her, but stopped short of contact.

'He's done nothing,' she protested. 'You don't have the right to do this.'

Losey looked at Blondie, handcuffed and held by two of his men. Subdued, sheepish, obviously he'd worked out what had happened. Losey nodded to them, and they headed towards the Met van with Blondie.

'Oh, but he has,' Losey said to the girl. 'And I think you'll find I do.' He smiled tightly and turned away.

'Where are you taking him?' she shouted.

'Marylebone Station, Seymour Street,' Losey said over his shoulder. He didn't look back. Let her spend half the night finding out where they'd *really* taken him. Teach her to be such a bolshy tart.

As they got into the car, Losey took out his cellphone and dialled. 'We've got him. Just picked him up a minute ago. We're taking him to Paddington Green.'

'I'm leaving right now,' Adel said. '*No* questioning until I get there.'

CHAPTER TWENTY

MONTPELLIER, FRANCE.

Jean-Pierre felt like a child in a sweet shop.

Vrellait was trying to finish up on the phone and a young female assistant was dealing with a shop customer – so Jean-Pierre gave a tight-lipped nod that he'd peruse the shelves for a moment. There were twelve aisles less than a metre wide, stacked floor to ceiling with old tomes, and Jean-Pierre noticed that from floor to eye-level were mostly Balzac, Daudet, Stendhal, Dumas and Baudelaire reprints from the 1880s to 1930s, but on the higher levels the books became older and rarer. He spotted something on a top shelf that caught his eye, and asked Vrellait about it as he put down the phone.

'Is that by any chance one of the 1672 reprints of *Les Prophéties*?'

'No. It's a 1724 edition.'

Jean-Pierre nodded. He already had a 1756 edition. Probably not worth it merely to gain thirty years. 'If you have any of the 1672s or earlier come in, let me know. I'd be interested.'

'Yes, yes. I will.' Vrellait smiled as he led the way to the back office. He raised an eyebrow as they sat down. 'But hopefully I might have something of far more interest for you.'

Vrellait didn't need to build up the significance for him. He'd thought of little else since Vrellait's call of the day before. He hadn't slept well with it on his mind, had woken up early and hit the coffee pot and downed probably seven cups by the time he left for Montpellier. As he noticed his hand trembling on the steering wheel, he wasn't sure if it was the caffeine overload or the anticipation of what might be in his grasp within the hour.

Cutting across the Camargue was one of his favourite drives: fields of lavender and vines one side, wild tundra and – if you were lucky enough to catch sight of them – equally wild groups of horses, the other. Jean-Pierre had tried to let the passing scenery soothe him.

He made sure now to keep that tremble out of his hand and his enthusiasm in check as he reached across and took the envelope from Vrellait.

'All eleven pages are there. All we have.' Vrellait smiled apologetically. 'And, as I say, only copies. The original right now is in Paris.'

'I understand.' Jean-Pierre didn't ask with whom. Vrellait had laid down the ground rules at the outset: one expert to examine the original papers for date and vellum authentication; two independent handwriting experts; two, including himself, to authenticate 'form, style and substance' of content. None of them were to be revealed to each other to 'avoid collusion or one party unduly swaying others'.

'What's the timescale?' Jean-Pierre asked.

'Two months. All the findings will then be collated, and an announcement made one way or the other. They're either real – part of Michel de Nostredame's long-lost code-guide – or they're forgeries.'

Jean-Pierre turned through the pages, and by the fourth the tremble was back in his hand. It would have been so much easier just to dismiss it as a forgery on first sight, not have to embark on this carousel of see-saw emotions and ambitions: his career boosted to new levels if it was proven real, abject disappointment if it wasn't; plus an equal slip from grace if he voiced his opinion the wrong way.

Yes, at first sight it looked real: that handwriting he now knew so well, almost as well as his own; turns of phrases and the rhythm and cadence of sentences too that struck an instant chord. He felt a tightening in his chest and tingling through his veins that said, '*Oh, God, yes, this is it!*'

Vrellait gestured towards the pages. 'The age of the *cassone* in which they were found points to César Nostredame rather than Michel himself. It was early baroque, end of sixteenth Century rather than mid.' Vrellait shrugged. 'And the other two false panels at the back of the chest were empty, I'm afraid. So we are simply left to wonder whether those originally held the remaining pages and they've since been removed and lost.'

'And discovered near Florence, you say?' Jean-Pierre confirmed.

'Yes, Empoli; about fifty kilometres west. But the provenance of the *cassone* traces back directly to Florence itself.'

Jean-Pierre nodded and returned to studying the pages. One of Michel de Nostredame's sons, César, had become an artist of repute and lived in Florence for several years. That part certainly fitted; something of this import Michel would have entrusted only to a close friend or family member. As Jean-Pierre got to the last pages, he saw the fresh quatrains Vrellait had mentioned.

'*If* it proves to be real, do you have any idea,' Vrellait asked, 'just how much of Nostradamus's code-book we might have here?'

Jean-Pierre pursed his lips. 'Most experts have always considered such a guide to be anything from fifteen to twenty-odd pages.' He leafed back through for a second. 'Seven pages of guide – so perhaps a third to a half.'

If it was real it would be the Nostradamus find of the century; five hundred years of wondering – with the two camps divided as to whether he'd written a code-guide or not – finally answered. Then the countless reassessments and reinterpretations that would no doubt follow.

But Vrellait was right to set the two-month time frame for cautious and thorough evaluation. In the past there'd been a number of hoaxes and misinterpretations; one of those, Jean-Pierre reminded himself, in fact involving some illustrations attributed to César Nostredame.

Jean-Pierre asked a few questions to fill in background, then finally nodded his approval. 'Yes, I would be more than pleased to take part in their evaluation.'

'And you would be most welcome to the team, my friend.' Vrellait sifted through some papers to one side. He finally dug out what he was looking for and passed it across. 'As I mentioned, this is just a small formality before I can let you leave with them. I'm sure you understand.'

Jean-Pierre perused the document: a standard non-disclosure agreement whereby he agreed not to share the papers with other parties; nor copy, disseminate or publicise them in any fashion. He read it swiftly, and signed with equal rapidity.

Like a long-sought-after lover, suddenly he couldn't wait to be alone with the papers; back to his study where, long into the night, he could immerse himself in them, caress and feast his eyes over every magical line and detail until he was satiated.

Blondie refused to talk for the first hour, so all they had was his name from a couple of credit cards he had on him: Benjamin G Corliss.

Adel decided to take a break and let Corliss stew while they ran his name through the system; perhaps he'd be more cooperative after cooling his heels for a while. And in that break, straight after his call home to tell Tahiya he'd be even later than he first thought, he received the call from Tariq about the third mosque bombing in Islamabad.

Adel sucked in his breath as he heard how close the Islamabad police had come to catching them. 'Well, one consolation, at least. They got *one* of them.'

'Not that much of a consolation either, I'm afraid.'

'Why's that?' Adel felt his blood run cold as Tariq

related what had happened. But, perversely, part of that gave him ammunition for the second part of his interview with Corliss.

'Looks like you were right,' he announced as he walked back in. 'Your friends executed the bombing exactly where you said they would – Kalatahn Mosque, Islamabad.'

'They're not my friends.' His first words.

'Oh, really? Doesn't look like that from where I am. In fact, seems to me that's the only way you'd know their plans.' Adel leant forward menacingly. 'If you were in on it with them.'

Back to silence.

'And did you know that your "friends" happened to take out one of their own during the bombing?'

'Like I said. *Not* my friends.'

'Used soft-nosed or oversized calibre, apparently. Nothing left of his face or head – so no chance of facial reconstruction to match against.' Adel smiled thinly. 'Probably got something similar planned for you down the line.'

Corliss clutched at his hair. 'How many times do I have to tell you?'

But for the first time Corliss looked rattled. Adel knew then that it was just a matter of time.

The first breakthrough came after fifteen minutes.

Adel said that if he walked out now, he'd

recommend Corliss be held for twenty-eight days under the Anti-Terrorism Act – possibly the Americans too would show an interest in him. Adel shrugged and smiled. 'Strange how such things have a way of happening between intelligence services. Then once you've been shipped to Guantanamo Bay, you're looking at a three-year fight with lawyers and appeals just to—'

Corliss sighed heavily, interjecting: 'I was only doing it for a friend. I have nothing to do with the bombers themselves.'

Adel held out a hand. 'That word again – *friend*. I say your friends are the bombers in Islamabad. You claim it's someone else. So if you insist on clinging to that story, then just who is this mystery friend?' Adel tapped his pen on a pad, impatient to write down the name. '*Who?*'

Silence again.

Adel went out and spoke with an SO15 officer. Then returned to Corliss and the questioning. Six minutes later, as arranged, the officer interrupted them.

'Just heard from Islamabad. One of the bombers they're holding has confirmed there was a London arm to their operation.'

'Thank you.' Adel looked back at Corliss. 'Full circle, it appears. And while you might wish to deny the Islamabad bombers as your "friends" – it seems they're awfully keen to include you.'

Corliss shook his head. 'I told you before – it's not them.'

'And I told *you*: if you wish to continue clinging to that account, then I need to know who. *Who?*'

Corliss's eyes shifted uncomfortably. 'Just an old friend who used to live in London.' He shook his head again. 'And I'm sure he had nothing to do with the bombings either.'

'Who?'

'I...I promised not to say anything – but that's not the only reason I've held back.' He looked at Adel with a plea in his eyes. 'He said he might be at risk if he passed on the information himself.'

'So meanwhile he puts *you* in the frame and at risk.' Adel narrowed his eyes. '*Who?*'

'I wasn't meant to get caught, you see,' he offered hesitantly.

Adel didn't respond, just kept his eyes steadily on Corliss as he watched the last of his resolve slide away. And as Corliss finally uttered a name, Adel sat back sharply. It was the second time in two days it had come up.

Adel called in an SO15 officer and went outside to make the call; there was no answer. He didn't leave a message, but kept trying again at ten-minute intervals. And on the third try, by which time he was in a cab heading to Victoria Station, Sam Tynnan answered.

After telling Tynnan that he'd just finished questioning his friend, Ben Corliss – 'who, I must say, remarkably, still spoke very well of you, despite being held for two hours in police custody' – Adel said simply, 'We need to talk.'

Sam sighed. 'Yes, I believe we do.'

CHAPTER TWENTY-ONE

SPRINGFIELD, MASSACHUSETTS.

Sam and Mike were quiet for most of the journey to Springfield, as if they were going to a wake. Mike drove.

Two hours after Ben Corliss had been released, Sam had managed to speak to him to get his take on what had gone wrong and what had been said in the interview. Mike came over to the cabin soon after.

'"We're a couple of the best plotmeisters in the business. If anyone can outwit half the Secret Service, we can." And first shot out the bag, we get caught.'

'Yeah, well, your "actorrr friend" was far from the

sharpest tool in the box – making the call from one of London's main streets wearing a distinctive jacket and scarf. I did say "discreetly"…'

Sam explained that he wasn't exactly spoilt for friends he could ask to do this sort of thing. 'It might have escaped your attention, but my address book is a bit light on spooks.'

They were frustrated although partly amused by the circus of it all. It was either laugh or cry. And after a couple of stiff Scotches they were calmer, and started to turn their thoughts to how best to handle the situation they now faced.

To protect identities, everyone in Adel's department was 'Emile' to outsiders. No surname, just a three-digit number following which most people calling assumed was their phone extension. To Sam, Adel had been simply 'Emile 238'.

Sam had called Emile back within the hour, 11.30 p.m., London time, with a 'neutral ground' meeting place. Mike had suggested Springfield, a fair-sized town just over the Massachusetts state line, which would then also make it easier for Vince to get a team there for back-up.

Emile in turn informed him that he'd have to be accompanied by one agent from their New York office: 'Regulations for all stateside visits, I'm afraid. But your name or any other details won't be shared with them.

As far as they're concerned, I'm simply meeting a Mr X in Springfield for something to do with a London operation.'

'OK.' Sam felt satisfied that enough precautions had been put in place; as many as he was going to get, at least. 'But he's obviously not to sit in on our conversation.'

'Obviously.' Emile asked if he'd also be there with a 'colleague', and they made the final arrangements: Glenwood Café, Springfield, 3.00 p.m. They'd sit in one booth and talk privately and their respective 'colleagues' in another, 'within eyesight but out of earshot.'

'Game on,' Mike said as the Glenwood Café came into view eighty yards away.

He drifted slowly, and thirty yards short of the café passed Barry Chilton and his sidekick, Phil Doughan, in a dark grey Buick Lucerne.

Chilton was slumped down in his seat so that his six-foot-seven-inch frame wasn't too apparent, and Mike made sure not to give them even a blink of acknowledgment which could link them for an onlooker. Instead, he glanced at Sam with a grim smile.

'Like I said before, if he *is* for real, maybe this was meant to happen.' Mike swung in and parked. 'The main positive force in your book – you were *meant* to help him. Sort of ordained, *karma* if you will.'

But Sam knew Mike was only saying it to make him feel better. Yes, that was one silver-lining way of looking at it. But it also struck Sam that it meant there was another option gone, one less choice he could make. More and more he was becoming simply a passenger aboard his own script rather than having any control over events.

In their phone call Ben had mentioned Emile's threat of being shipped off to Guantanamo Bay. Sam couldn't help but worry that, despite all their planning and safeguards, they were walking into a trap.

Mike scanned the café front and along the road for a moment, then glanced at his watch. 'OK, let's go.'

The first thing Adel found himself struggling to get to grips with was the extreme, fantastic nature of Tynnan's account; as he'd prefaced, fiction rather than fact. Tynnan's recounting was often slow, staccato, perhaps to ensure he got the facts across clearly and sequentially.

But at one point, like a broken-down car being pushed uphill and finally reaching the brow, Tynnan hit his stride and started rolling faster down the other side. Adel found himself hanging on to every word – *Washington, mosque bombings, girlfriend, Nostradamus, Mabus, Bahsem-Yahl—*

Adel stopped Sam at that point. 'And, in your book, Bahsem-Yahl becomes your "Mabus"?'

'Yes.'

'And how did he come into the picture, if I may ask? Why him in particular?'

'One of my Nostradamus contacts, Jean-Pierre Bourdin, proposed him as the most likely fit for Mabus. Though I'd already narrowed the choice down to five possible suspects.' Adel nodded acceptance but Sam had noticed a shadow cross his eyes at the mention of Bahsem-Yahl. 'Why? Is there something going on in the background with Bahsem-Yahl that I don't know about?'

'No, no. Nothing like that.' Adel shook his head hastily; possibly *too* hastily. He recalled one of his first concerns with the mosque bombings about pan-Arab claims of links to the West. So far, thankfully, no strong voices had been put to that. But Bahsem-Yahl was a strong voice that *would* rally wide support. If he proposed that the bombings were masterminded by the West, then that could dramatically tip the scales. 'But it's certainly one thing – *if* these people are using your manuscript to steer real events – that they have no control over. They can't exactly whisper in Bahsem-Yahl's ear that he should follow their lead.'

Sam nodded. *One thing at least left to fate.* Looking past Emile's shoulder, Sam tensed as he saw Mike – five seat booths down – on his cellphone. The arrangement was that if Barry or Phil saw anything untoward outside, they'd phone Mike. But Mike didn't look Sam's way. It was obviously just an unconnected, private call. Mike wound it up quickly to keep the line free.

Sam had been nervous at first. Each sideways glance from Emile, each beat of doubt he'd seen cross his face, made him worry that the agent was simply humouring him – biding his time and tapping his fingers until the prearranged vanload of armed SWATs arrived to take Sam away.

But as he got deeper into his account and Emile showed more interest, Sam started to feel more at ease. Emile was very different to the character in his book: quieter, less expressive, kept his own counsel more. Though something about that calm, reserved demeanour, Sam found himself warming to, liking – made him feel he could trust the man. As if he had any choice.

Then he reminded himself about Lorrena: liking and trust were not synonymous.

Emile made brief notes in Arabic as they went – six separate lines with only two or three words on each – and now Sam watched as for the first time he filled a line. Emile looked up.

'Now let us get to the next mosque bombings in your manuscript. The most vital things for us to get right are locations *and* sequence.'

Sam told him and Emile added five more lines with only a few words on each.

'So the first account you gave me with mosque locations was completely false?'

'Yes. Sorry about that.' Sam smiled edgily. 'But what with everything with Washington, then my girlfriend – I just didn't know who to trust any more. When you phoned, I feared you might be part of all that.'

'I understand.' Even without the nightmare tale, Adel would have understood: Tynnan's red-rimmed eyes, darting and shifting to shake away the ghosts as he talked, shoulders slumped with the weight of it all, spoke volumes. He *looked* like a man who'd been through hell, even if he hadn't told you how or why.

Sam glanced to one side as an elderly couple shifted into a booth on the next aisle. He leant forward, lowering his voice. 'But still I wanted to make sure you knew the right locations, to do the right thing – yet without any link to me. That's why I asked a favour of Ben.'

Emile nodded as if he understood that too, but said nothing.

Sam took a sip of his coffee; then, 'And did passing on the information help?'

'Yes, it did. Though not as much as we'd have liked, what with it coming in late. But at least the bombers were disturbed this time, even if we didn't manage to apprehend any of them alive.' Adel stopped himself short, a clear indication that was all the detail he'd share. 'And, tell me, in your manuscript, how did the final war-stage scenario play out?'

'Thankfully, events didn't get that far.' Sam shrugged, as if to emphasise: *no such guarantee in real life*. 'With Bahsem-Yahl's involvement, the most obvious scenario was from Iran. Though with the key question of whether they had fissionable material just for a suitcase or static nuclear bomb, or whether they'd reached the stage of developing missile warheads.' Sam looked at Emile for a second, as if he might embellish or offer an opinion on that. He didn't; he simply nodded with a slow blink.

'Another scenario,' Sam said, 'was with Pakistan: the electoral process collapses through civil unrest and radical Wahhabis within the military rise up and take over.' Sam held out a palm. 'From there, the options are open: suitcase nuclear "dirt bomb" attacks on major US and European cities or missile attacks on Israel. Or both.'

Adel became aware of the waitress looking at him; then realised it was because he'd been staring blankly in her direction. He looked away. They spent so much time worrying about already-radical nations going nuclear that often the option of an already-nuclear nation becoming worryingly radical was overlooked. But either way, the doomsday scenario of a largely Islamic alliance against the West was the same.

Sam took a fresh breath, breaking the uneasy

silence that had fallen. 'Strangely enough, there was a character in my book in an Arabic-language tracking unit. Not unlike yourself.'

'I see.' Adel wasn't sure why Tynnan was telling him this, except perhaps to try and forge some common ground. 'Yet another case of life imitating art,' he replied.

'Except he worked out of Fairfax, Virginia.'

'And where was he from originally?'

'Jordan.'

'Ah, and I'm from Egypt.' He smiled. 'So, you see – completely different.'

'Yes.' Mike had suggested that this be the only link mentioned. Revealing to Emile that his main character so closely resembled him might seem odd, and – given that his role now might mirror that character's – put too much pressure on him. 'What will you do? Will you be able to act on what I've given you?'

'I'll need a couple of days to consider it. But meanwhile I'll alert the authorities in Oman about the next bombing on the list, just in case.' Adel shrugged. 'And while I may well be able to do something about the planned mosque bombings, Washington looks a different matter. Particularly with you being concerned about stateside contact.' That wasn't Adel's only reason: the whole thing sounded like a heavily buried black-op which he'd have little chance of tracing in any case; and if he started digging, Washington would see his head above the parapet a country mile before Adel saw his.

Sam nodded. 'I understand.'

Adel's thoughts were divided. It would either end up a fantasy-driven wild goose chase or the most incredible high-stakes operation he'd ever encountered: *trying to second-guess an intricate chess game between the mosque bombers and Abu Khalish, using a fictional manuscript as guide.* And thinking about where that might lead – the doomsday portent of Bahsem-Yahl entering the fray – he prayed that it *wasn't* true.

And if Khalish now went ahead with the planned London bombing, despite the mosque bombers' warning, how would that play out? Adel desperately needed to keep his main focus on that these next few days.

He'd called Karam as soon as he'd landed in the US: still no activity spike. Then again just before walking in the café: still nothing.

He glanced at his watch. He spent seven or eight minutes clarifying some final details, then wound everything up.

As they stood and shook hands, Sam said, 'And, *please*, as I said – don't share this with anyone.'

'No, no. I won't. Rest assured.' Before, he hadn't fully appreciated Sam Tynnan's paranoia. Now he did.

'Where I have no choice but to share this information with the mosque cities concerned, the source shall remain anonymous.'

As Tynnan and his friend pulled away in their car, Adel called London again: still no spike.

Then again while he was waiting to board at JFK.

'Only three per cent rise,' Karam said.

Negligible. But with the echo of the loudspeaker announcements and bustle of people, he suddenly had a picture of London stations the following night, and people boarding trains already doomed because he'd done nothing. And by the time he landed, it might be too late.

Adel sighed heavily. 'For once I think we'll have to be guided by the information in hand rather than just spikes. Go straight to code red, critical, for all transport networks for London.'

Sam was anxious as they left the café.

As their meeting had ended, Emile was once more distracted, glancing at his watch. And then he'd been on the phone just as they drove away. What had that been about?

Just in case they were being tailed or there was a surprise waiting for them down the road, Barry and Phil followed from five cars back, watching for any cars in between that stayed with them for any length of time.

Forty miles out of Springfield, Barry called Mike's cellphone to tell him that everything was clear. 'Even if they changed cars three or four times, there's nobody still with you.'

'Thanks.' Mike watched in his mirror as Barry flashed twice and took the next turn-off back to Boston. Then to Sam: 'We're home clear.'

CHAPTER TWENTY-TWO

Akram favoured the Westbourne Grove Mosque for his regular prayers.

If the weather was fine, he'd often walk the mile from Lancaster Gate, otherwise he'd catch the tube. He'd been to other London mosques on occasion, but usually only when they had a particular imam whose sermons he liked.

Of late, though, Westbourne Grove had one imam, Ra'if Muhyi, whose sermons Akram had found increasingly inspiring. His words were fiery, touching on issues which the others stoically avoided: *Palestine, Iraq*. Westbourne Grove didn't have the same hard-line reputation as Finsbury Park Mosque, and Muhyi avoided the overt fire-and-brimstone rhetoric of archly radical imams. He was far more subtle: '*If you are invited into your brother's home, then you know you are welcome. But if you are not, you have to search in your soul and ask yourself some hard questions...*'

But it was enough – unbeknown to Akram – for MI5 and SO15 to keep a watchful eye on Ra'if Muhyi, taking photos as the mosque emptied to see who he might spend a moment talking to.

Allahu akbar...Allahu akbar...All praise and thanks are Allah's, the Lord of mankind, jinn and all that exists...the Most Gracious, the Most Merciful...

As always, Akram already felt soporific, his senses swimming, by the end of the chants and prayers; then the sermon, if strong, as it was today, would build on that layer by layer – each word and lilting phrase like a caress – making his heart soar. Akram was in his element. But then he noticed Wajd Masahran towards the back of the prayer hall, and his spirits sank back again.

When Masahran had first told him, he'd been incredulous: 'No, he couldn't possibly be involved in that. Omari and I go back half a century: we're not just master and servant, we're close friends. And, as you well know, he gives regularly to Palestinian charities. He would *never* sell his soul in this manner.'

Masahran had nodded solemnly. 'I can appreciate

you're upset at having to hear this. And, for now, it is *only* a suspicion. But soon we shall know for sure.' Masahran reached out and clasped one of Akram's hands at that stage. 'All I need to know, my brother, is if you are with us rather than against us in what we might have to do.'

Akram looked at his hand clasped in Masahran's, and he wasn't sure if he had any choice; that, if he said no, he would then also be labelled a traitor.

Akram had on occasion bowed and offered thanks to Imam Muhyi for his 'exalted' sermons as they exited; but today he spent a moment more in praise. Possibly because Muhyi's sermon that day had been particularly vibrant and heartfelt; though deep down Akram knew the truth: he was merely delaying the inevitable. Delaying what Masahran – whose eyes he could feel on him from five paces away, waiting for the moment to talk to him privately – had to tell him.

Home clear. Soon after Barry 'Chiller' Chilton flashed his car lights and turned off, he came into Sam and Mike's conversation.

'Chiller?' It was the first time Mike had used the nickname, but after 'Corky' Sam knew better than to ask whether it derived from his name.

'Yeah. Came from a stunt he pulled in a meat locker.' Mike explained that originally there were three crime families running Boston: Giuseppe Mazzone,

Neapolitan; Frank Doherty, Irish; and Vince Corcoran – half-Sicilian, half-Irish. The worst blood feuds and turf wars were always between the Mazzones and Dohertys, with Corcoran in the middle – perhaps because he had a bloodline in each camp – trying to calm the waters. 'That's why originally Vince's other nickname was "the peacemaker". But from each turf war between the two, Vince always benefited, and Giuseppe Mazzone got it into his head that Vince was purposely playing them against each other. Mazzone decided to play him at his own game. He took out one of Vince's capos and tried to pin it on Doherty. Except Vince worked out that it *wasn't* Doherty.'

'Chiller' was sent after the two Mazzone capos responsible. One he took straight out with a bullet to the head, the other he wanted information from – so he takes him to a local meat-packing station. 'The guy refuses to talk, so Chiller puts his hand on a block and chops off a finger with a meat cleaver. He then carefully takes the finger and puts it in the freezer. He comes back with a bowl of ice and shoves the guy's mangled hand in it, telling him that if both are kept cool, they'll still be able to sew the finger back on at the hospital. Chiller pumps him again for information.'

Two more fingers and he's got all the information he *wants*. 'Chiller kills the guy in the end in any case, because if he admitted to Mazzone he'd talked, their ace cards are gone. They used the information to pull Mazzone's organisation apart. Two more capos were taken out, but most of it was more subtle than that: police raids of his clubs, IRS and FINRA pulling apart one of Mazzone's money-laundering operations. Because, of course, Vince knows exactly where to point them. Within four years, Mazzone's operation is half what it used to be, and he sells out what's left to Vince. Heads down to Florida with his family.' Mike glanced at Sam. 'So if you're ever tempted to ask – no, I *don't* hold any illusions about either Vince or Barry. But they're certainly good guys to have on your side.'

Sam nodded numbly. The reverse side of that, not so good *against*, was crystal clear. But he reckoned he'd never have got through this without their help; rather the devil you know.

Mike picked up some groceries and brought them to the cabin. Robby Maschek had come over and put a scrambler link on both his cellphone and the cabin landline – so that neither could be traced or listened in to.

It was almost eleven by the time they got to the cabin. Mike had grabbed a takeaway pizza and some beers and stayed with him for almost an hour while they ate.

Mike nodded towards the corner. 'Feel free to use my computer whenever you want. Just make sure not to use your old email address, and be careful who you send to and what you say.' Mike waved his beer. 'Outside of that, like I say, feel free.'

Sam glanced at the computer warily for most of the next morning. He'd slept well that night – the first good night for a week. And, combined with the fact that he had nothing to do while he waited to hear from Emile, he finally decided to switch it on and continue with his Toby Wesley book. The words came slowly at first, but after a while the rhythm picked up.

As if by telepathy, mid-afternoon Elli phoned.

'How're you doing?'

'OK. Just starting to get into it more now.' The truth for once.

'I didn't mean the writing, Sam. I'm happy to get it *when you're ready*. Something like this takes time to get over. I asked how *you* are doing, Sam.' He'd called Elli and told him about Lorrena the day after her death. But, of course, he'd omitted all the background details. And, uncharitably, it had struck him that the tragedy with Lorrena gave him the excuse with Elli for all the writing that wasn't getting done because of everything else going on.

'Sorry. Well as can be expected, I suppose. Maybe why I've dived so quickly into the writing again – to try and push it all away. Forget.' Back to lying again. Safer ground.

271

'I know. I know.' Elli sighed. 'Like I said, Sam – when you're ready. You need some time to yourself after this.' Another sigh. 'And let me know when the funeral service is, Sam. Miriam and I would like to come and pay our respects.'

Sam felt a rock in his chest. He swallowed uncomfortably. 'Yes, I will. I will.' He hadn't thought about that. Perhaps he could cover by saying her father in Taranto was having the service there. He would cross that bridge later.

The writing flow slowed down after Elli's call – he felt guilty lying to Elli, but now he'd started he couldn't see an easy way of backtracking and explaining. By nightfall the inspiration had dried up completely, so he called it a day.

He watched TV for a couple of hours, then went to the fridge to peruse the wonderful array of microwaveable meals Mike had picked up at the mini-mart. *Sad-lonely-bastard-chicken-risotto-for-one* seemed to hit the mark.

Sam wasn't sure how much time had passed when he heard the sounds outside. Two hours, three? He wasn't even sure at first he *had* heard something. He turned down the TV.

Now it was clearer: the steady tread of boots on the ground, an occasional twig snapping. One advantage of the cabin was that it was so desolate and deathly silent outside that the faintest sound carried.

Sam held his breath. Through the front window he saw flickering torchlight on one side of the veranda and the trees in front, spilling onto the lake beyond.

Jesus. He shrank back towards the kitchen door, starting to check out escape routes.

Home clear. They'd been kidding themselves all along. Chopped fingers and checking for car tails. Government spooks were a different league. It would have taken two seconds for a casual passer-by to slip a device under Mike's car.

They'd then tracked it back here and simply waited for the best time to move in; last night Mike had been with him, tonight he was alone. Or maybe, on the one occasion Mike had gone to his house to pick up a few things he'd forgotten, Washington had him tailed back here.

The torchlight, one of those heavy-duty halogen lamps, swung across the front of the cabin, its beam moving in an arc across the lounge. Before it reached him, Sam slipped through to the kitchen and darted to the back door.

CHAPTER TWENTY-THREE

It was early evening when the call came through to Khalish in Costa Rica. As before, the conversation was conducted entirely in Spanish.

'Everything is in place with those London stock options. *Todo*.'

There was a moment's pause of deliberation. '*Bueno*. Go ahead. But ensure the purchase goes smoothly and cleanly. No stock options left loose and floating, as happened last time.'

'I understand. I shall supervise the matter personally.' The message was clear: no repetitions of Milan. A heavy pause. The other issue at hand, the mosque bombers and their demands, was more delicate. 'And what about that other party making noises regarding a takeover bid?'

'Other factors may well arise which will change the direction of that. So my inclination for now is simply to bide my time and see.' Another long pause at the other end, as if he was waiting for Khalish to elaborate what those 'other factors' might be. Khalish didn't elaborate. 'Let me know how those stock purchases go,' he said, and hung up.

LONDON.

Half the day gone and *still* no significant activity spike.

The pressure rose steadily hour by hour in the operations room. It rose when there were small increases – the peak so far had been six per cent – it rose when there weren't. And Adel's pacing up and down and every twenty minutes barking for an update from each sector didn't help.

By mid-afternoon, the operations room was a powder keg.

London activity had crept up another three per cent by then. Nine per cent overall.

Adel regularly sifted through photos of 'possible suspects and associates' taken at local mosques, madrassas and Muslim community and student gatherings. But today he found it hard to focus on them.

One face for a moment struck a chord, but he couldn't recall where from. He referenced quickly against the fifty or so prime targets imprinted indelibly on his brain. No match. Not relevant. He pushed the photos aside.

Only one thing was on his mind right now.

By the end of the afternoon, activity had edged up another two per cent. Eleven per cent. Not the sort of spike they'd associate with a major operation – that would normally be in the thirty to sixty per cent range. But something.

And Adel could still feel all that bubbling energy and tension from the operations room coursing through him when at 6.38 p.m. he walked through Victoria Station to catch his train home.

If he hadn't known from his day at work that something was happening, he'd have known it now as he crossed the station concourse. There was four times the normal armed police presence, earpieces networked, MP5 sub-machine guns quarter raised. The mantle passed on: *We've done all we can our end – now try and find them. Stop them!*

Seven minutes till his train left, it steadily filled after he got on. He'd taken the window seat of a group of three: at the aisle end was a middle-aged woman talking to a teenage girl directly opposite – Adel presumed her daughter – the only nearby seats occupied as he got on. Within two minutes of the train leaving, every seat was filled. By the time the departure whistle went, there were a dozen people standing in the aisle as well.

Adel didn't pay much notice to the man in the middle seat opposite until a minute before the train left. He was in his early thirties, Arabic or southern Mediterranean, heavily receding black hair, light-grey suit; just one of countless thousands similar working in the City. That on its own wouldn't have been cause to draw Adel's attention.

It was the way his eyes started darting anxiously to those around him: to Adel, to the women at his side; then to the people shuffling close to them in the aisle as the train filled. He seemed to be concerned, *overly concerned*, by who might be near him.

And the tan attaché case in his lap wasn't held loosely, normally: it was held in a death-grip, as if it contained gold bars or his very life depended on it. *Or the lives of those around him.*

A bead of sweat wormed its way down the man's brow. He caught Adel's eye. Adel looked away. The train started moving. *Too late.*

Adel closed his eyes, told himself it was nothing. The man was probably just an accountant wound up from the pressure of the day, with the heat and crowd of the train making it worse.

Adel recalled that not long after 7/7, he'd seen a couple of Arab-looking teenagers with backpacks get on his train home. He'd let the train go and caught the next one. And he was sure that countless Londoners had done similar over that period.

A week ago, prior to Milan, if an anxious-looking boy with a backpack had sat near him, he'd have felt as jumpy as now.

But then they'd seen those CCTV images from Milan of young men in smart cream and beige suits with attaché cases and Gucci loafers. And suddenly the message was: '*It could be that man in a suit who looks like an accountant or City broker sat right opposite you. It could be* anyone!' Obviously what Khalish had intended.

Adel opened his eyes again as he heard a baby crying. A tired-looking young woman, babe in arms, was standing in the aisle four yards away. Adel was about to get up and offer his seat, but then thought: if it *was* a bomb, the baby would be first to catch the blast. No chance of survival. Stark images from Milan assaulted his brain – *crumpled, mangled bodies, a woman clutching desperately to her child, already dead*. And as he paused – caught between those ghost images and rationality – a young man closer to her gave up his seat.

The man opposite's eyes settled on him again for

a second before continuing to dart anxiously to other passengers, another bead of sweat now trickling down his forehead. Adel turned and gazed absently through the train window as it hurtled along, telling himself it was nothing. Just his own demons. *It was nothing...*

But as he caught his haunted reflection in the glass, he realised he'd become a pathetic confirmation of Abu Khalish's success. For it wasn't the thirty or forty killed that counted to Khalish; it was the millions more he gripped in terror.

CHAPTER TWENTY-FOUR

'Just Jem, Sam. Nothing to worry about,' Mike reassured over his cellphone.

'Yeah, well, "just Jem" scared the shit out of me.'

'Sorry about that. I should have told you about him. Or, more to the point, Jem about you. He's the only one who stays in his cabin all year so he's become like an unofficial warden. I asked Jem to keep half an eye on my place. He sees a light on, but my car's not there...' Mike sighed. 'Sorry. Should have told him.'

Sam looked back at Jem, standing patiently outside. He was in his late fifties, with weathered features and some Red Indian blood; though you had to look close. And what little hair he had left was grade-one bristle.

A few minutes ago, Sam had tentatively opened the back door to see a 1950s Chevy open pickup truck parked ten yards away. Not the usual transport for a SWAT team – and it was empty. There were no other torchlights or signs of anyone else. Then Sam heard the man out front talking on the phone to whom he could only assume was Mike. '*Yeah, yeah. Tried to get you earlier, but you weren't answering – so I thought I'd better come over and check. A friend...OK. Yeah. Yeah. Will do.*'

Sam had made his way to the front door by then. The man smiled in acknowledgment as he opened it. 'He's here now, in fact...yeah. OK.' Then to Sam as he held out his cellphone: 'Mike wants a word.'

Sam took a few steps away as he talked to Mike.

'Certainly would have helped,' Sam now said.

'Again, sorry.' Mike risked a tentative chuckle. 'Just look at it as a good trial run for the real thing.'

'Oh, fuck off.'

Sam turned back and passed Jem his phone.

'Just let me know if you need anything,' Jem offered, and then he and his stadium lighting equipment left.

Mike filled in some background on Jem when he came over with the groceries the next day. 'He used to work for Vince Corcoran. Still does now and then, in between tooling around with custom cars and fishing

– as long as it's clean, "non-criminal".'

Claiming lineage all the way back to Mohawk chief John Deseronto, Jem used to live on the Akwesasne reservation on the New York/Ontario state border. 'And back then all his work with Corcoran *was* criminal, running contraband drink and tobacco – no drugs – across the Canadian border. The police raided the reservation four times, and finally got one of the charges to stick. The Akwesasne elders claimed that he'd "brought shame on their community" and while Jem was inside – he got three years – they barred him from the reservation and he lost his home there.

'A big blow personally to Jem for someone linked back to Deseronto. Corcoran felt responsible, so bought him the cabin here. I'd bought my place just the year before.' Mike shrugged. 'Probably good that you met up. He can keep half an eye on you at the same time. Jem's a pretty mean shot with a rifle.'

Crack SWAT team versus one old Indian with a pickup truck and a rifle. Yep, Sam felt *really* safe now. But he knew that Mike meant well.

After Mike left, Sam was reminded that there were a few people he'd yet to tell about Lorrena: Kate, Ashley, and his father, Ross. Widowed now for eight years, Ross Tynnan still lived in the Eastbourne bungalow on England's south coast that he'd shared with Sam's mum. Sam spoke to him at least once a month, and Ross particularly liked hearing from him when he'd seen Ashley. *How tall is he now? How's he doing at school?*

It was strange. When he thought about Lorrena – his girlfriend, *his love*, one of the warmest, gentlest people he'd ever known, now dead in a tragic accident – he'd feel as if his heart was breaking. But then when he thought of all the clandestine baggage and what she'd been a part of, his chest would freeze and he'd hear the change in his voice. It would suddenly be cool, distant, as if he was a detached newsreader relating what had happened. And so he had to keep fixed in his mind the *right* Lorrena when he made these calls.

He took a deep breath and picked up the phone.

The silence from our beloved friend, Abu Khalish, speaks volumes. We proclaimed at the outset that he had little care for Islam, but we were not to know then how strongly that would hold true from the passage of events.

Three of Islam's holy monuments desecrated, yet Abu Khalish – the great defender of Islam – sits by and does nothing. He considers himself to be of more worth. The ultimate insult, the ultimate arrogance. He puts himself above that of Allah's exalted places of worship. We see now with our own eyes what is most important to this man: himself and his misguided battle with the West. Islam, despite what he has asserted over the years, plays a poor third.

But Allah is nothing if not merciful. And so we hereby grant Abu Khalish a further forty-eight hours in which to redeem himself, his honour, and the continuing sanctity of Islam.

As with everyone in the operations room, Adel fell silent for a moment after the broadcast. Then the buzz slowly returned.

He'd tried to shut out the mosque bombers for two days to keep his focus on London activity, but they wouldn't let him. The video tape had been received by Al Jazeera TV in Qatar in the early hours, and from its time counter had been made four hours before that. So, thirty-eight hours left of the deadline.

Perhaps the bombers' intention, as with Milan, was to steal Khalish's thunder. If they were in any way plugged into intelligence networks – which Tynnan's account, if it held water, certainly suggested – then they'd know that Khalish had a London operation planned. In fact, they'd have known that simply from watching the news. It had been on the TV from early last night: '*Critical security alert on all transport networks around London.*' There'd even been brief shots of armed police at Heathrow Airport and King's Cross Station.

Adel had felt all that fresh anxiety amongst his fellow commuters on his way in that morning. He wasn't the only one checking out other passengers.

London activity hit a peak of thirteen per cent late morning. But then it started sliding back. By mid-afternoon, it was ten per cent. By 5 p.m., as commuters started to pack on trains to head home, only eight per cent. Adel was perplexed, much of his day so far had been spent double-checking and cross-referencing stats. Perhaps they'd finally found a way of bypassing *Echelon* and every other checking system. *Unlikely*.

And despite what the stats said now, Adel was sure the panic levels were still high. He'd noticed some commuters that morning staring daggers at a couple of middle-aged Arab men in thobes crossing Victoria Station. As if for a minute bombers would choose traditional—

Adel froze. *Thobes! Groups of worshippers in thobes exiting the Westbourne Grove Mosque.* Adel suddenly recalled where he'd seen that face in yesterday's photos.

He went over to the filing cabinet and dug them out. It wasn't someone on his normal security radar; probably why it hadn't registered the other day. But as he studied the photo now, there was little doubt: *Akram, Omari's servant*. They'd never met, but he'd seen enough photos from MI5's file on Omari with the comings and goings from his Lancaster Gate home to be able to put a face to the name.

And there was something else he noticed this time as he looked closer through the sequence: while someone else in the forefront met with Imam Muhyi, Akram was in the background talking with Wajd Masahran, one of Omari's main radical contacts.

Adel's chest tightened as it all suddenly gelled: *London. The lack of activity spikes. Omari the information source.* He only prayed he wasn't too late.

Akram stayed away from the house for much of the day.

He wanted to avoid Omari looking him in the eye, fearing what he might see there.

Fifty years their association, and for it to end like this! He thought about many of those days, especially when they were both younger, and felt slow tears run down his face as he sat on a bench in Hyde Park, staring blankly ahead. Passers-by criss-crossed his vision, but he saw none of them.

He shook the thoughts brusquely away. *No.* Omari is the one who has betrayed *me*! Betrayed me as he has all his brothers. Smiling and giving to Palestinian charities each year to keep up the pretence, when all along he'd sold his soul to the *infidels*. For how long had he been like that? When had the change come? Perhaps he'd been a Judas all along and Akram had *never* really known him.

Akram walked into Oxford Street, thronging with afternoon shoppers. There were a few people, like himself, wearing Arab thobes or jilbabs, but it was no more than a handful. The rest were in Western dress: jeans, T-shirts, girls in short skirts, low-cut tops or with their stomachs bare – navels jewelled or encircled with sunburst tattoos. Normally he found the atmosphere invigorating, but today he felt like screaming: *You've turned my brother's head, drawn him from me with your empty ways. Stolen his soul!*

He knew that none of them, with their empty hopes and ambitions – based on little more than shopping, sex and who was top of the football leagues – would ever truly comprehend the bond between Muslim brothers, drawn together under Allah.

They'd never therefore grasp just what they had broken. Perhaps that was why it had happened without him knowing or guessing, so *casually*, as with everything else in this throwaway society – sex, love, fidelity, honour – but Omari he had expected better of. They were the same, of the same background and cloth. Like twins. So this betrayal now was like staring in the mirror and seeing that half your face was suddenly different, unrecognisable.

And so he found himself not wanting to look at that new face now, averting his eyes so that he didn't have to accept it. That way he could cling to the old images and memories, before the betrayal.

Omari was in the drawing room when he returned to the house and Akram was able to drift quickly past with only a small nod of acknowledgment. *'Salaam.'*

He busied himself in the kitchen, but he could feel all the motion and activity of Oxford Street, all the *anger*, still coursing through his body. He had to brace himself against the kitchen counter to quell his body's trembling. He closed his eyes after a second. *Shut out the images too.*

'Are you OK?' Omari looked in from the hallway.

'Yes, I am fine.' He looked up slowly and forced a smile. 'Just running tonight's ingredients through my mind. Make sure I haven't forgotten anything.'

'If you don't remember how to cook lamb tagine by now, you never will.' Omari chuckled. 'I'm going down to the *hammam*.'

Akram nodded. 'I will bring the towels down shortly.' *Just as soon as my body has stopped trembling.*

What was coming, what he had to do, was weighing heavier with each passing minute.

He left it only five minutes before bringing the towels. *Get away quickly*, they'd said. *Leave as much of a time gap as possible.* Akram could hear the splashing of water as he reached the last few steps. The usual ritual: fifteen minutes in the pool, twenty minutes in the steam room, another fifteen or twenty in the pool.

'Ah, towels already.' Omari raised an eyebrow. 'Early today?'

As much a part of the ritual. Normally he'd bring the towels just after Omari had come out of the steam room.

'Yes, I...have to go back to Mukhtar's to get the lamb.'

'I thought that's where you'd been earlier?'

'The *halal* delivery had just arrived when I was there. Mukhtar said to give him twenty minutes to get it unpacked. I won't be long.' Akram nodded curtly and left to avoid more questions. *Before Omari saw the lie in his eyes.*

Omari shook his head and smiled to himself. Whatever was troubling his friend, it certainly was a big bee in his bonnet this time. Give it time, he thought as he drifted back and started to float. *Give it time.*

Akram went straight upstairs, his trembling almost out of control now, and grabbed the bag he'd packed the night before from under his bed.

He paused for only a second by the front door. Then left it, as arranged, an inch from the latch.

He paced rapidly away. The grey Mercedes was where they said it would be, eighty yards from the house. He nodded quickly towards the two men inside it as he passed. He couldn't look them in the eye either.

Adel tried Omari's cellphone. There was no answer; it went into message service after four rings. 'Call me urgently the second you get this.' He tried his landline.

After five rings with no answer, he rushed out, shouting to Malik, 'I've got to be somewhere.'

On the ninth ring, by which time he was going down in the elevator, he hung up.

Adel hailed a cab and tried ringing again as they got to the first set of lights. He bit at his lip, his chest tightening. Still no answer.

There was a three-minute delay to route a general alert through MI5 central and the Met, and if he was wrong an open message on the system was the last thing he wanted. Then he remembered he still had Bob Losey's number in memory from the Corliss op. He dialled.

'Bob. Adel at TAME again. I've got a possible problem in Lancaster Gate I need help with. Where are you now?'

'South Ken. Just finishing up on an embassy call.'

'Well, that's a mile closer than me.' Adel explained what he wanted and gave the address.

'No problem. I'll cut through the park – should be there in just five or six.'

'Oh, and Bob. Could you phone me the second you get there? Let me know the lay of the land.'

'Will do.'

Adel stared emptily at the London streets as they rolled by, praying that he was wrong or that he wasn't too late. But after a while, all they reminded him of was where he'd met with Omari. *Place three, place four...* The clandestine meetings that now had probably led to his death sentence.

He closed his eyes as he felt that cloak of responsibility settle on his shoulders. *An acceptable risk*, one life lost to save hundreds; the usual departmental take. But with what Adel knew about Omari's background and why he'd become an informant, this was one loss he simply couldn't accept.

Traffic was jammed as they hit Piccadilly, and as the cab finally swung onto Park Lane, Adel checked his watch. Losey should already be there by now, but no call back yet. Adel tried him again.

A burst of sirens was audible in the background as Losey answered. 'Yeah?'

'What's happening? Are you there yet?'

'Yeah, I'm here.' Losey was slightly out of breath, walking and talking at the same time. 'But, I...I need a minute to find out what's going on.'

'*Why?* What's happened? What do you see?' The sirens were getting louder, and there was a confusion of voices in the background. Adel felt his stomach dip. 'Talk to me, Bob!'

A heavy pause at Losey's end: Losey not wanting to comment, or simply unsure?

'Like I said – I need to talk to a few people here. Find out the score. I'll call you straight back.'

'Don't worry. I'll be there myself by then,' Adel said tersely, and ended the call.

He closed his eyes again for the remaining half-mile. Because already he knew – before his cab turned into the road and he saw the black stains around Omari's door from the explosion; before he took in the fire engines, the police and medics swarming; before Bob Losey headed towards him as he got out the taxi – that he was too late. Abu Khalish had got there before him.

CHAPTER TWENTY-FIVE

'That first stock option has been taken care of. The second will be purchased within the next few hours.'

The message was waiting on Abu Khalish's cellphone as he came out the pool. As before, obscure references in case *Echelon* was listening in. Stock option: assassination.

He always considered that the simplest plans were the best. With Copenhagen, Paris and then Milan, he was sure he had an informant somewhere in the network. The only question was: *where?*

He narrowed it down to eleven possibles, then arranged that each was fed a different target city. With no other activity to spark a security alert, he'd know – from which city put one out – where he had a weak link. In this case London, Fahim Omari.

In Khalish's house, half the furniture was covered in white sheets. By morning his servants would be loading suitcases into his car. Time to move on.

There was one other thing, apart from that last London stock option, that he'd needed to take care of before he left. He'd already seen some articles in the pan-Arab press regarding the mosque bombings, and so he'd put out feelers to five of his contacts to push that same angle of 'Western' involvement.

Khalish checked his computer. The answer was back from three of them: two had already put his suggestion into play, the other would do so forthwith. But the footnote from one of those first two intrigued him: '...*It appears from one source that someone has already made a similar suggestion.*'

Khalish felt gratified that someone else out there seemed to be looking after his interests. But what began to concern him was not only not knowing who was aiding him, but most importantly: *why?*

Early the following afternoon, Jean-Pierre phoned.

Sam said, 'I've got someone with me right now. I'll call you back in half an hour.'

Mike had suggested that if Jean-Pierre called again, he should talk to him. '*What*, thirty to forty people you spoke to for research – so those are your odds: one in thirty or forty that he's Washington's contact. But there's a simple test we can run.'

Sam called Mike in the interim; he wanted Mike there when he ran that test and also for on-the-spot input, if need be.

'I tried to get you before, but then I got busy with something else,' Jean-Pierre began. That 'something else', spending every available hour examining those eleven lost Nostradamus pages from Vrellait, had in fact been the main thing to finally spur him to try again now. 'I couldn't help noticing that these current mosque bombings have more or less followed those you mentioned last year. All that appears to have changed is the order of play with Alexandria and Islamabad.'

'Possibly not even that. In my early notes, Islamabad was first – but later on I switched those two. So if the bombings are following my later notes, they're *exactly* the same.'

There was a sharp intake of breath from Jean-Pierre. 'Oh my, worse than I thought.' Though he was actually thinking *better*. Once again his precognition had served him well. 'But that does bring me to the main reason for my call now. Because, you see, I'm planning a book of my own – all about prophecy and foretelling. And it struck me with these mosque bombings that in a fashion you yourself have foretold the future – indeed, with what you've told me now, *far* more accurately than I realised. And of course this would be given even more credence and relevance because of our contact. It might simply be combined with other similar factors and events – it might be worth a whole chapter on its own. I haven't decided as yet. But I thought—'

'I...I don't know if that *is* the case,' Sam cut in. His head had started reeling as Jean-Pierre ran off into the sunset with his book plans. Mike had advised to accurately relate the mosque-bombing sequence in case Jean-Pierre had some useful input on that, but to steer clear of the messy saga of being targeted and his manuscript taken. *Gloss over that by saying it happened at the research stage.* 'The thing is,' Sam continued, 'as with you knowing the mosque-bombing sequence from our contact – others did too. And those I contacted later when I'd refined my notes and reversed Alexandria and Islamabad – they'd have known the *exact* sequence. So it might not have been a case of foretelling at all. Simply someone passing information to another party that they shouldn't – perhaps even unwittingly.'

'Oh, I see.' Jean-Pierre sighed deflatedly and looked at the papers before him. Suddenly he wasn't so sure if the information was worth passing on. The night before, he'd shared with Corinne the new development with Vrellait and how it might be linked. Perhaps for once her advice had been wrong. But some of this chain of events was still vague, unclear. 'Forgive me if in the meantime I've forgotten – but, in your manuscript, just why were these mosque bombings taking place? To what purpose?'

Sam reminded himself that with each research contact he'd only imparted information in their own areas. To experts in Islam and terrorism, he'd given the background with Abu Khalish. With Jean-Pierre, the information shared had focused on Nostradamus and Mabus. No single research contact therefore had the *whole* picture.

'The initial purpose was to put pressure on Abu Khalish to give himself up.' Sam explained about the demands after each mosque bombing. 'Which later then leads to the announcement from Bahsem-Yahl – your suggested "Mabus" – that he believes the bombers are agents of the West. Which then of course threatens more conflict with Islam.'

'I recall you mentioning Khalish, but not all the details.' There was a pause as Jean-Pierre tied the threads together. 'So yet another aspect – the demand for Khalish to give himself up – appears to be playing out in real life?'

'Yes.'

'And, indeed, if Bahsem-Yahl comes out with a statement – we'll have a full house!' Jean-Pierre chuckled faintly; then, realising he might sound callous, coughed and cleared his throat. 'Though, of course, then we *would* be back in the realms of serious foretelling.'

'Yes, I suppose we would,' Sam agreed.

It was all becoming clear to Jean-Pierre. *Mabus!* Michel de Nostredame's third Antichrist, prophesied to unite Islam in a war against the West. It seemed incredible that now, five hundred years later, they were finally putting substance and a name to Mabus. His tone lifted. 'And tell me – when is your book due out?'

'Just finishing now, then the editing process.' Sam was almost a natural now with all this lying after playing the same duplicitous game with Washington and Lorrena. 'So probably not for another year, maybe more. You no doubt know the process yourself.'

'Very much so.' Jean-Pierre drew a fresh breath. 'One thing, though, I'd like you to think about. This theory of yours – that this has all come about through a research contact passing on information – you don't know that with any certainty?'

'No. No, I don't,' Sam had to concede. He wanted to shout at Jean-Pierre: '*I know the information was passed on, that it's not some fanciful foretelling, because I was purposely targeted and had my manuscript taken from me at gunpoint.*'

'I always advise people to keep an open mind on such things. It is all too easy to simply grasp for the first obvious or rational explanation. But the powers of precognition should never be underestimated.'

Sam cradled his forehead. Jean-Pierre was still clinging to it all revolving around his soothsaying. He shrugged and caught Mike's eye: *Another fine mess you've got me into*. But Mike looked anxious as he glared at his watch, tapping it theatrically. The message was clear: while Robby Maschek had linked a scrambler to Sam's cellphone, he'd warned that given enough time, a good hacker could bypass it and zone-track them.

Sam's head felt suddenly hot and cramped, his mouth dry. Perhaps that's what Jean-Pierre's waffling was for: to keep him on the line long enough. But he now had the ideal lead-in for Mike's test. Just one more minute and they'd know for sure.

'Strange you should mention that – because there's something else that in real life has mirrored my manuscript.' Sam told Jean-Pierre about the Muslim terrorist tracker at the centrepiece of *The Prophecy*. 'And now someone like that has been in touch in real life. What do you think – am I meant to pass on to him what I know or not?'

Mike had advised that if Jean-Pierre started digging about who he might be passing information on to or where he was staying, then they should start worrying that he was part of Washington's clique. '*And if he doesn't do either, there's one last crucial test.*'

'My God – more and more one is mirroring the

other.' Jean-Pierre lapsed into thought for a moment. 'And by passing information on to him, this might be a way of foiling these bombers?'

'*Exactly.*'

Another pause, then a measured sigh. 'Then I think you have only one choice – you *have* to pass information on.'

'Yes...I suppose you're right,' Sam said, the tightness easing from his chest. Jean-Pierre had passed the test. If he was Washington's contact, he'd have advised *against* passing on information.

'And, in fact, on that front – I believe I have something to pass on myself.' Jean-Pierre's eyes fell with a glint of reverence to the papers on his desk.

One quatrain amongst the twenty in those last four pages had leapt out at him immediately, turned his thoughts again to the mosque bombings and Sam Tynnan. So his deliberation over Vrellait's pages these past nights had been as much about whether to make contact and say something, as about their authenticity. He couldn't help thinking it was somehow ordained, predestined *fate*, that it should come into his hands at this juncture; he could almost feel Michel reaching out to him through the centuries.

A soupçon of discretion set against avoiding a possible cataclysm with countless lives lost? No contest. As he'd done with Corinne, he'd simply safeguard by insisting upon the same secrecy and discretion from this Sam Tynnan.

He started to explain what he had in mind.

They were still digging for Fahim Omari's body when Adel had all-points alerts put out for Akram Ghafur and Wajd Masahran.

The explosion had collapsed most of the columns surrounding the basement pool, two supporting walls and half the floor above. The pool and its surrounds were buried over two foot deep in concrete and plaster.

As Adel saw the first fireman emerging from the thick dust and smoke drifting up from the basement, Bob Losey had to hold him back. 'Nobody could possibly have survived down there, Adel. *Nobody.*'

Over the next hour, they'd pieced together what had happened. Omari had gone down to the *hammam* while Akram was upstairs – and Omari had probably assumed he was still there when the bomb went off. But Akram had meanwhile left the house, leaving the front-door latch open – there was no sign of forced entry – as he went.

One or two men had entered and placed a timed C4 device at the base of the stairs – the last steps still out of sight of the pool area. There had been possibly only two or three minutes delay on the timer – but by that time they'd have been a mile away.

Nothing back in, no leads, on either Akram or Masahran by the time Adel left the operations room that night. Omari's house was still teeming with firemen and bomb forensics. An hour after he got home, Tim McAuley, an SO15 officer heading clean-up and forensics, phoned to tell him that they'd stopped digging.

Adel sighed heavily as McAuley finished running through what they'd found. 'OK. Get the rest of forensics to do their bit. And don't forget, they should also follow the same line: a gas explosion.'

Adel didn't want Omari's status as a terrorist informant made public, which a bomb attack would hint at. A gas explosion therefore became the official version, and Adel insisted on tight control of all related reports. In turn, the alert put out on Akram and Masahran was linked to an '*attempted terrorist attack on London's transport network prevented by security services*'. Khalish's ruse would serve *some* useful purpose.

It had been a long night. Adel stared blankly at the ceiling as he lay in bed, images of Omari haunting him: *when they first met and became friends; the firemen's helmet lights piercing through the gloom of the dust and smoke; the clunk of masonry and plaster blocks from below as they dug for his body.*

Adel was in much the same position the following night when the tears finally came.

It had been a confusing, frustrating day.

Wajd Masahran had been on their radar for years, but Omari had always urged them to leave him be. '*He's too small a player to lead to any big fish. Besides, if you take him out – my main information source goes. More advantageous to leave him in place.*'

They'd traced Masahran as far as catching a flight to Bahrain late morning, six hours before the bombing. Nothing as yet from the Bahrain authorities.

But Akram had disappeared far swifter. They had him on CCTV at Paddington Station, but nothing after that. The assumption was that he'd caught a train to Heathrow, yet he wasn't visible there on any CCTVs, nor on any passenger lists for flights out.

After Paddington Station, Akram Ghafur had completely vanished.

Then just before 7 p.m., Sam Tynnan phoned with information about a 'fresh Nostradamus quatrain'. It had already been a manic day, *the worst*, and Adel's patience was worn; nevertheless he duly wrote down Tynnan's offering:

All shall fall in the wake of the crumbling domes
Their order changed for two braces to other, distant cities
Until the last domes which shall herald Armageddon
The pursuers shall be thwarted

After studying it for a moment, Adel commented, 'This appears to contradict what you've already given me about Oman for the next bombing.'

'I know. I know. I sometimes wonder myself if Jean-Pierre is travelling with a full load. But I thought I'd better pass it on, just in case.'

The message was clear: *do with it what you will*. Tynnan wasn't holding any store in it one way or the other.

Adel decided it was too vague, involving too many undefined mosques, to be able to act upon. Especially when right now they *did* have a defined target – Al-Jihwa Mosque, Muscat, Oman – and everything was already in place. He pushed the information aside.

But then at 11.09 p.m. they got the news. There'd been another bombing, this time at the Ras-Salwi Mosque in Karak, Jordan. Adel thought again about that quatrain. Was there more he could have done with it? Or had he given it short shrift because his thoughts were burdened with everything else?

Adel still felt jarred from this final turn of events when an hour later he got into bed beside Tahiya. The London bombing had been a ruse to trap Omari, and now the fourth mosque bombing hadn't followed Sam Tynnan's prediction. *Nothing was what it seemed any more*.

And then the tears came – not because of the confusion and frustration of the day, but rather from delayed shock. Only now, the first real respite in the past twenty-four hours from shouting orders down the phone or across the operations room, dealing with what had happened purely physically, was he able to take stock of what it meant to him emotionally. And as his heart finally opened to that, those emotions squeezed hard. Omari his friend. His *good* friend.

Tahiya reached out and touched his arm as the grief gently rocked his body. 'Are you OK, Adel...?'

He told her then about Omari, with good reason: Omari was a family friend first, an informant second. And as he admitted that he blamed himself, she said all the right things – albeit predictable, they still felt good – to salve his conscience: *You shouldn't. You couldn't possibly have known what they'd planned. I'm sure you did all you could.*

He talked then about his other problems and frustrations – Akram's and Masahran's disappearance and trying to track the mosque bombings; and for a moment he wondered why he was telling Tahiya: breaking their pact of never bringing his work home with him. Was it just because he'd had a nightmare day and wanted to unburden it?

She was understanding, though, stroking his brow, offering encouragement or advice where she could.

And suddenly it struck him why he was sharing this now with Tahiya.

The first pang of concern had come earlier that day – his suspicions that Omari had been targeted because of an internal leak. And the same thought had hit him again an hour ago with the mosque bombing being switched from Oman to Jordan; was there someone in his operations room he couldn't trust?

That's why he was sharing now with his wife: he was no longer sure who he could safely share information with.

He recalled how Tynnan looked when he met him at Springfield: the weight of the world on his shoulders, eyes haunted, not sure who was on his side. And within only two days, Adel had become the same. *Nothing was what it seemed any more.* The lines blurred between reality and fiction.

Unravelling Sam Tynnan's odyssey looked further out of reach now than ever.

CHAPTER TWENTY-SIX

Though an unavoidable necessity, Washington hated these meetings.

His ritual monthly sessions, in addition to any urgent summonses, with William – never 'Bill' or 'Will' – Grayford, head of Department 101.

Now touching sixty, at some point in his illustrious twenty-year CIA career Grayford had gained the nickname 'the shadow'. Some thought it was because if you scratched the surface of many a black-op, you'd find Grayford in the background. Like a shadow. Others thought it was because of his habit of having a lamp one side of his face with only one side slightly illuminated: a rough, puckered skin patch below his left cheekbone that he was keen to obscure. Rumour had it that he gained the injury as a marine in a fire-fight in Vietnam. But the truth was that he'd fallen on a metal picket fence as a child and two plastic surgery attempts still hadn't put it right.

The reasons given behind the naming of Department 101 were equally ambiguous. Some thought it was after George Orwell's Room 101, and yes, there was much about 101's activities that would make a Commie's toes curl. Others thought it was simply the door number on a Langley corridor from behind which its ops were masterminded.

The truth lay in the date of its inception – 20 days after 9/11. The day it was decided that another department was necessary to fight the new battle ahead: not predominantly focused on internal, national security, as the case with Homeland Security; conversely, not weighed so heavily towards international security repercussions, as with the CIA. What was required was a department that could swim comfortably in the waters in between.

Its funding came jointly through the CIA and Homeland Security, which therefore meant that it was also one step removed from Congress and Senate Committee vetting processes; this last advantage, though, was not freely admitted in political circles.

Today's meeting had been called impromptu, so

Washington was more anxious than normal. Like a buzzard fixing its prey, Grayford's eyes settled on him.

'You appreciate that we're now approaching the delicate final stages?'

Washington nodded swiftly. 'Yes, I do, sir. Very much so.'

'I see from your report that you've suffered some unexpected collateral damage?' Grayford perched gold pince-nez on the end of his nose as he perused the file on his desk. 'Two internal team personnel.' He peered above them as his eyes fixed again on Washington.

'Uh, yes, sir. Both unavoidable, I'm afraid – but very necessary to maintain the continuing security of the op.'

Grayford's gaze stayed fixed on Washington. After a moment he slowly nodded. 'Within the context given, that I can accept. But what I'm finding harder to comprehend is the fact that you let the main target slip through your fingers and go to ground.'

'We're checking possible options and putting some feelers out. It won't be long before we've found him.'

Again that steady gaze.

'And for the moment he's still proving useful,' Washington offered in hasty support. 'Playing the game we want.'

'And remind me, if you will, just why that might be?'

Washington paused for a second, swallowed. 'Because that's the way you set everything up.'

'Yes, that's right.' Grayford forced a patient smile. 'And as we also both know – pretty soon he'll stop being *useful*. So it might be a good idea to find him before that happens.' Grayford raised an eyebrow. 'Don't you think?'

Washington nodded. 'Yes, sir. I do.'

Grayford said nothing, rested back in his chair. *Fine. We understand each other.* His eyes shifted from Washington to other papers on his desk. The meeting was clearly over.

Washington got up and left.

Imams Sahkani, Al-Assan, Ghanil; Professors Al-Hital, Yousy, Karmal, Daoud...

Sam started making a list. Now they knew with near certainty that Jean-Pierre wasn't Washington's contact, his thoughts had turned again to *who*.

He got eighteen names down cleanly, then became unsure about the spelling of two names, and another – a professor at the University of Jordan – had gone totally from his mind.

He went online on Mike's computer to start googling, then abruptly stopped himself halfway through tapping out the first enquiry.

Washington's team probably had a list of all his research contacts. Those names had been in his research notes sitting right alongside copies of *The Prophecy* on his computer. One of those names tapped into a computer only twelve miles from his home – *Echelon* would pick it up in a heartbeat.

It was a reminder of how close he was to being uncovered – only a fingertip away – how straightjacketed his movements were. He jerked his hands back from the keyboard as if he'd touched an electric fence. He'd just have to work with what he had.

If the prime aim of Washington's op was to get Abu Khalish to give himself up, then it probably followed that whoever was Washington's contact was also sympathetic to that aim.

Sam tried to recall if any of his contacts had voiced anti-terrorist sentiments.

One imam – Mohammed Al-Esayi at the Umm Al-Qura Madrassa in Saudi – had commented that it was indeed 'lamentable that an increase in such activity had been almost directly proportional to an increase in the misunderstandings and misinterpretations of Islam.'

And Professor Barakeh at Beirut University had mentioned losing an uncle in a car bombing in Lebanon's civil war.

Outside of that, Sam couldn't recall anything else of note.

Sam's thoughts revolved for a while without any clear direction or answer, then it hit him: maybe they weren't meant to know! Caught up in their elaborate chess game to try and outsmart, outmanoeuvre Washington, they'd missed the obvious. Because while Emile obviously felt duty-bound to try and stop the mosque bombers, if indeed those bombings might lead to Abu Khalish giving himself up, would he want to impair that? Would *any* of them want to stop that possible outcome?

And with the news report yesterday – the fourth mosque bombing shifting location from his manuscript – there was something else vital he should pass on. He flicked on the scrambler before he switched on his phone and dialled Emile's number.

He stood up and moved away from Mike's computer and the window as Emile came on the line, and so he missed the police car pulling up by Jem's cabin on the far side of the lake while he was talking.

'Yes, of course,' Emile said, 'with Abu Khalish being their core target, that becomes an issue to consider... rather than necessarily a dilemma. A possible conflict of interests. But let me give more thought to that.'

As at their meeting, Sam sensed the guarded tone beneath the surface cordiality. He took a fresh breath; this was the trickier part. 'That fourth mosque bombing was also switched from the original one planned in my manuscript. And one other – the sixth in the sequence.'

'I see.' There was a marked pause. 'And why was that?'

'Because in the book the bombers feared that either an emerging pattern or some inside information had given those away.' The pause was longer this time at the other end. Was Emile concerned he was being fed a line? Sam should have told him earlier. 'Besides, apart from anything else, it's a standard writer's ploy – keep the plot twisting and turning. Keep the reader guessing.'

'So the fourth and sixth mosques you gave me were those finally bombed?'

'Yes.'

'And the original ones planned – before the bombers shifted locations?'

'The El-Mehbir Mosque in Rabat. And the Ab Sarikhan in Tabriz, Iran.'

'Well, at least they haven't done a double bluff and shifted back to the originals. And while the changed mosque now hasn't been the same – the fact alone that there's been a shift in locations *has* followed your manuscript.'

'Yes…I suppose.' The linked thought hit Sam then. 'And if they *had* kept the changed location the same – that would have gone against why it was done in the manuscript: to foil those tracking them.'

Emile sighed. 'Yes, there is that. Once they suspect someone might be on to them – whether just in your manuscript or in real life – odds-on they'd alter their plans.'

Emile thanked him and said goodbye, and as Sam turned back to Mike's computer he saw the scene across the lake. The conversation between Jem and the uniformed policeman was now in full swing, and Sam could see now a second officer seated in the blue and white car five yards behind.

Sam froze, hoping and praying that it was an unconnected visit, but as he saw the policeman look his way, that hope began to fade.

He shrank back from the window. Had he been seen?

It looked that way as he saw the policeman heading towards his cabin, Jem following closely behind.

Jem had known the local Utica PD policeman, Bill Burridge, for near on six years now. Sandy-haired and a florid seventeen stone already by his early thirties, he'd become a regular visitor since Jem's last parole. '*Just call me BB, like the gun or the jazz guitarist.*' Maybe 'BB' thought that would make him appear cool, a name that conjured up a jazz musician or a modern-day rapper – without really appreciating the fifty-year musical divide between the two.

But Jem thought 'BB Bill' was actually OK. His first visit after his parole had been more formal, a clear '*You make sure to behave now you're on my patch, yer hear?*' The visits had continued over the years, and while he'd mellowed and they'd become nodding acquaintances if still far from friends, Jem still found the drop-bys annoying as hell: thinly disguised check-ups because something local had gone down that could link to him.

A truckload of Marlboro Lights had been hijacked en route to Buffalo. If Jem heard about any being sold under the counter locally, 'You let me know, huh?'

'Yeah, sure.' Bill no longer asked him directly if he might be involved. Jem had told him enough times he didn't do that sort of stuff any more. So either Bill believed him or he didn't want to insult both their intelligences by asking the same question only to get the same answer.

Bill looked towards the lake. 'Catch anything worthwhile this year yet?' he asked casually.

'Steelhead trout a coupla weeks back.'

'Big?'

'Twelve-pounder. Second largest I've ever caught here.'

Bill whistled softly under his breath and looked again at the lake. Then his gaze lifted a fraction towards the cabins beyond, as if it was an afterthought. 'That Mike I saw at the window a moment ago?'

'Aaah...yeah.' Jem nodded. With the sunlight and reflections on the window, all Jem had been able to pick out was a vague shape when Sam had been by the window. Mike had confided in Jem the other day that Sam was 'laying low' and to keep half an eye out for anyone who might come snooping.

Bill kept his eyes fixed in the same direction. 'Don't see his car there.'

Jem felt his throat tighten. For the first time he began to worry that this visit might be about something else. 'No, ah...Cathy dropped him off a couple of hours back. She needed the car to do some shopping.'

'*Uh, huh.*' Bill's gaze stayed there a moment longer before he turned back to Jem. 'How's he doing these days? Finished his next book yet?'

''Fraid he doesn't keep me up to date with those things.' Jem shrugged non-committally. 'State secret.' Maybe that had been partly why Bill had mellowed in those later visits, when he'd discovered that Jem knew Mike Kiernan. Last summer, Mike had been at the cabin when Bill dropped by and, after introducing himself, he'd spent a while gushing to Mike about how he'd loved his last book. '*And who was that Boston police chief modelled on? Our own ballsy Len Macey, no doubt.*'

'Be good to say hello to him again, if it's no trouble.' And, clear from his tone that he wasn't waiting on Jem's approval, he started off round the lake.

Jem quickly fell in step behind, his mind spinning.

'Yeah, would be. Except...he asked not to be disturbed.'

Bill kept on walking as if he hadn't heard.

'...He was pretty pointed and insistent about it.'

Bill finally stopped, slowly turned.

'Apparently he's in the middle of writing a real important scene,' Jem offered. It was all he could think of.

'Oh, I see.' BB was visibly disappointed.

'Sorry. Maybe next time.'

Bill glanced at his shoes, then looked back at Jem. 'You sure everything's OK? Something ain't troublin' you?'

Jem felt his throat tighten another notch. 'Like what?'

'Maybe those cigarettes I mentioned. Maybe something to do with Mike.' Bill shrugged. 'You tell me.' This time Jem held Bill's gaze steadily with his best poker face, and after an uneasy pause, Bill added, 'You seem agitated, that's all.'

Jem chuckled disarmingly. 'Just keen to keep people from knocking on Mike's door, when he's made it clear: *no* visitors. *No* disturbances.'

Bill slowly nodded. 'Yeah, yeah. So you said.' He stared at Jem a second longer, then looked back towards the cabin.

Knife-edge. If Bill suspected something was wrong, he'd just bulldoze over Jem's protests and make sure he knocked at Mike's cabin door. Jem held his breath as Bill's gaze lingered on Mike's cabin.

* * *

Where, where, *where*?

Akram couldn't simply have evaporated after Paddington Station. So if he hadn't caught the Heathrow Express, perhaps he'd caught a train west: Devon, Cornwall, South Wales? Adel was sure they'd missed something. He put Malik and three others on trawling back frame by frame over the Paddington Station CCTV footage.

Last night, while Tahiya had soothed his brow, something she'd said had stuck in his mind: 'I'm sure as events unfold, you'll be guided to do the right thing. It will all become clear.' That was half the problem: the signals so far had been confusing. What if this *was* all some marvellously engineered black-op following the first half of Tynnan's plot – mosque bombings to pressure Abu Khalish to give himself up – and after this bombing or the next, as Tynnan had surmised in his last call, Khalish did just that? Billions of pounds and hundreds of lives saved. And by intervening now, he'd spoil the op. Khalish would stay at large. The ultimate betrayal to all those who'd lost loved ones *and* his friend Omari.

Which then meant that if there *was* an internal leak, in an obtuse way they were looking after the op's interests, and *his*. The mosque bombers could have changed venue purely from having seen the heavier security in place at the Al-Jihwa Mosque in Oman. And now Tynnan was saying that that shift in location had also been an element in his manuscript.

Either way, by design or default, that last quatrain Tynnan had passed on had been proven correct. Adel studied it again.

All shall fall in the wake of the crumbling domes
Their order changed for two braces to other, distant cities
Until the last domes which shall herald Armageddon
The pursuers shall be thwarted

'Braces' was *bracchia* in the original text, Tynnan had related from his Nostradamus contact, Jean-Pierre Bourdin – literally 'two arms' in Latin. So, according to this, four *domes*, mosques, in the sequence were meant to be in other, distant cities until the last 'domes'. But mosques, plural, did that mean two or three?

Adel shook his head after a moment. Even now in the cold light of day – without his thoughts swamped as they'd been when Tynnan first passed it on – he couldn't see a way of acting on it. There was nothing defined, nothing to grab on to. They couldn't put extra security on possibly hundreds of mosques.

'*Boss?* I think we've got that sequence now.'

Adel looked up. Malik by his shoulder. He nodded and followed Malik over to his computer.

On Malik's screen were five frozen frames. Malik clicked on the top left-hand frame and the frozen tableau of figures started moving.

'This is the first sighting we have of Akram Ghafur at Paddington Station.' Malik pointed with his pen.

'East entrance, coming off Praed Street. Wearing a beige-coloured thobe and carrying a dark-grey holdall. Time in the corner shows 17.48 p.m., only nine minutes after the bomb went off. The supposition is that he walked straight to the station after leaving Omari's house.' Malik clicked open the next frame. 'Then we have him again here, a minute later, crossing the main station concourse.' As Akram went out of frame, Malik opened the next. 'Then here, approaching a food kiosk. Appears to buy some bottled water...'

Adel followed Akram's on-screen progress at Paddington Station as Malik opened and played the successive CCTV frames.

'The last one we see him on is here.' Malik tapped the screen with his pen. 'Going into the station washrooms on the south side.'

Adel surveyed the sequence again. 'And you've obviously checked later? I'm thinking as long as perhaps two hours.'

'We've gone up to three hours later. Nothing. One guy we thought for a moment was Akram on platform four, so we blew the frame up close. *Not* him.'

Adel slowly nodded, eyes still shifting between the frames. 'And is there a blind spot on the washroom cam? Otherwise surely he'd have been seen coming out.'

'A small one. But we'd have still been able to see part of a shoulder, *something*. We can't see even that.'

Malik looked up with a tight-lipped grimace. 'And even if we'd missed him there, we'd have picked him up on one of these two.' Malik pointed. 'Nothing on those either. After the washrooms, Akram Ghafur simply vanishes into thin air!'

But Adel knew that Akram had to be there somewhere, only they'd missed it. Akram was shielded by other people in frame at a vital juncture, or some other simple explanation. His eyes continued to dart between the frames. Where, where, *where*?

Akram had arranged to meet his contact, Al Hakam – Abu Khalish's right-hand man for this operation – an hour and forty minutes after the bombing.

He'd questioned the time gap at first – he wanted to get away as quickly as possible. But Al Hakam said he needed the time to arrange the last details: *Akram's final payment and instructions. His flight ticket.* 'Besides, you need to get changed in the meantime. Your new identity.'

The arranged meeting place was a mile west of Paddington Station. Akram decided to walk to the station and change.

His passport with his new identity and half the payment, seventy-five thousand pounds, were already in his bag. Now he needed to change and put on the wig and make-up to match that passport photo. He used a washroom cubicle at Paddington Station and within thirty-five minutes was finished. His own beard and moustache were quite trim; the new growths were far bushier, the beard longer.

The two prosthetics below his cheekbones, making him look fatter, he stuck on before the beard – as he'd been instructed step by step earlier for his new passport photo.

Black trousers and a dark-green kaftan top replaced his thobe. His bag collapsed into a small square, and there was another brown bag which folded out to replace it. Exiting the washroom, he was a different man: Abdul Radwan, Libyan national.

Despite the disguise, he still felt conspicuous and vulnerable out on the street, and there were fifty minutes to go until the meeting. He found an Italian café a quarter mile down the road and buried himself at the back, ordering a couple of strong espressos to kill the time. He observed his hand as he lifted the cup: it was still shaking.

Criticising Omari for being a Judas, when this was no different: Judas money for betrayal. Akram wondered how much MI5 had paid Omari to betray his fellow *fedayeen*?

Except there *was* a difference, Akram reminded himself. Omari didn't need the money, it was just betrayal for betrayal's sake. When Al Hakam had seen Akram's concern when payment had first been mentioned, he reminded him that this was his survival fund, his means of making his own way without Omari's salary or roof over his head.

He shook his head after a moment. It didn't seem to matter. He'd spun it through his mind scores of ways, each with a good, strong justification – but still felt the guilt like a heavy hand on his heart.

He paid the bill and hailed a taxi twenty yards along the road to go to his meeting.

Dusk had fallen, street lamps and lit shop fronts now the stronger light. Akram closed his eyes as the taxi passed an antique shop Omari and he used to frequent. *Shut it from your mind*.

Akram got the taxi to drop him at the end of the road, as Al Hakam instructed. He walked the remaining distance. Eighty yards from the main road the street turned to form an L-shaped dead-end, wire fence bordering rail lines one side, garages and small industrial units the other, now locked up for the past two hours. Al Hakam had stressed they needed somewhere quiet, no passers-by looking on, for the transaction.

As Akram turned into the dead-end, he could see Al Hakam waiting twenty yards ahead.

Al Hakam nodded and smiled as he approached. '*Salaam*. You are well?'

'As well as can be.' Akram forced a weak smile in return. *Shut it from your mind*. 'I suppose I will be headed to Libya now? Home of Abdul Radwan.'

'Yes. Al Bayda. Not too far from the border – so you'll still be able to visit your beloved Egypt now and then. And we've created a good back-story for you. Egyptian father, plus also time spent working in Cairo and London as a servant. So your accent should not seem untoward.'

'I understand.' Akram made an attempt at a gracious shrug. Having agreed to do Masahran's and Al Hakam's bidding, he felt numb to all the details. Al Hakam could have said he was going to Patagonia and he'd have hardly complained. He noticed that Al Hakam wasn't dressed that differently to himself: black trousers and dark-blue kaftan top. He was a powerfully built man, his beard and moustache bushy.

Al Hakam reached into the pocket of his kaftan. 'Here is the flight ticket – to Benghazi. There's coach transport from there to Al Bayda.'

Akram nodded as he took the ticket. 'OK.' He gave it only a cursory glance.

Al Hakam took two thick envelopes from his left-hand pocket. 'And this is the final payment.'

But Al Hakam purposely held the envelopes to the side of Akram's vision, so that he had to shift his focus to take them; a distraction from the movement of the ice pick already in Al Hakam's right grip.

It was a thrust he'd done a hundred times before, in fact he'd been the one to help Youssef perfect it. Executed well, it left no bloodstains on the assailant's clothes. And today should have been no different – except that at the last second Akram was distracted by something over Al Hakam's shoulder, and moved.

The blade hit a rib, snapped in half. Akram grunted, eyes suddenly wider over Al Hakam's shoulder before shifting in horror to his kaftan front.

Al Hakam thrust again, grabbing Akram and swivelling at the same time so that he had sight of what had caught Akram's attention. Three boys, no more than seventeen, were clambering over the railway fence near the end of the road, returning from their latest graffiti outing.

Two frozen montages sixty yards apart as the blade sank home. The second boy was still only halfway over the fence – not sure just who had caught who.

Al Hakam felt the blade go cleanly between the ribs this time; but now only half-length, it couldn't reach the heart. He tried again, ramming harder. He felt a rib crack as his hand connected, but still the blade didn't reach Akram's heart.

Akram's groaning verged into a strangled bellow as the air shunted out of him.

One of the boys shouted, '*Hey!*'

The second boy jumped to the ground, but still they waited until their last friend clambered over before moving their way. And then only a half-hearted jog;

obviously apprehensive about confronting someone with a blade, even with three of them. Though their shouting now was bolder, more insistent.

Before the boys got too close Al Hakam got in three more good stabs to Akram's abdomen, hoping to puncture something – stomach, liver, colon. He was meant to take the first batch of money and the passport from Akram's bag – the final envelopes were just paper – but there was no time now! When the boys were about thirty yards away, he let Akram slump to the ground, and ran.

He had a stolen moped wedged between two garage units twenty yards round the corner. By the time he heard one of the boys running after him shouting, he was near the end of the road on the moped. As he turned into the main road, he glanced back: the boy wasn't following.

He had a lot of Akram's blood on him, though it was difficult to pick out at night against the dark-blue kaftan. He turned off three roads along – another industrial rail-side street, dead at night – dumped the moped and kaftan, and tore off the beard and moustache.

Underneath he had a black jacket to match his trousers, white shirt and navy tie. Within minutes he was just another clean-shaven office worker hailing a cab to head home.

* * *

Bill Burridge took his time contemplating Mike's cabin before looking back at Jem.

'Yeah, sure,' he said, smiling thinly. 'Next time.'

But Jem wondered if Bill suspected something as he watched his squad car head off – and Sam too voiced his concern when minutes later Jem went across.

'Do you think he might have been sent to sniff around and find out if someone was at Mike's cabin?'

'Don't know.' Jem explained how he'd hopefully covered by saying it was Mike staying there, busy with some work. 'Trouble is, we won't know if he's bought that story unless someone else comes to pay you a visit. And if that's to happen, it'll probably be these coming hours or by the latest tonight. Best you stay at my place for a spell.'

Sam was glad of the break from being at Mike's on his own. *Cabin fever.* But he was still forced to hide out of sight in a back room while Jem kept a vigil at the front window, binoculars trained on Mike's cabin, rifle at his side. If he saw a team moving in, the plan was to hightail it out of there in Jem's Chevy.

They'd left the kitchen light on at Mike's and the connecting door to the front room ajar, so that as it got dark Jem could pick out any figures moving around.

Nothing happened during daylight, no vehicles approaching or movement, and the first hours of darkness passed slowly too. Then it started raining, a mist steadily rising from the lake as it got heavier, reducing visibility. A few times Jem tensed, thinking he'd picked out something amongst the shadows, but then he'd relax again as he realised it was nothing. Finally, just after eleven-thirty, a stiffer rod of tension squared his shoulders. He rasped urgently to Sam, '*Someone coming!*'

Car headlights were approaching on the road behind Mike's cabin. Fifty yards, thirty. Jem followed them intently with his binoculars.

'Who is it?' Sam pressed, his pulse racing.

'Not sure.' But the car didn't slow, and as the lights swept past Mike's and veered off to the left, Jem could pick out who it was.

He eased out his breath. 'Frank Highton, that's all. He swings by every now and then when he strikes lucky with a pick-up at a singles bar.'

Jem kept up his vigil until 4 a.m. – fearing they might wait to be sure Sam was asleep before moving in – then called it a night.

But Sam didn't sleep well; fearful that they might still come in the hours of darkness remaining, he listened out for every small sound: faint rustling, footsteps, engine thrum or tyre tread on the approach road, anything out of place amongst the steady rain patter outside.

And the next day and night were even worse because he was back at Mike's cabin and alone again. *Maybe*

they'd decided to strike tonight rather than last night,
somehow had picked up that he'd stayed at Jem's then.
Finally, after fours hours of restlessness, he gave up the
ghost on getting any sleep.

He made a coffee and took it over to Mike's desk,
contemplating the dark, still lake.

Cabin fever. He'd felt that dull, grating stillness
ticking down every heavy second of every minute of
every hour these past few days. Yet throughout that
tense, piano-tinkling build-up, it had felt as if nothing
he could do was right.

Mindless TV shows bored him, and in any case
they weren't nearly enough to stop his mind drifting
to what had happened, trawling yet again through the
wreckage of his predicament. And when the news came
on, any coverage on Khalish or the mosque bombings
would bring back his anxiety.

Perhaps this was why he'd started to try and work
out who Washington's contact was. Not only to ease
the boredom, but also the guilt – he should be doing
something to help; especially as the unwitting architect
of that chain of events.

But now that too seemed futile. Because apart from
the fact that indeed it might be best if they all sat
by and didn't foil the op – either way it would do
little to help his own plight. Even if this was some
silver-lining op and soon Khalish, under pressure of
the mosque bombings, gave himself up, Sam would

still be the man who knew how they'd done it. The man who knew too much.

And if Bahsem-Yahl or some other hard-line cleric spoke out and linked the mosque bombings to the West, yet the bombings still continued – it would be even worse. He'd then be the man who knew too much about the black-lining op that had sparked off World War Three. Either way, they couldn't possibly risk leaving him alive.

So whatever happened, he faced more of the same: long hours, days and – if he was lucky enough to survive that long – years stretched out ahead at cabins and hideaways like this. The endless solitude and pregnant tension grinding his will down nerve by nerve, bone by bone, so that after a while he'd probably be past caring if they finally found him and put a bullet through his head to end it all.

He looked out at the black, lifeless lake, pale in comparison to his mood at that moment, and thought: *You weren't to know it at the time, Lorrena, but you were probably the lucky one.* While what he'd passed to Emile might or might not be able to save the world from calamity, he had yet to work out how to save himself.

CHAPTER TWENTY-SEVEN

My sons and brethren, united under the benign light of Allah. You will have seen these past weeks dark clouds threatening that light, darker and more worrying than many seen before. Because while we have seen desecration of Allah's sacred places of worship in the past – unfortunate wayward acts between brothers who have temporarily lost their way, stepped outside of His exalted light – never before have we seen such organised and wilful acts of destruction against His holy shrines and, in turn, against His name.

Yet we are told that this is meant to be in the name of Islam, to test the faith and devotion of one

Abu Khalish. This, in my eyes – in the eyes of one who has devoted his life to following the wishes and decrees of Allah as proclaimed by His one and only exalted messenger, Mohammed – cannot be. For one brother of Islam to test the faith of another through the destruction of its holy monuments is a miscreant act of untold proportions. A sin against the name of Islam and Allah Himself.

So it is with a heavy heart that I make this statement now – with the grace and will of Allah, this divine proclamation – that no devout sons of Islam would indulge in such acts. If indeed born of Islam and Allah, then they have become agents of the devil and the West by torturous routes beyond imagination; we can but pray for their souls. But it is my belief that they have never been sons of Islam, they have been servants of the Western devils, infidels, from the outset – which is why they have been able to indulge in such abominations without due conscience. Without feeling the grip of Allah's wrath crushing their hearts.

And so I beseech all true brothers of Islam to rise up as one against these unholy acts, one voice rising as would a mighty sword against these abominations. One voice to loudly proclaim: an attack against one of Allah's sacred monuments is an attack on Allah Himself. An attack on Allah is an attack against all His people.

* * *

Two months ago, Bahsem-Yahl had stood on the podium in Azadi (Freedom) Square for the anniversary of the Revolution, but today's speech was made from his study. On his desk sat the Koran and Hadiths alongside a vase of freshly cut flowers, and the Iranian flag hung on the wall behind him.

In Washington, DC, David Stennell played the brief clip again, looking for any small details or nuances he might have missed on the first three plays. Nothing. At least for now. He started flicking through news channels for reactions. It looked like it was going to be a long day.

He hardly lifted his head over the next fifteen hours, except to tell his secretary what type of deli sandwich, muffin and coffee he wanted brought to his desk. At-desk meals were *de rigueur* too for much of Stennell's section after the announcement, and for them the first respite from that head-down, round-the-clock schedule was, in the end, almost three days later. It was the first moment they had any real handle on the effects of the broadcast, the 'general mood out there' in White House parlance.

Because that's what Stennell's NSA department did, they measured 'effect and reaction', or 'mood', if you will, from various events: elections, government changes, troop movements, diplomatic – or sometimes not-so-diplomatic – gestures; or, as now, simple political announcements. Except that this announcement, from the reaction so far, was proving to be far from 'simple'.

Stennell looked at the frozen news clips on his computer screen. The first street demonstrations had been in Tehran and Bushehr, but within hours had spread to Cairo, Islamabad, Riyadh, Amman, Damascus and Gaza. The first Christian church attacked had been late the first night in Sudan, the next twenty hours later in the Christian Ashrafieh neighbourhood of Beirut. By then the demonstrations had also spread to many Western cities: Paris, London, Stockholm, Amsterdam.

The eight Farsi and fifteen Arabic-language experts in his team were still busy sifting through the reams of newspaper reports and TV news transcripts; but he had enough for now to provide an interim report, which countless departments had been screaming for the past forty-eight hours.

That volume of material delay, though, plus the fact that reactions were still 'in progress', allowed him to hedge his bets, not use overt, conclusive terms which might nail his opinion too firmly. It was the cautious language of intelligence operatives or diplomats. So he said 'worrying' rather than 'alarming', 'concern' rather than 'fear', 'anxiety' rather than 'distress'; even though his heart, what his gut told him, swayed towards the latter expressions. '...*It will be interesting to see how things develop over the next few days. And, of course, if and when there* is *another mosque bombing, matters could well escalate.*' Subtext: looks like the whole caboodle could go haywire of its own accord, but if there's another mosque bombing it *definitely* would.

Stennell gave his report one last read-through, then scanned the request list. There were almost sixty in total, half of them coming in straight after the announcement. The rest were long-term general requests for notification of 'any activity in the region'. Various sectors and parties within the State Department, CIA, Homeland Security, or senators or congressmen with interests in Middle East affairs. The phrasing of one of those early requests caught Stennell's eye – almost as if they'd been expecting something like this from Bahsem-Yahl's quarter. He shook his head after a second. Perhaps they simply had Bahsem-Yahl in their sights for reasons of their own. Wouldn't be the first or last time. He started sending his report through.

Adel could hardly face the news broadcasts any more.

After Bahsem-Yahl's speech the day before, each fresh news bulletin broadcasting increasingly volatile demonstrations etched the concern deeper on his face. Before long someone was bound to pick up that he knew more than he was letting on.

And he couldn't share his thoughts with anyone. Not least because he'd promised Tynnan, with *good* reason. If Washington's tentacles spread any distance, it would be the first thing to get Tynnan targeted. Plus the repercussions for his own team. If he showed his hand, those same tentacles would ensure their efforts to track the bombers were thwarted or shut down in short order. His *only* ace card right now was his inside-track information from Tynnan.

But with the requisite secrecy of that pact, it struck Adel for the first time how alone he was: there was nobody in the operations room he could share his burden with. Not that they'd believe him in any case: *'I've got this inside information from a British writer. He wrote exactly this scenario in a manuscript last year, and now fears this is all being copied from that. A blueprint for Armageddon, if you will.'*

Alone. Adel turned his attention back to tracking Akram and Masahran. Safer ground, where his reaction didn't risk betraying his secret.

'How's it going?' he asked Malik.

'I've eliminated the first twenty minutes – seventy-eight people in total. *Busy* washroom.'

The suggestion had come from Bahir early afternoon: if Akram didn't exit the washroom looking the same, then perhaps he'd used one of the cubicles to change, 'put on some sort of disguise.'

It was a reasonable suggestion, but painstakingly slow putting it to the test. CCTV shots had to be scrutinised frame by frame, matching people going in and out, until finally, hopefully, they'd find an *out* with no *in* to match it. Since the same person had to visually match, it was a one-man task. Malik had been working through the washroom CCTV footage now for almost two hours.

Adel patted Malik's shoulder with a tight grin. 'If you still haven't found anything up to an hour after Akram entering, we'll call it a day. Start looking at other options.'

Forty minutes later Karam grabbed his attention as a fresh news item came on the large plasma screen. '...Another retaliatory attack on a Christian church, this time in Ashrafieh, Beirut.'

Adel looked at it as long as he could bear, nodding numbly. He was still in the same position two minutes later at his desk, one hand cradling his forehead to shield his closed eyes, when Malik's excited yelp rang out.

'Got him...*Got him*!'

Adel went over. On Malik's screen was a man in a dark-green kaftan, heavy-jowled with a thick black beard and moustache with grey tinges. Malik blew it up two sizes larger, and only then, as Adel leant in closer, could he pick out the resemblance to Akram.

'Are you sure?' Adel pressed.

'*Absolutely*. I've tracked back through every single person going in after Akram. This man's definitely not amongst them.'

Adel's eyes fixed more intently on the frozen image on screen. He slowly exhaled. '*OK*, looks like we've got our man. Lift as close a mugshot as you can from this and put it out on all-points.'

One of the teenagers stayed close to Akram, muttering reassurances. 'You'll be alright. Just hang on. They won't be long.'

The other two were just out of his field of vision behind him. One of them called 999 on his cellphone to get an ambulance and police there. 'And *quick*! There's loads of blood!' Then as he hung up the other was saying that he wasn't sure he could hang around, he had to get home.

Akram didn't know whether the boy had left by the time the ambulance crew arrived because he blacked out seconds later.

The next thing he remembered was feeling cold; a cold so intense that it felt as if an icy lance had been run through him. He started shivering uncontrollably, and as that lance hit his stomach, the pain was excruciating, arching his body off the gurney. Two medics fought to press his body back down with more words of reassurance. 'Stay calm...you'll be OK. Just keep *still*.'

But he knew this time that they were just empty words because he could see his own blood soaking the blanket in the stark flashing light as the ambulance sped along. And he could see it too from their faces. He was dying!

A part of him welcomed the cold and the pain – seemed fitting punishment for what he'd done, his betrayal. After all, Fahim Omari had suffered no less for *his* betrayal; why should he be any different? And then when they met in the hereafter they could discuss their respective betrayals, where they'd strayed and gone wrong; and perhaps finally they'd embrace and be friends again. As they'd *always* been.

He coughed then, though it was difficult with the oxygen mask and the plastic pipe in the corner of his mouth. And on the third cough, something surged from his stomach. The medic standing closest, a girl no more than twenty-four, lifted the oxygen mask and wiped him clean. He tried to focus on her, but she faded into a grey blur; and suddenly he was back with Omari hugging him with tears in his eyes as he doused the last of the flames with the cement sacks and saw Akram was OK. And then they were both side by side, the sun hot on their backs as they skimmed stones across the still Nile waters, putting a couple of herons into flight. 'I'm sorry, Fahim...*so sorry*. Please forgive me.' The images faded to dark grey, then finally black again.

The young medic looked worriedly towards her male colleague after wiping away the vomit. It had been heavy with blood. She looked at the blood pressure and pulse readings. Both had dropped sharply in the last few minutes, the pulse now just forty-two. They were losing him.

There was a buzz from the breakthrough with Akram's disguise. The photo was put out on all-points, while Malik ran a sequence of Akram's new figure from other cams: *crossing the station concourse, exiting again on Praed Street*. The new lead kept spirits buoyed in the operations room for the next hour or so.

Until the newscast with the latest drama in the wake of Bahsem-Yahl's speech: a two-thousand-strong demo in Paris running amok where eventually water cannons had to be brought in. The operations room was subdued again.

This time there was nowhere for Adel to take refuge; nothing left to do now with Akram except await responses on the APB.

It struck Adel then that he wasn't just hiding away from the unfolding drama because his reaction might give away his secret pact with Tynnan, but also because he was at a loss what to do about it. *Powerless*.

Last night after the announcement, Tahiya had sensed something was wrong beyond it being just a 'tough day'. And once the kids were in bed, she'd finally asked him what it was. 'If you feel you can or indeed *want* to share it, that is?'

He'd shaken his head. 'No, no. It's OK. Hopefully it will work itself out. Perhaps later.'

Except that he couldn't see it getting any better later, or being any easier to talk about. *Pathetic*. He wasn't even able to talk to Tahiya now. Truly *alone*.

There was one factor over which no one had any control and that was whether or not Bahsem-Yahl would make an announcement; this couldn't be steered from the manuscript and was purely left to fate. He could try and rationalise it numerous ways: if you *were* to pick a fit for Mabus out the hat, Bahsem-Yahl would probably be one of only three good choices. There'd also now been two further Middle Eastern newspaper editorials claiming likely 'Western influence' behind the mosque bombings, one of them also quoting a leading Lebanese cleric. But by far the strongest voice on that – the one with any chance of garnering wide Islamic support – had come from Bahsem-Yahl. And regardless of any rationalisation that could be applied, it had now shifted from the fiction of Tynnan's manuscript to *fact*.

Adel had told himself at the outset that if and when an announcement came from Bahsem-Yahl, it would represent the point of no return. Even if this *was* some well-intentioned black-op to get Abu Khalish to give himself up, once that announcement was made, that moment was gone: it was the last thing Abu Khalish would then do. He'd just sit by and watch with fascination as the battle between the alleged 'Western-led' mosque bombers and Bahsem-Yahl played out. The op's main aim from that point on had failed, and so nothing Adel did could possibly spoil it; at least *one* less pressure. The race then, as in Tynnan's manuscript, was purely to track the mosque bombers and hopefully uncover that they *were* Muslim, *no* Western affiliations, before the cauldron of Islamic wrath Bahsem-Yahl had started boiling spilt over.

Except that Adel was no longer sure how to start. With the last mosque bombing and now a quatrain denoting a change 'for two braces to other, distant cities,' the next mosque targets could be practically anywhere.

And so, as Sam Tynnan had protested only days ago, Adel too now found himself simply a passenger aboard that same manuscript, feeling powerless to do anything as he watched newscasts showing those first seeds of World War Three being sown.

CHAPTER TWENTY-EIGHT

Sam also used distractions to hide away from Bahsem-Yahl's announcement and what it signified; but in his case it was the joys of customising a 1954 Chevy pick-up truck as related by Jem.

'I went for a 355 seven hundred horsepower in the end. Hooked that up to a four hundred trans and threw in a BDS blower and nitrous oxide for extra zip.'

'Right.' Sam hardly had a clue what Jem was talking about, it was a language all of its own. He simply smiled and nodded at what he hoped were the right moments as Jem proudly displayed his labour of love.

'Some aluminium heads and high-rise intakes, a

converter and shift kit, and she was ready to go.' Jem gave the hood a gentle pat and smiled fondly at the engine before closing it again.

Sam had spent half the day watching the news of demonstrations and banner waving in the wake of Bahsem-Yahl's speech with morbid fascination, channel-surfing to catch the latest but then not *wanting* to watch it. He'd noticed Jem fishing on the small lake jetty as he'd looked out from the cabin, so decided to join him. He needed some air.

Two nights back they'd swapped notes on their respective friendships with Mike, and Jem had talked about his time at the cabin as well as his years spent on the Akwesasne reservation. Then they'd discussed fish and best methods to catch them before finally getting round to his Chevy truck.

'My dad used to have one. Would take me into town in it at weekends and park right out front of the ice cream parlour while he bought me my favourite cherry milkshake with double scoop.' There was a soft gleam of nostalgia in Jem's eyes as he said it. He smiled. 'But to the likes of you, it's probably best known as the lonely teenage buck's truck in *American Pie*. I'm heading into Utica to pick up a few things. Wanna ride in with me?'

'Thanks, but better not – especially after the other day. Murphy's Law your friendly policeman would be in town at the same time.'

Jem nodded. But still he didn't ask just why Sam was 'laying low'. Perhaps an unspoken rule, a line never crossed with those on the run.

There were a couple of things Sam was running low on though, so after the guided tour of his Chevy truck Jem offered to pick them up for him.

When Jem left, it was just Sam and the newscasts again. Sam hiding away in a cabin while the world outside fell apart to act three of his manuscript. The cabin fever starting to bite again, *hard*.

Not long after, he hit the Scotch bottle, and after a few stiff ones – he lost count – he ambled out onto the veranda. He leant on its front rail, gently swirling his glass, looking at it pensively contrasted against the lake beyond. The clarity that was once in his life and the dark mire it had become. He stayed there for a while, and as he turned to go back inside he saw the car: a dark-grey Pontiac G6, at a thirty-degree tangent on the back road, partly shielded by the trees. The car's windows were tinted, so he couldn't tell if there was one person inside or a carful.

Trying to look casual, he sauntered inside and sat himself where he had a good view of the road through the front window. It was four full minutes before the Pontiac drifted past, did a three-point turn at the next road fork two hundred yards along, then headed back the way it had come.

Sam was listening to the last of the engine drone

to make sure it had gone when his phone rang. It was Jean-Pierre again. All he needed! And as Jean-Pierre started pushing his soothsaying book plans with renewed vigour, Sam hardly had any resistance left: the unfolding Bahsem-Yahl drama had half-numbed him, half a bottle of Bushmills had done the rest.

'When I first saw that Bahsem-Yahl announcement, I was astounded,' Jean-Pierre said. 'I couldn't think straight for a while afterwards.'

I still can't now, Sam thought; though, from what he sensed was coming, for different reasons. 'I can appreciate.'

'I think we both have to accept that this now has gone far beyond simple coincidence.'

'Yes.' Sam's temples started throbbing, and for a moment he felt dizzy. *Whatever you say*. Sam's thoughts were still on that car.

'This without doubt warrants more in my upcoming book than just the chapter I mentioned the other day. Probably a whole section of its own. This is an incredibly unique situation.'

Unique? 'Yes...I suppose it is.' *Certainly a whole new one to me.*

'And tell me. Did the last mosque bombing also follow that of your manuscript?'

'No, no. It didn't.' Sam swallowed back a belch. 'Though that's the first where it's been different.' Was this how they'd planned it? Wait for Jem to leave, then get Jean-Pierre to phone and distract him while they moved in?

'Aaah – so that quatrain I passed on was correct. Different cities *have* been chosen for the last ones.'

'Yes, it...it appears so.' The room tilted for a second, and Sam leant against a side table to steady himself. He shook his head. Without the drink, he might have seen where Jean-Pierre was headed, decided he wanted to keep that card up his sleeve. It probably didn't matter, but he wasn't lucid enough now to determine that. He tried to listen out for sounds from outside again. *Was that Pontiac returning?*

'I've also been preparing some fresh quatrains – modern-day renderings of Michel's thoughts if he were still prophesising now. And, as I mentioned to you last year, I use *all* the same devices he did then: charts and quadrants, astrolabe and armillary sphere. I'll continue preparing those, but now I'll also review how they might best serve this new situation.'

'I see...yes.' But they'd all but discounted Jean-Pierre from any involvement, hadn't they? Was this his mind finally snapping, or just the drink? Sam cradled his forehead. He wasn't feeling well at all.

'But obviously I'd like to ponder the matter some more. Let's talk again tomorrow.'

'Obviously. *Yes*...let's do that.'

Sam closed his eyes and massaged his throbbing

temples as he hung up. Then, realising where his next belch was heading, he rushed to the bathroom to be sick.

Jean-Pierre had sensed that Sam Tynnan was distracted as he spoke, not really paying attention. Perhaps he hadn't yet adjusted to the situation. So he'd decided to break off with an excuse and he'd pick things up again the next day.

He'd also felt heady with it all, but perhaps with good reason. Because while he'd run through every possible contingency after last speaking to Tynnan, if Bahsem-Yahl *did* take any such stance, he, Jean-Pierre Bourdin, had been the one to predict it and link Bahsem-Yahl to Mabus!

It would not only be a real-life prophecy, as he'd been working towards with fresh quatrains for his next book, but one – *if* events unfolded as Tynnan had depicted in his manuscript – with vast, portentous implications.

Then there was the timing. Vrellait contacting him about the lost code-book and fresh quatrains, involving him in authentication of probably the most vital Nostradamus find in five centuries. Then as the full extent of the odyssey with Sam Tynnan's manuscript was revealed and Bahsem-Yahl's proclamation suddenly became a fateful reality, yet again he found himself centre stage in a vital revelation. Now the icing on the cake: one of those long-lost Nostradamus quatrains had also been proven right.

The planets, luminar transits and quadrants – which he'd spent so many nights exploring for fresh prophetic insight – were all conspiring as if to say: *this is your time!*

His senses literally swam with it, lifted his spirits and put a bounce in his step as he headed off for lunch at Henri's. It was a bright day with a touch of spring warmth in the air, and within minutes he was in his favourite part of Salon: the heart of the old town with its narrow lanes leading to the main clock tower, the *Tour de l'Horloge*. He knew many of the traders in the lanes – the *charcuterie* and *épicerie*, the *boulangerie* where he bought his morning bread and pastries – and today he greeted them more cheerfully than usual.

Jean-Pierre bought a copy of *Le Soir* at a news kiosk, turned off at the clock tower, then sixty yards along paused by the Nostradamus statue. He gave that too a firmer, more reverent nod, and stayed by it a moment longer than usual in contemplation, tilting his head and closing his eyes as he felt the sun on him. *His* time, his moment in the sun.

A trace of his smile still lingered when he arrived at Henri's, opening out *Le Soir* as he took a seat at a pavement table. Twenty yards away the Moussue fountain gently burbled.

He could hardly recall a time when he'd felt so good, so spirited, and even Henri didn't seem as surly as usual when he took his order.

He found the news item he was seeking on page five: a two-column article on Bahsem-Yahl's speech and the aftermath reaction. After reading it, he folded the paper on the table. It confirmed what he'd suspected from watching news reports: the demonstrations would likely get worse, especially if there was another mosque bombing.

He felt a moment's pang of guilt that his spirits might lift at an unfolding calamity; but then if he played his cards wisely with this Sam Tynnan, his role might be vital in *avoiding* that calamity.

He could see it all clearly: two big books at least, newspaper and TV interviews, his status rising to without question the leading Nostradamus expert in France, if not worldwide. He certainly couldn't think of any other who'd been at the centre of such a chain of events.

He had a rare celebratory brandy to finish his lunch at Henri's, then another when he met Corinne for a coffee after work to bring her up to date on everything.

'That's wonderful news, Jean-Pierre...*wonderful*,' she exclaimed, matching his excitement as he poured out the story.

Again her hand reached across to touch his arm.

And, feeling suddenly bold, as if nothing he did could be wrong at that moment, he leant across and kissed her on the forehead. 'And *you're* wonderful too...I've felt that for a while now. I should have told you before.'

There was a frozen moment in which she looked faintly bewildered, and he feared that he might have read the signals wrong, pushed his run of luck too far. But then the soft glow in her eyes told him everything was all right – *more* than all right – and took him to another level entirely.

An hour later when he kissed Corinne goodbye, that fever – a raw, intense excitement and the feeling that all the heavens were smiling on him at once – carried him on a magic carpet into the solitude of the night. Just him alone with the stars.

The first two hours went slowly, only random words, part sentences, nothing cohesive. Barely a line for each hour. Then things started to flow. Over the next three hours, he finished that quatrain and produced two more complete ones.

Then he hit a dead-end again, nothing. But Jean-Pierre had the feeling that something was there: elusive, just out of reach.

He was feeling tired now as well, so forty minutes later he finally called it a day.

The thought awoke him. Snapped his eyes suddenly open like an electric shock. Blinking, adjusting – that first suspended moment between sleep and consciousness – then he leapt out of bed and grabbed a pen and pad from a side table.

The message, quatrain, he'd sensed just out of reach last night, was suddenly there, clear as a bell. And he feared that if he didn't write it down quickly it would go, fade away and slip through his fingers.

He changed only two words before he was happy, felt that it accurately conveyed what had reached him. A tingle ran through him as he read it. Undoubtedly, *his* time.

When Jem came back from Utica, Sam asked him about the dark grey Pontiac.

'Nope.' Jem shook his head. 'Don't know the car. Not among the regulars here, at least.' He shrugged after a second. 'But that ain't to say someone hasn't got a new car since last year, and it's impossible to keep track of all their guests and friends. Also, some people drop by just for a view of the lake now and then. Quick sandwich or a smoke, then off again.'

'Yeah, I suppose.'

'Catch its license plate?'

'No. It was shielded behind the trees.'

Jem nodded. He could tell that Sam was still unsettled. 'Best you stay at my place again tonight. Just in case.'

* * *

'Hi, Namir. How are you? How's the family?'

'*Salaam*, Adel. Well, all well. Good to hear from you. All well with you too, I trust?'

'Yes. Everyone's fine.'

'My, Jibril will be old enough soon to come out in the summer on his own. Nasuh would be glad of the company.'

'Yes. Maybe next year.' His brother Namir's eldest son, Nasuh, was almost the same age as his Jibril, and they'd bonded instantly on past family holidays.

Namir was younger than Adel by only eighteen months, but sometimes that gap had felt like a chasm. Their greeting now was still tense, even after all these years, Adel fearing that one day when enquiring after his health, Namir would retort, '*How do you think I am? You stay in London and break our father's heart. And meanwhile, in covering for you, I have to give up my own hopes and ambitions.*'

Their father's plan had been for Adel to study for two years at London's exalted School of Economics, then return to Dumyat to help him run the business, eventually taking over.

But then Adel had fallen in love: with London, with Tahiya. And besides, at no time had he seen himself as a marble and stone merchant, yet he'd never had the heart to tell his father. The three-thousand mile gap to break that news had made it easier: the coward's route.

Namir's ambition had been to study Islam and become an imam – he was already two years into his studies at the Sultan Hassan Madrassa in Cairo when Adel made that fateful call to their father. And so Namir had to jettison his dreams and take Adel's intended place in the business when the following year their father became ill. Four years later they buried him.

Namir had never hurled that rebuke, though in all the phone calls and summer visits since, Adel had felt it hanging in the air between them. *Guilt*.

Even just from those few years at a madrassa, Namir was one of the most knowledgeable people Adel knew regarding Islam.

He got to the point of his call: the mosque bombings. 'You've probably seen the news about them.'

'Yes, of course. One of them at the El-Qelef Mosque in Alexandria, not far away.'

'Yes. But I wondered if there might be any sort of pattern in them?' Adel gave a quick rundown of the mosques bombed so far.

'Well. Each one appears to be of rising significance within Islam.'

'Yes, OK.' Even if Adel hadn't already known from Tynnan, a few in his section had picked that out. 'But apart from that?'

Namir considered for a moment. 'All of them, apart from the Kalatahn Mosque in Islamabad, are Sunni.

Outside of that, nothing really strikes me.'

'How about any links between the last mosque bombed, the Ras-Salwi Mosque in Jordan, and, say, a mosque like the Al-Jihwa in Muscat, Oman?' The shift from Tynnan's proposed mosque to the one actually bombed.

Brief pause. 'They are both of similar stature within Islam. And, of course, as these rise in importance, there will be less of equivalent rank.'

The seed of an idea ignited in Adel's mind. 'The mosque in Oman. How many would be of similar stature?'

'A dozen, perhaps fifteen.'

Adel went to the next in Tynnan's list. 'What about the Dayahli Mosque in Doha, Qatar? How many there of equivalent rank?'

'Quite a significant mosque. Four minarets, if I recall.' A gentle hum as Namir mulled over his answer. 'Probably no more than eight to ten of similar rank.'

Eight to ten. Not an unwieldy number to arrange extra security for, Adel thought.

'But if you want to pin it down further,' Namir said, 'I know someone you could call: Hanif al-Nabighah. He used to be in my old madrassa, he's an imam now at the Al-Azhar Mosque in Cairo. He'll be able to give you the exact number, along with the name and location of each mosque.'

'Ah, excellent. Thanks.' Adel sensed this was the

closest Namir would ever come to a rebuke: '*This man from my past knows far more than me, all the things, in fact, I'd planned to learn before your own plans reorganised my life for me.*'

Adel took al-Nabighah's contact details and thanked Namir again before he hung up.

He called the number straight away, and within ten minutes he had a list of mosques: nine directly equivalent, and two more which, '*with a benign, fortuitous blessing from Allah,*' could be included.

There was no time to lose. He handed the list to Karam and told him to instruct his team to put out alerts. Then he paused and took stock, tapping one finger by the phone for a moment before making his call to Sam Tynnan.

The call that Sam had been waiting on most had in fact been from 'Emile' in London.

So late the next morning, after touching base with Mike, he was disappointed to get another call instead from Jean-Pierre.

Sam was sober this time, albeit tired – so as Jean-Pierre rolled on with his book plans, Sam was better prepared to handle it. 'How long before it's finished?' Sam asked.

'Four or five months.'

Sam knew the rest: a year to eighteen months publishing timeline, at a push four to five for something topical. If events unfolded as per his manuscript, the last mosque bombing would take place in only ten to fifteen days. This whole drama would be wrapped long before then. But still he should tread carefully.

'There are certain things – because parties I'm in contact with are bound by official secret acts – that I won't be able to divulge. It might also be necessary, because of the sensitive nature, that my name's kept out of it. Perhaps a pseudonym used.'

'I understand.' Jean-Pierre sounded faintly deflated.

'But the main facts can still be used. There's no problem with that. As matters progress, I'm sure it will become clear just what would be wise to reveal or not. Where we might have to be discreet.'

'Yes, of course. I can see the perfect sense in that.'

Sam didn't want to completely stonewall Jean-Pierre. After all, he *had* been the one to pin Bahsem-Yahl to Mabus. Plus the quatrain he'd passed on had proven correct, so he didn't want to discount him as just a madcap Nostradamus prophesier. He might have some other useful input, which, indeed, Jean-Pierre now revealed he did: another fresh quatrain.

Sam wrote it down. 'Thanks for that. I'll pass it on.'

'Whatever else comes up, I'll let you know, of course. Also I'll keep you up to date with my book progress. How it's shaping up.'

'Yes, yes. I'd appreciate it.' He could hardly stop Jean-Pierre in any case from publishing *his* account of events. Meanwhile Sam sensed it was best to keep him sweet, keep the lines of communication open. 'And I'll let you know how everything progresses my end.'

Emile's call had finally come through three hours later.

'I'm sorry I didn't phone you before. Bahsem-Yahl's announcement threw me off balance, yes; I wanted time to adjust to that. But the main reason – with the location shift on the last mosque bombing – was that I no longer had a clear plan of attack with future mosque bombings. I think I finally have that now.' Adel explained his 'equivalent ranking' theory. 'Extra security for eleven mosques should be manageable. I've already put out the alerts.'

'Sounds good. Certainly a hundred per cent better than *no* plan.' Sam was reminded that at each stage Emile appeared to be resembling the main character of *The Prophecy* more and more. Just when it looked like he'd been sidelined, he'd thrust himself centre stage again. *Life mirroring art*. He wondered if he'd ever reveal that phenomenon to Emile. 'And on the same subject, I've received another quatrain from Jean-Pierre he feels might be relevant.'

Adel repeated a couple of words to make sure he'd written it down correctly, then: 'You appreciate this doesn't appear to correlate with the last quatrain we had from Jean-Pierre. In fact, I'm not immediately sure what it *does* mean.'

'I know. What can I say? I'm just the messenger here.'

Adel chuckled lightly. 'You're a bit more than that, Mr Tynnan. But I know what you mean.'

WASHINGTON, DC.

'You remember that film *Three Days of the Condor* with Robert Redford and Max Von Sydow. Where this little CIA department sifts through news cuttings and books, looking for something worrying and subversive which everyone else might have overlooked. Well, that's what we do here. Except half the time you're directed what to look for, and eighty per cent of that searching is now electronic. You might be looking for news reports on Sudanese troop movements, Argentinian elections, a Gaddafi or Putin speech, or a Chechen rebel comment or action. But your job will be to collate all the news reports and distil from that just how worrying that event might or might not be. But the devil's in the

detail. The devil's in the detail. If you see something
that concerns you, no matter how small, don't let
it pass. Because sometimes it's those small, buried
details that end up far more significant than you
might think. And those are also often the ones that
everyone else has overlooked. So here we *do* sweat
the small stuff.'

David Stennell recalled the words of their section
head, Kenny Verbeck, when he'd first transferred from
another NSA department five years ago. It wasn't hard
to remember, because Verbeck still used variations of
that for new recruits; and if they were joining Stennell's
team, he'd sit in on those initial briefings to throw in
his two cents.

The wording of Department 101's request had
nagged at him, so finally he'd pulled the item back
on screen. Was he reading too much into it? *Small
stuff*. Perhaps if he hadn't viewed it alongside all the
others it wouldn't have stood out: '*Please inform of
the reaction from the Middle East and Arab press to
the recent mosque bombings. Particularly interested
also in reactions, if any, from the area's political
leaders and hard-line clerics such as Bahsem-
Yahl.*'

All other parties and departments had just made
general requests, no specific names. Possibly 101 had a
particular interest in Bahsem-Yahl, that's why. He did a
quick keyword search to see how many 101 documents

Bahsem-Yahl's name featured in: forty-seven. He ran comparison searches with equivalent-sized sectors in the CIA, Homeland Security and his parent NSA: twenty-six, nine and twenty-one respectively.

OK, so they did have more of an interest in Bahsem-Yahl than most. The question now was: why?

CHAPTER TWENTY-NINE

It took hearing his son's voice to finally break Sam.

He'd told his father, Ross, about Lorrena's death two days ago, but when he'd tried Kate's number it had gone through to voicemail. Late evening when her return call came, she apologised that she'd been away on location.

'I'm sorry, Sam...so *sorry*.' Marked pause, then: 'How are you coping?'

'Don't know. Still mostly in shock, trying to come to terms with it.' He sighed heavily. 'Don't think it's fully hit me yet.' One way of explaining, he supposed, why he came across as numbed and shell-shocked rather than a blubbering emotional wreck. 'Is Ashley there?'

'Yeah…sure,' she said after a second. She was still gathering her thoughts after the shocking news. 'But give me a minute with him, will you? You probably don't want to go through saying that all again.'

'OK, yeah. Thanks.' A more poignant *thanks* than he'd like to admit. Kate could lend the right tone and emotional gravitas that right now wasn't in Sam's heart to muster. All he'd manage was another numbed, distant, still-in-shock account.

He closed his eyes as he heard her break the news gently to their son. Ashley's voice was disbelieving, a cracked plea to it – though Sam couldn't hear the words.

But when Ashley came on the line a minute later, his tone was calmer. Perhaps Kate had coached him: '*When you talk to your father, try and be calm – he's having enough trouble dealing with this as it is.*'

'So sorry to hear that, Dad.' There was a pause as he weighed up what other words might be considered 'adult' and non-hysterical. 'You really liked Lorrena, didn't you?'

'Yeah…yeah. I did.'

'Me too.'

An awkward silence settled, both of them trying to be low-key about what had happened; though for different reasons, Sam thought.

'Are you going to be OK, Dad?'

He sighed. 'I don't know...I suppose so.' And suddenly it hit him. Not what he had to avoid saying because of Lorrena – '*I haven't come to terms with what she'd been a part of myself, let alone explaining to anyone else...that's why I have no clue how to emote her death*' – but because of everything else he was holding back from his son: '*I'm in danger and have been for a while. I'm hiding away right now, and have no idea when I'll be able to come out of hiding; or, in fact, if I ever will make it out of this mess and be able to see you again.*'

As if the three thousand-mile gap wasn't enough, he was adding another million miles with all the things he wasn't able to say. It was perhaps the last time he would speak to his son, yet he daren't give that away.

And as he felt the terrible crushing weight of those emotions press in on him, finally the tears came.

'Are you sure you're OK, Dad?'

He swallowed hard against the ton weight in his chest as he bit the tears back. 'Yeah, I'll be OK. I'm fine.' Ironic, he thought: it had taken the emotional weight of everything else going on to finally hit the right emotional note over Lorrena.

He wanted desperately to say something to Ashley, even if it was just one last 'I love you', or 'You take care now'. But that might unnecessarily alarm the boy, or, worse still, he'd tell Kate and she'd phone back with twenty questions. So in the end he just kept it to a simple, 'Goodbye. Catch you later.'

SANA'A, YEMEN.

They chose 4.30 a.m. for the time of their assault. Not only because it was apparently when the body was at its lowest ebb – but because it was six and a half hours into the guards' shift, who'd come on duty at 10 p.m. They'd be tired, attention starting to wane, already half an eye on their shift's end in ninety minutes.

There were six guards assigned to the al-Dahia Mosque in Sana'a, Yemen. Four at each corner sentry post, two permanently patrolling the mosque's perimeter, floodlit as brightly as a football stadium.

Their own assault team had been increased to six to compensate, but still they needed to milk every possible advantage.

They'd broken into a storage warehouse opposite from which to launch their attack, having cased it the previous day and immobilised the alarm.

Sacks of grain, flour, rice and spices were stacked in racks, with not much space in between: just enough for the two men to squat shoulder by shoulder as they aimed their stun grenade launchers through one of three front warehouse windows.

They waited for the signal from their team leader, Faraj. Both had to be fired at precisely the same time at each front corner sentry point.

Faraj took one last check of the mosque front for anything out of place, then lifted one hand. They launched, and barely had the grenades landed before their two C4 men were rushing across the road wearing percussion-guard helmets.

As the two front-corner guards were brought to their knees by the stun grenades, they set their charges either side of the mosque's central entrance. The guards would be outside of the arc of the explosions, so there was no need to drag them clear.

The rear and perimeter-patrolling guards had been alerted by the first two bangs and were running towards the commotion when two more sharp flashes and bangs from the stun charges brought them to a halt.

Faraj surveyed the scene. Everything was going well.

Until the arrival – no sirens or warning – of three Land Cruisers full of COS military police. And everything suddenly changed.

The mosque entrance bombs went off then, and Faraj cringed as he watched the unfolding drama – everything suddenly diffused through a fine mist of stone dust.

Three stun grenades fired in quick succession halted

almost half the police in their tracks, but the rest, ten-men strong, were still advancing.

One of the C4 team managed to get clear and would join them at the warehouse rear, but the other caught a bullet halfway across the road, and fell. He rolled over and drew and pointed his gun at his two closest assailants, catching two more bullets in the stomach before it fell from his grip.

Faraj nodded solemnly to Dhakir.

Dhakir aimed his rifle at their fallen colleague's head, but as he squeezed off the shot one of the policemen got in between. Through Dhakir's sights the policeman's left thigh erupted as he crumpled.

He reloaded, but then two more policemen, running in their direction, blocked his line of fire.

Faraj was shouting and waving frantically. '*Yalla!* Let's go...*let's go!*'

The police had worked out where they were firing from and were rapidly approaching, two of their return shots ricocheting off the window edge and a side wall. As it was, they might have left it too late to escape through the back.

The news from Sana'a set the London operations room ablaze.

A vibrant, expectant buzz that Adel hadn't seen for a while. Or perhaps it was simply the contrast with the lull on other fronts: still nothing in from Akram's new photo identity put out on APB, and Cunningham's Mehri-language trace list had stalled at six hundred and twelve names, with chances remote of further narrowing the list.

An expectant, nail-biting wait – in the end it was almost four hours of Adel pacing anxiously, trying to absorb himself with other work, grabbing the phone as soon as it rang – before the call he was waiting for finally came through.

'I'm sorry, Adel. He didn't make it.' Masrur at TAME15 in Riyadh had promised to phone as soon as he had news on the mosque bomber from his Sana'a hospital contact. 'They lost him on the operating table only minutes ago.'

Adel closed his eyes momentarily. So they were left with a dead rather than live suspect again. Although this time there was one important difference.

'But facially he's fine, unmarked, you say?'

'Yes, perfect. The wounds were to the stomach and one leg.'

'One saving grace, I suppose.' Adel requested that the suspect be cleaned and photographed. 'And get those photos through to me as soon as possible so we can run matches. Along with anything else from the scene which might seem worthwhile.'

'My police contact mentioned stun grenade types they hadn't seen before. The manufacturer, Clayton Industries, they knew – but the model number markings were new to them.'

'Mmm. Could be something. Let me have that model number, and get the grenade casings photographed too if you think it will help.'

The stun grenade model number came through within half an hour; the mosque bomber photos he had to wait for over four hours.

Adel recalled a photo of Che Guevara on a slab he'd seen while at college, taken by Bolivian police to prove that the notorious revolutionary was, without question, dead. He'd looked like the mosque bomber did now, facial muscles collapsed, two shades whiter. It was not the best condition for a mugshot match but at least it was *something* to work from. Small mercies.

And his 'equivalent mosque' gambit had paid off, if only partially. Twenty seconds earlier, and they might have captured more of the bombers with hopefully one still alive. Most importantly the bombers would now have the message that they were on to them – their shifting venue plans had been foiled.

But one thing above all else had been proven: there was obviously no internal leak. At least not within his immediate surroundings. Karam's team had liaised directly with each police force, with those in turn told to keep the alert secure. There'd been no general network alerts.

The dead mosque bomber's photo *was* put out on a wider network – there was little secret, any minute his death would be on news networks – including all TAME offices as well as GCHQ and NSA. The stun-grenade model number Adel passed solely to GCHQ's Paul Cunningham to share with his NSA counterpart.

The first feedback came at 9.18 a.m. the next morning: Paul Cunningham with news on the stun grenades.

'We had some records here, but I wanted to get input from the States too – just to be sure. Belt and braces. They sent me a message overnight. Clayton Industries is a well-known US small-munitions manufacturer, but this stun grenade model was only released two months ago. It's far from in general use with US forces, let alone NATO or elsewhere. Right now it has trial-use status with four US Army and two Marine combat units, and three city SWATs.' Cunningham ran through them by name, but none of them prompted any helpful links with Adel.

'I suppose a terrorist group getting hold of them might seem unlikely then?'

'Given the short time frame and limited distribution, yes. But not *totally* out of the question. It's been known for even prototypes and pre-sale samples to have been stolen or go "missing", ending up in the wrong hands.'

'OK. Read you.' The chances were slim. 'Keep this under your hat for now, Paul. With Bahsem-Yahl shouting about US-linked involvement, the last thing we want to do is let loose this little hot potato.' Adel sighed. 'Meanwhile I'll work out how to handle the Yemeni police when they come back to me.'

Adel rang off. Either he'd tell them they were still checking or that distribution network was wider than it was. Adel noticed his hand as he pulled it back from the phone. It was shaking.

Since the news from Sana'a, he'd been living on raw adrenaline, too many coffees and too little sleep. His nerves were shot. Last night, tossing and turning to get to sleep, with every possible outcome spinning through his mind, Tahiya had asked again if there was something troubling him he wanted to share. And again he'd fobbed her off, told her it was OK, it would sort itself out.

Alone. Holding things back from Tahiya, holding things back from his colleagues. And it had reached a new level with them. While he could admit he was keen to bury any US links because of Bahsem-Yahl's speech, he had to be careful not to voice that too strongly. Otherwise they might suspect that something deeper was troubling him: that he already knew how it might play out from Tynnan's doomsday scenario.

The tension in the operations room intensified as the day progressed, or perhaps it was just him. Adel toyed with the idea of having lunch out, but he didn't want to spend a whole hour in a restaurant and possibly miss something. Instead he grabbed a chicken salsa wrap at the local deli and went for a walk.

The Embankment was only eighty yards away. He sat on a bench as he ate, idly watching the tugs and tourist launches sail past. But as his gaze drifted east he could see St Paul's in the distance and was reminded of meeting Omari by the riverside at The Anchor. *Place four*. He closed his eyes for a moment as he chewed the last couple of mouthfuls and swallowed. *Too many ghosts.*

He threw his sandwich packaging in the nearest bin and headed back to the office.

CEBU ISLAND, PHILIPPINES.

When the call came through, Abu Khalish was in the back of a taxi heading out of Cebu City towards his newly rented villa in Cordova Reef. The hustle and bustle thinned on the city outskirts, fewer brightly coloured jeepneys and pedicabs jousting and weaving to the rhythm of intermittent beeps.

He pondered whether to take the call for a moment: no doubt Al Hakam would try again later when he was at the villa. But with his move, he hadn't yet had a chance to speak to him – all he'd got the past thirty-six hours had been messages. He was keen to speak to him directly.

'I missed you the last few calls,' Al Hakam said. 'You got my messages?'

'*Si, si.* I was travelling yesterday.' The most he would impart, even to Al Hakam. 'I understand that second stock option has now also been taken care of?'

'Yes...it went smoothly as well, like the first. No problems.'

'That's good.'

'It's been buried in a portfolio, so will remain private. Not easily uncovered.'

'*De acuerdo*. As always, I leave such details in your capable hands.'

At the other end, Al Hakam honed in on every nuance and inflection. Was there any hint that Khalish might be suspicious? He'd added the last in case Khalish had checked London newspapers online and seen no record of Akram Ghafur's death; a missing person would take longer to surface and might not even make the papers.

'And, as always, your trust is appreciated. And in turn repaid.' Three years now he'd been Khalish's main clean-up man ensuring every last trace was buried. But he knew that if his screw-up with Akram came to light, that status would swiftly disappear. As with Youssef, the man who'd recruited the Milan bombers and had been the last on Al Hakam's list; he'd walk into his apartment one day to find everything gone and a timer flashing red on his ceiling.

Khalish could sense that Al Hakam was anxious about something, or perhaps was simply waiting for a return pat on the head. He gave it. 'Yes, you did well. We'll speak again soon.' He had more pressing things on his mind now than Al Hakam's sensitivities.

Bahsem-Yahl's announcement had taken the main pressure off. After all, no reason why he should give himself up with the suggestion now that the West was behind the mosque bombings. But it looked unlikely that his own contacts had been much influence there; someone else had pulled the main strings.

He glanced out thoughtfully across the harbour waters as his taxi crossed the bridge towards Mactan Island. There was a cabin cruiser returning to a city marina, and two fishing junks heading out in the dusk light for night fishing. *Calm. Order.* A stark contrast to the mayhem of the city only a mile away.

He'd always thought he was the main player in that respect; the key puppet master controlling where and when there was order or mayhem. But as he thought about the turn events had taken with Bahsem-Yahl and the mosque bombers, he suddenly realised there was another puppet master in the game. One with an even grander plan in mind.

* * *

Malik swivelled in his seat and hit Adel with the news as he walked in.

'They've got a match on that photo, boss. Iraqi national by the name of Rashad Nasrahi. Came in from the NSA just ten minutes ago.'

'Matched from their terrorist database?'

'No. They had him on their Iraqi forces list. Nasrahi joined the post-coalition Iraqi police two years ago and left five months back. There's nothing on their records for what he's been up to since.'

Adel's spirits, lifted by the initial news, dipped again. 'Sunni or Shiite?'

'Shiite.'

Adel nodded as he sat at his desk. *Iraqi. Shiite.* At least *one* plus. Shiite would score strong favour with Bahsem-Yahl due to Iran's eagerness to see rising Shiite influence in Iraq. And by no means were all the new Iraqi forces seen as American lackeys. Many had joined purely for the money, but Shiites in particular to redress the jackboot minority Sunni rule they'd been under for so long. Still, for now it might be best to keep Nasrahi's spell with the Iraqi police under wraps. More buried secrets.

Adel spent a few minutes reading the NSA data on Nasrahi, then started his calls. First up was the NSA contact name on Nasrahi's file, Giles Schofield, to inform him that Nasrahi's Iraqi police details should be kept strictly 'eyes only'. Then he phoned and asked

Masrur to confirm with the Sana'a morgue the file's identification details. Height: 184 cm. Weight: 91 kilos. Scar under right-hand side of chin.

Masrur's return call came eighty minutes later. Match on the height and chin scar. 'Weight two kilos under.'

Close enough. 'Thanks, Masrur.'

Adel needed another coffee. His ninth or tenth of the day, he'd lost count. And he was halfway through sipping it, mulling over the wording of an official notice about Nasrahi and what should be included – or, more importantly, left out – when he saw the alert notice on his screen.

He opened it, and felt his stomach sink as he read. He grabbed the phone.

The day after meeting Tynnan, he'd thought again about Washington. Apart from the danger of digging, Washington was the sort of name that would bring up a million cross references. He wouldn't find anything. But Sam Tynnan could be a different matter, as long as he searched discreetly. He'd gone through a central GCHQ scrambled feed which wouldn't even link back to his department, let alone himself. It could be anyone in the MI5, MI6, GCHQ or police network. *Nothing.* Obviously they'd used a generic- or code-name – writer, scribe, author – or maybe a number. Or Tynnan was simply imagining it all. But Adel had left a request on the system to be alerted if anything *did* come up. And now it had, in the worst possible way.

He chewed at his lip as the phone started ringing, praying that Tynnan answered. If he didn't, it looked like game, set and match to Washington before they'd even got into their stride.

CHAPTER THIRTY

Sam ran full pelt round the lakeside to Jem's cabin, a light rain cool on his face, Adel's frantic words still spinning in his head: 'If you're at any of the following addresses, get out of there now!'

The first had been his home address, the second Kate's in Laurel Canyon, the third and fourth Mike's home and cabin, then Vince Corcoran's Lakeville house and three addresses he didn't recognise. Sam presumed they were other houses of Corcoran's, or perhaps Robby Maschek's.

'Christ's sake, what's happened?' Sam demanded. With still that nagging doubt that Emile might be in on it with them, Sam didn't let on where he was.

'A general APB has gone out stateside just a minute ago. "Accomplice in an act of terrorism. Armed and possibly dangerous. Approach with caution." One consolation, at least, is that they don't know *exactly* where you are. That's why they've put out "all known addresses" to cover the bases. But that's not going to be much help when in two minutes the police bang your door down! So, like I say, if you're at any of those – get out now! *Now!*'

Sam rang Jem's bell, knocked, rang again, and seconds later a bewildered Jem answered.

Gasping like a landed fish, Sam shared only the bare bones: APB just put out, got to get away, 'Like *now*!' It took only forty seconds for Jem to grab jacket, keys and a couple of things from a drawer, and they were wheel-spinning mud and gravel as his Chevy truck headed out on the cabin's only access road.

The main road was three hundred yards away, then another seven miles to Highway 90. Sam's heart was in his mouth. If they were confronted by squad cars on the access road, they'd be blocked in.

They made it to the main road, but after a short while on it Sam started to feel anxious again. The road was quiet with little passing traffic. He felt conspicuous, vulnerable. Any police cars passing en route to the cabin couldn't miss them.

Only two cars and a truck passed over the next four miles, and Sam had started counting the seconds to reaching the highway when he heard the siren. He wasn't sure whether to duck down or turn his head. In the end he turned away, as if he was talking to Jem.

'Just an ambulance,' Jem announced as it became clearer. It swept past them heading towards Westernville. Sam released his caught breath.

As they turned onto Highway 90, Sam phoned Mike. They needed a plan of where to head. Some direction.

Sam gave Mike the unedited version, aware of Jem glancing at him as he said, 'Accomplice in an act of terrorism.'

Mike sucked in his breath. '*Jesus*. Looks like they finally tired of playing with you. Or perhaps it just took them this time to work out your contacts and possible hideouts. Where are you now?'

'On Highway 90 heading east, about eight miles from Utica.'

There was a moment's deliberation at Mike's end. 'The only person I know who could help with this sort of situation is Vince. He's the only one with a bunch of safe houses up his sleeve they won't find. And even if they *do* get lucky, he's got another dozen to pull out his sleeve. Let me call him.'

'Sounds like an option.' As if he had any choice. 'But Boston? Long gauntlet to run to get there.'

'I know. Maybe he'll have somewhere closer. Or, at least to give you some early back-up and cover, Barry and Phil could meet up with you halfway somewhere: Albany or Hudson.'

Jem cut in. 'I can only go as far as Little Falls, max. I've got to get back for something.'

'You hear that?' Sam repeated it to Mike anyway.

'Yeah, *yeah*. OK. Let me call Vince and—' Mike broke off then, and even from Sam's end he could hear the heavy door-banging which had distracted him: his wife Cathy's voice questioning, defensive, then a couple of sharp, insistent male voices. 'Gotta go! *Problems*.'

The line went dead.

It looked like the police had already arrived at his door.

Nadeem Shoaib busily tended her patients on the ward. Only twenty-three, her family had originally hailed from Lahore, though she was born and bred British and so was more familiar with the streets of Limehouse, Hounslow and Hammersmith than her native Pakistan.

She was Sunni Muslim from her parents although far from adherent, and every spare bit of her nurse's pay was spent on holidays to Ibiza or Faliraki. My goodness, how her parents would blush if they knew half the things she got up to.

But Nadeem always felt she gained enough favour points to compensate in Allah's eyes because of her work, her daily caring for people. She felt she had a true gift.

Genuinely unaware of her beauty, with doe eyes the shade of pale copper and black hair almost to her waist, she didn't realise that her sweet face and warm, disarming smile did half the job right there. Purely her presence at their bedside lifted patients' spirits, made them feel better.

Her favourite patients, though she'd never tell anyone, were the ones 'on the brink'. Those who'd hovered close to death or for whom it was still a close call; those who might not have much time left. She gave them her utmost attention, as if purely through her caring and warmth, she could convince them to hang on to life. And if she failed, and sometimes she had shed bitter tears over those failures, at least she'd know she'd done her best and made their last days comfortable; given them a sense of being cared for, *loved*.

Not that this one brought in the night before last would notice. He was still on oxygen and intravenous, and apart from a few grunts and splutters, he'd been out of it since. Apparently they'd lost him for almost thirty seconds on the operating table and it was still touch and go now.

An 'on the brink' case if ever there was one. But there was another reason she paid him special attention. He was a Libyan national according to his records, but with that thick beard and moustache, he reminded her of her favourite uncle in Lahore.

As he was still listed as 'critical', he had his own private annexe room at the end of the general ward. He coughed and she leant across to do her checks. It was the same routine every time: check heart rate and blood pressure, lift the oxygen pipe and clear his airway, then wipe away any mucus that had run onto his beard.

Except that this time as she lifted the pipe it felt stuck, a small part of his beard lifting with it. She put it back and lifted again, in case it had been an optical illusion. It did the same.

She tentatively pulled at the area of lifted beard. More of it pulled away. She headed to the end of the ward to get her matron.

Access Denied. Access Denied. Access Restricted to Level 8.

Of the forty-seven Bahsem-Yahl files, thirty-six *Denied*, five *Level 8*, three *General Access*; leaving only three that Stennell was able to open.

Nothing juicy. Just general reports from post-revolution until now which looked like they'd been cobbled together from the *CIA Factbook* and *Wiki* by a couple of undergrads.

Their department had keyword-checking access across all files, regardless of the security level, so they could determine which departments had interest in which subjects – not only to supply them with updates on said subject, but for cross-referencing with other departments. But opening and reading the full files was another matter.

Stennell stroked his chin. He'd seen a fair few level 6 and 7 restrictions in his time, but 8 was rarer; only CIA, NSA and State Department hierarchy. He ran a check to see if other departments outside of 101 had the same level of blockage with Bahsem-Yahl files. fifty-four per cent restricted access, but most were levels 4 and 5, a handful level 6 and 7, one 8. More in line with normal ratios.

He reached for his phone and buzzed Kenny Verbeck's line. He'd gone as far as he could with it. Perhaps at Verbeck's level of clearance he'd be able to open more files and see what was going on.

Twenty-five minutes later Mike called back. It *had* been the police at his door.

'They left ten minutes ago. I gave them a quick tour of the house to satisfy them you weren't hiding in any cupboards or under a bed – otherwise they might have hung around. But I also wanted to have a word with Vince before calling back.'

'Any luck?' Sam asked.

'Yeah, all arranged. Vince had them there too, but they never got further than the entrance gate. Sent Barry and a couple of the guys down to get rid of them: "The guy you're looking for ain't here! Now if you wanna take it further, you know what to do. Be good boys and go get warrants. And remember to bring torches, because Vince ain't turning the fuckin' lights on for yer."'

Sam laughed.

Mike took a fresh breath. 'Now the plan is for Barry and Phil to meet up with you, and the best place *would* be Albany. But if Jem can only make it to Little Falls, you're going to have to hang on longer so that—'

'It's OK,' Sam cut in. 'Jem's going to hire a car for me there, *his* licence, so I can continue on.' In the wait for Mike's call they'd worked out the details. 'With a terrorist APB out, driving on someone else's hire details is the least of my worries.'

'OK.' Mike ran through the arrangements. Barry and Phil would meet him at Broadway Joe's bar on Albany's Pearl Street. 'Pool tables, sports screens, usually very busy. Nobody will pay you much attention. But bury yourself at the back just in case. You'll get there as much as thirty or forty minutes before them, but just hang on. They'll be there.'

'Never been there, but I know where it is. Thanks, Mike.'

'No problems. And Sam?' But as Sam said *yeah?* Mike paused a second, as if it might come across as too maudlin or press home Sam's nightmare situation, when a reminder was the last thing he needed. 'Good luck.'

Jem glanced across a couple of times after he hung up. Sam had sensed something was on Jem's mind earlier, and now he'd said that dreaded word again: *terrorist*. Though it was a minute more before Jem got round to saying anything.

'Look, Sam. I don't mean to pry in your business. And any friend of Mike's and Vince's is a friend of mine and all that. But I want to tell you – I don't hold no truck with people who fly planes into buildings and plant bombs in cafés and malls. If my blood brothers on my father's side did that because of every past land dispute and injustice, there wouldn't be much of this fine nation left.'

'I doubt if Mike would have anything to do with me either, if that was the case. No worries. The closest I've come to that is writing a book about terrorists. Some people have been using that in ways they shouldn't, and now they want me out the way to bury what they've done. It's a long story.'

'I get it.' Jem nodded, risking a tentative smile. 'And if you tell me, then you'd have to kill me.'

Jem confessed that the reason he had to get back was because his daughter was coming over to the cabin. She was thirteen now and he only saw her once a week.

So they had one thing in common, Sam considered: being part-time fathers. In turn he told Jem about Ashley living with his ex-wife on the West Coast. 'I'd love to see him more, but what can you do?'

There was a conversational lull then. Perhaps because they'd both started thinking about their kids. After a minute, Jem turned on the radio. It was an easy-listening station and the Bellamy Brothers' 'Let your Love Flow' was playing.

There wasn't much else to say. They were two part-time fathers: one with a chequered petty-criminal past who spent most of his days fishing, the other with a terrorist APB hanging over his head and his days numbered. And with that, more poignantly for Sam, the reminder of when, or *if*, he'd see Ashley again.

With the radio on, they didn't hear the sirens at first. It had been forty miles since the ambulance siren and they'd become complacent.

Jem turned down the radio, and they were all too clear, moving rapidly closer. Sam felt his neck tense up as he stared stonily ahead.

Jem glanced in his mirror. 'Police cars this time. Two of them. Sixty yards. Forty. Hanging on our tail now.'

Sam closed his eyes, a shudder running up his spine.

They'd obviously worked out that Jem was one of the only people at the cabins this time of year, then got his registration and found him on the highway; not too difficult, it was the main route south-east to Boston and New York. They hadn't got that far, Sam thought ruefully: less than fifty miles. But then what had he expected with half the police of NY State looking for him?

'They're still hanging there,' Jem said. 'Looks like they want us to pull over. What do you want me to do?'

'What do you mean, want to do?' Sam arched an eyebrow. 'Doesn't look like we have much choice.' It all ended here, he thought, his stomach sinking. Prison, Guantanamo Bay, or far worse once he was in Washington's clutches: dumped at the bottom of a lake alongside Lorrena.

But Jem was smiling slyly, one finger hovering by a switch below the dashboard. 'Well, that's where you're wrong. One thing I learnt from running contraband on the Akwesasne. Always have something extra under the hood for when you need it. Flick of this switch and the blower and nitrous oxide kick in. In no time we'll have left them behind for dust.'

'I don't know.' The sound of the sirens smothered them, cramping Sam's thoughts. All options seemed hopeless. 'Now they're onto us, they'll just radio ahead. What will we gain? Twenty, thirty minutes at most.'

Jem shrugged. 'Or we might just lose 'em. It's your call, Sam. Not my butt on the line. Pull over now and let them take you, or flick the switch and gain some time or possibly even get away?'

CHAPTER THIRTY-ONE

The streets of London flashed by Adel's taxi window as he headed to Hammersmith.

From when the ward matron observed Akram's fake beard, it took them only twenty minutes to piece everything together. First they looked in his holdall – where they'd found his passport for his identity – for any clues. When they opened an envelope and saw the thick wad of cash inside, they checked back through the missing persons and police notices regularly received and this time spotted the bulletin they'd missed before.

The hospital secretary, Michael Grierley, apologised

for that earlier oversight as he escorted Adel towards the room.

'The first person who checked on the system unfortunately didn't make the match. Patients are listed by name only, and they don't have sight of people on the wards. We had the patient listed as Abdul Radwan, not the Akram Ghafur on your alert. Then with the irregularity with his beard, we checked back and saw the note: "*possibly using an alias*". Lucky we did.' Grierley beamed broadly, as if taking personal credit for that last due diligence.

Adel was hardly listening, all his focus was just on one thing.

Adel sucked in his breath as Grierley opened the door at the end of the ward. There was no doubt that it *was* Akram, but the sight of him, his condition, hit hard. He was as pale as death and surrounded by tubes monitoring and feeding him. Looking at the man in front of him, Adel could see that the hope of him pulling through was slim.

Sam tried to steady his hand as he sipped at his beer.

As Mike had said, the bar was busy, and nobody was paying him much attention. But Sam was still shaky from their earlier close encounter.

Jem had flicked the switch as the first car swung out to overtake. 'Looks like they're going for a one-front, one-back jam-in!'

Along with a throatier engine roar, Sam felt the surge as the nitrous oxide blower kicked in. But then Jem saw the second car swing out to overtake – it looked like they weren't pursuing them after all. Just as quickly, Jem flicked the switch off.

The police cars passed and were a hundred yards ahead of them before Jem relaxed. They'd obviously simply been waiting for a gap in the oncoming traffic to pass them.

Sam had been on edge since the very beginning of this nightmare ordeal, but the squad cars on their tail had pushed it to a new level. Perhaps it was all finally hitting him now: an APB out with half the state's police hunting him down. There was nowhere left to run. No more time to buy. It all ended here, *now*.

He brought his glass up with both hands to steady it, gently closing his eyes as he sipped. Oh *God*. As he'd waited round the corner for Jem to get his rental car his nerves had started jumping again, then hit fever pitch as he'd parked in the multi-storey two blocks away and heard sirens nearby. He'd sat stock-still, breath frozen for a moment before he finally heard them fade away into the distance.

That tremble was still there as he'd walked into the bar, and it occurred to him that after his solitude in the cabin, he hadn't been amongst crowds for a while. His mouth was dry as he'd ordered, each glance that lingered for a second making his heart leap. The bar crowd was two hundred strong or more. What were the odds of a policeman amongst them who'd seen the APB photo? Maybe meeting Barry and Phil here hadn't been such a good idea.

Sam glanced at his watch: twenty to thirty minutes more to wait. He took another slug of beer.

At least in the last five minutes he'd become more invisible to people in the bar, sunk more into the background. It was a dedicated sports bar and a local ice hockey game had come on, displaying on most of the thirty-five screens in the bar, with the remainder carrying highlights of recent NFL matches or CNN and WNBC local news.

Sam was happy just to sit back and watch the screens ahead with the hockey game. He'd seen enough news these past days and political-pundit analyses of where all this riot mayhem might lead, when he already half-knew.

The bar crowd became steadily louder, jeering and shouting with the ebb and flow of the game. And Sam suddenly realised that the sounds of the city beyond had been drowned out. If police cars, sirens wailing, pulled up right in front to come and get him, he wouldn't be able to hear them. He stole another anxious glance at his watch.

On the TV screens, a fight broke out between two players, the bar crowd's jeers and shouts rising as more players jumped in and it became a free-for-all.

But one screen tuned to news was showing the latest Arab street riots.

A crowd were pulling and tugging at an American flag, one man finally winning the day and stamping on the now torn flag before setting it alight to the shouts of the others, the noise from the bar crowd for a moment seeming to match their rising chants: *Allahu akbar...Allahu akbar. The desecrators of Islam shall die...die!* Stones were thrown at cars as they surged past, a rock smashing the windscreen of one, a Molotov cocktail hitting another, setting it alight.

Sam looked away, suddenly concerned that someone might pick up on his agitation at the on-screen riots. The bar crowd were all still staring towards the game on screen, jeers subsiding as the referee broke up the fight. Although as Sam cast his eyes over the crowd, he noticed that one man *was* staring at him: the barman who'd served him earlier. The man quickly averted his eyes as Sam met his gaze, but just before he'd brought his attention back to the draught he was pulling, Sam saw his eyes shift to one of the TV screens suspended from the ceiling.

Sam couldn't see that screen from where he was, its back was to him. Some action on the hockey game, or something else? Sam leant forward and looked at the only other news screen in his view: CNN. *Discussion on that week's Dow Jones ups and downs.*

The barman took the money for the beer, but instead

of serving the next customer he headed to the end of the bar and through an open arch to the staff area. Just before he disappeared from view, he glanced again towards Sam, as if making sure he was still there. Sam knew then that something was wrong. *Very* wrong. What *was* on that screen?

He got up hurriedly, leaving half his beer on the table, and headed towards a slot machine to the left of the bar. From there, he could see what was on that screen; if nothing, just the hockey game or CNN, he could return to his table and continue waiting for Barry and Phil. If not, he'd already be halfway towards the door and out.

His legs felt unsteady as he moved through the crowds, his pulse a rapid drumbeat at his temples.

And as that screen finally came into view, it all fell into place: it was a WNBC local news bulletin, and the clip they were now showing was about a warehouse fire in Rochester – but obviously a moment before *he'd* been on screen. They'd put his APB photo out to local news networks!

Sam had that sense of eyes on him again, and pulled his gaze away from the screen. Through the open arch at the end of the bar, the barman was looking anxiously his way as he spoke on the phone. And another man at the bar Sam had just passed now did a double take.

Oh, *Jesus*. Sam felt the ground fall away. Breathless,

heart pounding heavier with each stride, he headed swiftly towards the bar exit.

The double doors and the crowds in between tilted and swayed in his vision for a moment. His legs threatened to buckle and he felt suddenly dizzy, fearing he wouldn't make it even that far. He'd faint and crumple before he reached them, would awake to see policemen reaching hands down to lift him to his feet.

More eyes were on him now. But perhaps that was because his gaze was fixed intently on the exit as he strode like a linebacker on a power-walk, ready to flatten anyone who dared get in his way.

He burst through the doors into the street. It was crisp outside, but it did little to clear his head; the hum and buzz of the bar stayed with him, made him feel hot and pressured. Four people outside the bar were having a smoke break and Sam hustled quickly past them, checking over his shoulder after ten paces to make sure nobody was following him from the bar. Then again after fifteen: still nobody.

But then he heard a police siren and his heart leapt into his mouth. It was *close*, no more than a hundred yards away. He glanced over his shoulder to see a squad car turn in from a side street behind him. He fixed his eyes straight ahead again: *Don't look back any more. And don't, whatever you do, start running. They'll know then something's wrong!*

The siren moved closer, *closer* and it took all of Sam's will not to break into a run. He kept his footsteps steady, despite his pulse doing double time to their tread. Finally the siren stopped, about thirty yards behind him. Still he kept his pace steady. Don't look back...*don't look back*. But with the long, expectant silence and only the clip of his step on the pavement, the tick-tick of the squad car's idling engine, and now a murmur of voices, Sam sensed that something was wrong.

His resolve finally broke as he looked back and saw the barman talking with the police through their open window. And as the barman lifted a hand and pointed towards him, Sam knew then that his earlier fear had been right. It did all end here, *now*.

WASHINGTON, DC..

Kenny Verbeck leant back from the screen and scratched at his chin. Dave Stennell sat the other side of his desk watching his superior's reaction as he took in the information Stennell had found.

Verbeck was in his late fifties and dome-smooth bald, his sour bulldog features belying his sharp wit. An NSA veteran dating back to Reagan's doomed 'Star Wars' policy, Verbeck felt he'd proudly earned every follicle lost from each drama since.

And now one of his staff had dropped a possible fresh drama in his lap. Verbeck had only been able to open four more 101 files. Three of those hadn't shed much light but the fourth had been an entirely different matter, more worrying. Still it was just hints and shadow phrases – the language of diplomacy – nothing concrete. But Verbeck knew that if he went higher with it, he wouldn't get anywhere; worse still, the hatches might all quickly batten down and the files would disappear.

'OK, this is how it will go down. An hour from now, your computer will have problems.'

'It will?'

'Yep. Suspected virus. A guy named Hank will come down to sort it out.'

'OK.' Stennell nodded, but he still had little idea where this was headed.

'He'll link up to his own laptop to search through and hopefully zap the virus. In reality, he'll be running those 101 files through the best encryption code-breakers around.' Verbeck smiled conspiratorially. 'Nothing like using the firm's own code-breakers to get into their own files.'

Shadows of concern crept into Stennell's face. 'But this will all link back to my computer. *Me*.'

'Don't worry. Hank's an old master. He'll spin it through so many remote servers between here and Tokyo, they won't know whether they're coming or going. In the end they'll think they've been hacked by some guy in Belarus or Mumbai. When all the time it's been happening right under their noses.'

Stennell nodded but said nothing. He still looked uneasy.

'Hank will bury every link and trace here and email me those 101 files through whatever far-flung server he's meant to have hacked from. You won't even be in the loop.' Verbeck held his gaze. 'And, of course, goes without saying: we never had this conversation.'

Stennell finally shook off his concern and managed a tentative smile. 'Already forgotten.'

Sam ran. Nothing left to do. But the squad car would catch him in no time; he needed some quick options.

His heart racing and his breath short after only a half-dozen strides, the siren wound up again as the squad car surged after him.

Nine yards more to the next turn, he'd make it easily – but they'd swing in and catch him soon after. Then another thirty yards to the one after that.

Pounding his legs hard, he was only a few yards to the turn now – but the squad car had already closed half the gap between them and was bearing down, *fast*.

As he came to the side street, he could see a service alley eighteen yards up. He ran towards it, had gone twelve paces before they swung in behind him. They'd slowed for the turn, but the revs were high again now, siren deafeningly close.

The squad car was ten yards behind as he came to the alley. A dark-blue van was parked sixteen yards up, but he wouldn't make it past the van before they reached him. Sam was desperate. He ran on; he had a plan.

Loudhailer boomed then: 'Police! Stop...*stop*! Stay where you are.'

Finally, eight yards past the alley, as the squad car swept in alongside him just past a parked car, Sam stopped. He turned and slowly raised his hands. Breathless, heart pounding, he hoped he appeared submissive; prayed he'd timed it right. As the passenger cop went to open his door, Sam darted back to the alley. He knew that once the cop was out the car, he'd unclip his holster and it would all be over.

'Hey, stop!' the policeman shouted through the partly open door. Then came the sound of it shutting and the siren winding up again.

By then Sam was already nine strides into the alley, legs pumping hard.

They swung in after him in a squealing circle. Angry now. Revs higher, screaming, a maniacal surge forward, they screeched to a halt a yard short of the van. One door swung wildly open, loudhailer booming again.

'I said *Police*. Stop where you are! *Now!*'

Sam was already twenty yards past the van, and gaining. Then his stomach dropped as he saw the driver-seat cop levelling his gun at him.

There was a silver car on the left and Sam cut in sharply after it and kept close to the wall, crouching as he ran to kill the angle.

No clearly beaded line as Sam glanced back, and now it looked almost a forty-yard shot.

So Sam was surprised, heart leaping, when the shot came. An echoing boom in the narrow alley, the bullet zinged off the wall a foot above his head. Sam crouched lower still, kept running.

The cop steadied to fire again, then thought better of it and reholstered. They both got back in the car and hastily backed up.

Sam tried to pick out the squad car's position from its siren as the next cross street loomed close. They appeared to be swinging round the block. But he'd be clear and hopefully into another service alley by then.

Then came the sounds of more sirens; they'd obviously radioed for help. Sam gauged them as still a fair distance away – he had eighty, ninety seconds grace if he was lucky.

There was a service alley directly opposite with two more facing each other thirty yards to his right. Half a dozen people walking on the street. He headed for the alley his side. It was the last thing they'd expect him to do, double back on himself, and it was vital he got to his car. He wouldn't last much longer running the streets of Albany.

Though now one of the distant sirens sounded as if it was swinging round to where he was headed. It was touch and go whether he'd make it to the next cross street before it. He put on an extra spurt and, as he reached the end – chest heaving, aching hard – the road was clear. There was a service alley diagonally opposite and if he'd got his geography right, the multi-storey with his car was directly across from its far end.

But his legs were like jelly, felt as if they'd hardly be able to carry him five paces, let alone the fifty more to the multi-storey car park. Then halfway down the alley, making his stumbling run falter, he heard the sound of another siren. It seemed to have come from the road directly ahead by the multi-storey. Yet he hadn't seen a squad car pass.

Sam slowed as he came to the end of the alley, approaching cautiously. He stopped at the end and peeked out. Then pulled back as quickly again, his heart racing.

A squad car was parked forty yards away; the only plus was that it was faced away from him.

Sam could hear other sirens closing in. Within two minutes, the street would be a complete no-go. Right now it was just reasonable-to-high risk. Sam closed his eyes for a second, steeling himself. He took off his windbreaker and turned it inside out to show the white satin lining; it wasn't reversible, but at that distance they probably wouldn't notice.

There were any number of similarly aged Caucasian males in the city, but hopefully the white instead of beige windbreaker and the fact that he'd be *walking* instead of running would mark enough difference from their radio alert. Sam felt as if he was crossing a tightrope; he could feel the cops' eyes checking him out in their wing mirrors as he walked.

The second he was out of sight, he darted to the elevator. He pressed for it once, twice. *Nothing.* He looked up at its indicator lights. Broken, or it was stuck on the fourth floor.

He started up the stairs, leg muscles screaming with every step, and, as he reached the first floor, he suddenly remembered: *Barry and Phil!* They'd be at the bar any second. He dialled Mike on his cellphone.

'Yeah, Sam. How's it going? Barry and Phil with you yet?'

'No, *no*. That's why I'm calling. Got problems, *big* problems.' He related the nightmare with the barman and the police alert. 'I've spent the last ten minutes running from them. Got clear by the skin of my teeth.'

'*Clear?* I can still hear sirens in the background.'

'Yeah, yeah. Not far away.' Sam kept his voice hushed, as if ears might be pressed to the car park walls. 'But I think I've lost them now.'

'*Jesus*, Sam. What a mess. I'm sorry.' He'd got in just twenty minutes ago and hadn't seen any local news yet. 'I had *no* idea. OK. So a new venue for you to meet up with Barry and Phil. Somewhere *without* people who might have seen the local news. Perhaps—'

'Let me get clear here first,' Sam cut in. 'I might not have many free options on routes out of here. Just tell them to hang on until I know what—' Sam broke off. He'd heard a siren swinging into the road below. 'Hold on, Mike.'

Sam ran up the last five steps to the third floor. He went over to the edge and looked down. There was now a second squad car alongside the first. His heart froze. He'd thought the first car hadn't ID'd him as he'd gone past. But maybe they had; they'd simply waited for back-up before moving in.

'Gotta go, Mike.' *While he still could.* 'Tell Barry I'll call again in ten or fifteen when I know where I'm at.'

Silence as he rang off, just the steady clip of his footsteps across the car park. *Did ID him, didn't?* Sam's head was boiling with it.

He could see his car now over the far side: grey Dodge Caliber just beyond a Nissan Pathfinder. He picked up pace towards it. Clip, clop. *Did, didn't.*

Then as he heard the siren wind up again and enter the ground floor of the car park, he had his answer: *did*. He didn't need to go to the edge this time to make sure. The siren echoed up clearly through the car park, as if amplified threefold.

The siren switched off as the squad car cruised the ground floor, then wound up again as it went up the ramp to the first floor, as if announcing: *We're coming for you, Sam...we're coming for you!* It all ends here, *now*!

He broke into a run again. His only hope was to sink down low in his car. Stay out of sight until they'd gone, pray that they didn't see him. Then his eyes picked out the CCTV cameras: one in each corner. It would take them only minutes in the security kiosk to work out what he'd done. There might already be a cop there watching.

He took out his car keys and pressed the button from five yards away to unlock the doors. Or maybe he could pass them as they made their way up. If he timed it right, swinging down a ramp just as they were heading up the other side, he'd get a healthy lead before they could turn round. And if a squad car blocked the exit, he could swing over and go out the entrance lane. He'd seen that on a film once.

Heart pounding, *frantic*, he reached for his car door.

Suddenly an arm clamped hard around his neck.

Sam's muscles dissolved, every last screaming nerve in his body collapsed: no resistance left. The police had obviously worked out the link with Jem and the rental car, had staked it out knowing that he'd return at some stage. The cuffs would go on and another cop would appear to read him his rights. They always came in twos.

But instead a cloth was clasped over his mouth and nose, acrid fumes stinging high in his sinuses, making his eyes water.

And as the light faded, the car park sinking into a grey blur, Sam knew then that it wasn't the police after all. Washington's men had got him.

CHAPTER THIRTY-TWO

Adel paused for a second as the nurse opened the door to Akram Ghafur's room. This wasn't going to be easy.

'Don't be too long,' she requested. 'He's still very weak.'

There was a slow blink of acknowledgment from Akram. He still had intravenous feed and monitoring wires attached, the heart-rate machine gently pulsing to one side, but the oxygen feed to his mouth had gone, Adel noted. And he looked a shade less white; only half-dead. Adel nodded to the nurse as she shut the door behind him, and took a seat at Akram's bedside.

Akram had finally come round eight hours after Adel had first seen him, close to midnight, and Adel received a call from the SO15 officer keeping guard. '...*But the doctors apparently need another hour or so to run tests.*' Adel said that by the time the tests were finished, he'd be there.

He introduced himself as Emile, a friend of Fahim Omari's. 'And there are some questions we need to ask, Akram. We need to know who has done this to you.'

'*We?*' Akram quizzed. 'Are you a friend of Fahim's, or with the police? I think you need to make up your mind.'

'I'm not with the police. But, in my capacity, it has fallen to me to talk to you and pass to them what you tell me.'

'Aaah,' Akram said. His eyes glinted. 'So you are Fahim's contact. The one he's been passing information to.'

'If you will.' Adel shrugged. There was little point denying it; with where their conversation had to head that would quickly become apparent. 'But I was Fahim's friend first, his contact second.' Adel leant forward in his chair. 'So let us return to my question: who did this to you, Akram? Who tried to kill you?'

But Akram's eyes simply glazed over and he looked away.

The steady beep-beep of the heart monitor counted

off ten seconds, fifteen. And when it became clear that Akram wasn't about to answer, Adel said, 'I daresay it was the same people who planted the bomb and killed Fahim Omari – though I am presuming here, of course. So, who, Akram? Because this wasn't just some sneak mugger who came out of the dark and knifed you. It was people you had dealings with. *Who?*'

Akram moistened his top lip with his tongue as he turned back to Adel. 'Even if I felt inclined to tell you, which I don't – you think I'm *crazy?* They'd make sure to find me, finish the job off next time.'

Adel smiled wryly. 'Seems to me like they're going to do that anyway. It's obvious you know more than they're comfortable with.' He shrugged. 'But, fine. If you think you'll be OK without any protection.'

Akram's eyes flickered as the first seeds of worry took hold. But the bluster quickly returned. '*Pah!* Protection. Like the protection you gave to your precious contact, Omari, no doubt. *Worthless!*'

'We had no idea he was at risk. With you we *do*.' Adel smiled tightly. He knew he'd struck a chord; Akram felt vulnerable. 'We have half of the equation in any case: photos of you talking with Wajd Masahran in front of the Westbourne Grove Mosque. We have enough on Masahran to lock him up and throw away the key – but Masahran for the moment has flown the coop. So now we're just left with *you*. And with your part in Omari's bombing – terrorism and accomplice to murder – it looks like we'll be throwing away the key on you too. A good ten to fifteen in Belmarsh.' Adel held out one hand. 'Then, yes, you'd have no worries about them getting to you.' He shrugged. 'Unless of course we *wanted* them to. Made sure you were put in the right part of Belmarsh.'

Akram's eyes widened. His heart monitor crept up a notch. But Adel saw he at least had the situation clear: his fate rested entirely in Adel's hands, and hinged on what he said next. For a moment it looked like he was ready to throw in the towel. But then a defiant gleam crept into his eyes.

'You assume, of course, that I'm not so tired of life that that would hold any relevance for me. That, indeed, while I still draw breath, other things might be more important: honour, conscience, and not crossing certain lines to make it difficult to live with oneself. Such as *betrayal*.' Akram fixed his eyes steadily on Adel. 'And I am guessing too, my friend, that you don't have quite enough information to throw away the key as you suggest.'

Adel had hoped to get Akram's cooperation through the standard route: kid glove one hand, boxing glove the other. Because the other route meant imparting a secret he'd kept for over six years; one that he'd sworn to Omari he'd never share with *anyone*, not even Tahiya. Though now, given the circumstances, perhaps it was finally time for that.

Adel drew a long breath. 'Good words, Akram: honour, conscience, *betrayal*. It's such a shame that *none* of those apply to Masahran and his cohorts; that, having gained your trust, they betrayed you and left you for dead in the gutter. So certainly you owe them none of those in return.' Adel sighed. 'But let's get to the *real* betrayal, shall we? Betraying the man whose family took you in from the streets. Who fed and clothed you, ensured you wanted for nothing. Who, over forty long years, became more than just a master: he became a friend, like a brother. Because *that* betrayal, my dear Akram, is far harder to comprehend.'

'You know I'm not talking about that betrayal,' Akram spluttered, a fleck of spittle landing on his bottom lip. 'I'm talking about Omari's betrayal – of *all* his brothers. *That* is what I speak of now.' But Adel could see that he'd struck a chord again: Akram's eyes had glassed over, close to tears at being confronted with what he'd done. 'Don't you think I took all of that into account? Fought hard with my conscience before making such a decision? And, besides, if I'd refused to help – you think that would have made any difference? I'd have simply been labelled a traitor as well. They'd have made sure that *two* of us were there when the bomb went off.' Akram shook his head. 'This problem now is because of Omari's betrayal, not mine!'

Adel said nothing, he simply held Akram with the

same steady, contemplative gaze. He wanted him to talk more, exorcise his demons; hopefully *overtalk* and provide him with more ammunition. He'd reel him in when the time was right.

Eight beeps sounded on the heart monitor before Akram spoke again. 'All those years of giving to Palestinian causes, fooling his brothers that he was helping them – when all the time his aim was to betray them. When I found out, it felt as if I'd *never* known him.' Akram shook his head again. 'Did you know that Layth's mother was Palestinian?'

Adel stayed silent. He nodded, closing his eyes for a second as if in penance. Layth's mother had died of a brain tumour when he was only twelve. *Layth. Yes, it had all started with Layth.*

'...And her brother still lives in Gaza City to this day. A rising star in Hamas, word has it. And when Layth's father died just five years after – did you know about the solemn promises Fahim Omari made to his beloved brother, Ihsan, on his deathbed?'

Adel nodded solemnly, eyes slightly downcast.

'Oh, yes – everyone knows about the first promise,' Akram said. 'That he'd take care of Layth and love and raise him as his own – as is often the custom between blood brothers in Islam. But there was another promise made at the time. In the old days, Ihsan and Fahim used to court the likes of Arafat, and Ihsan kept up regular contributions to Palestinian causes; even more so later in memory of his wife and her family still there. Fahim solemnly promised to continue with those – in the spirit and memory of *both* of them.' Akram's eyes clenched shut for a moment. 'But in the end he betrayed their brothers, betrayed their cause. *Betrayed* their memory.' Akram mimed a dry spit to one side.

Adel nodded gently. 'A promise that for the first years he kept to. Indeed, with what was most important – the true spirit of that promise – it was kept to throughout.' Adel watched Akram's brow knit. *Time to reel him in.* 'But did you ever trouble to ask yourself why the change? Why Fahim might suddenly decide to betray the memory of his brother and nephew?'

Akram thought for a moment, his brow furrowing deeper. 'You are talking in riddles now. You make no sense.'

'Think about it. Did he not love them? Or perhaps he didn't really care for them that much after all? That's why the betrayal was so easy.'

'Don't be a fool!' Akram's tone was as sharp as his look. 'Fahim was very close to Ihsan. And Layth became like a son.' Akram glanced away for a second. 'After the death of his own son, Nasib, Layth was the bright light he desperately needed. But Fahim came to love Layth for being Layth – not merely as a replacement for Nasib. He was such a generous, bright spirit, we *both* came to love him. Those years he spent with us, I've never seen Fahim quite as happy and content.'

Akram's eyes moistened at the memory of better times. *We both came to love him.* Adel's throat tightened at what he was about to do.

'So think about it, Akram. All that love. Not something you'd betray simply at the drop of a hat. It must have taken something momentous.' Akram's eyes shifted again, as if his mind was trying to grasp something just out of reach. *The precipice edge Adel was about to push him over.* Adel swallowed. 'But I *can* tell you that that change – the decision to "*betray his brothers*", as you put it – came with Layth's death. That was the key event that changed Fahim Omari's thinking. Contemplate that for a moment – Layth's death – then ask yourself why that might have brought about such a change.'

Akram's thoughts continued to churn, eyes searching, before he finally lost patience. 'What are you talking about? You're talking in riddles again. Layth died in a car accident on Long Island. What on earth could *that* have to do with Fahim making such a decision?'

'Yes, that was the story he put out. But think about the timing, Akram. The *timing*. What else happened in New York the week that Layth died?'

After another rapid eye-shift, Akram finally hit it, like a brick wall. He gasped: 'The Twin Towers.' But then he caught himself and just as quickly dismissed the idea. 'No, *no*. It couldn't have been. Layth's accident was a week after that.'

'Five days. That was the time it took them to go through work records and be sure that he was there that day and didn't get out.'

Akram's eyes continued to shift for escape routes. 'But that can't be. He *couldn't* have been there. He worked for UBS – they didn't have offices in the World Trade Centre.'

'And *that* was the part of the story that Layth himself constructed – *before* his death.' There was a pleading tone now in Akram's protestations, and Adel could see it too in his eyes – as if Akram knew it was the truth, knew that he was clinging now to little more than desperate straws. It was time to stop jousting. Adel took a deep breath.

'Layth's initial intention had been to go to New York with UBS, who he in fact worked for in London. But then a stronger opportunity arose with another investment bank, Armell-Levy. There was only one problem – Armell-Levy was a predominantly Jewish company. Its main directors were all Jewish and, worse still, a significant part of its foreign investment portfolio comprised Israeli companies.

'None of that background with the *Nakba*, the catastrophe, on his mother's side meant anything personally to Layth. He'd had Jewish friends while at

UBS, after all, and saw carrying such grievances into this modern age as preposterous. But he nevertheless felt he'd be defying his parents' core beliefs, tainting their memory. And, as a result, his Uncle Fahim also wouldn't approve. So Layth said nothing about it, kept up the pretence that he was joining UBS.'

Adel shrugged. 'Fahim didn't discover the truth until almost two years later. He had Layth's cellphone and apartment number, but one day Layth's cellphone was down and Fahim tried him at work and it all came out then. Though he didn't confront Layth with what he knew until four months after that.

'Layth told him everything, didn't hold back. And, in turn, Fahim was understanding. While he'd sympathised with his brother's adherence to "the cause", in turn he didn't see why Layth should have to carry that cross in today's age. It played little part in Layth's life now. Fahim learnt then where Layth worked – Armell-Levy's ninety-eighth floor office in the North Tower – and Layth talked also about his friends there. Some Jewish, some Christian and, yes, a few Muslim like himself. But Layth didn't look at race and creed, he looked at them as *people*. He saw the possibilities for this generation: how they could teach past generations – those still clinging to hate based on race and creed – a thing or two. To Fahim, Layth was pure goodness through and through.'

Akram's eyes had filled with tears and now they began to trickle down his cheeks.

'...So when Layth died, when those planes hit the towers, Fahim's world fell apart. Not only had he lost Layth, but all those other young hopeful lives had been lost too – those friends Layth had talked of. And for what, *what*? "The cause" made less sense then to Fahim than ever.' Adel held out his hand. 'Do you know how many Muslims were killed in 9/11, Akram?'

'I...I...uuh.' Akram swallowed hard, unable to answer. Everything he'd held true had been demolished in only minutes, the rubble of it strewn around him. Layth and Fahim's double lives, and now the terrible realisation that he'd betrayed his best friend of forty years, condemned him to death on a lie.

'More than three hundred,' Adel said. 'Mostly American Muslims, but a few also from Arab nations. Three hundred! That's a lot of *brothers* to have to die for the cause, is it not, Akram?'

Akram didn't answer, he simply scrunched his eyes shut and shook his head as if he couldn't bear to hear what Adel had to tell him any longer.

Looking at Akram's anguished, quivering state, Adel felt a stab of guilt. But there'd been no other way; and this had also been a difficult exorcism for himself, unburdening a secret he'd held for so long. He stroked his forehead.

'Fahim called me when it happened to make all

the arrangements. Layth's name was removed from 9/11 death records and a car accident became the cover story. If it was known Layth had died in 9/11, suspicions might have been raised with the likes of Masahran. The first few months, Fahim did nothing. He was still too shell-shocked to act out his plan. But he knew his position was unique: he could continue aiding Palestinian causes while also using his contacts to gain vital information on bombings. For him, Layth's death had separated the two. He told me that he'd never before had such clarity on the issue.'

As Akram finally opened his eyes, a half-murmur, half-wail escaped his lips. 'Please forgive me...*please*!' But his plea wasn't for Adel. His eyes were fixed, unseeing, on the ceiling.

'Bin Laden had by then hidden away, was mostly a spent force. And Abu Khalish had risen to take over the "terrorist king" mantle with his bombing campaign. But to Fahim, they became reminders of what had happened to Layth, and he began to see it as a personal battle against Khalish. Each bombing thwarted by passing on information, he saw as a step towards avenging Layth's death; a repayment, a penance, if you will.'

Akram's wail had descended into gentle sobbing.

'You see, Akram, Fahim *never* did betray the promises he made to his brother. He kept giving to

Palestinian causes and charities. If it was for a school wing damaged by the IDF or for an orphanage – he gave. But if it was for mortars, bombs and AK-47s, he refused. Because all that reminded him of was what had happened to Layth. *That* was the separation made in his mind. The only way he felt he could stay true to the spirit of his brother *and* Layth. In the end, he betrayed neither of them.'

As Adel had continued, Akram's sobbing had become steadily heavier, until it racked his whole body. A nurse appeared at the door, alarmed.

Akram got his sobbing back under control, wiping at his tears as he held his other hand towards her. 'It's OK...*OK*. Just a little longer.'

She backed out reluctantly, her eyes resting on Adel for a second accusingly. A reminder that he'd already stayed longer than he should.

As the door clicked shut, Akram wiped away the rest of his tears and got his breathing back under control. 'What can I do...*what can I do*?' And as Akram's eyes rested on him, Adel wished that this plea too hadn't been aimed his way, because it was pitiful.

To help, or to save your own soul and conscience? At this moment, they were one and the same. He could have just said, 'What I wanted when I first walked in here – *who* did this to you?' But this had all been about penance so far: Fahim Omari's penance for his brother *and* Layth; for self and others. So perhaps also the best way to sweeten the pill now. *Two doses of penance and one of 'attachment to a cause'.*

'I think you know what Fahim would want of you now,' he began.

CHAPTER THIRTY-THREE

SALON, PROVENCE.

One day while going back over some early quatrains, Jean-Pierre suddenly burst into tears. One of them had mentioned *plague*, and he had a sudden sharp, vivid picture of Michel's grief at the loss of his first wife and young son and daughter to the plague in Agen. Not just a clear image of Michel kneeling by their bedsides, tearful as the last rites were read, but how he'd felt in that moment.

In reliving Michel's life as closely as possible, sometimes the images crept over the edge, became too acute. After all, the main markers of his life were all around him in the town, his ghost on practically every

421

street corner: his old house on Rue Moulin d'Isnard – now renamed Rue Nostradamus in his honour – where he'd lived with his wife Anne and their six children; the traders of the Rue de l'Horloge where he'd got his daily provisions; the site of the Franciscan chapel where he'd regularly prayed and was finally buried; the church of St Laurent where his remains were moved after the 1789 Revolution; the plague pit by the canal – Michel had tended to plague victims when he first arrived in Salon, and before that in Marseilles, Lyon and Aix.

It was perhaps to be expected, that occasional emotional overload, a knock-on symptom, backlash from delving too deeply. Because while most researchers were happy just dealing with the known, proven history of Michel's life, he was more interested in cross-linking those events to discover what might have driven Michel: that tragic loss of his first family to the plague driving him to study its treatment to save others from that calamity; a close scrape with inquisitors in Toulouse in his early years urging later caution not to be too overt or direct in his prophecies; his interest in astronomy leading in turn to astrology, and then his success with his early 'Almanac' prophecies encouraging him to continue.

Jean-Pierre hoped he better understood not only how Michel felt during those key life stages – losing his first family, his father's death within a year of his arrival in Salon, the birth of his six children to Anne all within a ten-year span, 1551–1561 – but also their effect on his writing, his quatrains.

Michel's quatrain about Mabus had been written in 1557, two years after his prophecy about the French king had first made his name. Conflict between Islam and Christianity had been very much a concern of that period as well. The *Reconquista* in Spain had shaken off the last vestiges of Islamic rule only sixty years previously, and clashes between Ottoman Empire and Christian forces were a regular event in the eastern Mediterranean, leading finally to the Great Siege of Malta in 1565. How much might all of that have influenced Michel?

And part of that was still on Jean-Pierre's mind when he met Corinne for dinner that night.

'Are you OK?' she asked, reaching over to touch his hand reassuringly.

'Yes, I'm fine.' Then, when he saw that his curt answer hadn't satisfied her, he explained about his earlier emotional overload.

'It's perhaps to be expected right now,' she said, 'what with everything else going on. Your focus is far more intense than normal, passions running high.'

'Yes. I suppose.'

Passion. The main thing that had initially attracted her to Jean-Pierre beyond his unconventional eccentricity – the embroidered tunics, hippy-style hair, his at times infuriating detachment from the world outside and the emotions of others – the passion and intensity of his work with Nostradamus. Though she'd almost given up ever getting any of that focused on herself.

They'd gone to La Brocherie, the restaurant on the site of the Franciscan chapel where Michel de Nostredame was first laid to rest, the walls ordained with memorial plaques, portraits and old quatrains on parchment.

Corinne pursed her lips. 'You know, I was always intrigued why Mabus was such an important figure in Michel's quatrains. I could find only *one* reference to him.'

'Yes, that's true. But once that name had been established, all of Michel's other references to that same "third Antichrist" then linked in.'

Corinne nodded slowly. 'And from those it was postulated that this third Antichrist, Mabus, would hail from the Arabian peninsula, Persia or the Levant?'

'That's right.' After a year of attending his lectures, it was little surprise that she wasn't far behind him at times. Corinne bit her lip. Obviously something was on her mind. '*Why?*'

'I was just curious – what made you pick Bahsem-Yahl to link to Mabus? There are so many others you could have chosen.'

'True. But I think what nailed it for me was first of all getting pointed towards Iran – *Persia* as it was –

by Michel's epistle to Henry II in which he described that third Antichrist as the new Xerxes – the ancient king of Persia. Then finally because Bahsem-Yahl was the most worrying voice coming out of Iran, one that *could* unite all of Islam.'

'I see.' She lapsed into thought again momentarily. *Xerxes.* 'And now with this fresh quatrain mentioning Saladin, it appears we have yet another ancient Islamic warrior.'

'I suppose, yes...we...' Jean-Pierre suddenly trailed off as the final link in that chain hit him. He ran the sequence through again in case he'd missed something, apologising to Corinne as he took out his cellphone. '*Sorry*...quick call to make.'

But Tynnan didn't answer, and it went into his service provider's voicemail.

It was the same again when Jean-Pierre tried as they left the restaurant, though this time he left a message. And when after twenty-four hours there was still no return call, he tried one last time. Again, message service.

'OK. So what have we got?' Adel asked.

First thing that morning Adel had passed on the information he'd gained from Akram to a team of four, then convened with them again just after lunch.

There were three key locations to check: the first was Akram's attack scene, the other two where he'd previously met up with his attacker. They were both park benches: one by the Italian Garden in Hyde Park, the other on the south side of the lake in St James's Park – though the only CCTVs were by the main entrances or restaurants in each. Then anything on Al Hakam from travel connections.

Isam held up his notepad. 'From all flights and Eurostar since the attack, there are only two matches for Al Hakam or the three possible pseudonyms we have for him on file. They're *both* outside the age frame: a fifty-nine-year-old on a flight to Kuwait late the following day, and a twenty-eight-year-old early this morning to Toronto.'

Adel stroked his forehead. Akram put his attacker's age at between mid-thirties and early forties. 'Follow up only on the twenty-eight-year-old.'

'He was also with his wife and five-year-old son, so unlikely.'

'True.' Adel shrugged. 'But you've got to admit, it's a good cover. And we've seen crazier things.' He looked to the others. 'Scene of attack and parks? What there?'

'Not much luck with narrowing down at Hyde Park, I'm afraid.' Bahir sighed dramatically. 'Forty-six possibles.'

Siraj said that he hadn't fared much better at St James's Park.

'How many?'

'Thirty-eight.'

Adel nodded. He wasn't surprised. All Akram had been able to recall was that Al Hakam wore a dark jacket – but couldn't specify colour – and light shirt, no tie, at each of the park meetings. So the main defining feature was a heavy beard and moustache.

'And you've got better news for us, I suppose?' Adel said, noting Karam's wry grin.

'Didn't think I would at first.' Karam glanced at his notes. 'There was no CCTV anywhere near where he was attacked – so I had to widen out until I did hit some, particularly on the main roads feeding that area. In the end I came up with these.' He passed a batch of photos to Adel. 'Eight in all. The main thing to help pin it down was the kaftan top. Otherwise we might have been talking about forty or more.'

Adel looked through them. All the pictures were of men with heavy beards in kaftan tops riding mopeds or small motorbikes. Akram's description on that occasion had been more precise, and they also had the input of the teenager who'd seen Al Hakam jump on a moped. 'This is good...this is *good*.' Adel glanced at his watch. He instructed them to complete their 'possibles' list, then put their heads together for cross-reference matching. 'Let me know the second we hit one, *if* we do. Deadline 4 p.m. That's when I plan to head out to the hospital again and go through these with Akram Ghafur.' Meeting finished.

As they went back to their desks, Adel cradled his forehead. It was 9.18 a.m. in New York. Tynnan had said that he'd phone again in a few hours, 'Once I've got clear.' Now, eighteen hours had passed. He tried Tynnan's number, but it went into voicemail. Adel didn't leave a message. If Tynnan *had* been picked up by the police, it could open up an awkward can of worms as to why they'd had contact.

His team hit a possible match between one of the moped and Hyde Park photos just over an hour later. Then another possible hit eighteen minutes after that: not the same moped photo and yet another shot from Hyde Park.

Adel was looking between the two options when Malik's voice interrupted him.

'Boss? You might want to see this.'

Adel lifted his head as the sound was turned up to match the scenes on screen: a large crowd chanting, two cars burning behind them, another to one side. Flames were also billowing from a shop window where a petrol bomb had been thrown.

'Karachi this time,' Malik prompted. 'Thirty thousand strong, apparently.'

It was the third of the day. The Middle East had been awake for five hours before them; more time to rally protestors and cause mayhem, Adel thought sourly. And they seemed to be getting larger and stronger each time, reminding him that he didn't have much time left. He resisted the temptation to bury his head in his hands, simply closed his eyes briefly as he nodded.

'I know...*I know*,' he said. But even that felt like a cipher of sorts. *I know*, because I've watched these demonstrations for the past few days now and I'm sick of them, can't bear to look at them any more. Or *I know*, because I've already seen this whole scenario mapped out in a manuscript, so I know where it's all headed. The pressure of not being able to share his secret was stifling.

Adel grabbed his jacket a minute later and collected the rest of the photos from his team, saying that he'd decided to head to see Akram at the hospital twenty minutes early. 'We've gone as far as we can with the photos in any case.' But his exit had more to do with escaping the mounting volatility of the demonstration on screen. Half the operations room was transfixed by it, some of them now on their feet, mouths slack, eyes glassy as the images bombarded them, wondering how much worse it could get or where it all might end – when Adel already half knew that answer.

As Adel travelled down in the elevator, alone, finally he did bury his face in his hands.

Hank was able to access all but seven of Department 101's Bahsem-Yahl files.

Kenny Verbeck spent over an hour going through them before finally lifting his head. Again the language was diplomatic, often vague, but there was still more than enough both above and between the lines to ring alarm bells.

One name in particular leapt out at Verbeck and gave him cause for concern: Matt Calvinson. Of all the nuts in the born-again Christian 'end-timers' bowl, Calvinson was a prize Brazil.

Some might argue that was unfair; that indeed there were other more extreme end-timer nuts out there, it was just that Calvinson was the best-known, most 'media visible' nut, *and* the richest: his TV evangelist shows regularly attracted audiences in the millions.

But it was his sizeable contributions to the Republican Party and his, at times, uncomfortably close association with the President that had made the security services twitch. And so they'd made sure to monitor every Calvinson word and deed. If Calvinson put his foot in it – which he did regularly – they wanted to know how it might reflect on that association. Whether any White House disassociation or counter statement might be required.

Verbeck checked on his computer to see who at the NSA handled Calvinson related data. George Caffrey.

He buzzed Caffrey's line and explained what he was after: Calvinson's meetings and key comments of the past year. 'Those with the President we already all know about, they're well documented. But there are some others I'm interested in.' Verbeck ran through them, two senators, an arms contractor and a Halliburton executive from the 101 files, making notes as he went; but as he came to the last name, William Grayford, Caffrey fell silent. 'What's wrong?' Verbeck prompted.

'Er...we've picked up Grayford in three meetings over the past fourteen months. And we were starting to wonder why.'

It was Verbeck's turn to fall quiet. He wasn't about to fill that gap, even if he *did* know. Caffrey knew how it worked given their respective positions: Verbeck asked, Caffrey answered. 'So, those meetings with Grayford. Where and when?'

After noting the three meetings, Verbeck asked about copies of Calvinson's most recent sermons. 'Say, over the last two months?'

'Yeah, got those. Up to two years back, if you want.'

'The two months will be fine. By the way, when's his next TV sermon?'

'Tomorrow night at seven and Sunday morning at eleven. Always the same two slots. Be there or risk eternal fire!' Caffrey chuckled briefly, then decided to chance his arm again. 'Any particular reason for the interest?'

'Yep. Because, praise the Lord, I think I've finally seen the light.' He thanked him and hung up.

Normally that fire and brimstone crap would have

his eyes glazing over within minutes, but he was going to make sure to hang on every word of that coming sermon.

No escape.

There'd been a group of demonstrators on Speakers' Corner every day since Bahsem-Yahl's speech, but now they'd swelled to a few hundred strong. They chanted and waved their placards at passing traffic as Adel's taxi edged into Park Lane on his way back from seeing Akram.

Under the heading IRATE ISLAM, the topic also filled the front page of his *Evening Standard* on the train journey home. There were pictures of the latest demos in Karachi, Medina and Bushehr on the first few pages, then four smaller European demos, including Speakers' Corner, on the next two. *Fair enough*. But then the following three pages were filled with rehashed flashbacks to 7/7, the aftermath of last week's London bomb alert, current figures for *Hizb ut-Tahrir* members in the UK, and the latest outrageous comment from the Muslim Council of Great Britain.

Adel gave the newspaper short shrift, folding it aside with a sigh. After a moment he closed his eyes to the gentle rocking of the train. Reading the papers, you'd get the impression that most of the Muslims in Britain, and the world beyond, were radical. At times, Adel felt the separation of his work more starkly.

Days ago he'd been desperately trying to save the lives of those around him, yet he could never tell anyone what he did, least of all his own people: many would consider him a traitor for betraying his own. And now, with having to keep Tynnan's odyssey close to his chest, he was divided even from his work colleagues. Adel smiled to himself at the irony of it.

Bright lights from a station flashed past and Adel opened his eyes. They'd had a breakthrough with Akram, yes, but still nothing from Tynnan. Where *was* he? He took out his cellphone to try him again.

An hour later Adel picked at his dinner, the momentum of the day still with him. Akram had identified one of the moped photos as Al Hakam; but Akram was equally sure that Al Hakam's beard had also been false. So now they had to run computer image progressions to see what Al Hakam might look like without the beard to get an idea how he might appear in his passport and passing through customs.

Adel had called back into the office and sent the photo through to Max Redmond at GCHQ before heading home. 'Back to you hopefully mid-morning tomorrow.'

As he looked across the table, Tahiya smiled half-heartedly. While she could sense he was distracted, she'd obviously given up the ghost on asking what was wrong. But something about tonight – perhaps because he finally had a positive ID on the Omari front – made him decide to finally tell her about *everything* troubling him these past days, not just the bare bones he'd previously given her on the Omari bombing.

Though in observation of *one* rule, *not in front of the children*, he waited until after he'd given Farah and Jibril a hug goodnight and Tahiya had put them to bed.

He poured them each a glass of *Zibib*, a blend made with fermented dates rather than aniseed. Neither of them adhered to the extent of giving up all alcohol and, while they drank sparingly, *Zibib* was one of Tahiya's favourites, kept only for special occasions.

Adel explained everything in sequence – the mosque bombings, Sam Tynnan, Nostradamus and Jean-Pierre, Bahsem-Yahl – and watched Tahiya's expression become graver with each sentence.

They sat in silence after he finished, Tahiya looking down at her hands. On the rare occasions he shared work information with her, it had always fallen into two categories: either he'd already gained work colleagues' opinions and was looking for concurrence; or he mistrusted that consensus, so was seeking the reverse, a reinforcement of his doubt. But this was different, she realised; she was the *only* one he'd shared with, and now she felt the weight of that responsibility: the two of them the only gatekeepers of such a profound secret.

She lifted her eyes to his. 'I can see now why this has been a difficult burden for you to shoulder alone.'

He nodded, closing his eyes fleetingly. 'And the worry now, compounding everything, is that this Sam Tynnan has disappeared. There was an APB put out for him in the States, and he said he'd phone me in a few hours when hopefully he'd got clear. I've heard nothing now for over twenty-four hours.' Maybe that had been the final factor to tip him over the edge into sharing with Tahiya. As the day had progressed, each passing hour with still nothing from Tynnan had tightened his concern. Yet he couldn't bounce it off anyone in his office: Sam Tynnan simply didn't exist on their radar.

Tahiya shrugged. 'Perhaps the police got him after all.'

'No, don't think so. I checked just before I left the office. There's no note of an arrest; the APB is still open, yet to be satisfied. And he's not answering his phone.'

Tahiya's eyes shifted for a second. 'Give it a little longer. Hopefully he'll resurface, make contact again.'

'*Hopefully*.' He took a heavier sip of *Zibib* before getting to his other worry: the mosque bombings and whether he was doing enough. 'If I get this next one wrong, it might be too late to pull back from the brink.' He shrugged helplessly. 'You've seen the demonstrations out there?'

'Yes, I have.' She glanced at her glass, as if for inspiration. 'But do you feel in your heart you're doing everything you can?'

'Yes, I…I think so.' He rubbed at his forehead, then explained his 'equivalent mosque' theory. 'My brother Namir in fact gave me the clue to it. And certainly it worked last time. We got one of them, albeit not alive.'

Still in thought, Tahiya leant forward and touched his arm. 'If you truly feel you're doing all you can, Adel, then you can't do more. It's not your job to save the world.' She stroked his hand. 'And certainly not alone, as you have been so far with this.'

'I suppose so.' And as some of the weight lifted from his chest, he felt glad he'd shared with Tahiya. Perhaps that was what he'd been seeking all along: not so much advice, but rather reassurance that he was handling things right. *Absolution.* He shook his head. 'But still I can't help feeling I'm missing something with the mosque bombings. Something vital.'

Late the previous night, he'd dug out the second quatrain from Jean-Pierre to study it again:

Of the last fiery domes,
The order of one shall be reversed,
The other replaced by that of higher order,
Saladin shall be confounded.

Still it made little sense. Not least because it contradicted the first quatrain from Jean-Pierre which suggested that the last two mosque targets in Damascus and Medina would remain the same as in Tynnan's manuscript. The one stable element in it all. Both had heavy standard security, but they'd put through alerts in any case; and still there was the question of *when*.

Tahiya traced a finger absently round the rim of her glass. 'That's one thing I can't help you with, I'm afraid, Adel: unravelling your thoughts. One area where we're all truly *alone*.' She raised an eyebrow. 'The only advice I could give is that, perversely, when you don't think about something, when you don't try and force it, invariably the clearest thoughts come.'

He nodded. 'Often true.'

They lapsed into small talk, mostly about her day and the kids, as they finished their drinks, and when they went to bed Adel followed that advice: for almost two hours he lay staring at the ceiling, trying not to think about what had happened to Sam Tynnan and what he might have missed with the mosque bombings, before he finally fell asleep.

CHAPTER THIRTY-FOUR

There was nobody in the room when Sam woke up. He shook off a dull ache in his head as he looked around slowly. The room was twelve foot square and he was on a single bed, his left wrist handcuffed to its frame that side. The only furniture was a pine side table and matching drawer set. A basic, functional bedroom.

It was night-time and the curtains were drawn, with no light at their edges. But the bedroom door was open, light spilling in from a hallway; the only light in the room. Some sounds now from across the hallway. Gentle clatter of plates, cutlery, a drawer being closed. Sam leant over, and through a half-open door the other side of the hallway he could see kitchen cabinets. The light was starker there and he could hear someone moving around.

He pulled back sharply as someone came into view. From that split-second profile he could see that she was female, slim, blonde.

More plates clattering, a couple of kitchen cupboard doors opening and closing. Then the sound of padding footsteps.

After a moment, Sam risked another glance. She was out of view at first, but as she reappeared she turned in his direction.

Too late in pulling back, his heart raced; not so much from getting caught peeking, but because of what he thought he'd seen.

With the light behind her as she walked in, making Sam squint, it took a moment for him to be sure: *Lorrena!*

Yet it all still had a dreamlike quality about it. As if with a quick head shake he'd awake to the reality: Washington or one of his henchmen would be walking towards him. And as the pieces fell into place, he realised that the dream wasn't that different to the nightmare reality. They were no doubt down the hallway in another room, waiting for her to tell them he was awake.

'Sam…*Sam*.' Her face was soft and concerned; how he remembered her. 'Are you OK?'

She reached towards him, and he shrank back – as far as he could with the cuff on.

She touched his cheek, gently stroked it, and he shuddered against her touch. He turned his head, closing his eyes. Shut her out.

She pulled her hand away and he felt the mattress sink as she sat beside him. He opened his eyes after a second, slowly shaking his head.

'So that was all a lie too – your car accident? You drowning? Just like the eighteen months you spent with me.' His jaw set tight. 'Fitting, I suppose. Start with a lie, finish with one.'

Her brow creased. 'No, no. The first was a lie, *yes*. But not the car accident. Washington really did try to kill me.'

He held her look. 'Yeah, sure. *Sure*. I forgot for a moment how good you are at this. So what's the plan this time? You chat to me for a while. Butter me up. Get the last bit of vital information needed.' He glanced past her shoulder. 'Then Washington and the rest of the goons come in to cement my legs into lake-ready waders? Come on, Lorrena, you were with me a *fucking* year and a half! What possible secret could be left for you to drag out of me?'

Lorrena shook her head, and even in the half light Sam could see her eyes glistening. 'No, it wasn't like that.' She paused, shrugged. 'Well, yeah, at the beginning it was. But then things changed.'

'*Changed?*' he demanded incredulously, his eyes narrowing.

She met his gaze then looked away. All the times she'd spun the words through her mind these past days, now they just froze in her throat. It would just sound trite, ridiculous. He'd think it was simply another 'story'. But Sam had shifted back to her car accident.

'So, if it wasn't a set-up, how come you're here? The police found blood on the windscreen glass from your car pulled out the lake.'

'Oh, I went in the lake all right. Doped up as one of Washington's men steered my car towards the lake and jumped out just before the edge. I hit the lake *and* the windscreen – hard! *See?*' She turned her cheek and took Sam's hand to touch it.

Sam could see a cluster of eight or nine small pitted scars, his fingers trembling as he touched them. 'I'm sorry,' he said, though not sure immediately why: *Sorry that this happened to you, or sorry I disbelieved you?* He swallowed. 'But still you managed to get out? You weren't unconscious?' And immediately he knew which. His tone said it: he still had strong doubts.

'For a moment, *yes* – ten seconds, thirty – I had no idea. But I was lucky. The currents worked in my favour.' It sounded so simple like that: *the currents worked in my favour*. It had felt like being in a washing machine tumbler. Not knowing which was up, down, sideways. And cold, *so cold* it took her breath away, her lungs bursting for air as she felt herself tossed and dragged through the murky water. 'It seemed to take for ever to surface, by which time I'd taken a fair few mouthfuls.' She bit her lip. 'The only advantage was that, with the current, by then I was a couple of hundred yards downstream. And I'm assuming Washington and his sidekick were still looking straight ahead to make sure I hadn't made it.'

Sam nodded slowly. That was the other thing he'd wondered about. She was either telling the truth, or it was the mostly perfectly constructed lie; one that covered all the bases. *Like the one she'd acted out for the eighteen months she'd lived with him.* 'So, if as you say Washington and his goons aren't lurking in the other room – then why the chloroform to knock me out? Why the cuffs?' He tugged at his left hand, rattling the metal cuff against the bed frame.

'There wasn't much choice about the chloroform, I knew you wouldn't come with me easily. I'd been tracking you from the day before when I discovered you were at Mike's cabin, and the cops were going to get you any second. And once they did, they'd have handed you to Washington. His department put out the APB.' She gestured. 'And the cuffs? I knew that once you awoke, you'd probably fear the worst. Might simply attack me, try and escape.' She shrugged and glanced to one side. 'There's nobody else here, Sam. But if when I've finished talking you still don't believe me, fine. I'll take off the cuffs and you're free to go. Take your chances out there again.'

That Pontiac by Mike's the other day. Sam nodded. As if he had any choice. *Captive audience.* 'OK.' Then, in contradiction to what she'd just said, sounds came from the hallway. A door closing and footsteps heading their way.

Sam tensed, expecting Washington to appear in the doorway any second, smug smile in place: *You're such an easy touch, Mr Tynnan. She got you going all over again.* But the guy who leant into the doorway was in his late twenties with gelled, spiky blond hair, trendy pink-rimmed glasses, nose- and ear-rings and tie-dyed lime-green T-shirt.

'Oh, except for Chris,' Lorrena said. 'A friend. He helped me carry you in and out of the SUV.'

Sam was trying to take it all in. *The Nissan Pathfinder next to him in the multi-storey.* Chris was slim and gawky-looking; even with help from Lorrena, carrying Sam's weight must have been a stretch for this guy. He clearly wasn't one of Washington's men. The only thing he'd make was a fly SWAT team.

'You OK?' the young guy asked.

Lorrena nodded, and he headed back along the corridor.

As the door clicked shut along the hallway, Lorrena took a deep breath. Where to start? That first day they met at the library? No, it went back almost four months before that; and so that's where she started, when one of Sam's research sources – she was never let in on exactly who, not at her level – contacted Washington's department. The first moment of concern that what he was writing could have wider implications. Then came their meeting set-up, having monitored his regular visits to Albany Library. Sam nodded mutely, his only reaction so far, before he started quizzing about her background. Who she *really* was.

Yes, her father was originally from Taranto, but he wasn't there now; he lived in San Francisco, where her family had resided most of their lives. But she knew the Oneida area well because an uncle had lived in Syracuse for years. That was one of the reasons she was chosen. She pulled at a strand of hair. 'And in my late teens, I used to lighten my hair. My natural colour is mid-brown, but for my "history" with you I went two shades darker. Almost black.' First name the same, surname changed from Perello to Presutti. She grimaced. 'They like to keep histories close, if they can. Reduces the chances of slip-ups.'

Finally, she got to her moving in with him to keep day-to-day tabs on his progress with *The Prophecy*.

'Along with who you might have sent parts of the manuscript or shared vital details with.'

Sam blinked slowly as he assimilated, tried to make sense of it all. 'So all that crap with them asking me where I'd sent the manuscript, they already knew?'

'Well, eighty per cent of it. I wasn't there all the time – so there was a chance you might have sent chunks out without my knowing.' She shrugged. 'Although I regularly checked your email history for that.'

Sam closed his eyes for a second, even now a shudder rising as he thought about it. 'And you knew too that they'd come that day? Stick a gun in my face and play Russian roulette?'

'I knew that they'd go in, yeah. But I had no idea they'd be so brutal. Details like that I wasn't in the loop on, like I say, "at my level". Not important enough. *Expendable*, as it turned out.' She shrugged helplessly. 'Even if they *had* told me, it wouldn't have helped – because if I'd protested, that would have given away that I cared about you. Become closer to you than I should.'

Sam slowly shook his head; he had even more trouble getting to grips with that. '*What?* Having spent a year getting me to bare my heart and soul, my *life* to you, only for you to put a wrecking ball through on behalf of "God and country" – you suddenly decided you *liked* me?' Voice rising, incredulous.

'No, it went deeper than that.' Then she quickly bit her tongue. As it was, they were just skirting round their real feelings: *Liked*. *Become closer*. Even that, Sam was struggling to grasp, the chasm between those emotions and the lie he'd discovered their relationship to be – without widening it with talk of anything *deeper*. But her feelings for him had built slowly, in stages, she reminded herself; so maybe that was how to tackle it: take Sam step by step. She sighed. 'You know, when I was first sent in – as with most assignments – they tell you you're doing it for the common good. The nation. Your little bit in putting the world right. So, you're made to feel good about what you're doing. In your case, we were told that your manuscript had worrying implications for the War on Terror. That it could ignite Islamic passions and lead to serious conflict. In other words, stir up the hottest hornets' nest of the day. You needed keeping tabs on, watching. But then bit by bit, the heat was turned up. Check this, check that; monitor this, monitor that... *"It's more serious than we first thought!"* And every few chapters of *The Prophecy* you finished, I had to copy and send to Washington.'

She cradled her forehead, gently rubbing her temples. 'When they finally told me they were going to take the manuscript from you and destroy *all* possible copies – I had no idea that's what they planned. Let alone in the way it happened.' She held her eyes steady on Sam. 'But by then I'd seen the work you put in on *The Prophecy*. Slaving at it day by day. Putting everything you had into it. I knew that, to you, it would be like having your new-born baby wrenched away.'

She watched Sam flinch then and look away. Was he still harbouring doubt, or was the memory still too painful?

But she kept her gaze steady on him; because when he looked back at her, she wanted him to see that she meant these words. They weren't just more lies to add to the mountain she'd told him during their time together. 'And I saw too, Sam, how you were with your son. With your friends and others...and, most importantly, with *me*. You made me feel good, Sam. Wanted. *Loved*. I haven't felt that way before. Not like that.' But as Sam looked back at her, she could see why he'd turned away. His eyes were glistening, tears welling.

'Maybe that's because I *did* love you,' he said.

'I know...' She closed her eyes for a second, wishing the floor could swallow her up for what she'd done. She felt her own emotions welling up and bit back the tears. 'That's why, Sam, as I saw all of that – got to know you – that's why in turn I came to—'

But he reached out to her then, pressing two fingers gently against her lips. 'Don't...*don't*!'

For a moment there was silence, with only the falling of their breaths, Sam's eyes desperately searching hers. She felt suddenly empty inside, not sure what else she could tell him, what was left of her soul to bare that might convince him. But what had she expected? For eighteen months, she'd been party to pulling his life apart. Had she hoped to patch that all up simply in a twenty-minute conversation? Then she remembered something her father had said years ago. '*A gift can sometimes help prove your love. Not necessarily expensive, but something it's clear you've put a lot of thought into. One thing they really want, will* mean *something to them.*' She couldn't think of anything that Sam would want more.

'I made a copy,' she said.

'*What?*' He stared as if this might be another lie, a trick – or perhaps he hadn't heard right.

'When I found out they were going to take *The Prophecy* from you – having seen all you put into it, knowing what it meant to you – I put a copy on a memory stick. And put it somewhere safe.'

Sam's eyes kept searching hers, as if, of all the things she'd told him, this was hardest of all to believe.

She fished in her pocket for the key, leant over and

unlocked the handcuffs, pecking him softly on one cheek as she pulled back. And she saw then something in Sam's eyes finally settling, adjusting. Perhaps he was ready for the next stage; *perhaps*.

'But for all this to stop, Sam,' she said, 'we need to get that copy. Let me explain.'

CHAPTER THIRTY-FIVE

'Find him, find him...*find him*!'

Aside from the ass-chewing – hell, he was used to those now from Grayford – Washington had gained a certain satisfaction seeing Grayford break into a cold panic, lose his rag. Mr urbane-charming-cool – correct that, *ice-cold* – was the essence of Grayford. The sort of guy Washington imagined surgically removing your heart while you were still alive and, without as much as a blink or sweat bead broken, hold it up to you for casual conversation. *'Isn't the heart a fascinating thing?'*

Nothing ever rattled Grayford. Except now.

That satisfaction had at least taken some of the sting out of Grayford's verbal whipping. Some payback mileage too as he passed Grayford's message on to his team.

'The powers on high have spoken. And their instructions are pretty detailed and complex – so pay *real* good attention now.' He pitched his voice three octaves higher in a camp impression of Grayford. 'Find him, find him...*find him*!'

That got a few laughs all round. Then his expression became more sober as he went into detail as to just how that might be achieved. Playing Mr Intelligent to Grayford's oaf. Redressing the balance of only moments ago.

Orders over, he went through to the adjoining office to his own computer and tapped out his report on the whole sorry APB/Albany saga Grayford had requested.

Once they'd traced all possible addresses for Tynnan, putting out an APB had seemed the best, not to mention *only* way to handle it. Theirs was a small unit: they could only hit four possible addresses at the same time, max. Especially with one of those seven addresses being Vince Corcoran's Lakefield mansion – no doubt guarded like Fort Knox so demanding double their normal strike team. And if they'd run the strikes out of sync, word would have spread from one to the other like a bush fire. They'd have simply shifted

Tynnan one step ahead of them each time.

No, a blanket APB had been best, with the advice that they all strike at the same time. Which he'd been halfway through explaining when Grayford lost it.

Oregon was first up with news just over an hour later.

'Albany police have pinned it down to three likely places they lost Tynnan. Two streets where he might have jumped in a cab and a multi-storey car park. There are security cams in the multi-storey and one street, but if it's the other we're outta luck.'

'When can they get the tapes to us?'

'Originally they were talking about tomorrow morning by messenger, but I told them we didn't have the time. So they'll copy and JPEG them, then email the files straight to my computer. Should be through in an hour.'

'Good work.'

Seven snapped paper clips later, Cali was next to put his head in the door, though from his expression it looked like bad news.

'We've had another raid on the system.'

'When?'

'Just fifteen minutes ago.' Washington arched his eyebrow as if to ask: *why wasn't I told immediately?* Cali held a hand out. 'Spent that time working out what we might be dealing with.'

'Same guy as last time?' Late the previous afternoon

they'd had the first raid, Cali waxing lyrical about the ingenuity of the hacker. '*Shit-hot code-breaker. The few footprints left evaporated in some remote server in Surinam. Whoever he is, he's good. We ain't gonna track this guy.*'

'No, that's the thing.' Cali shrugged. 'No code-breaker used this time. Whoever it was went straight in with a known code – and *not* the one hit on by yesterday's hacker. It was different on the last three digits.' Cali explained how access codes were the same for the first fourteen digits, then differed on the last three. 'Many agents think they're the same for everyone through the whole seventeen, but they're not. Those last three in fact identify just who's accessing the—'

Washington cut in impatiently. 'Spare me the nerd lingo, willya – just cut to the chase: *who* you think was raiding the system?'

'You're not going to like it.'

'No, obviously not.' Washington fixed him with a glare. 'And even less now with your faux build-up.'

As Cali told him who he thought it was, Washington felt his chest tighten. 'That's not possible.' He shook his head. '*Not* possible.'

'*...so that they may know me when I show myself Holy through you before his eyes. I will summon a sword against Gog on all my mountains...every sword will be against his brother. I will execute judgement upon* *him with plague and bloodshed; I will pour torrents of rain, hailstones and burning sulphur upon him and on his troops and on the many nations with him.'*

Kenny Verbeck sat back and rubbed at his eyes. He'd started playing Matt Calvinson's sermons late the previous afternoon, headed home, and only had time to grab a quick coffee before settling down in his home study for round two: Calvinson's 7 p.m. live sermon. In between coffee refills and a quick spoon-taste of the dinner his wife had simmering on the stove, he watched most of it. He was recording it in any case: the main thing was the sequence, how the rhetoric had built over the past few weeks, and he still had four recordings to watch in the middle.

So that morning he'd settled down for that vital back-to-back play, and was seventy per cent through when Hank phoned. He was glad of the interruption. Twelve hours of Matt Calvinson's hell and damnation, with Satan, demons and trumpeting angels as supporting cast, was too much for any man to take.

'I managed to get into another five 101 files,' Hank said.

'Oh, right.' Hank had said he'd hoped to crack more of them. But as Hank told him what he'd found, Verbeck wasn't sure he was glad after all. 'Thanks.'

Hank sent the files through, and Verbeck spent half an hour reading them, making notes as he went, before getting back to the rest of Calvinson's sermons.

'*...they came out of the mouth of the dragon and out of the mouth of the beast and out of the mouth of the false prophet – spirits of demons performing miraculous signs, and they go out to the kings of the whole world to gather them for the battle in the place they call Armageddon...*'

Verbeck massaged his temples. He'd noticed a decided rhythm and momentum to Calvinson's recent speeches. He'd been talking for years about the '*End Times*' and '*The Rapture*' in loose terms; but now it was as if he knew with certainty that time was approaching. His smile increasingly smug, satisfied, as if to say: *I know something you don't!*

'*...And we see all of those events coming down upon us now as we witness the words of the false prophet in Tehran, Bahsem-Yahl – summoning his people too for those final battles in the Valley of Jehoshaphat, in Damascus...as has been written...*'

And now those 101 files had put texture and substance to it; just why Calvinson thought he might know something.

Verbeck went back through his notes and circled one of the names: Adel Al-Shaffir. The third time now that the name had come up, and he was probably the most viable contact. According to the 101 files he was also in touch with the others, so could in turn alert them; *if* he thought that was the best action.

But the other urgent call Verbeck had to make posed more of a dilemma. There was no point in going to his boss and, in turn, the NSA chief with this. Grayford pulled equivalent rank, so it would just be a Mexican stand-off. A few weeks of sandbagging with 'internal enquiry' threats, and already it would be too late. No, it had to go higher, and quickly. But there was only one person Verbeck knew who might be able to get the President's ear at the drop of a hat.

True to his word, Max Redmond at GCHQ got back to Adel mid-morning with computer renderings of what Al Hakam would look like without a beard or moustache. 'Or with just a moustache, if you prefer.'

The minute they came through, Adel passed them on to Isam and Siraj. 'Possible CCTV matches for all London airports and Eurostar.'

'For how long? Isam asked.

'Forty-eight hours after the attack. If we find nothing, we'll rethink: stretch the time frame or check other regional airports.'

Siraj picked up a match an hour after lunch: Heathrow Airport.

Adel went over to Siraj's computer as he ran the sequence.

'We pick him up first of all here. Terminal 4 concourse. Then here – this is the clearest shot.' Siraj zoomed in, and Adel nodded slowly. There was little doubt; it was almost an exact match of the computer photo: dark navy suit, white shirt, tie. Without that facial match he'd have merged with the throng of business travellers and been impossible to pick out. 'We lose him here for a while...then pick him up again here, joining the KLM queue.'

Adel looked at the timer in the corner: 21.08. Ninety minutes after Akram's attack. 'Certainly didn't waste any time getting his backside on the first flight out.' Al Hakam was one of Abu Khalish's main lieutenants and they'd never been this close before. Adel looked at the frozen frame; after four years of hunting down Khalish, it felt almost surreal. 'Get on to KLM and find out where that flight was headed.'

'No need.' Siraj smiled. A few deft key taps and another frame popped up with the check-in desk front-on. Siraj zoomed in until the desk sign was clear: *KLM. 22.15 to Amsterdam Schiphol.*

Adel went back to his desk and phoned his counterpart at TAME9 in Holland. 'Hayyan. Big fish just landed in your pond. And he might well still be there.'

Impossible! She was dead...*dead*!

He'd stood alongside Ohio and they'd watched for several minutes without a ripple or movement on the lake surface ahead.

They'd got the security cam tapes from Albany PD half an hour ago and started looking through them. They saw Tynnan cut swiftly across the street cam's view; there were no cabs in sight at that moment. They concentrated on the multi-storey, following his progress up the stairs: starting to speak on his cellphone halfway up, looking over the side as he reached the third floor, hanging up seconds after. He appeared increasingly agitated, then finally broke into a run.

They thought they'd pinpointed where he'd disappeared, just as he was getting into his car, a grey Dodge Caliber – but the view was mostly obscured by the Pathfinder with tinted windows alongside. All that was caught on cam was a flicker of arm movement to hint at a tussle behind.

They watched the squad car come into view and coast slowly along the floor. The Pathfinder glass was tinted, nothing could be seen – but Washington's guess was that they already had Tynnan laid low on the back seat, out of sight.

The Pathfinder pulled out shortly after the squad car disappeared from view. Tynnan's car behind was now fully visible, clear glass: no Sam Tynnan.

They went back on the tapes to when Tynnan's Dodge Caliber pulled in and parked thirty-four minutes earlier. Eighty-two seconds later on the cam timer, as Tynnan was going down in the car park elevator, the Pathfinder appeared and pulled in alongside.

As they watched the Pathfinder door open and a young spiky-haired blond guy step out, Washington eased an audible sigh of relief. Not Lorrena! His eyes hadn't deceived him. He *had* seen her drown in the lake.

Then a few paces from the Pathfinder someone else came into view and started talking to spiky-hair: female, platinum blonde, slim. Washington presumed she'd followed in another car just out of view of that cam. But something about her, the way she moved, caught his attention. And as she turned and started walking alongside spiky-hair towards the camera, he was almost sure. *Almost.*

'Freeze that frame and move in!' he instructed Cali.

And each frame as it moved closer, 5x, 10x, 20x – until her face filled the screen – he felt the hammering in his chest: no, no...*no*!

Washington closed his eyes for a second to compose himself. Then he got Cali to go back to when the Pathfinder first came into view for a similar freeze-frame blow-up of its license plate.

Minutes later, Washington made the call – perhaps it would make the payback more personal, an exorcism of sorts – and the plate number was out on the network linked to Tynnan's APB; along with two pictures of Lorrena Presutti/Perello, *whatever your name might be right now*: one blonde, one with dark hair. 'Could be travelling separately or together. Approach with caution. Both armed and highly dangerous.'

CHAPTER THIRTY-SIX

'All arranged. New Hampshire Union Bank, Lancaster,' Mike confirmed. 'Barry and Phil will meet up with you there – well, a discreet distance away. Three and a half hours, you reckon?'

'Yeah, three and a half.' This was the timing Lorrena had given Sam for the drive from Chris's place in Binghamton. Glancing across as she drove, she gestured, 'Give or take.'

'They'll probably get there a bit before you. If not, hang on. Don't risk going in without them watching your tail – too risky! They won't be long.'

'Sure, but not too long. Sitting in front of a bank

with the engine running, with an APB still out on yours truly – probably not the wisest move.'

Mike chuckled. 'You've been watching too many *Dirty Harry* movies. And, Sam – break a leg, huh?'

'Yeah. And if it all goes wrong, no doubt someone else will do that for me.'

An hour before setting off for Lancaster, over a couple of strong coffees, Lorrena had filled in the details and explained why getting the memory stick copy would change everything.

'Like I said, at my level I was only told so much. And that changed and evolved as things progressed. After that first stage – when I was told your manuscript could have cataclysmic impact on Islam's relationship with the West – the next was after they'd taken it. "OK, you've got it now," I said. "Why doesn't the op end and you ship me out of here?" They said I had to hang on to make sure you didn't have hidden copies or didn't feel inclined to rewrite it. Which then meant liaising regularly with the fake-Arab hit squad – because if you'd suddenly become a threat, they'd have been the ones to take you out rather than Washington's main team. All neatly put down to a terrorist attack.'

Lorrena closed her eyes for a second with the reminder, took a fresh breath. 'Finally, when parts of your manuscript started being played out in real life with mosque bombings – they dropped the last shoe: that what you'd laid down was an ingenious scenario to flush out Khalish, judged by the powers that be,' Lorrena mimed parenthesis with two fingers, 'as "too great an opportunity to pass up playing out in real life". The way Washington put it, it wasn't clear whether I was being told at that stage only because events on the ground necessitated that "need to know". Or whether he'd also just been let in on the loop himself. So I can't say, hand on heart, whether that was the plan from the start.' Lorrena shrugged. 'Or, if it was, just *who* was in on it, including Washington.'

'So how would getting that stick with *The Prophecy* now scuttle all that?'

'Because that was the main worry, especially at the Abu Khalish stage. If you *did* dig out a copy of *The Prophecy* from somewhere, or rewrite it, *whatever* – if it was suddenly out there in the public domain – Khalish would then know all he had to do was get the likes of Bahsem-Yahl to come out with an opposed declaration to take the heat off.'

'And now that he *has* come out with that announcement?'

'Different effect, same end result. Can you imagine the great Bahsem-Yahl suddenly hit with the revelation that he's been no more than a bit player in a fictional manuscript which a CIA department have decided to play out? Certainly he'd avoid any more "grand proclamations", unless he was keen for more egg on his face. And, once he'd folded his tent, no doubt the current furore would die down too.' Lorrena frowned. 'Sure, he'd probably bleat that was all part of the same "grand conspiracy of the Western devils", but copies of *The Prophecy* to a couple of major newspapers – along with its creation and editing dates, all on that same stick – should quickly stifle that.'

Mike had been incredulous when Sam had brought him up to date: *Jeez – Lorrena's still alive? Are you sure you can trust her? That she's not spinning you another line?*

'Can you think of another good reason why she'd tell me all this? Bother to run the gauntlet now to try and get this stick?' Mike didn't have any good answers to that, and so the arrangements were made: Barry and Phil would meet them at the bank for back-up. The bank where six months ago Lorrena had deposited a copy – all but four pages he'd written on the last day.

Mike was the only call he'd made. Lorrena was against him calling Emile in London until *after* they'd got the disk. 'I hear you loud and clear that you trust him. But he's still part of the same extended security network. Might not be him, but it only takes one word slipped to the wrong person in his department and we'd find a reception committee waiting for us at the bank. Once we've got the disk, it's different. Then it's a done deal.'

Lorrena drove. Chris in the back on his laptop.

'He'll keep us up to speed on whether the police or Washington get on our tail.'

The farm fields and rolling hills of Vermont drifted by; a signpost, *Claremont 3 miles,* just ahead.

But one part of Lorrena's account didn't add up, Sam contemplated. 'Knowing all this, why didn't you get the stick earlier?'

'As much as I might hate Washington for what he did to me, and *you* – you think I'd want to spoil an op like that? The possibility of Abu Khalish giving himself up. All those lives saved?' Lorrena tightened her grip on the wheel. 'And the Bahsem-Yahl announcement was *what* – five, six days ago? It's only now, as we see those street demos gaining steam, that it looks unlikely Khalish will give himself up. He'll just sit tight and see how all this pans out between Islam and the West.'

Sam nodded. 'That certainly changed everything. Question is, was that also part of the plan from the outset? And, if so, why?'

'I don't know, Sam. As you can see, I too was played – only not to the same degree as you. And it's taken me until now to unravel even this part, let alone anything else. That's something which neither of us might ever get to find out.'

'Just had a couple of cam recognitions in on that license plate: Bellow Falls and Claremont. Both on Highway 91, Vermont.'

Washington nodded and followed Indiana back to his computer, looking over his shoulder as he traced a finger over an on-screen Google map.

Washington asked, 'Which was the last one in?'

'Claremont, recorded just seven minutes ago. Bellow Falls, twenty-three minutes. So they're heading north.'

'What's up the line from there?'

Indiana scrolled up. 'Hanover, St Johnsbury, Lyndonville and Lancaster.'

Washington studied the map for a second. 'OK. Let's get ourselves in the zone. Nearest military airstrip where we could land?'

Indiana searched through the list. 'Nothing nearby. But there's a private airfield just south of St Johnsbury. Should be able to take a C-37 or Bombardier at a push.'

Minutes later, the arrangements were all made: a Bombardier CL-605 would be fuelled and ready for take off from Langley Air Force Base. Cali checked he had everything he needed between two laptops to maintain tracking and communications, and, the last Kevlar vest slipped on, boot strap tightened and rifle bolt checked, Washington's team of twelve were packed in two Hummer H3s rolling furiously towards it.

CHAPTER THIRTY-SEVEN

'You shouldn't call me here! It's too risky.' Adel's breath came short as he spoke, not just from surprise, but from leaving his house in a rush the second he recognised the voice. He started heading up the road.

'I got the message you left about Al Hakam,' his caller said.

'Yes. I left that between work and home, when I was able to speak. But that's all the news there was. You shouldn't have called me back.'

At the other end, the man was silent for a moment. It was night-time and the sea between the palm trees was now like black soup, the only light from a hazy moon and some fishing boats on the horizon. Distant pinprick lights from their lamps shone into the water to attract fish. 'That was our arrangement from the outset. You'd keep me informed.'

'Yes, of course. And I *have*. But that's all there's been for now.'

There was another heavy pause. 'You'll let me know the moment there's anything more on Al Hakam? If they start getting close?'

'Without question. Of course.'

'Then I shall leave everything, as usual, once again in your capable hands. *Salaam*.'

'Salaam.'

It was the second call of the day to rattle Adel. The first, from Kenny Verbeck of the NSA, had come through an hour before he'd left work, and he'd spent practically every minute since juggling the words in his brain like so many hot potatoes.

'We've been looking at the records of another department in relation to Bahsem-Yahl. And your name has come up in those files, along with a certain Sam Tynnan and Jean-Pierre Bourdin. Both of them known to you, I believe?'

'Yes. Yes, they are.' Verbeck obviously already knew.

'Now it's our belief that an op originally aimed at

flushing out Abu Khalish at some stage got derailed to head elsewhere.'

'And where might that be?'

Verbeck took a step back. 'We're not entirely sure yet. Still putting together all the pieces. But suffice to say that while we spend much of our time focusing on extremities of Islam as they pertain to terrorism, there are extremities too on the other side, in Christianity. "End-timers" as they're known. Some of whom, indeed, might feel well served by escalated conflict between Islam and the West, because it satisfies certain Bible prophecies they hold good and true.'

As Adel tried to draw Verbeck out, he'd taken another step back. 'As I say, we're still in the midst of unravelling it all – so it would be neither fair nor wise to say more than I already have. But to the main reason for my call now: you're obviously aware how Sam Tynnan has been played and manipulated in all this. Well, the thing is, from what we can see on file, it appears you and Bourdin have been as well.'

Adel had felt the floor fall away. 'In *what* way?'

'Again, we don't have all the specifics. But I think you should be aware of that: some of the information you've been fed might not be reliable. Particularly if you're hinging key decisions on that information. You're in contact with Tynnan and Bourdin?'

'Only Tynnan. But not for the last couple of days. There's an APB out on him, and it appears he's gone to ground.'

'Yes, I've seen that. I'll see what we can do this end to try and remedy that situation.'

'I'm sure Mr Tynnan would much appreciate it.' Adel put an edge to his tone. *See what we can do... try and...* It sounded tenuous. Certainly didn't appear that Verbeck had compelling influence over Sam's fate. Which made Adel wonder just how much sway he held with everything else.

'But if you are able to have contact with either of them, their input could throw a spotlight on just what information might be reliable, and what might have been guided by an outside hand.'

Adel was out of breath. He'd been walking steadily up the hillside road from his home, and now, as he reached the brow, he turned and admired the view.

He was at the top of Epsom Downs and ahead of him the land gently rolled away. There was no dramatic cliff drop or lover's leap, but spread before him on the horizon were the lights of London.

He used to come here a lot with Tahiya, particularly when they first met. They'd have late lunch or drinks at a local pub and make sure to get to the car park just before dusk. Then sit there in his battered nine-year-old Toyota Corolla – all he could afford back then – and watch the sun dip down and the lights of London slowly rise.

It was partly the reason they'd chosen the area. They could enjoy that same view a short walk from the house, and at weekends they often came with the kids.

He'd checked Verbeck on the system and seen that he headed up a sizeable NSA section. He looked for real. But what if Verbeck was part of it all? They knew he, Adel, was on track with foiling the final mosque bombings, so something else was needed to throw him off. Something to make him doubt his current information. So Washington gets one of his cronies to make a call.

Information? All he'd had to work on had been Tynnan's mosque list and a couple of quatrains from a latter-day Nostradamus seer, the rest he'd cobbled together himself with some help from Namir.

Derailed? Christian extremists and Bible prophecies. End-timers?

It sounded even more ridiculous and far-fetched than Tynnan's manuscript. If Washington was going to get one of his buddies to try and throw him off track, he should at least have troubled to put together a half-believable—

Adel stopped himself. *Exactly.* Which meant the opposite applied: this was the last story they'd concoct if they wanted him to swallow it. Which, de facto, meant that it was probably true.

The lights ahead glimmered and twinkled. Teasing, *elusive*. Something he was missing, just out of reach…

End-timers? The last fiery domes…Saladin?

And finally as that light reached him, the last piece of missing mosaic, it froze the breath in his chest. But he still needed to check to be certain. He started back to the house, striding purposefully. Within twenty paces, he was at a half-run.

Mike Kiernan's coffee cup was halfway up to his lips when he saw the news item. He put it down again.

The kids were at school and Cathy at her aerobics class. *Peace*. Ideal writing time. The panic with Sam had shot a few holes in his own writing schedule these past days and he needed to catch up.

But he couldn't just close the shutters. Block out the world outside. Not while they were still in the midst of it all.

In the end he'd found a good compromise. The local news was interminably boring: new shopping mall being opened, nursing home closing down, NY Giants cheerleader dropped from the line-up because it was discovered she'd previously posed for *Hustler*.

So he'd have the TV on with just the picture, no

sound. A mindless, endless real-life visual soap opera to make the mind swiftly switch channels to something else. *Anything* else.

He'd had a good run of two hours when the item came on: a full face shot of Lorrena with dark hair, as Mike knew her. Then one with a blonde wig or dyed.

Mike turned up the sound and caught the tail end. '...*Linked to terrorist suspect Samuel Tynnan. Last seen in the Albany area and still at large.*' There was another quick shot of Sam to remind everyone as the item ended. '*And today at Rosamond Gifford Zoo in Syracuse, a surprise for newly arrived panda—*' Mike hit the mute button.

When he'd spoken to Sam earlier, Sam had reassured him he should be fine. '*The glass of the Pathfinder is heavily tinted, but as an extra precaution my hair's been dyed blond – like Lorrena's. In any case, nobody's going to see me. She's going into the bank alone. And she's not even remotely on anyone's radar. She's meant to be dead, remember?*'

But somehow they *had* put all the pieces together, worked it out. He reached for the phone.

Adel was breathless. Both from his run back from the Downs and his frantic key-tapping and searching on his home computer.

Of the last fiery domes,

The order of one shall be reversed,
The other replaced by that of higher order,
Saladin shall be confounded

Adel had originally discounted the second quatrain from Jean-Pierre. Mainly because it contradicted the earlier quatrain which had rung true and they'd struck gold on with his 'equivalent mosque' theory. Which then also meant, from that same quatrain, that the final two mosque targets in Damascus and Medina would remain the same.

He'd started to wonder whether Saladin might relate to himself. Yet another Arab trying to fend off the forces rallied against Islam; save those last 'fiery domes'. Yet finally *confounded* by their plot, by the information presented. *Played and manipulated?... It appears you and Bourdin have been as well.*

Verbeck's mention of 'Christian extremism' had sparked the thought. Saladin had been the legendary warrior leading Islam against the onslaught of Christian forces in the Crusades. And one of Saladin's most famous battles had been the siege of Jerusalem. *End-timers?* Adel recalled from somewhere that Jerusalem also featured in their final prophecies. He started searching on his computer.

At one point, as he was furiously tapping away, Jibril peeked his head in the door. Adel's at-home computer was also used regularly by his kids for school project work. Adel waved him away impatiently.

'Not now...*not now*!' *Can't you see your father's busy trying to save the world?*

Tahiya popped her head in straight after him. 'It's late, Adel. He's going to bed. He only wanted to say goodnight.'

Adel brought Jibril close and hugged him, probably far tighter than normal. 'Sorry...sorry!' Suddenly realising that the pressure of everything had led to his over-reaction. As Tahiya led Jibril out, she shot Adel a look as if to say: *'We made a pact that you'd never bring all this home with you. Perhaps now you can see why.'*

Adel looked back at the screen:

Saladin reclaimed Jerusalem in 1187 after 88 years of Crusader rule. Saladin initially was unwilling to give any quarter to the European occupants of Jerusalem until Balian of Ibelin threatened to kill every Muslim in the city and destroy Islam's holy shrines of the Dome of the Rock *and* Al-Aqsa Mosque *if quarter was not given.*

Adel sifted through the 'End-Times' pages he'd Googled, found the reference: '*And when ye shall see Jerusalem compassed with armies, then know that the desolation thereof is nigh... For these be the days of vengeance, that all things which are written may be fulfilled...for there shall be great distress in the land, and wrath upon the people. And they shall fall by the edge of the sword, and shall be led away captive into all nations; and Jerusalem shall be trodden down...'*

Damascus, as Adel saw now as he scanned through, followed Jerusalem in the 'End-Times' doomsday clock: the last two cities destroyed before Armageddon. Damascus was the last but one mosque site from Tynnan's list; but Jerusalem he hadn't mentioned. *The order of one shall be reversed... The other replaced by that of higher order.*

More worrying still, Adel read from those pages, many end-timers believed that the destruction of the Dome of the Rock was necessary to make way for the building of the Third Temple, the event which would herald the return of the Messiah.

He did one last Google search to be sure: *Jean-Pierre Bourdin. Nostradamus prophesier.* Fifty-three hits, Bourdin's home page was sixth on the list. An email address and telephone number were at the bottom. Adel picked up the phone.

It answered late, on the fourth ring. Adel launched quickly into the reason for his call.

'Ah, you are Sam Tynnan's contact?' Jean-Pierre confirmed. 'I tried to get him a couple of times the other day, but his phone's not answering. I was beginning to—'

'He's got problems right now,' Adel cut in. 'Hopefully all cleared up in a few days. It's a long story. But that's partly why I'm calling now rather than him. Those two quatrains you passed to him. Where did you get them from?'

Jean-Pierre suddenly became wary, recalling Vrellait's warning not to share with any other parties. *The non-disclosure he'd signed.* 'I...I'm afraid I can't say. It's confidential where they came from.'

'So they *did* come from somewhere else?' Adel pressed. 'That's what you're saying?'

Jean-Pierre became flustered. 'It's a...a delicate situation. One involving a pledge of discretion to another party.'

Adel took a deep breath. Losing patience. 'Look – I don't need to know *where* they came from. Only that they were fed to you by an outside party.'

They? 'Yes, yes it was – but *only* the first quatrain. The second was my own.'

'*OK.* Only the first, you say. That last quatrain wasn't given to you, fed or suggested to you in any way by an outside source? You're sure of that?'

'No. It was all of my own doing, my own creation.' Jean-Pierre explained that he was preparing a volume of modern-day Nostradamus prophecies using the same ancient methods. 'Consulting the stars and heavens exactly as the great Michel would have done five hundred years ago. Pure inspiration!' Jean-Pierre's voice rose with excitement. 'But that is in fact why I was trying to get hold of Sam. You see, Michel's three Antichrists have always been seen as Napoleon, Hitler and then Mabus. But he also mentioned the "new Xerxes" in relation to Mabus, and now with this fresh quatrain of mine adding Saladin, we also have a chain of three leaders from what is now Islam: Xerxes, Saladin...finally Mabus. So, given that context, *three* Antichrists might hold another significance. I thought he, *you*, should know – in case it was important.'

'I see.' While no doubt solid grandstanding for the sort of books Jean-Pierre wrote, nothing immediately hit Adel from that link – and he had what he wanted already. He thanked Jean-Pierre for his help, and the second he hung up he started dialling again.

Dome of the Rock, Jerusalem. Adel prayed he wasn't too late.

LANCASTER, NEW HAMPSHIRE.

Lorrena coasted along slower as she came into the street with the bank.

Fifty yards before it, Barry and Phil sat in their dark-grey Buick – Sam reminded of that day at Springfield when he'd met Emile. They barely got a nod from Barry as they rolled past; as before they gave no overt recognition which might tie them together.

The town was quiet. Busy only in the winter – the

skiing and log cabin season, or the height of summer – for the nearby lakes, now it was that awkward dead period in between.

Lorrena had chosen Lancaster because she wanted somewhere remote from the Oneida area. '*Nowhere Washington might possibly make a connection.*' She'd been to Lancaster only twice as a young kid when she'd visited her uncle in Syracuse and he'd driven up at the weekend for her first skiing experiences.

Lorrena parked twenty yards past the bank in the first available space. She checked herself briefly in the mirror and got out.

'Wish me luck!'

She didn't wait for a response before shutting the door, so Sam was left only with willing it as he watched her in the wing mirror. She sauntered along casually, making sure she didn't appear too hasty or on edge, then paused a moment to compose herself before entering the bank. Then she was gone from view.

The wait was nerve-racking. Only one other person went in the bank over the following minutes, and two came out – one a teller from her navy blazer. Sam watched each of them like a hawk. The teller, a short-cropped redhead in her early thirties, went into a café four doors away. The exiting customer, a paunchy, mid-fifties man, receded in Sam's mirror before finally turning into a side street a hundred yards behind them.

Then everything was quiet for a moment, nobody in or out.

It seemed incredible, unreal that any minute Lorrena would reappear with the memory stick and all would be made good as she'd said. The whole nightmare would end and he'd regain the eighteen months of his life lost writing *The Prophecy*. His eyes transfixed to the wing mirror following every movement from Lancaster's main street, it seemed almost too much to hope for.

Sam jumped as his phone rang. He looked at the display: *Mike*. The only person he'd picked up for the past forty-eight hours.

'Yeah?' Then Sam felt the ground open up as Mike told him about the news item just on.

'Whatever you do, don't let Lorrena go into that bank!'

'It...it's *too late*! She's already in there.' Sam looked in the wing mirror again, this time more anxiously; imagining wailing sirens and squad cars winging round the corner any second.

'How long ago?'

'*What?*' Sam glanced back as Chris murmured something. He'd picked up the news item on line. He turned his laptop screen towards Sam. The photo with blonde hair was hazy, but unmistakably Lorrena. 'Uh...three or four minutes ago. No more.'

Mike sighed. 'This was on just a minute ago.

Perhaps it's the first time it's been up. All we can do is pray nobody in that bank has seen it yet.'

'Yeah, I suppose.' Sam swallowed hard. Ahead, the red-headed teller was coming out of the café with a sandwich or cake bag. 'All we can do.' And after Mike signed off, Sam did just that. Closed his eyes and silently prayed.

CHAPTER THIRTY-EIGHT

THE WHITE HOUSE, WASHINGTON, DC.

Carl Miller was a legend. Retired now for six years, he'd been CIA chief for so many years – twenty-two to be precise – that many people thought he was still at the helm.

The last ten years of his tenure hadn't been easy. Plagued by arthritis, it had finally got to his spine and hunched him over, bent and gnarled his hands and fingers so that they looked like twisted tree roots.

Then came the cruel names, the 'twisted toad', the 'caustic cripple', along with the push to get him out – claiming that his illness no longer made him fit for duty. Largely ambition driven by those pushing than any true reflection on Miller's ability, successive presidents had resisted that push; for them, the CIA and Miller were synonymous. It became difficult for them to imagine anyone else adequately filling those shoes.

Despite the names and the acid reputation bandied about by some, Verbeck had found Miller – from a four-year spell with the CIA before he'd joined the NSA – one of the kindest, warmest bosses he'd ever worked with. He was also one of the only people Verbeck knew who could get the President's ear at short notice.

They waited only a few minutes before being shown into the Roosevelt Room by the chief usher. Miller was stick-thin and close to six foot, but his bent spine robbed him of a few inches. He walked with the aid of a cane.

The President sat at the head of a long mahogany table. He gestured towards two seats to his left. Miller took the closest.

After the pleasantries and Miller asking how the President's father was – that's how far he went back with the family – he started laying out his case. He ran through the events sequentially: Bahsem-Yahl, 101 files, Grayford, Washington, Tynnan, Adel Al-Shaffir, Matt Calvinson – pretty much how Verbeck had laid it out for him earlier. He passed across the relevant 101 files as he spoke, but the President only glanced at portions. For most of the time his eyes stayed fixed on Miller.

It was a consummate performance. Over the years, Miller had learnt to play his illness to advantage. A pained grimace or sudden catching of breath, as if he'd just been hit with a sharp pang, often worked wonders.

There was silence as he finished, the President summoning his thoughts or uncertain whether there was more.

Finally: 'And this second scenario you *suspect* – it's your belief this is in play right now?'

'Yes. As we speak. No time to lose – and all the other worn clichés.' Miller forced a smile.

A few more questions to clarify the situation, then the President sat back, his eyes going between Miller and the files. He waved a hand towards them.

'Now I'm not even going to attempt to claim I didn't have knowledge of the first part of this op. That would be ingenious of me to do so.'

'Disingenuous,' Miller corrected.

The President smiled. 'Just testing. Like I was saying, you'd find that hard to believe. It would give the message I don't know what's going on in my own security networks. But are you truly suggesting I might have had knowledge of this latter part and *still* approved it?'

'No. Not at all, Mr President.' Miller grimaced with

an unexpected pang. 'In fact, the opposite. I believe they only presented the first part of this op, knowing it had high chances of getting rubber-stamped. Then at some stage they hijacked it to head to stage two – probably where they'd intended it to go from the outset. A case of starting off as one thing and ending up as something else entirely.' He forced a smile. 'And, after Iraq, we all probably have a better understanding of how that can happen.'

The President nodded slowly. 'But it's still all just a *theory*, Carl. That's what you're saying? A hotchpotch joining of dots from these 101 files. You don't have any hard facts yet?'

Miller shrugged. 'Oh, sure. In a few weeks or months, no doubt we'll have those *facts*. By which time it will be too late. And a year from now there'll probably be a senate enquiry – while we're also busy counting the rubble and bodies from Islamic riots for bombing their prized mosques and Bahsem-Yahl has found the justification to fire those missiles you fear Iran has. Or maybe Israel will get antsy and do it first! You want to wait for all that to happen, fine.'

'I hear you loud and clear, Carl. But there's also a flip side: if I cut this op – based right now, like I say, on little more than a *theory* – we could be losing the best opportunity we've ever had of getting Abu Khalish to come out with his hands up. Bunch of lives saved there too, in case you haven't noticed.'

'Of course. Every op has its upside and downside. And over the years I've probably spent more time weighing that than most.' Miller shifted in his seat, wheezing softly from the exertion. 'But I believe this one's gone beyond that now. After Bahsem-Yahl's proclamation, the odds on Khalish giving himself up are remote. Further mosque bombings, and he'll just sit by and watch with interest to see which way Bahsem-Yahl jumps next.'

The President glanced towards the side-wall portraits, as if hoping to draw inspiration from past presidents. 'So what you're saying is I'm damned if I do, damned if I don't?'

Miller simply nodded, said nothing. *Wouldn't be the first time*, he reflected.

The President took a moment to collect his thoughts. 'As always, Carl, you lay out a good case. But I need a little time to consider this.'

'*Time?* That's one thing we don't have a lot of.'

'I know. I appreciate that.' But there was little beyond the President's strained smile to indicate which way his decision would go.

'And talking about damned – or *damnation*, as he likes to put it. It might be prudent to be arm's length from Calvinson when this blows, which I believe it will. There'll be strong focus on his Party contributions of the past years, as if there hasn't been enough already.'

'I'll take that under good advisement too, Carl. Thank you.' He smiled tightly, his poker face starting to strain.

They left and as their footsteps echoed along the West Colonnade, Miller turned to Verbeck.

'We've done all we can. Pushed it as far as we're able, or *dare* to go. Now it all rests in God's hands.'

'You mean the President's?'

Miller smiled. 'Just testing.'

In-flight, Washington arranged by phone for two BMW X5s to be waiting at the airfield.

Cali picked up another plate identification read just before they landed. 'On the ramp heading off of 91. Looks like they're headed for Lancaster.'

In the lead X5 with Washington, Cali and Indiana handled communications. Nevada and Montana sat with rifles at the ready, Ohio drove. The other six, rifles and M16s primed and ready, rode in the second vehicle.

Twenty-eight minutes later they were headed down the same ramp, Cali's mood improving as he studied his laptop.

'Got them again. And this time it's a fixed read. Looks like they've parked.' He turned his screen so Washington could see. 'Cam in front of a bank in Lancaster.'

'How far away are we?'

Cali clicked his on-screen map back to the forefront. 'Twenty-seven miles.'

Washington looked at their speedo: 89 mph. Eighteen minutes away.

Everything about bank manager Colin Finch was compact, thought Lorrena: not tall, five-four max, a trim compact frame; no fat, but not an ounce of muscle either.

His papers were piled neatly and compactly to one side, his reading glasses were slim, compact, which indeed he'd just taken from a compact case to compare her receipt against the register open on his desk.

She smiled as Finch looked up from the register.

'All seems to be in order, Miss Pres...Presutti. One year paid in advance, so no fees owing.' He peered closer at the screen. 'Still five months left, in fact.' He looked at her as if that might hold some significance.

She held the smile. *It didn't*. With it being the last half-hour of banking business that day, she'd had to wait ten minutes while Finch finished with his last customer. Before walking in, she'd managed to calm her nerves, but as the seconds dragged she'd felt herself tensing up again. She glanced at her watch.

'Sorry, Mr Finch. But I've left things tight for another appointment.'

'Yes. Yes, of course.' Flushing faintly, *he hadn't been compact enough with his time*, he quickly scanned a document to one side. He passed it across. 'The release form. Sign and date at the bottom, and that concludes everything.'

She did as instructed and passed it back. 'Thanks.'

'And identification?'

She handed across her passport.

He compared signatures, *OK*, but his eyes did a fleeting double check between her and her passport photo.

She touched her hair. 'Blondes have more fun, as they say.' She smiled.

He passed her passport back. 'Everything appears to be in order.' Then he unclipped the envelope with the memory stick from another form and slid it across. 'All done, I believe. I don't want to hold you up more than need be.'

They stood.

But as they came out of Finch's office and Lorrena caught the eye of one of the cashiers – a short-cropped redhead – she knew there was a problem.

The woman did a quick double take, looked like she had just seen a ghost.

'Mr Finch!' the woman called out, panic in her eyes. The photo had just been on the TV in the café. She was sure she wasn't mistaken.

'One minute,' Finch replied tersely. 'I'm finishing with a customer.' Finch opened the cashier's gate for Lorrena. 'If we can be of any assistance in the future, don't hesitate.'

'Certainly.' She nodded. 'Thank you.' But the blood-rush to her head was so heavy she could hardly hear her own voice.

She strode away as quickly as she could without making it evident there was a problem – and was two-thirds of the way across the bank when Finch called after her.

'Miss Presutti. *Hold on!*'

She kept walking as she glanced back – the expressions on Finch and the cashier's faces told her all she needed to know – and with a muttered, 'I don't think so,' she ran the last few yards to the door.

Finch hit the door lock a beat too late, Lorrena heard it buzz as she swung it open to make her escape. The alarm rang out a second after, waking Lancaster from its normal calm.

DOME OF THE ROCK, JERUSALEM.

The Dome of the Rock and Al-Aqsa mosques comprise Islam's third most holy sites after Mecca and Medina. They are also among its most fiercely guarded: not only from the contingent of Muslim *Waqf* guards within the Temple Mount compound, but the Israeli guards by its main entrance, the Mughrabi Gate, and beyond on its Western, 'Wailing', Wall. In addition, countless security cams around its perimeter and in the Old City fed back to a control centre half a mile away, headed by Choam Weisel.

Israel took security of the Dome of the Rock very seriously. Not least because an attack on the Dome would undoubtedly give rise to Islamic cries that they'd purposely been lax so that an attack could take place. The possible repercussions were too horrendous to contemplate.

The first thing to alert Weisel's team watching the banks of cams that night was a grey van stopping near the eastern perimeter wall. The operator, Mikhel, watched it for a moment without alerting Weisel – then beckoned him over frantically as four men wearing ski masks burst out.

Three ran to the wall, throwing grappling hooks up, the other ran south and was quickly out of sight of the cam.

'What's the nearest patrol we can get there?' Weisel barked.

'Via Dolorosa, I think.' Mikhel picked up the phone. 'Also alert the Mughrabi Gate guards?'

'No. The *Waqf* patrols will see this lot first.' With a Dolorosa unit from the rear and *Waqf* guards in front, they weren't going to get far, thought Weisel.

But halfway through dialling, Mikhel froze as a Sufa police jeep appeared on the same cam and pulled up twenty yards behind the van. One policeman stayed in the jeep and five leapt out, the lead two drawing their guns, shouting up at the three now halfway up the ropes on the wall.

'*Mazel tov!*' Weisel held both palms out, glancing heavenward. 'Some days God reads your mind.'

As Mikhel hung up, another of his other men, Yaniv, held out his phone. On the line was one of the policemen at the eastern wall.

'Choam Weisel.'

'As I was saying to your man – we picked up on the van in the Muslim quarter. Didn't like the look of it, so we followed. Lucky we did.'

'Certainly was.' Yaniv had switched a screen to the same cam, so Weisel could see the policeman talking in his jeep, his men to one side beckoning the wall climbers down at gunpoint. Then he remembered the fourth man and told him, 'He ran to the south. We lost him on the cams behind some trees, so you might not have seen him either.'

'Oh, *right*.' The policeman glanced over his shoulder. 'We'll go and check.'

Suddenly there was a flash and a small explosion from seventy yards behind his jeep. All the screens in the operations room went blank.

'What's happened?' Weisel yelped.

'Uh…*yeah*. I'm still here. Looks like the guy you mentioned just took out the nearby substation. But don't worry, we're on it. And the three on the wall are starting to come down now.' In the background, Weisel could hear excitable shouts in Hebrew and Arabic. 'They're not going anywhere. Look, I've got to join my men and help out. I'll call again in two minutes when I know everything's a hundred per cent secure.'

'Ah, yes. *Sure.*'

But in the following silence, with every screen in the operations room blank and no eyes and now no ears on what was happening, Weisel started to feel uneasy. *What if they didn't get that last guy? What if it wasn't as secure as they thought?* He looked back at Mikhel.

'Let's go with that suggestion after all. Alert the Mughrabi Gate guards. This lot might need the back-up.'

Mikhel started speaking on the phone, and Weisel watched his face drop in utter disbelief.

'*Eh?*' Weisel turned sharply as one of his other men tried to grab his attention. It was Gabriel Chayat of *Shin Bet* on the line for him. *Certainly was all happening tonight.* 'Ask Mr Chayat to hold on one minute. Just finishing up with something else.' The great *Angel Gabriel* would have to wait for once. Whatever was happening at the Mughrabi Gate suddenly looked more intriguing.

Mikhel put one hand over the mouthpiece as he turned to Weisel. 'You're not going to believe this.'

* * *

Adel's call was to TAME12 in Tel Aviv, who in turn called Gabriel Chayat, head of *Shin Bet*, Israel's internal intelligence. Chayat made three calls: The first was to instantly mobilise a 20-strong *Yassam* strike unit to the Dome of the Rock; the second was to inform the security minister what was happening, and why; the third to tell Choam Weisel what he would any second see on his Temple Mount security screens.

That third call took place as the *Yassam* team, headed by Avrim Talmi, were storming the Mughrabi Gate, one of the gate guards having just taken Mikhel's call. Talmi's second in command, Jaron, spoke briefly with Mikhel and, hearing about the assault by the east wall, commented, 'I'm sure they're all in on it together. Can't see them trying to take on a dozen or more *Waqf* guards with just four men.' Then he put on his own headgear, integral gas and night-vision mask, and brought up the rear of his team already at a half-run.

Talmi was one of the first out onto the flat stone platform of the Temple Mount, a few of his men flanking each side. To his right was the Al-Aqsa Mosque, to his left the Dome of the Rock. The main floodlights were out, but generator-powered emergency lights provided some brighter light-spikes in the soft green fluorescence of his night vision.

He could hear voices, frantic footsteps, some gunfire, but couldn't match those sounds to people until he'd run twenty yards out – the Dome itself blocked most of the activity.

Then it became clear. Two men were running from the far side of the Dome, one ten yards behind the other. A number of guards on the ground, Talmi presumed were the *Waqf* patrol, knocked out by the gas drifting from a nearby canister.

One *Waqf* guard was not quite fully under, and managed to raise his upper body to fire at the two running men. The return fire was instant, two shots kicking up stone dust close to him, the third hitting his rifle shoulder.

They'd hardly be able to move an inch without taking out that position, Talmi considered: from the rampart top of the east wall, a few men were firing rifles and had ropes dangling down the wall below them, the two men now scurrying across the courtyard headed frantically towards those ropes.

Talmi directed ten of his men to hit the wall-top position with a barrage of fire, and another two to aim at the two men running. 'Leg shots – we want them alive, if possible.'

He'd already broken into a run, beckoning Jaron to follow him – he wasn't sure he could ask anyone else to do this duty.

'*Short time fuses*' on the C4, that's all he'd been told. *But did that mean forty seconds, a minute, two minutes?* The difference now would be critical.

A shot zinged close by, the answer fire from his men heavier still. His breath rasped loudly inside the gas mask, the ghostly green Cinerama strip of his night vision jolting as he ran.

And then he saw the *plastique*. Pale grey packs either side of the portico facing the Dome of the Chain. Talmi went for the furthest – he was three yards ahead – and pointed Jaron to the other.

They didn't check the timers, simply took a few frantic steps and launched the C4 as far away as possible. Jaron's pack reached the trees beyond the steps that side before exploding. Talmi wasn't so lucky. Hardly had it left his fingertips before he felt its blast, felt it burn the hair from his head and the air from his lungs as it hurled him back against the Dome of the Rock wall. Then everything went black.

All gone wrong. Sam was convinced the game was up two minutes before the bank alarm went off when he saw a squad car pull up forty yards behind them on the opposite side.

His first thought was that they'd made Lorrena's number plate. Chris had just accessed the latest APB broadcast and seen the update on their details. Or perhaps someone inside the bank had recognised her and alerted them. But then the cop in the passenger seat got out and went into a Starbucks.

Sam's held breath eased.

Though as the cop returned with two coffees and they sat drinking them, again Sam was convinced that his first thought was right and it was all a ruse: *Terrorist alert. Wait for back-up. Meanwhile grab a couple of coffees, act nonchalant. Make sure not to frighten them off before the cavalry arrives.*

Sam's eyes cannoned between the two wing mirrors, praying that the squad car shifted and proved him wrong or that Lorrena came out before the back-up arrived and half a dozen sirens descended on them.

The bank alarm ringing killed any further speculation.

The squad car driver slammed into DRIVE on reflex. He didn't think he'd ever had an easier bust. The alarm bell ringing, the smoking gun of the girl running out. All the time a police car sitting across the road. *Boy, they had some dumb robbers these days.*

The only casualty was his partner's shirt from some spilt coffee as he'd lurched forward. Barely a full wind-up of their siren before they were there, doors swung open, guns out. The girl had only just opened the Pathfinder driver's door.

'Hands up. *Don't move!*' She froze. Tentatively, she raised her hands.

Two men inside, he could see now. 'Get those hands where I can see them. Get out! *Out!*' They too raised their hands. The back door opened.

Yep, an easier bust he'd never known. Back slaps all round in the squad room. *Correction,* now a guy from the bank was out on the sidewalk bleating about a 'suspected terrorist alert'. *Terrorists,* huh? Maybe they were looking at a couple of commendation badges.

Something else should have struck him about all this, he realised: it was *too easy.* But that final thought didn't click until he heard a familiar sound behind him: two guns being cocked.

'Now be good boys and put those guns to the ground, *slowly,*' Barry Chilton said. 'And nobody will get hurt.'

Adel got a return call from Yoav Zahavi at 12.16 a.m., 2.16 a.m. in Israel, with a rundown of what had happened at the Temple Mount that night.

'...Minimal damage to the Dome of the Chain, but three guards injured. One shoulder wound, another with a leg wound; the third, unfortunately, caught part of the explosion: second-degree burns, lost three fingers, fractured collarbone and a burst eardrum.'

'Will he be OK?'

'Well, he'll make it through, if that's what you mean,' Zahavi confirmed. 'And the bombers' toll: one dead, one injured.'

Adel closed his eyes, hardly daring to wish. 'And will he be OK? Will *he* make it?'

'He certainly will. Only a superficial leg wound. Medics reckon he'll be fit and ready to talk in three or four hours.'

Yes, yes! Adel shook a clenched fist skyward. 'I'm heading straight out there – should be with you before first light. Don't let anyone question him until I get there!'

'I'm not sure that will—'

'Yoav, this is political dynamite,' Adel cut him short. 'These men are responsible for the worst series of attacks against Islamic shrines ever known. Whatever Israel comes out with about this, Muslims will *never* accept or believe it – least of all Bahsem-Yahl, who has appointed himself prime spokesman condemning them. Worse yet, if what comes out isn't favourable, Israel could end up partly getting blamed.' Adel sighed. 'Believe me, it's in Israel's best interests to keep a healthy distance on this one. Only a Muslim like myself might be trusted as mediator. Even then, I might not be seen as sufficiently aligned, I'll need to involve the other authorities who've had bombings: Egypt, Jordan, Yemen, et al. But at least I'm in touch with them and they've so far accepted my mediation and efforts in tracking the bombers.'

'Since you put it like that.' There was a smile in Yoav's voice.

'Sorry to remind you that your country's not flavour of the month in the Muslim world.'

'You could at least have let us down gently.' Yoav chuckled. It looked like another call to Gabriel Chayat. 'I'll see what I can do.'

CHAPTER THIRTY-NINE

'What *is* that she's passing across?'

Washington and his team had seen the whole sorry drama on the live cam through Cali's laptop: the bank alarm ringing, Lorrena running out, the cops swinging in and drawing their guns, the two goons coming up behind the cops. The goons moved the cops forward at gunpoint a couple of yards, picked up their .38s and pocketed them. Finally, they shot out the squad car's back tyres, and the two cars headed off – the Pathfinder leading the way, the goons' grey Buick just behind.

Washington sighed, shaking his head.

But he'd seen Lorrena take something out of her pocket as she'd opened the driver's door, then slip it quickly back as the police arrived. Then just before they'd headed off, she'd taken it out again and passed it to the guy in the back seat. He asked Cali to go back to those frames.

'There. That's the one, right *there*! Now zoom in on the left hand. What's she holding there?'

At ten times magnification, the object could be made out, but Cali pulled it up to 15x and put on a filter to soften the grain to be sure.

'Looks like it could be a flash drive, a memory stick.'

Washington felt as if a knife had been plunged in his gut. He asked Cali to roll forward to make sure that's what she'd passed to the guy in the back seat. It was. It all gelled in that instant: why visit a bank so far away? She'd have been able to make cash arrangements through another bank or draw from any ATM machine. No, it had to be something physical deposited there. Something important.

'If that's what I think it is…' he hissed. As if they didn't have enough reason to shut them down, and *fast*, now they had been given a rocket boost. 'How far from them now?'

Cali brought his map back up. 'Seven miles to Lancaster, and they're *what* – maybe two miles the other side?'

Washington nodded slowly.

But a second later Cali's brow furrowed. 'Got another problem now, though. If they've got a laptop with wireless modem with them, they can send whatever's on that stick wherever they want right away.' He watched Washington's expression drop like a stone, then smiled slyly. 'However, that's something I might just be able to help with.'

AMSTERDAM, HOLLAND.

Building manager Luke Haartman had never known twelve large men move so deftly, so quietly. Like ballerinas.

Weighed down with rifles, helmets, flak jackets, heavy boots, still they moved up the marble staircase without a sound. Having just let them in the main door to the building, he watched their progress anxiously.

It was half-three in the morning and the building was eerily silent with only a faint thrum of traffic from the city beyond. The sound of a pin drop would carry.

Al Hakam had first been seen just before 1 a.m. by an undercover MIVD agent meeting an informant at a café in the de Pijp area. He kept half an eye on Al Hakam over his contact's shoulder, then when he saw him leave half an hour later, politely made an excuse and hailed a taxi to follow him.

That was the first moment he was able to phone in an alert for back-up. But nobody had arrived yet by the time he watched the taxi ahead drop off Al Hakam at an apartment building just off Hoofdweg, two blocks from Rembrandt Park.

It was a short-stay serviced block and they got hold of the building manager and showed him a photo of Al Hakam to find out which apartment he was in. 'B5, first floor.' Then they arranged the strike team. The news fed back to Hayyan Melki at TAME9, but when he tried Adel's line to bring him up to date, it went straight to his messaging service.

The building manager was keen to let them in – he didn't want doors broken unnecessarily. In turn, the strike team didn't want the noise. But now their leader looked back at him expectantly as he approached the top of the stairs. The manager was still fixed to the spot in the entrance foyer. No words were spoken, but the leader's gaze shifting between the manager and the first-floor door made it clear. *Aren't you going to open this one as well?*

The manager wasn't so sure about the upstairs door. *Terrorist?* Standing just the other side of the door as a welter of bullets flew through or a bomb exploded probably wasn't the wisest move. With a sheepish grin, he handed the electronic key card to the nearest man to pass up the line.

The team leader held one hand up expectantly

as another poised the card to swipe. As soon as the tumbler clicked, Al Hakam might awaken; they'd have to move swiftly.

As it turned out he didn't stir, despite the flurry of rapid footsteps in the wake of the door click. One of the team touched the barrel of his MP5 against Al Hakam's cheek.

Al Hakam felt the tickling on his cheek and, as he opened his eyes, the gun barrel was pressed hard against it, pinning his face to the pillow. Five BBE guards were in his line of sight, and no doubt there were more behind. Panicked instructions flew in Dutch and English. But he could only raise one hand in his position, the other was trapped under his pillow – an inch from his gun, a Browning HP.

He remembered reading about Abu Nidal, one of his heroes; how he'd slept every night with a gun under his pillow. Al Hakam had done the same now for almost the past decade. But he couldn't raise up to fire the gun, he could hardly move with the rifle barrel pressing him down – so he did the only thing allowed him: he snaked his left hand that final inch and fired the gun from where it was.

A gout of blood exploded from the guard's thigh, the return shot firing in instant reflex: the bullet went through Al Hakam's cheek and took out two teeth and part of his left jawbone before exiting the other side.

* * *

'The mosque bombers and Bahsem-Yahl story, you say?'

'Yeah. What I'm about to send through will blow the lid off it like you wouldn't believe. Biggest thing since Watergate.' Lorrena was on her hands-free as they sped along. Chris had looked up the number, dialled, then passed the headset across. 'Why do you think I called you rather than the *New York Times*?'

'Certainly appreciate it. Like to get the jump on them if we can.' Tone upbeat, positive, but the sub who'd taken the call at the *Post*'s Middle East desk, Gill Altmann, was thinking: dime for each time someone had mentioned Watergate, he'd be a rich man. Most of these calls ended nowhere, but for that two per cent which *did* end up having substance, he acted as if each might be the story of the year. 'And what was your name again?'

'Lorrena. But I'm not important in this. The guy centre stage – the one you want to put bold, upfront and make sure you spell his name right – is Tynnan. Sam Tynnan.' She glanced across at Sam, and wondered if she was trumpeting as much for herself: still desperately trying to make good on what she'd done to him, make amends. 'He's the author of the manuscript I'll send through in a minute. Which you'll see, as you go through it, ninety per cent of these events have been based on.' As Altmann gave her the email address, Lorrena repeated it aloud for Chris to type straight in. 'Through to you in just a minute. Woodward and Bernstein still with you, by the way?'

Altmann laughed. That one he hadn't heard before. 'I'll get on it as soon as it comes through. Back to you shortly.'

Chris tapped a one-line note, '*As just arranged with Lorrena,*' attached the file and hit SEND.

But a third of the way through, the email froze. He waited a moment, thinking it might be a network overload problem, then hit a couple of keys to try and free it. *No response.* In fact, nothing on his computer seemed to be responding any more. Then seconds later everything on screen started to merge and melt, the words sliding down his screen like hot treacle.

In her mirror, Lorrena saw the shock on Chris's face. 'What's wrong?'

'I don't know. I don't know.'

They heard then the first strains of sirens behind them. Distant, but audible.

Adel got a call back from Yoav while he was at Heathrow Airport, forty minutes before his flight. '*Angel Gabriel* of *Shin Bet* is at one with your mode of thinking: attacks against Islam's most holy sites? Best for Israel to keep a back seat on this one, as arm's length as possible. The prisoner awaits you.'

So Adel's first call after going through customs

at Ben-Gurion Airport was to Hayyan Melki, who'd called and left a message while he was in flight.

Adel wasn't sure whether to laugh or cry when Melki told him the events of that night in Amsterdam. '...so, unfortunately, Al Hakam's cheeks ended up getting "ventilated".'

'And here was I about to say I can't interview him because I'm in Israel. Looks like he won't be speaking to *anyone* for a few days.'

'Five, the doctors say. With jaw reconstruction – scheduled for later today – *and* fresh stitches each side, they're apparently putting in a fixed brace before relying just on wiring.'

Five days? Al Hakam's arrest would be in the papers later that day and Abu Khalish would know then he was at risk. He'd immediately change locations and erase any last contact points or details.

'Everything with Khalish will have gone cold by then, even if Al Hakam finally does say anything,' Adel sighed. The information would be worthless. *To get so close to Khalish, yet still he'd elude them.*

'Perhaps we should look at it philosophically. He'd have probably stayed close-mouthed for that time anyway. We've had many a prisoner, and I'm sure you've had the same, say nothing for months on end – if indeed they talk at all.'

'True.' But as Adel lifted a hand for a taxi in front of Ben-Gurion Airport, he was struck with a thought.

'Did they find his cellphone in what they took from the apartment?'

'I don't know. I'll check the inventory. Why?'

'If they did, there's one thing we might be able to try.'

CHAPTER FORTY

'Two squad cars just joined the party ahead of us,' Indiana announced. He'd tuned into the local police radio band. 'As we thought, the guys left stranded at Lancaster called for the posse.'

Washington nodded, but his eyes stayed fixed on Cali playing a sonata on his laptop. His concern at that moment was more with how he'd got on. 'Did you get them?'

'Yeah, think so,' Cali gloated. 'Nifty bit of kit that. We call it "Colon the Barbarian". Sneaks up the ass of your computer, blocks all network connections and starts eating it from the inside. Then, following the same path, we go in with *this*.' With a quick keyboard flurry, Cali switched to another page. 'Assuming, that is, this is the same guy who hacked us using Lorrena's old code the other day. If not, we're screwed!'

After a second, a luminous green dot appeared on screen. He tilted it towards Washington. 'That's them, right there!'

Washington smiled, his first in the past hour. 'How far?'

'Five miles, and closing.'

He turned to Indiana. 'And the squad cars?'

'Don't have an exact fix. But from the chatter I'd reckon about two miles.'

'Al Hakam has been arrested.'

At the other end, Abu Khalish froze. After a second: 'Who *is* this?'

'Sharaf Farhi. A close friend of Al Hakam's.'

There was another heavy silence. Karam, along with the rest of the operations room, waited with bated breath, fearing that Khalish had smelt a rat and would hang up.

'He didn't mention you.'

'No reason why he should. After all, you pay him to be discreet. But he did ask me to call you if anything should happen to him. To warn you.'

Khalish exhaled softly. 'That's very kind of

him. But I would assume, especially since he's had the courtesy to have me called, that he's not about to say anything in any case. So why the worry?'

Karam swallowed. They'd run the conversation through a number of possible scenarios. This wasn't one of them. Across the room, Siraj held up a finger. First hurdle crossed: *Broad regional network*. Malik stood over Siraj, eyes shifting anxiously between his computer and Karam making the call.

They'd found Al Hakam's cellphone and Melki in Holland had sent it to Adel's team in London. They'd focused on numbers called immediately after the attacks on the handler Youssef in Milan and Akram in London. One number had stood out.

Malik, unit leader while Adel was away, coordinated everything; Karam made the call because his Arabic dialect was closest to Al Hakam's – who they believed hailed originally from Jordan – and Siraj tracked the phone network's progress on his computer. Now they had to pray that they could keep Khalish on the phone long enough to trace where the network signal ended. Three more stages to go.

'Because whatever information the police used to trace Al Hakam might also lead to yourself.' There was a weighted silence again from the other end. Karam continued hesitantly, 'I don't know. I'm only filling in the gaps here, guessing. All I was asked to do was call you.'

'Yes, yes. I understand. And where was he arrested?'

'In Amsterdam. An apartment near Rembrandt Park.' Karam's heart skipped as Siraj held up another finger: *Country network*.

'Indeed. Very unfortunate.' Khalish sighed with resignation. 'Thank you for letting me know.'

Karam panicked, sensing a winding-down in Khalish's tone. The next stage, *Local regional network*, would pin it down to fifty thousand to two hundred and fifty thousand people, depending on the population density. Only if they hit the last phase, *Neighbourhood network*, did they stand a chance of tracing Khalish. He had to keep him on the line.

'I suppose, with this information, you will make other plans now?'

'Yes, of course. Without question. But thank you, your call is appreciated.'

This time there was a decided edge to Khalish's voice: *my* business. Karam wouldn't have been surprised to hear the call click off straight away. He needed something more revealing and dramatic to hold Khalish.

'Al Hakam told me something else important to pass on.'

'Yes?' Khalish was losing patience.

Karam let out a slow dramatic sigh, drawing it out. 'He said that Akram Ghafur wasn't killed in the end – just badly wounded.'

'*What?*' Khalish was angry, incredulous. Then an edge of suspicion crept into his voice. 'And just why would he trouble to pass on such information at this stage?'

'Because...*because*...' Karam's mind spun for possible options. Siraj held up a third finger: *Local regional network*. Just *one* more minute. '...he felt he'd let you down. It weighed heavy on him. That's why he stayed close in an Amsterdam apartment. He hoped to go back and finish the job.'

'I see.'

'And now that he's unable to do that, I suppose the only thing left was to say sorry. Make amends. It might also have been Ghafur remaining alive which led the authorities to him. That may have been his downfall.'

'Yes, I...I suppose so,' Khalish murmured. In the background he could hear the pulsing of crickets and lapping of surf eighty yards away. At least that would tie in with what Al Hakam had spun in their last call about the body (stock option) being buried, '*Not easily uncovered.*' He was trying to cover for the fact that no body had been found, nothing had appeared in the newspapers. But something bothered him about this call now. He was eager to get off the line and be alone with his own thoughts to determine what that might be. 'Again, thank you.'

'It was the least I could do. Respect Al Hakam's wishes at this difficult moment. Ensure that—'

'And you have,' Khalish cut in. 'Thank you. Goodbye.'

The line went dead.

Malik's eyes shifted sharply from Karam to Siraj on his computer. 'Did we get him? *Did we get him?*'

'They're coming in from Colebrook,' Indiana said. 'They'll cut them off by the junction with route twenty-six. Three squad cars.'

Washington grimaced. Surely they had them now. At his suggestion, Indiana had patched in to the local police network. With Cali's on-screen tracking, they'd been able to give them vital input.

As soon as Lorrena and crew knew the police were on their tails, they'd sped up. From Cali's on-screen dot, they hadn't reduced the gap on them much in the past half-hour, and the light was starting to close in. Shutting them off at a junction ahead became a necessary option.

Faint mist started to roll in off the lakes they passed intermittently; glimpses of grey-blue between firs and spruces flashing by each side.

'They say they're just a mile from the junction.' Indiana held his phone a foot away, relaying the information as it reached him. 'So just a minute from now.'

'And how far are our motley crew from the cut-off?'

Cali checked his screen. 'Five and a half miles.'

He turned it so that Washington could also watch the progress of the green dot: four miles, three, *two*... pulses quickening as they watched the gap close. As soon as they saw the dot slow and finally stop, it was effectively all over. They could just coast along then. The cops ahead would have them roped and tied by the time they arrived.

But a mile before the cut-off, the green dot shifted, headed at a north-east diagonal on another road.

'*Oh boy!*' Cali shouted instructions to Indiana who, in turn, barked them at the police.

Washington cradled his head at the back and forth fiasco. He could hear the frantic voices of the police regrouping through Indiana's cellphone. By the time they had, the three new squad cars were no closer than the two already on their tail on the diverted route.

'Looks like they knew or guessed there were cops ahead,' Indiana said.

Washington glared at him wearily. 'You don't say?'

For the first time that day Washington began to worry that they might not catch them; at least not easily. There were no nearby military bases in Vermont or New Hampshire. 'But what about Maine?' he asked Cali. He'd noticed from the map that the Maine county line was close.

'No military bases, but there's a naval airbase not far away at New Brunswick.'

'OK. Get them on the line for me.' It was time to bring in some bigger guns.

CHAPTER FORTY-ONE

'So, what do you think of her?' Barry asked Phil. 'Vince's latest squeeze?'

As the frantic squawks on the police band died down, they returned to their previous conversation: Vince Corcoran's new girlfriend, Ivana, twenty-six and fresh over from the Czech Republic ten months back.

'Seems OK to me.' Phil thought for a second. 'Nice smile.'

'Nice smile?' Barry grinned incredulously, tilting one hand off the steering wheel. 'That's *all* you noticed? That waist thinner than your neck and that pair of fully loaded forty-fours about to pop at any moment went right by yer?'

'Sure, I noticed them.' Phil shrugged. 'But I didn't want to be indelicate.'

'*Indelicate?*' Barry arched an eyebrow. Raise the flags. Phil had managed a four-syllable word. 'You know what some of the guys are calling her, what with that rack an' all?'

'No?'

Barry paused for effect. 'The bouncing cheque!' They laughed, Barry's guffaw, despite having spun the same line a dozen times to others, rising louder. But his laugh died quickly, eyes narrowing as he watched the Pathfinder ahead indicate and overtake a gasoline truck.

For a while now he'd carried a PB scanner in his car; it had given him the jump on many a scrape. So when Sam had phoned and told him their computer was down, 'We've got no idea of police movements any more,' he'd been able to oblige. 'No sweat, got it all coming through loud and clear on the PB. Anything worrying ahead, I'll call you.' He had.

But while the roadblock had been sidestepped, now they had another three squad cars behind them. The initial plan of them running interference if the police got too close wasn't going to work any more. They might be able to hold up a couple of cars, but the rest would get through.

Barry listened out for the sirens for a second, trying to gauge distance. At moments, depending on the wind-shift, they sounded as if they were pressing in closer.

As Barry indicated to overtake the gasoline truck, he made his decision. Just the other side of it, he swung in sharply, slamming on the brakes.

Phil's eyes widened, not only from the unexpected action, but from the gas-truck bearing down on them, brakes screaming.

It came to rest a foot from them.

Barry leapt out, waving his gun. 'Out, and leave the engine running. Out! *Now!*'

The driver stepped down, hands half-raised, unsure what to do with them. 'What do you want with me?'

Barry saw that he was only a couple of inches shorter than himself. 'We're trying to get together a fuckin' basketball team – whaddya think?' He waved the gun. 'Now keep walking thataway, and don't stop till I tell yer.'

The sirens edged closer, flashing lights visible now.

Barry jumped up into the cab, slammed into reverse and swung the truck back round until it blocked the road.

The police cars were eight hundred yards away, seven...*six* as he jumped down.

He undid the fuel cap underneath. Five, *four*. He ran back to his car, surged forward thirty yards, and stopped.

And as he aimed at the spilt fuel, the police were only two hundred yards away and closing rapidly. The first two bullets sparked against the asphalt but didn't catch. The third did. He turned, shielding his face as the air blast and wall of heat hit him. *Hundred yards.*

He jumped in and floored it, eyes glued in his mirror to the police cars beyond the billowing flames and black smoke. Winding-down of sirens, they stopped twenty yards short of the truck. Doors opened and some cops jumped out.

Barry braced himself, expecting shots zinging after them, but none came. Obviously they were too far away by then for the cops to even bother trying. He noticed the gas-truck driver still walking by the roadside.

'You can stop now!' he shouted from the window. Then with a shrug at Phil. 'Some people...'

'With all due, that *is* what you said to him. Don't stop until I tell you.'

'Literal, Phil. You're not meant to take literal everything said. Or maybe one day when I tell yer to take a hike or drop dead, I'll get lucky.' He grinned, but from Phil's expression it looked like it might take him a while to work out that one.

'I wonder,' Phil said. 'If you hadn't told him to stop, whether he'd have just kept on walking?'

'We'll never know now, will we?' He shrugged. 'Just another of life's great mysteries.'

* * *

As Indiana relayed from the police what had happened, Cali frantically checked his on-screen map.

'Turn off here! *Here!*' he snapped, panic in his voice.

Ohio braked hard and, still doing sixty, swung the wheel. The X5 lurched, the back starting to slide before he accelerated out of the turn and, with a quick fishtail, righted it again.

Cali exhaled. If they'd missed that turn, that was it. There wasn't another before the gas-truck blockage ahead. As with the squad cars, they'd have been trapped.

He looked ahead, then back at his screen. 'Seven hundred yards along, turn left.'

As Ohio made the turn, Cali traced the new road with one finger on screen. It ran parallel with the original road, at one stage only four hundred yards between them. Then that gap widened again to half a mile before another cross-road linked the two fifteen miles ahead.

'What are you thinking?' Washington pressed.

'I'm thinking we've got no other choice but to take this route.' Cali sighed. 'We can cut back on the other road up ahead, but by then we'll have slipped back another mile and a half behind them.'

Again the thought: *they weren't going to catch them*. Washington asked Cali to pass his phone. He wanted an update from the Apache pilot heading out of New Brunswick.

'What's your position now?' the pilot asked Washington.

'Eight miles north of Oquossoc, more or less following the line of the Canadian border ten miles in. Heading north-east.'

'OK, read you.' Washington could only just make out what the pilot was saying above the heavy rotors and engine thrum. 'I'm just over Farmington now. Should be with you in twelve to fifteen.'

'Good. Let's speak again when you're in the zone.' Washington broke the connection, and noticed then Cali's expression change, a smug leer rising. 'What is it?'

'They've slowed. The green dot's hardly moving.'

'But not stopped?' That had been one of their worries. As soon as they worked out they were being tracked, they might ditch the computer.

'No, but slooooowww. At a crawl.'

'Chance of catching them, then?'

'If they keep this up long, yeah.' Cali nodded. 'Fair chance.'

The mist had become heavier as it got dark, their headlamps churning fog patches into milky billows as they rolled across.

Lorrena was slow in responding to the flashing

523

lights ahead, emerging suddenly through a mist patch. At first she panicked that it was another police roadblock, one that Barry hadn't picked up on. But as it cleared ahead she saw it was a house in sections on two low-loaders, the convoy fronted and backed by two warning vehicles with flashing lights.

She braked hard, watched their speedo plummet. It bottomed out at 18 mph.

All they needed! Her hands gripped tighter to the steering wheel, noticing for the first time they were trembling. They probably had been for a while, but with their breakneck speed and the vibrations of the car she hadn't noticed it.

Traffic had been light on the road, but as it approached six o'clock and people started to return home from work, more cars had started coming the other way. One car passed, then another two hundred yards behind. Then another. She had to keep her nerves under control and wait on them passing.

Sam picked up on her edginess. 'At least with that gas-tanker blocking, the panic of the police right behind us has gone.'

'Yeah, there is that.' She glanced in her mirror as Barry's grey Buick came into view again. He flashed at them as he came within a hundred yards: '*I'm here now,*' or perhaps: '*What the fuck's happening ahead*?'

She tapped a finger anxiously on the wheel. After a moment, a gap opened in the oncoming traffic. She swung out. But then after only twenty yards she had to brake sharply, pull back in again behind the convoy. There was another set of lights looming ahead suddenly round a slow curve.

She'd have to wait until the road straightened again. She needed at least a clear four-hundred-yard stretch to make sure of getting past the convoy. It seemed to take for ever, but finally it was there. After the last oncoming car, she swung out and floored it.

Two-thirds past the convoy, she saw another set of lights on the horizon. She made it easily, but kept half an eye on Barry behind. He did too, just; the oncoming driver was forced to slow, beeping twice in protest as he passed. Barry swung back in forty yards behind them.

Lorrena's nerves bristled as she heard a rustling, branches snapping and crunching, in the forest to their right. She glanced across – was it a moose or perhaps a horse running through? But she could see nothing. Then it came again: a rapid crunching and tearing lasting only seconds, then gone.

Barry was flashing at them again. *What now?* As it came once more, a snapping and tearing through the tree branches, then something whistling close by with an air-pop, she realised what it was. *They were being shot at!*

They got another flash from Barry, and she turned

and saw them then: lights flickering through the trees four or five hundred yards away, seventy yards back from parallel with them.

As they'd seen themselves get closer to the green dot on the parallel road, Nevada had been struck with the idea. Along with his M16, he'd brought a TAC-50 in case they were faced with a long-range sniper situation.

'With all the trees, think you'll be able to get them?' Washington pressed.

'Be hit and miss.' Nevada grimaced wryly as he steadied and aimed through the X5 window. 'But worth a try.'

Part of the challenge, Nevada thought. The TAC-50 was high-powered, its .50 calibre bullet heavy; it would rip easily through tree branches, would even split through a small tree. Only a large tree would stop it.

So it was a question of how many small or large trees there were in between. A lottery.

The motion of the target vehicle and theirs – the rapid vibrations Nevada braced against as he aimed – made it all the more difficult. A challenge. One thing Nevada, an ex-Green Berets sharpshooter, relished.

The next shot made it halfway, slicing through twigs and branches before hitting a fifty-foot-high spruce. The second was stopped far earlier by a thick trunk.

The third made it most of the way through.

Sam and Lorrena heard its thud clearly, saw the bark, wood splinters and dust explode into the air only twenty yards to their side.

'We've got to do something,' Sam said, hands clenched into fists, nerves wire-taut. 'If one of those hits us.'

'*What?*' Lorrena held a hand out helplessly. 'We're going as fast as we can.'

'I know, but we need to do *something*!'

Two more shots: one dying early, the other stopping forty yards away.

'Turn the lights off!' Sam said.

'Are you *crazy?*' Lorrena glanced across sharply. 'With the mist, I'm having trouble seeing as it is.'

'I know. It's a risk. Maybe slow a bit to compensate. But probably less of a—'

The bullet hit then and Lorrena was thrown against him, some of her blood splattering against his cheek. A blizzard of glass spun past them, the *Pathfinder* veering wildly.

Sam feared for a moment she was dead or unconscious. Her head lolled and her eyes closed briefly. But then he saw her left hand still gripped tight to the wheel, struggling to get the car straight again.

'Only a flesh wound, as they say,' she hissed breathlessly.

The bullet had hit her side window and ripped

through the top of her collarbone, taking a chunk of flesh with it, before blowing out the windscreen on exit.

She cut their speed on reflex, to just over 70 mph, but the air-rush buffeting them still felt like being in a wind vortex.

Two more shots: one made it midway, the other two-thirds through, flying wood dust just visible.

'OK. Kill the lights,' Lorrena said. 'You'll have to do it. This arm's screwed.'

'You need to get a tourniquet on that,' Chris said, taking off his tie-dye and starting to rip it.

Blood was streaming heavily from her shoulder, Sam saw as he leant across and switched off the lights. But he saw something else then too in her eyes: sorrow, regret, more than fear. As if she knew in that moment they were going to die, but wanted to tell him how sorry she was for her part in it. *If I die now on this last fool's errand, will you believe then that I was telling the truth? I'd fallen in love with you.*

Behind, Barry beeped as he killed his lights too, getting the message; otherwise the sniper would still pick out the Pathfinder in his beam.

Darkness. Only a faint glimmer of moonlight struggling through thick cloud cover picked out the road ahead.

Lorrena cut their speed another notch. Beyond the thirty yards of road ahead, there was nothing but a black void. She couldn't adjust quickly enough to any curves or turns in the road, especially steering with one arm.

Chris leant over and tied a crude tourniquet around her collarbone, strapping it under her armpit.

Then came three more shots: two buried themselves in the forest, but the third winged clear.

They held their breath, but it seemed to pass at least three yards ahead of them.

Suddenly, the road was floodlit by an oncoming car. It beeped at them twice to tell them they had no lights as it passed.

They waited out four more shots, none of them making it all the way through, then in the following frozen silence dared to speculate that they'd given up.

Surely they must solely be firing blind now?

They waited a full forty seconds of silence, the billowing mist and blanket darkness of northern Maine rolling by, before Lorrena finally spoke.

'Looks like they've stopped. Given up on us.'

'Yeah, looks like it,' Sam agreed.

Then seconds later he felt those words turn to ashes in his mouth as they heard the thud-thud of a helicopter break the silence above them.

CHAPTER FORTY-TWO

Adel felt as if the world was raging around him.

Mosque bombings, Sunni-Shiite, Muslim-Christian, right-left, right-wrong. The raging in the streets in the wake of Bahsem-Yahl's pronouncement mirrored in his frantic calls and conversations that morning, each of them fighting for jurisdiction over the fate, the *blood*, of the captured mosque bomber.

'*My name is Muhab Haidar and I come from the village of Shehabiyeh in southern Lebanon, where my family still live...*'

It had taken almost two hours to get the prisoner talking. And another hour after that, Adel wished he hadn't. He knew that what he had in his hands was dynamite. He'd started making his calls.

Haidar was ahead of him as they headed across the tarmac at the military section of Lod Airport towards the waiting helicopter. Three guards each side of him; Israeli one side, Egyptian the other.

Israel had already made it clear they had no interest in trial jurisdiction on something involving Islamic property and territory, Dome of the Rock included; also viewed, per se, as exclusively Islamic holy ground. The information Adel had garnered during the interview made that an absolute. Israel wanted this hot coal as far away as possible.

Most of Adel's conversations had been with Gabriel Chayat, head of *Shin Bet*, who in turn had apparently conferred with Ari Dahan and other Kadima ministers.

Once Israel's position had been confirmed, Adel started calling the other mosque bombing locations: Turkey, Egypt, Jordan, Pakistan and Yemen.

'*We're holding one of the mosque bombers, and some hard and fast decisions need to be made regarding trial location and arrangements.*'

Five hours of jousting and jurisdiction preference posturing between prosecutors, ministers and sometimes local imams, and the arrangements were decided: the trial would take place in Alexandria, Egypt, the site of the second mosque bombing.

Five judges would sit on the bench: one each from Egypt, Turkey, Pakistan, Jordan and Yemen. Israel would send an advising prosecutor to cover their interests.

Three Egyptian guards would be despatched immediately to assist in escorting the prisoner. Diplomatically, he was already partially viewed as an Islamic prisoner and ward. As soon as he landed on Egyptian soil, he would be considered fully so.

Adel hadn't shared details of the prisoner or any information gleaned from their interview, in any of his calls, except with Gabriel Chayat. This was divulged in a one-hour meeting behind closed doors while they waited on the Egyptian guards' arrival. The information was seen as too sensitive to risk discussing over the phone.

They got into the helicopter, a Bell V-22, through its tailgate ramp. On each side were seats facing each other, with parachute straps at the rear. The engines started and the tailgate closed.

It was a chopper/aircraft hybrid, and so took off vertically, but its small wings below two rotors provided a flight more akin to an aircraft.

Adel closed his eyes. The day had been wearying, and he'd grabbed less than an hour's sleep in his early flight from London.

'My name is Muhab Haidar and I come from the village of Shehabiyeh in southern Lebanon...

'Shehabiyeh is predominantly a Muslim village. And I too am Muslim. A Shiite...

'In the late 90s, I was involved in Hezbollah militia activity, mostly against Israel, but also some terrorist attacks against Falangists and foreign interests there. Mainly US and French. I worked as a munitions and explosives expert for them, and still, officially, I am listed as a member of Hezbollah.'

Haidar had given his age as thirty-four, but with his heavy beard he looked a few years older. A tape ran as they spoke. The room they were in was ten foot square, no windows. One of Chayat's men had spent twenty minutes beforehand checking for bugs; Chayat was also keen that what came out in the interview didn't reach unwanted ears.

The only bright light of the day had been Malik's call from London, shortly after he came out of his final meeting with Gabriel Chayat.

'We might well have got him, Adel! The phone network tracked the signal down to half a dozen villas in a place called Cebu Island in the Philippines. Local police are arranging a strike force right now.'

'Indeed, great news, Malik. *Marvellous!*' But after four years of tracking Khalish, all he felt inside was numb. *Why couldn't this have happened last week?* With the main target gone, the mosque bombings would have stopped. In particular this last attempt in Jerusalem and the cataclysm it could lead to. 'Let me know how it goes.'

Adel had finally started drifting into a restless sleep when he heard the commotion. His eyes snapped open.

On the flight so far the guards had been quiet with only brief, muted conversations between them. But now both sets of guards were on their feet screaming at each other.

Adel saw the reason for the panic: Haidar, his hands cuffed in front of him, had grabbed a grenade from the adjacent Israeli guard's belt and had it clutched tight to his chest, screaming as the guard fought to wrestle it back from him.

One of the other Israeli guards leapt back a yard, flipped up the lid on a side-mounted box and pressed the red button inside.

The tailgate started opening slowly.

Someone shouted frantically towards the pilot. 'Egroph Gohvah! *Egroph!*'

The CV-22 dipped sharply and started losing height. The intention was obviously to get the grenade out of the open tailgate.

But as Adel looked at Haidar and the guard locked in their death-struggle, screaming at each other from only inches away, he saw that the grenade pin was already out. And Haidar's grip on the grenade looked tight, immovable. There hardly appeared time to wrestle it from him, let alone out the tailgate to safety.

A cold shudder ran through Adel. It was too late; they weren't going to make it.

'As soon as you're in position, you'll see two sets of vehicles,' Washington instructed the pilot. 'Just under half a mile apart on parallel roads, heading north-east. Got them yet?'

The AH-64 pilot checked his PNVS screen. With the heavy cloud cover, he was relying solely on infrared heat recognition. After a moment he saw the four vehicles come into view. 'Yeah, got them.'

'OK. Our team are the two right-hand vehicles.' After Washington's initial contact with the New Brunswick base, a quick flurry of calls between department and Navy brass had put the chopper under his guidance and command to take out a target, if necessary. 'The target's the front vehicle of the left-hand two vehicles. The one taking the lead. Got that?'

'Roger. Lead vehicle, left hand. Just getting into position for a lock-on.'

As the thudding of the helicopter became louder in the night sky above them, Lorrena sighed resignedly: 'Doesn't sound like just reconnaissance to me. More like an attack helicopter.'

Its reverberations were heavy, all-consuming. Sam

could feel them in his chest, merging with his laden heartbeat. He closed his eyes for a second. 'If this part had been scripted, I might have been able to help, tell you what to do. But the manuscript didn't get taken in *The Prophecy*, and you or I never featured in it – even in alter ego form.'

'See. It's all your fault.' She smiled fondly at him. 'You missed out the best parts.'

But Sam knew it was a last-ditch attempt at light-heartedness to ease the hollow sense of loss – that this was it. It was all over. They were both about to die.

Die? Never seeing Ashley again, never holding him in his arms. And Lorrena, well; he'd already lost her twice: first, when he discovered their relationship had been a sham, a lie; then again with the news of her drowning. And now, just when he realised that she'd loved him after all – with everything she'd put herself through in penance, risking her life when she could have just walked away – she was to be lost from him again, along with all else. Cruel fate.

Part of him wanted to scream in protest. But another part thought: maybe this was meant to be, karma, repayment for all the lives lost due to *The Prophecy*. After all, rightly, wrongly, indirectly, unwittingly, and all the other ad nauseam justifications – it *had* been his creation. He only hoped that by catching on to what was happening and feeding the information to Emile, in the end they'd been able to save the day. But even that he began to doubt. If Washington had successfully shut down his and Lorrena's endeavours, no doubt he'd done the same with Emile. They'd been fooling themselves all along.

But his emotions felt worn; on the same treadmill between blind hope and fear for so long now – he felt he hardly had any reserves left. His anguish for his lost life and the son he'd never see again reduced to no more than numb resignation as he stared up at the sky in silent defiance.

'Do you have a fix yet on that target vehicle?' Washington asked. 'Left-hand lead.'

'Yeah. Locked on.' The pilot's eyes flicked between his two rocket options. Probably the Hydra-70 would be best. It would destroy the vehicle without leaving too large a hole in the road.

'OK, soldier. Take out the target!'

The pilot put one hand to his helmet earpiece for a moment, as if ensuring with the static on the line he'd heard the instruction correctly. 'Affirmative.'

He pressed the button to launch his rocket.

The surrounding guards' shouts and screams became increasingly frantic as Haidar and the guard tussled.

One of them went to help, but the pair clutched

tight together spun and grappled away from him. They rolled a yard closer to the half-open tailgate, but the grenade was still gripped in a death-lock between them.

Something changed in that instant in the Israeli guard's face. He suddenly realised he wouldn't get the grenade free and there was only one option left. Haidar saw it too, or perhaps he felt the shift in the guard's body, because Haidar shouted at him in Hebrew; as if only by using the guard's own language could he snap him out of what he was about to do.

Too late. Haidar was already off balance and the guard's weight carried the momentum.

They lurched back towards the open tailgate. Haidar's feet shuffled wildly for purchase to resist, his shouts becoming a strangled scream as with one last thrust the guard wrestled and tumbled them out.

They hit the side of the tailgate, now two-thirds down, seeming to suspend on one edge for a moment before sailing free into the air.

The explosion came a second later, rocking and bucking the helicopter wildly.

Adel expected it to stabilise soon after, but it didn't. The rocking and side-to-side lurching continued. He realised then that they were in difficulty. Either something vital had been damaged, or the tailgate dropping too early for their altitude, combined with the explosion, had caused serious problems.

As the pilot fought to bring the helicopter back under control, Adel closed his eyes and prayed.

CHAPTER FORTY-THREE

CORDOVA REEF, CEBU ISLAND, PHILIPPINES.

Al Hakam captured? This was the first thing to check.

Abu Khalish searched online. The report wasn't in any main newspaper articles yet, but he found it on a couple of Internet news sites, one Dutch, one English. Arrested in a dawn raid, he'd been shot and wounded and was currently in hospital. Expected to recover. The details were pretty much as Al Hakam's 'friend' had imparted.

He thought it unlikely Al Hakam would talk, but it was probably best to move on. The humidity was too high for him here in any case, like a warm, sticky blanket wrapped around him day and night. He felt himself sweating with it now from just this bit of key-tapping on the computer. Next time, he'd choose somewhere with a dry heat, more like his native Jordan.

The use of Al Hakam's cellphone, though, perturbed him. Khalish had only picked up because he'd seen the caller ID. But how had Al Hakam got that phone to his 'friend'? A *dawn raid*? If Al Hakam had really been surprised like that, he'd have had no opportunity, or indeed reason, to pass it to his friend beforehand.

So the police were probably prime suspects to have that phone. But why on earth would they warn him early of Al Hakam's arrest and also urge him to up-pegs and shift?

Suddenly the drawn-out nature of the conversation dawned on him, the man keeping him on the line by revealing that in fact Akram Ghafur hadn't been killed. The main thing not to have rung true. Why on earth gain favour on one hand by calling and warning him, then on the other draw disfavour by divulging that Al Hakam's last assignment had been unsuccessful?

Abu Khalish leapt up, looking at his watch: twelve minutes had passed since the call. It would take him three short minutes to pack essentials in a light bag and get clear. The only forces of any size were in Cebu City. Would they be able to get them organised and over the bridge to the reef in that time?

Only a minute into his packing he had his answer.
A searchlight drifted briefly across a front window then
was joined by another. Keeping out of sight, Khalish
went to the window and peered out. Six or seven
police and army jeeps, thirty or so men spreading out
from them, rifles in hand. Some were also positioning
at a neighbouring villa in view.

He ran to the back of the house. A dozen men
were already there, a mixture of navy and camouflage
uniforms, more running from the front. He sighed
resignedly. He'd known this moment would come one
day. The only irony was that it had come now, just
when he'd worked out that he was only part of a
much bigger picture. He smiled wryly. They'd put on
this big show thinking he was still a kingpin, when
he'd just been a pawn all along.

There was only one thing left to do. He went over
to a side cabinet, took out the gun there and headed
out.

Senior Inspector Andres Morua was taking no
chances. He'd called out a full complement from three
city police stations plus support infantry from the local
53rd barracks for the operation.

Abu Khalish. He was expecting heavy guns in
support, a strong show of guarding terrorist militia. So
when he saw a lone figure walk out, it was unexpected.
He remained cautious; eyes narrowing as he scanned
the villa's windows, expecting gun barrels to sneak out

and a barrage of fire to start at any second. But all he could see behind the man was a Filipino servant and maid peering nervously through a French window.

The approaching man was dressed in beige trousers and a white cotton kaftan top. With his long, dark hair swept back and clean-shaven face, there was no clear resemblance to the heavily bearded photos of Khalish he'd been emailed.

He held one hand out to his men, urging caution, as he lifted his loudhailer.

'Raise your hands! *Levanta tus manos!*'

Khalish had no intention of doing so, of subjugating himself in that manner. He simply nodded politely, and kept walking steadily towards the soldiers with his hands by his side.

There was no point in saying anything to this group of soldiers. They were just hired minions, and they wouldn't believe him in any case. And there'd be an endless chain of other minions between here and Guantanamo Bay who equally wouldn't listen to him, would discard his words as just the ramblings of a lunatic as they shoved him in handcuffs from one monkey cage to another.

Morua repeated his order to Khalish in English and Spanish, a sharper edge now to his voice.

Khalish stopped and, smiling graciously again, slowly raised them. The fact that he was cheating them of that information, that they might now never get to find out, was satisfaction enough. His only regret was that he himself wouldn't now get to see how it played out. Once he'd worked it out, it had begun to intrigue him: would everything go as they'd planned with Bahsem-Yahl, or would it, as he suspected, backfire spectacularly?

'It is indeed shameful the manner in which you have all been fooled!' Khalish shouted towards the bank of soldiers. 'And that, once again, the final satisfaction, the last joker played, has been mine.'

With a last smile and nod, he brought his raised hands down in a dramatic '*Salamu Alaykum*' bow; and, as he straightened, his right hand reached behind for the gun tucked into his trouser waistband. He pointed his gun at the soldiers.

Three shots came from the bank of soldiers in quick succession; then an avalanche of thirty or more from semi-automatic fire before Morua raised a hand to stop them.

Khalish lay on the grass twenty yards away, a crumpled, bloodied mess, barely recognisable from the stay-pressed Martini advert man of only seconds ago.

Morua went over and crouched down by the body. He looked at the gun in Khalish's hand: it was a toy replica, and not even a good one at that. '*The last joker played has been mine.*' The glory announcement that he and his men had closed the final chapter on the infamous Abu Khalish would certainly have the shine taken off it by them turning him into a colander for holding no more than a toy pistol. He had between now and when he got back to the station to make his calls to consider what to do about that.

When William Grayford heard the sirens approaching his gate, he already knew that they were coming for him.

He'd seen the earlier news: '...*In light of recent comments by TV evangelist, Matt Calvinson – White House spokesman, Jeff Baumann, has today announced that all past Republican Party donations received from Mr Calvinson will be returned. Mr Baumann said, and I quote, "We have stated clearly several times before that receipt of such donations does not mean that members of the Republican Party or the President in any way support or endorse Mr Calvinson's views, which are entirely his own. However, to avoid any such further incorrect and wasteful speculation, we have decided that said donated funds should be returned forthwith to Mr Calvinson."*'

Obviously they were trying to create as much distance as possible from Calvinson before it all hit the fan.

As Grayford's servant turned from the video entry phone to tell him that a Lieutenant Blandford was at the gate, he was already halfway up the stairs. 'Shall I let him in?'

'Yes, by all means. Show them into the drawing room and tell them I shall be down to join them in just a minute.'

It had all started not long after his father died four years ago. A young marine sergeant in the Pacific arena during WW2, rising to a 3-star lieutenant general before retirement, he was one of the strongest men he'd ever known. His rock. The one he'd always gone to in difficult times for sage advice. Probably, many people thought he too was strong, but he got most of that from his father; only he didn't realise how much until his father's death.

He'd gone off the rails for almost two years. No favouritism: he gave all four vices – drink, gambling, women, a few lines of coke at the right parties – an equal crack of the whip. Then one day he fell victim to a clumsy honeytrap and blackmail from a hooker – oh, add murder – and decided it was time to straighten himself out.

His father had been very religious. A Bible in one hand, gun in the other, straight and true scything through of the often misty mire of life; there was no lack of clarity where his father was concerned. Maybe it would work for him too; simple clarity was certainly what he'd needed at that moment. Then after dallying with the local Presbyterian church for a while, which still hadn't got him completely clean, he saw one of Calvinson's sermons; saw that same, uncompromising, clear-cut conviction he'd seen in his father.

Voices raised downstairs, insistent. The police officers were making it clear that they hadn't come for coffee and a polite chat. They had an arrest warrant. He went over to his desk and took the gun from a drawer.

For a while, he didn't wholly buy into Calvinson's more radical fire and brimstone doctrines. Then one day there was sudden clarity – *as if hit by a blinding light*, Calvinson would no doubt proclaim. In that moment of revelation, he saw where his views and Calvinson's coalesced.

For years within 101, Grayford had been warning that Islam had to be confronted full on in the short rather than long term, that if they bided their time while unstable Islamic regimes gained nuclear arms, it would be too late. Many would no doubt accuse him of stirring up a hornets' nest unnecessarily. But he considered it purely prudent gardening. The way he saw it, a final conflict with Islam was inevitable; only by bringing it about early could the West confront it on their own terms, be assured of victory.

Warmonger? Hell, no; he was simply ensuring that the final, inevitable Armageddon would be smaller, the body count far less. And, increasingly convinced of that, Calvinson's sermons and warnings started to hold stronger meaning and portent. He began to see a design in God's will, as Calvinson portrayed it, that Armageddon was indeed meant to be imminent.

He also saw himself as a key instrument in that: why else would his father's death have thrown him through Calvinson's church door at this time? Who else was in a position to both interpret those prophecies correctly and set them into motion, ensure that God's will was enacted?

Footsteps starting up the stairs. He handled the gun reverently. Colt M1911, the gun his father had carried in the 5th Marines the day they'd liberated Iwo Jima.

God's will? The stages of play had been so ingenuous and inspired that he couldn't possibly take sole credit for it; he felt sure that God's hand had guided him through much of it: Tynnan's manuscript, the mosque bombings, Adel Al-Shaffir, Jean-Pierre Bourdin, finally Bahsem-Yahl. With Tynnan in contact with Al-Shaffir, and Bourdin still a key source, all they'd needed was a false quatrain fed through Bourdin – a long-lost Nostradamus code-book along with some fresh, never-before-seen quatrains would prove irresistible – to provide the necessary tilt on the rudder steering away from those last vital mosque bombings.

Footsteps moving urgently along the corridor. His father had regularly oiled and cleaned the gun, kept it in working order.

As for Bahsem-Yahl making the pronouncement as they hoped: already there'd been suggestions of 'Western collusion' in the Arab press. That simply required more impetus, those early seeds nurtured through Arab contacts in their pocket – one an Iranian junior minister who had Bahsem-Yahl's ear, the other a prominent pro-Shiite Iraqi journalist: '*A claim has come to my notice which I believe has great credence. But at present it has little strength of voice behind it. It is my firm belief that if such a voice was lent to it, it would gain much support within Islam, with two key aims: to deflect from the unlikelihood that any true son of Islam could possibly harm their own sacred monuments; and to further unite Islam against Western interference in Islamic affairs. It is my belief that such a pronouncement would reflect upon the individual making it both strong foresight and wisdom. It would do much for their personal standing. Yet, caution: this person should be deemed to already hold these qualities, otherwise the pronouncement might not carry adequate weight. And, indeed, few within Islam could lay claim to such esteemed qualities as highly as yourself.*' Bahsem-Yahl's vanity had done the rest.

Playing God? He preferred to see it purely as executing God's will. And even if he was, it was a darn sight preferable to what would happen now without him doing so. Having to face a delayed

Armageddon, when Islam was stronger, better prepared. Mercifully, he wouldn't be around to see that.

Footsteps close to the door, pressing in.

He put the gun barrel in his mouth and pulled the trigger.

CHAPTER FORTY-FOUR

DUMYAT, EGYPT.

After saying *du'aa*, grace, at the table, Namir raised his glass to his brother. 'It is good to see you, Adel. So good. You should come on official business to Alexandria more often.'

'It appears that the pleasure is all mine.' Adel waved one hand towards the food spread, and smiled gratefully at Inayah who'd prepared it. *Batarekh* and *mortah* to start and, according to Namir, who'd leant close conspiringly while Inayah was in the kitchen, as if it was a secret he wasn't meant to impart, '*Prawn molokheya to follow, your favourite. Remember how our mother used to cook it, often with prawns we'd caught that very morning with father.'*

Adel remembered. As it was, this visit was more poignant than the many in the past. Perhaps because the last chapter had now closed on the events burdening him these past weeks, or simply because he felt glad to be alive – everything appearing somehow brighter, fresher on the train journey he knew so well from Alexandria to Dumyat, one his family had often made when he was a child.

The sounds of Namir's and Inayah's children drifted from the kitchen. Namir was old-school formal in that respect. The children were fed separately in the kitchen by their servant, who'd helped Inayah prepare the meal. When their eldest, Nasuh, was fourteen, he'd be allowed to sit with the grown-ups.

Adel had never before kissed the ground after a flight, as he knew many a panicky flyer did, but he had earlier that day. Once the tailgate had closed, stability had been partially restored, but it had still been a jolting, uneven flight the rest of the way.

After he'd dealt with the paperwork and statements about the incident, his first call once on the train had been to Gabriel Chayat.

'My name is Muhab Haidar and I come from the village of Shehabiyeh in southern Lebanon...

'What was the guard's name?' Adel asked Chayat.

'David. David Shapira. Only thirty-one. The doctors gave him the diagnosis just days ago: inoperable brain tumour. He hadn't even told his wife yet.'

'...*and still, officially, I am listed as a member of Hezbollah – but seven years ago I was recruited by the CIA as an informant. I passed on invaluable information from the inside about Hezbollah activities.*'

'So you selected him, put him forward for this?'

'No, he volunteered. There were two other choices.' Silence. A moment's respect for the soul of David Shapira. Chayat cleared his throat. 'His widow and two children will be well taken care of. A life insurance policy with a payout of five million shekels will magically appear.'

Adel closed his eyes, nodded. The end justified the means.

'...*All of our group, like myself, are Muslim, except one – a Maronite Christian – and all with much the same background: recruited by the CIA at some point. We were told that the mosque bombings assignment was through a special ops division, but many of the same handlers were used. We were never given a division name...*'

As Haidar had opened up, Adel knew that to release the information would be suicide. Bahsem-Yahl's claims would be proven right and the cataclysm they'd been frantically striving to hold at bay would be unavoidable. Worse still, and here was the cruel irony, the warped aims of those behind the mosque bombings would end up satisfied. Everything he and his team had done would be for nothing. But how could they suppress the information?

It was then that he'd had his hour-long private meeting with Gabriel Chayat and they'd made their plans. Apart from wishing to avoid Muslim uprisings, Israel had strong interests in hiding an American link to the bombers. Israel was viewed by many Arab states as simply an American proxy in the Middle East. The fact that the captured bomber was also apprehended on Israeli soil would drive home the final coffin nail. 'However we tried to spin it, there would be talk of collusion,' Chayat said with a resigned sigh. 'Unfortunately there's only one way to bury something like this. But it has to look like an accident, and it has to also be witnessed by Muslim guards. Only their testimony would be completely trusted in a situation like this.'

Shapira had clutched Haidar's cuffed hands to the grenade, then grasped them in his own as they wrestled, the action so quick it was impossible to tell which had come first. With everything on file still listing Haidar as a fully fledged member of Hezbollah, the last link would be buried. Everything with Bahsem-Yahl would quickly die down.

'Thanks for the help, Gabriel.'

'No. I should be thanking you. We had as much to gain. At least we've done our bit towards proving that Arab-Israeli cooperation can sometimes work.'

As Inayah cleared away the dinner plates, Adel and Namir retired to the terrace. Namir lit a large Cuban cigar, his only vice; Adel declined with thanks. If he took only a few puffs, he'd be back to the thirty a day he'd smoked through most of his twenties.

Poignancy. Their father used to smoke similar cigars, and their old family home was only three blocks away. The warm night air, the smell of hibiscus, jasmine and perfumed *shisha* smoke tempered by a gentle sea-salt breeze, exactly as Adel remembered it.

And whether from the poignancy of that moment, or because David Shapira had brought to mind 'sacrifice for others', he finally apologised to Namir for having deserted him, left him to run their father's business.

Namir looked at him, drew at his cigar. 'It was a long time ago, Adel.'

'I know. But it was wrong all the same. You had to give up your dream of being an imam. What you'd set your heart on.'

Namir was thoughtful for a second. Then he blew out a soft plume of smoke and waved his cigar hand. 'You think that I am unhappy with all this? With how things have turned out?'

'That's not the point. The fact that you've made good of the cloth left you. I still put myself first. And that meant you were left with little or no choice. Your ambitions were sacrificed because of mine. That was wrong.'

Namir raised an eyebrow. 'You think I'd have insisted you put your ambitions second? Put everything you'd found in London, your love for Tahiya, aside?'

Adel said nothing. Namir's eyes stayed on him.

'We all make choices, Adel. And if I'd really wanted to pursue becoming an imam, I could have got a manager in. Certainly when father died.' He smiled. 'As things turned out, with my contacts, I've become probably the largest supplier of stone and marble to mosques in northern Egypt. There's a bit of me in all of them. And will be still a hundred years from now.' His smile widened. 'I have more presence in mosques than I could have ever hoped to achieve as an imam.'

Adel knew that Namir was trying to ease his guilt, but it felt good all the same. He gestured with one hand. 'Since you put it so eloquently.'

'My pleasure.' Namir blew out a fresh plume of smoke. 'But what concerns me, Adel, is that this still troubled you after so long. This burden.' He tapped ash from his cigar. 'So let me pass on to you some advice I was given long ago: in any action, if you can't be true to Allah, then at least be true to yourself. To his voice within you. Your *conscience*. And if you can do neither, then that action is best avoided. Otherwise it may weigh heavy on you for many years. But in this case your concern is misplaced, my brother.' Namir stood, beckoned Adel. They embraced. 'Whatever might have settled in your own heart about that incident – all is forgiven. Even though I never personally felt there was anything to forgive.'

Be true to yourself and Allah.

And as Adel felt his brother gently pat his back, felt the tears welling in his eyes, it wasn't so much for that final forgiveness, but for the souls of Muhab Haidar and David Shapira. Both sacrificed, at his request, on the altar of a greater good. *Means to an end.*

At that last second, Haidar had screamed at Shapira in Hebrew: *'Why are you doing this? I am on your side!'* Unable to comprehend just why he was being sacrificed.

Perhaps that was why now he was finally releasing that old burden with his brother; he couldn't possibly shoulder both.

'We got on to what was happening a bit late in the day for comfort, I'm afraid,' Verbeck said. 'But at least we got there.'

'Yeah, you did at that.' Sam was reminded of Washington's team on that first day: *We got here just in time.*

Verbeck didn't want to give details of just how close, make Tynnan sweat any more than he already had.

The President had decided to finally do something two hours after he and Carl Miller visited him. But another hour had been lost tracking what was in progress, part of that trail ending with an Apache AH-64 called out of a New Brunswick navy base. They got hold of the base commander and explained the situation. He in turn contacted the pilot and ascertained that 'lock-on to fire' positions were being provided by the 'front right-hand vehicle in regard to a front *left*-hand vehicle.' When the pilot came back to his commander a minute later to say that he now had a final fire order, he countermanded it: 'You are to fire at the right-hand lead vehicle. They are the renegades in this particular situation. Repeat: *right*-hand lead!' '*Affirmative!*'

The second X5 apparently hit the fireball and ditch of the first vehicle, and was effectively taken out as well.

Verbeck took a fresh breath. 'So, Mr Tynnan. What decision have you finally come to?'

Sam had to give it to Verbeck. He ran a smooth operation. Three hours ago he received a call from someone in his department, an NSA lawyer – Sam didn't catch his name – outlining what the official position would be: '*A group of Muslim terrorists took the manuscript of one Samuel Tynnan and used portions of it to perpetrate a series of mosque bombings with the aim of putting pressure on terrorist leader Abu Khalish. At some point this group also infiltrated members of Department 101, a CIA wing. The extent of that infiltration is now the subject of a State Department enquiry.*'

Nothing would be said beyond that. Furthermore, Sam would be asked to sign a non-disclosure agreement – as his caller keenly reminded him, *'issues of national security generally push aside any First Amendment rights'* – promising to say nothing outside of that. In return for signing, he would receive a one-off compensatory payment of two million dollars. *'...for any losses incurred by your manuscript being held. Possible trauma suffered won't be mentioned. After all, we can't be held responsible for the actions of terrorists, and those of errant 101 staffers would end up a moot and complex legal point.'*

'And if I refuse to sign?'

'Well, you wouldn't get the payment, of course. Then lawyers would go to it on each side. But meanwhile we would insist that your manuscript was held and embargoed from publication for two good reasons: one, assessment of security risk caused by its publication; two, material evidence, and also to see if there might be cause to charge you for incitement of terrorism for what you'd written.'

Sam didn't think they'd be able to make those charges stick, but the damage would already be done. *The Prophecy* would be held up for another year or more. The message was clear: quick signature and fat cheque on one hand, pile of hassle on the other.

Following that call, he'd phoned Elli and asked his advice, who'd already waxed lyrical when they'd spoken earlier about the market potential of *The Prophecy.*

'*Like I say, Sam, this is a big book. The biggest. So we don't want anything else possibly holding it up from the marketplace. Besides, the elbow room they've left you is enough. The fact that it ends up as "terrorist-affiliated parties unknown" is neither here nor there. The big story driving interest and sales is the fact that the manuscript was taken for seven months and used as a blueprint for these mosque bombings and against Abu Khalish, one of the hottest news topics recently – especially now with this final showdown with Khalish. The fine details behind that aren't important. In fact, might provide extra intrigue: more people reading the book hoping to work out just who was behind everything.*'

Sam smiled, reminded of why Elli Roschler was his agent. *Incorrigible.* Market thrust first, second and third. Mike had said pretty much the same when he'd phoned him for a second opinion.

'*You don't know enough of what's going on in the background to say anything in any case. Just guesswork. Elli's right: great back-story. Puts a whole new meaning to the "pain" us writers go through producing a book. Looks like I'll be getting some competition on the NYT list.*'

Sam brought his attention back to Verbeck. 'So, the bottom line is: a bunch of Muslim terrorists took my manuscript as a guide to a mosque-bombing campaign, and at the same time infiltrated a CIA department. The two of them then skipped happily down the road hand in hand towards a hopeful Armageddon?'

'Yeah, more or less. If you're happy with the Yellow Brick Road version.' Verbeck's faint chuckle died quickly. 'Trouble is, there isn't much more can be said outside of that. I'm tied by the same "national security" secrecy agreement you'll sign. So even if you pushed me, all I could say is that there are extremities on both sides of the fence, and sometimes, just *sometimes*, increased conflict is seen to serve *both* their interests. But that's as far as I could go, and even that would be *off* the record.'

'So, in the end, all that's being admitted to is act one of what happened. Act two is being glossed over, or perhaps is even being given a complete back-spin: the terrorists influencing this CIA department rather than the reverse.'

Verbeck fell silent for a moment. 'I think we understand each other perfectly well, Sam, on just what can and can't be said. And even if what you say *did* have any substance – it wouldn't serve anyone's interests to claim that now, would it?'

Sam nodded. He heard Verbeck loud and clear. That had in fact been the final crucial element to sway Sam. 'I know. If anything is said on that front, then it feeds Bahsem-Yahl's claim and leads to more conflict. These crazies – at present "unspecified" – would get what they wanted after all. And what we've all been trying to avoid, all our efforts, will have been for nothing.' Sam sighed. 'That's why, yes, I'd feel inclined to accept your offer and sign. No other reason.'

'There you go,' Verbeck said. 'A shitpile of money *and* a noble cause. It doesn't get much better than that.'

Sam smiled. He liked Verbeck. He was no doubt as slippery as a box of toads, but it was all done with such panache that it was almost a pleasure getting shafted.

Towards the end of them wrapping up the arrangements, Verbeck asked, 'By the way, how is she?'

Elli and Mike had also enquired earlier, and Sam answered much the same now: fine. The operation on her shoulder had gone well. 'The surgeon expects her to regain full use of it.' He was planning to head to the hospital later.

Mike had also asked: 'And how are *you*?'

The leading question. He'd gone through so many emotions with Lorrena the past forty-eight hours, he wasn't sure what to think any more. His doubts because of her early betrayal had largely been salved by her risking her life to finally help him, but the truth was, despite everything, he'd never really stopped loving her. 'I'm good about it. Good.'

Their plan was to head to California for a year. Get away from Oneida and all the ghosts of what had happened there. He'd see more of Ashley, and she'd also be closer to her father in San Francisco. They'd find somewhere on the coast in between: Santa Barbara or San Luis Obispo.

Sam looked at his watch. He had one last call to make before he headed to the hospital to see Lorrena.

'Is it safe to talk now?'

'Yes, it's safe.'

Adel had spent a couple of hours after dinner at Namir's, who'd then run him to the station for the last night express train to Cairo. His flight from Cairo to London left at 2.15 a.m. The call came through twenty minutes into his train journey.

'I saw the news about Khalish. That's why I called. It seems almost too good to be true.'

'Oh, it's true alright. There's no possible doubt.' Adel had received the news from Malik shortly after he'd landed in Alexandria. 'That's why it's indeed safe for you to call now, my dear Fahim. Oh, *so safe*. And it happened not far from where you are, it appears.' Omari's chosen far-flung location had been Langkawi, Malaysia. Ironic that in order to keep clear of Khalish's possible clutches, he'd ended up living much the same life as him.

'Yes, not far,' Omari said reflectively, and as he looked towards the lapping surf through the palm trees, it became the gentle swish of water as he swam in the *hammam* on that last day in London.

The phone had rung incessantly. First his cellphone which had been left upstairs, then the house line. When he finally realised that Akram had gone out and wasn't going to get it, he got out and slipped on his robe to answer it.

Straight away, he saw the device on the third step up, flashing red. He dared not touch it, so just ran straight out; the explosion came when he was half a block away.

Jalal Haboush, one of his *Mahbusa* playing group, lived two streets away. He ran there and, after a couple of coffees and stiff *araqs*, he phoned Adel.

Their plan was mapped out: if he surfaced, Khalish would simply try and kill him again. So a new identity was chosen and Haboush sworn to secrecy. Adel covered his end with a gas explosion – a murder investigation would have rapidly exposed the cover-up over the body.

'So, it's all over,' Omari said with a sigh.

'The main event, yes. But there are still residual Khalish cells to worry about. Two more years of hiding away and hopefully those will have died down too. It will be safe for you to resurface.'

'And what will happen to him?' Omari asked. '*Akram?*'

It touched Adel that with all Omari had had to give up and how close he'd come to death, never mind the *betrayal*, Akram was still his main concern.

'Because he supplied information, we were able to cut him a deal. Conspiracy to terrorism charge at the lowest possible level – he'll get three years. With good behaviour, he'll be out in a year to eighteen months.'

'I see.' Omari's voice was hollow.

And it struck Adel again just how much Omari had lost: his son, his young nephew, Layth, then – through this ultimate betrayal – his best friend of forty years. And in having to hide away from Khalish's grasp, he'd had to cut himself off from London and all else he'd known for so many years. All his other friends.

The poignancy of that loss had made it easier for Adel to keep up the pretence of Omari's death to Tahiya and others. It had been a death of sorts for Omari.

'Thank you, Adel, for getting Khalish – for all those future lives saved. All those other Layths. But also, if you hadn't, that shadow would have stayed hanging over me. I'd have found myself consigned to Mai Tai land for ever.'

They laughed gently. 'We couldn't possibly have that.'

'And with the *hammam* bombing, I lay blame there too wholly with Khalish. He was a scourge, a cancer befouling everything he touched. Akram became little more than a pathetic pawn of his will, left with little choice. I find it hard to hold in my heart grievance against him.'

Adel closed his eyes. Omari was still desperately trying to shift the blame from his good friend to lessen the sting of that betrayal. 'I know.'

'So what made you think of Jerusalem?'

Sam had already seen the news: the dramatic attack on the Dome of the Rock foiled at the last minute by Israeli police. The report covered the one bomber captured who later killed himself along with an Israeli guard. '*The bomber has been named as Muhab Haidar, a Shiite Muslim from southern Lebanon with active links to Hezbollah. And the Israeli guard as David Shapira...*' Adel had only needed to fill in the gaps.

Adel related the thought processes he'd gone through with Jean-Pierre Bourdin. 'When Verbeck told me that some information had likely been manipulated and Bourdin said that only the first quatrain had come from an outside source, my focus naturally went to the second one. That apparently was his own creation. And one of Saladin's main battles was the siege of Jerusalem. "Liberated" is the term used in Islamic texts. Though I'm sure Jews and Christians have other terms for it. So it appears that at least on this occasion Bourdin has been an accurate seer.'

'I'm sure he'll be pleased to hear it. Will make

up for him being misled over the first quatrain.' He talked briefly about this odyssey featuring in part of Jean-Pierre's upcoming book. But there was only so much Sam could say with his hands tied by Verbeck's agreement. He'd let Jean-Pierre down gently.

Sam paused at that point to get the right words in place, composing himself for the main reason for his call: the secret he'd withheld from Emile all along. 'There's something perhaps I should have told you before. You know the character in *The Prophecy* who I mentioned was like you?'

'Yes, I remember you saying something about that.'

'Well, he was more than just a bit character. He was the main protagonist. As with you in real life, in the book he played the main part in saving everything.'

'Oh, I see.' The night train was not far away from Cairo now. The tracks followed the Nile Delta, but the river was only visible in patches. Clusters of palms and limestone-washed villages clinging to its edge. 'And why didn't you say anything before?'

'Because I thought it might be too daunting, might put too much pressure on you.'

'Yes, I suppose.' It had been daunting as it was. Would knowing that have made it more difficult? The uncomfortable sense that life might be mirroring art too closely? Adel remembered the first time he'd done this train journey. He'd been no more than five and they'd travelled third class: rough wooden seats or often no seats, cheek by jowl, goats and chickens herded in along with bicycles. Then four years later, as his father's business started doing well, they'd gone second class; finally, in his teens, first class. How they'd taken this journey had in many ways mirrored his family's transition.

Sam continued. 'But he ends up doing things very differently to you. Perhaps because he has to make one final, tough decision.' Sam paused, hoping that hadn't come across as derisory. Emile had probably had to make 'tough' decisions all the way through. 'Because, in the book, one of the bombers ends up having clear links to the West. And so he has to lie and cover up for that.'

'Oh, right.' Adel's heart skipped a beat. It felt as if all the moisture had suddenly been sucked out his mouth. He looked at his reflection in the darkness of the train window. A week ago he'd seen a man, like millions of others, gripped in the fear of Abu Khalish's terror attacks. What did he see now? A face that would for ever reflect the ghosts of what he'd done?

Sam sighed resignedly, as if making nothing of the most vital decision his protagonist had to make in *The Prophecy*. 'It seemed the right thing for him to do at the time: one lie to save the world from calamity. Fair trade. But that lie, and what he's done, weighs heavy on him for a while after. Affects him very badly.'

'I can see how such a thing might weigh on his conscience.' *He could still see Haidar's face in those last seconds, hear his screams.* Adel gently closed his eyes, swallowing. He could hardly breathe. 'And tell me, does he eventually survive this?'

'Yes, he survives this,' Sam said.

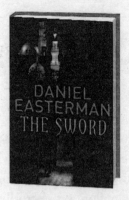

THE SWORD

BY DANIEL EASTERMAN

His heart was beating like a drum at dawn.
Something clawed at his stomach, something
with talons from his worst nightmares.

An invitation to visit one of Cairo's antiquarian booksellers sets in train a series of terrifying ordeals for Jack Goodrich. Having been shown a priceless sword claimed to have belonged to the Prophet Muhammad, Jack returns home brimming with excitement. But that's when the nightmare begins...

A dangerous new movement within the ranks of fundamentalist Islam wishes to put a new Caliph on the throne, to rule the Muslim world. To do this they require the Sword, and they will stop at nothing to get it. With the deadliest of weapons in his hands, if the new Caliph were to declare jihad, the consequences would be catastrophic.

A tense and gripping thriller on a truly international scale that poses a chilling question: how can you stop a holy war before it starts...?

SPEAR OF DESTINY

BY DANIEL EASTERMAN

The explosive new thriller from the bestselling author of
THE SWORD.

The untimely and brutal death of an old man sparks a
chain of events that will put his nephew in danger as he
races across Europe to Egypt, to solve one of the oldest
mysteries in the world: the location of the tomb of Christ
and the sword that pierced his body on the Cross.

In 1942 Gerald Usherwood and his platoon discover
a mysterious crypt and it becomes clear they've stumbled
upon something extraordinary. Sixty years later, his
nephew Ethan discovers his body, slumped over his desk,
clutching a small, ancient relic. As Ethan begins piecing
together the events of sixty years before, guided by
Gerald's diaries, he finds himself hurtling across Europe,
just one step ahead of the killer who will stop at nothing
to discover the final resting place of Jesus Christ...and
the ultimate religious icon that could spearhead a violent
campaign to revive the Nazi legacy...

a&b